PRAISE FOR G.A. McKEVETT AND THE SAVANNAH REID MYSTERIES!

CORPSE SUZETTE

"Savannah's as feisty as ever."
—*Kirkus Reviews*

MURDER À LA MODE

"Added to a well-plotted mystery, the very funny depiction of a different side of reality television makes *Murder à la Mode* a delight."
—*Mystery Scene*

CEREAL KILLER

"Food lore, a good puzzle, an exciting climax and cats with their therapeutic purring all add to the fun."
—*Publishers Weekly*

DEATH BY CHOCOLATE

"*Death by Chocolate* is G.A. McKevett at her very best."
—*Midwest Book Review*

PEACHES AND SCREAMS

"A luscious heroine, humor, and down-home characters."
—*Library Journal*

SOUR GRAPES

"A delicious addition to the series . . . this cozy is as crisp and sparkling as Villa Rosa's best white zinfandel."
—*Publishers Weekly*

Books by G.A. McKevett

Just Desserts

Bitter Sweets

Killer Calories

Cooked Goose

Sugar and Spite

Sour Grapes

Peaches and Screams

Death by Chocolate

Cereal Killer

Murder à la Mode

Corpse Suzette

Fat Free and Fatal

Poisoned Tarts

A Body to Die For

Wicked Craving

Published by Kensington Publishing Corporation

G.A. McKEVETT

A BODY
TO DIE FOR

A SAVANNAH REID MYSTERY

KENSINGTON BOOKS
www.kensingtonbooks.com

KENSINGTON BOOKS are published by

Kensington Publishing Corp.
850 Third Avenue
New York, NY 10022

All Kensington titles, imprints and distributed lines are available at special quantity discounts for bulk purchases for sales promotion, premiums, fund-raising, educational or institutional use.

Special book excerpts or customized printings can also be created to fit specific needs. For details, write or phone the office of the Kensington Special Sales Manager: Kensington Publishing Corp., 850 Third Avenue, New York, NY 10022. Attn. Special Sales Department. Phone: 1-800-221-2647.

Kensington and the K logo Reg. U.S. Pat. & TM Off.

ISBN-13: 978-0-7582-1555-0
ISBN-10: 0-7582-1555-X

First Hardcover Printing: January 2009
First Mass Market Printing: January 2010

10 9 8 7 6 5 4 3 2 1

Printed in the United States of America

For Lillyan Rose,
The newest flower in our garden.
May you grow and blossom all your days
In sunlight and love.

Acknowledgments

I would like to thank Leslie Connell for her friendship and support, year after year. Leslie, the Moonlight Magnolia team couldn't function without you!

I also want to thank all the fans who write to me, sharing their thoughts and offering endless encouragement. Your stories touch my heart, and I enjoy your letters more than you know. I can be reached at: http://www. sonjamassie.com.

Chapter 1

"**Y**ou call this place a 'health' club? It looks like a medieval torture chamber. What's so bloomin' healthy about it?" Savannah Reid said as she and her friend, Tammy Hart, stepped out of the women's locker room and into Savannah's idea of "fitness hell."

She shuddered as she looked around the controversial, militaristic gym with its prison-gray walls, bare cement floor, and jungle of sinister-looking workout equipment. Overhead florescent lights sputtered, while a frenetic noise that might have been called "music" boomed around them. The nerve-jarring racket was interspersed with an abrasive, brassy, female voice, screaming at those who were working out to "Go! Go! Go, you tub-o! Move! Move! Move that lard! Work that lazy ass! Don't you *dare* stop!"

The only thing that might even remotely be considered "décor" was an eight-foot-tall poster on one wall, a picture of a woman with flowing blond hair, wearing thigh-high boots and a camouflage-print latex bodysuit. Savannah could only classify her as a cross between a Marine drill sergeant and a dominatrix.

Savannah elbowed Tammy and nodded toward the

sweat-drenched men and women, slaving away at the gleaming steel devices. "They actually pay money to do this . . . to listen to her mouth, to get insulted and demeaned like that?"

"They pay *big* money. Pain doesn't come cheap in Clarissa's House of Pain and Gain."

They walked to the far end of the room, which was slightly less crowded, and found a couple of machines that were side by side and unoccupied.

Tammy removed her camouflage-print sweat suit—the club uniform—revealing a T-shirt, shorts, and a svelte, trim body that even Clarissa Jardin would have to declare "nearly perfect."

She sat on the seat of one of the machines, placed her arms between some cushioned pads, and began to expertly push them together in front of her chest, then release them back to her sides.

Savannah lowered herself onto the machine next to Tammy's and began to do the same.

As Savannah worked muscles that she'd forgotten she had, she glanced down at her own khaki and olive drab sweat suit that she had donned for this undercover gig and began to question her commitment to the assignment.

No doubt, the founder of this fine establishment—and all of its sister franchises across the nation—would not consider her robust figure "perfect." In fact, although Savannah was quite happy with her own body and its curves, she was pretty sure that Clarissa Jardin would consider her a "tub-o." And if you listened to Clarissa's shtick on the talk show circuit, being not-so-svelte put you at the bottom of the human barrel, along with serial killers, puppy drowners, and cupcake eaters.

About a year ago, the fitness diva had moved from Los Angeles to Savannah's hometown, the quaint, Southern California village of San Carmelita. A small, seaside community, its citizenry consisted of wealthy celebs escaping the smog and congestion of the City of Angels; weekend tourists, who were also seeking fresh air and relaxation; and common folks like Savannah and Dirk who made their livings catering to the celebs and tourists.

San Carmelita had buzzed with gossip when Clarissa had moved there. Savannah's opinion had been: *Big whoopty-do. Just what we needed . . . another loudmouthed luminary with an attitude.*

"I'm hating this already," she muttered to herself. "Dirk's going to owe me, big time, for this one."

On the opposite side of the room, their friend, Detective Sergeant Dirk Coulter was already deeply immersed in his undercover persona. Grunting, groaning, and red in the face, he was quite successfully manipulating some sort of contraption with wires, pulleys, and weights.

Not bad for an old fart, Savannah thought as she watched his arm and shoulder muscles bulge with the effort. She had to admit, he still looked pretty darned good in a tank top. She amended the thought to *semi-old fart*, remembering that, in his mid-forties, he was only a couple of years older than she.

They were really just kids. Okay, kids with twenty-plus years of hardcore life experience. His were cop years. Hers were cop and private investigator years. And, like dog years, those added up fast.

"Yeah," Tammy said. "We ladies of the Moonlight Magnolia Detective Agency don't work cheap."

Savannah didn't reply. There was no point in stating the obvious—that the members of the Moonlight Magnolia Detective Agency hadn't been working at all lately.

No clients. No income. Hence the opportunity to do freebies for Dirk.

"Yes," Tammy said. "After this, old Dirko is going to owe us both a nice dinner at Chez Antoine." She motioned toward one of the nearest machines. "But even better than that, think how much fun it'll be if we nail the perv."

"True. So true." Smiling a nasty little grin, Savannah chuckled to herself as she perused the possible suspects working the rows of equipment.

If they could nab the guy who was somehow taking candid shots of the gym's female clients in various stages of nakedness and posting the pictures on the Internet, it would all be worth it. Heck, Dirk wouldn't even have to buy them dessert at Antoine's.

Savannah had a mental flash of the French chef's dessert cart and quickly modified that thought, too. No, whether they caught this guy or not, Dirk was going to pay, and the fee would be expensive, highly saturated fat calories.

Savannah watched as he paused between repetitions and glanced over at the cute, twenty-something, chickie-poo on the machine next to him. He sucked in his belly, flexed his biceps, and gave the young woman what he no doubt thought was a sexy, come-hither grin.

It was all Savannah could do not to stomp across the room, smack him on the head with a barbell, and remind him that he was old enough to be the gal's father. But she fought down the urge. She was nothing if not the model of self-restraint.

Besides, she had to give him a little credit for the self-confidence—okay, delusions of grandeur—that enabled him to think he had a chance with the girl.

The thought occurred to her: If women could remain as confident in their own beauty as men were in their studliness for so long in life, the world would be a happier place.

"Anybody look suspicious to you?" Tammy asked.

"Not really," Savannah said as she considered their possible culprits.

Clarissa's devotees were a wide demographic, judging from the group assembled in the House of Pain and Gain today. On the rowing machine, a seventy-ish lady in a bright purple and red sweat suit worked those handles like a Roman galley slave. She had a fanatical gleam in her eyes as she stroked in time to the pulsing music, punctuated with Clarissa's admonitions to "Work! Work! Get the rust out of those joints! Get that ugly cellulite off your lazy butt!"

Savannah thought of her own octogenarian grandmother, Granny Reid, and chuckled to think of how the feisty Southern lady would react to Clarissa's brand of encouragement. If anyone were to suggest to Gran that she was lazy or carried any excess baggage, they might just receive a skillet greased with bacon fat upside the head. And along with the corrective smack, they'd get a lecture about how "sportin' a few extra pounds to begin with got a lot of good folks through the dark days of the Great Depression."

Gran was big on stories about the Great Depression, skillet smacking, and the incalculable culinary value of fresh bacon grease.

But Savannah couldn't stop and think about Gran at the moment for two reasons: One, she would start missing her grandmother and be tempted to hop a plane to Georgia. And two, she had a peeping, picture-taking Tom to catch and a life to live here in sunny Southern California . . . not to mention a dessert cart full of éclairs and napoleons to eat.

With her priorities firmly in place, she continued to scan the Clarissa Jardin exercise fiends.

The twenty-something hunk hefting barbells near Dirk was a possibility. He was gorgeous, probably of Mediterranean descent, obviously a serious bodybuilder. As he lifted first one weight, then the other, he watched his own reflection in a nearby mirror.

Savannah doubted that he had time or inclination to gawk at anybody's bod but his own.

Tammy seemed to read her thoughts. She leaned close to Savannah, her mouth close to her ear, and shouted above the booming music. "I don't think it's him. He's just into himself."

"Yeah, and who can blame him?"

Tammy giggled. "Dirk's watching you watch him. He's got his jealous puss on."

Looking over at Dirk, Savannah saw that he was, indeed, wearing a frown. And it probably was a jealous scowl, though, with Dirk it was hard to tell. Ninety percent of his facial expressions were scowls.

Savannah grinned and winked at him. "It's okay for him to check out the babes," she shouted back to Tammy, "but heaven forbid we should peruse the dudes."

"He wouldn't care if *I* were the one looking. He's only jealous of *you*."

"We're trying to catch a perv here and—"

"Dirk's got it for you bad."

"Nobody's got nothin' for nobody. End of subject."

Tammy snickered. "Whatever you say, boss lady."

"I say . . . I think we should keep an eye on the creepo with the potbelly in the too-tight shorts over there." She discreetly nodded toward a middle-aged guy on a stationary bicycle near the window. His electric-blue latex shorts announced to the world that he was neither well-endowed nor circumcised. And both facts were bits of information that Savannah would have gladly lived and died without knowing.

"Dirk should arrest him for wearing those shorts, if nothing else," Tammy added. "If that isn't indecent public exposure, I don't know what is."

"Yeah, really. With any luck, it'll be him."

Savannah continued to hope and work the machines,

as she and Tammy moved around the room, trying first one apparatus, then another.

Dirk stuck with his weird pulley contraption, and Savannah was pretty sure he did so to remain close to the bimbo next to him. She made a mental note to mention the fact to him later, to point out what a fool he had made of himself.

Hey, he didn't have a *wife* to do it. *Somebody* had to build the guy's character.

And all the time, Savannah watched the weirdo in the blue shorts and hoped he would do something suspicious . . . other than dress grotesquely.

But he didn't.

She kept constant tabs on him throughout his short and nonexhaustive workout, but he finished, disappeared into the men's locker room, and left the establishment, wearing skintight jeans and a mesh tank top. And he never passed within ten feet of the women's locker room entrance.

Meanwhile, Savannah's muscles were starting to complain. Bitterly. "This bites," she told Tammy. "Whoever our guy is, he's not here today. We might as well leave."

"Yeah, really." Tammy paused and dabbed a couple of barely there drops of sweat from her brow with a towel. "I need to get out of here and go on my daily run. I want to help Dirk, but this is seriously cutting into my own personal workout time."

Soaking wet with sweat, hurting in every atom of her body, feeling every one of her forty-plus years, Savannah decided not to tumble off the machine, fall onto the floor, and curl into a fetal position. Doing so would lack a certain . . . dignity.

"*Daily run*, my ass," she muttered.

"Huh?"

Tammy looked so sweet and innocent. Savannah also

decided not to slap her. "Why don't you run along?" she said. "Make it obvious to Mr. Muscles and those older guys in the corner over there that you're on your way to the locker room. Maybe we'll get lucky and one of them will follow you. I'll keep an eye on them while I tell Dirk this gig is over. At least for today."

"You got it."

Tammy gathered her towel, clothes, and water bottle and sashayed toward the women's locker room door. At least, she tried to sashay. Savannah smiled, thinking that she really couldn't expect a Yankee gal to priss properly. If a girl wasn't raised on sweet tea and buttermilk biscuits, a certain wiggle was missing from her walk. 'Twas a shame, but it couldn't be helped.

However, Tammy was fulfilling her duties as bimbo bait quite well. Savannah couldn't help noticing how every set of male eyes followed her friend as she left the room. Undoubtedly, if there was a hardcore, lawbreaking, dirty picture–snapping pervert among them, Tammy's tight, size-zero heinie would draw him out.

Savannah picked up her gym bag, walked over to Dirk, leaned down, and said in his ear, "Okay, big boy. Your girls have enjoyed about as much of this bullpucky as we can stand. We're pulling the plug and heading home."

"Gotcha," he replied, looking as tired and disgusted as she felt. "The magic is pretty much gone for me, too."

She followed his eyes as he watched the girl who had been next to him walk away and head toward the locker room herself. On the way, she stopped and said something to Mr. Bulging Biceps, then gave him a quick kiss.

"Hm-m-m," Dirk grumbled. "And I figured he was gay."

"You think all muscular guys with great hair are gay."

His feathers instantly ruffled. "You like his hair?"

She sighed. "He's got hair, Dirk. Hair is hair. Frankly, I think it's overrated, but—"

"Go shower."

"I'm going to. And I've gotta keep an eye on the kid, in case it's a janitor or somebody who works here sneaking in the back door or whatever."

"Give a yell if you need me."

She gave him a sweet smile. Sweeter than he deserved, considering how he'd been ogling the barely legal female next to him. "We always holler out for you, sugar, when we need to be rescued by a burnin' hunk o' manhood."

He lit up so brightly that she felt guilty and didn't have the heart to tell him she was pulling his leg. The only time she "hollered out" for him was when she needed someone to hold down her sofa, eat her popcorn, drink her beer, and watch boxing on her TV.

Or when she needed a dear friend.

She left him and made her way to the door in the back marked "Women's Locker Room." And even though Clarissa was still screeching about the horrors of lard and cellulite, Savannah couldn't help noticing that male eyes followed her own figure, too. Maybe not as many as Tammy's, but she still had her share of admirers.

A good sashay mixed with a hearty dash of self-confidence went a long way when it came to attraction and sex appeal.

She was feeling tired and lazy and relaxed when she entered the locker room, ready to just shower, go home, and kick back.

But the moment she passed through the dressing area and into the showers, a creepy, apprehensive feeling washed over her. The hair wasn't exactly standing up on the back of her neck, but she had the sensation that some sort of threat was nearby.

It was an intuitive warning that she had felt many times before as a police officer and since, as a private investigator. And she had learned, long ago, not to ignore it.

She opened her mouth to call out to Tammy, but

thought better of it. Instead, she glanced around, taking in the closed door on the back wall of the long, narrow room, the two rows of shower stalls on either side.

She could hear more than one shower running. The odor of disinfectants, mixed with the floral smells of soaps and shampoos, scented the humid air.

Only three stalls were being used, their plastic curtains drawn. She walked quietly between the rows, bending over to peek at the bare feet exposed between the bottom of the curtain and the floor.

Tammy's perfectly pedicured, hot pink toenails made identification easy. Three stalls away from Tammy were a pair of feet wearing bright red and purple flip-flops—the senior lady from the rowing machine, no doubt.

But it was the feet wearing the sneakers that caught her eye.

Sneakers and jeans.

In the stall right next to Tammy's pink toes.

Silently, Savannah crept up to the curtain of Tammy's stall and pulled it aside a few inches.

A wet, sudsy Tammy whirled around, but Savannah pressed her finger against her lips in a silent "Sh-h-h," then pointed to the plastic curtain that separated her shower stall from the one next to it.

Tammy's eyes widened, but she nodded.

At least twenty thoughts and decisions processed in Savannah's brain in the next few seconds, the major ones being: *Weapon's in my gym bag. Don't pull it yet. Handcuffs in waistband. No time to call Dirk. Tammy's wet and slippery. Won't be much help.*

The most satisfying thought: *Gotcha now, you dirt-sucking perv . . .*

And the uppermost thought any time she was getting ready to apprehend a perpetrator: *Don't get killed!*

A moment later, all conscious decision making was

over, because an arm reached beneath the plastic curtain. And in its hand was an open cell phone.

A video camera cell phone.

And the user was pointing it up at them.

Savannah felt, more than heard, Tammy's sharp intake of breath as she instinctively moved back away from the camera and against the curtain on the other side of the stall.

Stepping into the stream of the shower, Savannah reached down, grabbed the wrist, and yanked with all her might.

Someone yelled.

She felt him fall. Hard.

But she hung on.

The camera fell with a clatter, and Savannah was dimly aware of Tammy scooping it up and holding it to her bare chest.

Savannah braced herself and gave the arm another jerk.

Her illicit photographer came sliding, facedown, across the floor, under the curtain, and into their stall.

Tammy squealed and tried to gather the curtain around her as Savannah twisted his arms behind him. A second later, she had him cuffed.

"You got him!" Tammy shouted.

Savannah flipped him over . . . and looked down into the frightened, youthful, pretty face of Dirk's bimbo exercise companion.

"And *he's* a *she*!" Tammy added.

When it came to stating the obvious, Tammy was gifted.

Savannah loved her anyway.

"What the hell do you think you're doing?" Savannah asked the girl, reaching up to turn off the shower, now that they were all three thoroughly drenched.

"Nothing! I wasn't doing anything!"

"You were taking dirty pictures."

"I was not! I was calling my mom!"

Savannah turned to Tammy, who was now cocooned in shower curtain. "Check that phone," she told her. "Was the camera on?"

Tammy nodded. "Still is."

"Turn it off and check to see what she got."

Good with techno gadgets, it didn't take Tammy long to do as she was told. She squealed. "Oh, my gawd! She got my butt and from that angle, it looks as big as a bus!"

"Don't you dare delete it! That's our evidence!" Savannah reached down and hauled the weeping girl to her feet. "What are you doing, taking pictures of women's naughty bits? You're not into girls; I saw you smooching Mr. Universe out there a few minutes ago. And you sure looked like you meant it."

"I . . . I . . . it isn't that big a deal. I mean, it's just some silly pictures and—"

"Are you kidding me?" Savannah wished she had a bacon-greased skillet in her hand. "There's a sixteen-year-old girl who's afraid to leave her house now because you took some of your 'silly' pictures, posted them on the Web, and turned her into an overnight porn star."

The woman didn't answer, just continued to sob.

"She's been downloaded thousands of times in the past few weeks. How do you think that makes her feel? How do you think her parents feel? I'll warn you right now, girlie, her daddy wants a piece of you."

Tammy was holding the camera phone, watching her X-rated footage over and over again and shaking her head. "How can you do this to another woman . . . violate someone's privacy like this?" she asked her. "Why?"

"I didn't want to," she said, snuffling. "Really, I didn't. He made me."

"*Who* made you?" Savannah asked, already knowing the answer.

"Vittorio."

Savannah glanced over at Tammy and nodded toward the cell phone in her hand. Tammy caught her meaning and discreetly flipped on the phone's camera, pointing it in their confessor's direction.

"Vittorio made you take pictures of naked women in public showers?" Savannah stated . . . for the record.

"Yeah. He made me. Really he did."

"And how, exactly, did he force you to do this?"

"He told me that if I didn't do it, if I didn't love him enough to do that one little thing for him, he'd break up with me."

Savannah gave her a long, steady, piercing look, until finally, the young woman broke eye contact and stared down at her wet shoes, shame and fear all over her face.

"You think I'm disgusting," she said, crying softly. "You think I'm worthless, total crap, giving in to a guy like that."

Savannah weighed the thoughts and emotions sweeping over her. "No," she said, "I'm disgusted by what you did. I'm angry at you for hurting other women, but I don't think you're crap." She sighed, removed one of the handcuff manacles from the girl's wrist and attached it to the shower's cold-water handle. "*You're* the one who thinks you're crap," she said, "not me. Somewhere along the line somebody told you that you're worthless, and you took it to heart. That's the problem here. Otherwise, if you loved yourself, and some jackass like Vito suggested you do such a thing, you would've told him to turn those barbells of his into suppositories and then dive off the end of the city pier."

Savannah turned to Tammy. "Watch her till I get back."

"Sure." Tammy nodded, as always, too eagerly. "And can I dry off and get dressed?"

"No, you have to keep wearing that shower curtain until the CSI unit gets here and fingerprints it and swabs it for DNA."

Tammy's big eyes widened and mouth opened and closed several times before she finally said, "You *are* kidding, right?"

Savannah chuckled and shook her head as she walked away. She wouldn't go back to being young again for anything in the world. Having the odd wrinkle and cellulite bump was a good exchange for bits and pieces of accumulated common sense.

When she exited the locker room, she was relieved to see that both Dirk and Vittorio the Magnificent were still working out. But when the young man saw her, he got a wary look on his face. He set down his barbells, picked up his towel, and tossed it over one shoulder.

Donning an unconvincing pseudo-nonchalant expression, he began to stroll toward the men's locker room door.

Savannah hurried over to Dirk and said in his ear. "It's him. Mr. Biceps."

"The *big* guy?" Dirk asked.

"Yeah."

"Damn."

"Yeah."

Neither of them was averse to a little hard work in the call of duty, but Savannah had to admit she didn't blame Dirk for this momentary lapse in enthusiasm. The guy was enormous, not to mention young. And she could usually tell which ones would give them a hard time, resist, run, fight, or all of the above.

Vito looked like a resistor.

As he walked toward the men's shower room, he had a swagger to his step that announced to the world that he was, indeed, an "alpha male." Or at least that he considered himself one, and that was an attitude that frequently caused problems. Law enforcement officials had ways of dealing with the Alpha Vitos of the world, but they often went home nursing bruises and sprains after dealing with them.

And Savannah had gone home and soaked battered parts of her body in hot Epsom salt baths too many times in the past to relish the thought now.

"Slip me your cuffs," Savannah said. "Quick."

"Why?"

Dirk wasn't a materialistic sort of guy, but the half a dozen things he owned, he guarded like a rottweiler with a supper dish full of chopped sirloin.

Savannah elbowed him. "I used mine on the bimbo. Hand them over now."

"Oh, yeah. You're gonna take that guy down by yourself. . . ."

"I'll get the job half done. The rest is up to you."

"This I gotta see."

He followed her as she headed toward the men's shower room, where their quarry had just disappeared.

At the door, she turned back to him and held up her hand. He stopped and she mouthed, "One minute," to him. He nodded.

She reached for the zipper on her sweat suit top, gave it a tug downward, three or four inches, and went inside alone.

Other than one naked little fellow in the back of the room, who scrambled for a towel at the sight of a female entering the locker room, the only other occupant was Vittorio. He had peeled off his T-shirt, and Savannah didn't have to fake the light of lust in her eyes as she looked him over.

To get a gander at a body that good looking, a gal usually had to go to a strip club on "Ladies' Night," pay a cover charge, and be prepared to stick bills in some pseudo-fireman's G-string.

He gave her a suspicious, and somewhat hostile, look as she hurried over to him.

"Hey," she said, "my boyfriend and I are having an argument about you, and I've gotta ask you something."

She walked across the small room and stood quite close to him, making sure he had a clear view straight down the front of her sweat suit.

Savannah would be the first to admit she was a few pounds over what the charts suggested even a tall woman should weigh. But she would also be the first to point out that at least ten pounds of that excess was in her bra, and therefore, not altogether something to be scoffed at.

And Vittorio seemed to agree.

He was obviously enjoying the pectoral view as much as she had been.

Enjoy it while you can, you dirty little peeper, she thought. _Where you're going, you're not going to see any real girlie parts for a long time._

"You and your boyfriend are fighting over me?" he asked, all too pleased at the prospect.

"Oh, yes," she said in her breathiest, phone-sex voice— the one she never got to use for anything other than distracting perps . . . unfortunately. "We were arguing something fierce about you."

In her peripheral vision, she could see Dirk. He had stepped into the room and was moving slowly toward them.

She moved slightly to her right, causing Vittorio to have to turn his back to Dirk in order to maintain his clear view of her feminine assets.

Giving him her best, dimpled smile, she reached out and ran one hand lightly from his shoulder to his elbow, her fingertips skimming over his biceps. "Maybe you can settle the argument for me."

He gulped, his eyes glued to her cleavage. "Ah, sure . . . I mean . . . I'll try."

Her hand moved further down, along his forearms, and she leaned closer still, until her chest was nearly brushing his. "My boyfriend said that to get a body like this, you *must* do steroids. But I said, 'No way. He gets all those gorgeous muscles from working out. I can just tell.' "

Vito was breathing hard . . . hard enough for her to congratulate herself on being able to seduce a guy half her age.

She'd like to think it was because she was just so danged hot, but she reminded herself that Pretty Vito had this felony voyeurism problem and was, no doubt, a pretty easy mark.

Dirk was only a few feet behind him.

It was time.

She reached down and in a practiced move, snapped one of the handcuffs onto Vito's right wrist.

A split second later, she twisted his arm behind his back, and Dirk was ready to grab it.

Vittorio was so shocked at going from "seduced" to "cuffed" in a heartbeat that he was captured before he knew it.

And even then, he didn't seem to get it.

"What is this?" he asked Savannah, indignant. "You and your boyfriend . . . you two into something kinky here?"

"Nope," said Dirk as he spun him around to face him. "Only one perv-o here, buddy. And you're it." He flashed him his badge. "San Carmelita Police Department. And you're under arrest."

"What am I supposed to have done? What are you arresting me for?"

"Taking naughty pictures," Savannah told him. "Or should I say, talking some nitwit girl into doing it for you."

Vito bristled. "I did no such thing. If she was doing something like that, it was all her own idea! It's *her*! Arrest *her*!"

As they led him from the locker room, Savannah shook her head. "Shoot, there goes tonight's fantasy."

"What?" Dirk asked, cranky.

"The chivalrous knight fighting the dragon to rescue the fair damsel fantasy. Sir Galahad here just ruined it." She sighed and shook her head sadly. "Dadgummit. And with that body he would've looked so good in a suit of armor, too."

Chapter 2

"When the hell is she gonna be done messing with that?" Dirk grumbled as he sat on Savannah's sofa, petting her oversized black cat, Diamante, who was sprawled across his lap.

Diamante's only reaction to his complaint was a slight tail twitch to show her own irritation. Diamante and her sister, Cleopatra, held the firm conviction that when a human petted a cat, they should give the task their full, undivided attention.

Dirk was falling down on the job.

Besides his preoccupation with Tammy, he had one eye on the television. The Dodgers were down four runs at the bottom of the eighth, which made him even grumpier than usual. And grumpy, distracted guys didn't give the best pets.

In the corner of Savannah's living room, sitting at the rolltop desk, Tammy was working intently at the computer. She had banned everyone, even Savannah, from coming near her while she completed her task.

As Savannah walked by the desk, on her way from the kitchen, a tray of assorted desserts in hand, Tammy grabbed a manila folder from the desktop and held it over the computer screen.

"Oh, please," Savannah said, "it's not like I haven't seen your bare butt in person plenty of times before." She held out the tray. "Here, eat something before you grow faint from hunger."

"Like *that* would ever happen to anybody around *here*."

With a critical eye Tammy glanced over the plate laden with fudge brownies, a piece of pecan pie, a bowl of Ben and Jerry's Chunky Monkey, and something that looked like a strawberry sundae. "Eh, it's all poison. Pure poison. You really shouldn't contaminate your body with—"

"Yours is the one in the corner," Savannah told her, tamping down her irritation. "It's strawberries over yogurt over a sliced banana, sprinkled with chopped pecans. I made it just for you."

Tammy hesitated, laid down the envelope, and reached for the dish. "You put sugar in it, didn't you?"

"Don't you snerl up your nose at *my* food, girlie. You'll eat it or wear it!" Savannah glanced at the computer screen. "And believe you me, it'll cover a lot more of you than that bar of soap did."

Tammy squealed and slapped the folder back over the screen.

Savannah walked over to Dirk, chuckling. "Here you go, big boy," she said, setting the tray on the coffee table in front of him. "A little something to take the edge off that ravenous hunger of yours . . . the one you worked up while pushing away from my dinner table fifteen minutes ago."

He merely grunted and continued to stare at the television. That was a bad sign. Dirk ignoring free food? She wondered if she should waste time trying to find his pulse or just go straight to CPR.

She glanced at the screen. "That bad?"

"They suck. They just stinkin' suck."

"O-o-okay."

Dirk had a real gift for making succinct, pithy, insightful comments; it was part of the wonder that was him.

But he wasn't so deeply entrenched in despair that he couldn't rally enough to reach for a brownie. "She'd better not be ruining my evidence over there," he grumbled, nodding toward Tammy.

"She's not. She's just fuzzying out her . . . um . . ."

"Her fuzzy."

"Sh-h-h!" Savannah sat down on her favorite over-stuffed, cushy chair next to him. "If she hears you say something like that, she'll delete the pictures altogether."

"She will not. She enjoys nabbing and prosecuting a perv as much as we do."

"True." Savannah smiled as she scooped Cleopatra, her other black mini-panther, onto her lap.

Tammy appeared to be a gentle, peaceful, loving soul to those who met her. And most of the time, she was pure human sunshine.

But, like Savannah, she also had a fierce streak, and her persona could change to Warrior Queen in a heartbeat . . . in defense of herself and others whom she deemed innocent and in need of protection.

Savannah knew that, given no alternative, Tammy would have "bared it all" in a courtroom—if there had been no other way to prosecute Vittorio the Peeporio. But Tammy was handy with the computer, and she was particularly good with manipulating photos, so why shouldn't she guard her own modesty with a few well-placed defocused circles?

"I mean it," Dirk said, biting into a brownie, "her messin' around with those pictures better not jeopardize my case. I want this guy. You should've heard the lip he gave me when I was booking him. Comes from a rich family in Twin Oaks. Considers himself above such things as getting arrested: It's time he had a reality check, and I'm happy to be the one writing it."

"Tammy's not going to ruin your evidence. She knows what she's doing. She'll leave enough that it'll be obvious what happened. Besides, she's keeping a copy of the original, untouched movie. Her in all her nudie glory."

"Yeah, but what if I get Judge O'Fallon? You know how *he* is."

"O'Fallon?" Savannah sniffed and looked disgusted. "Oh, yeah. He's the one who insisted on watching those whorehouse tapes over and over when we were prosecuting that madam."

"He even took them home with him when the case closed."

"If you get O'Fallon," Tammy said, obviously listening to their every word, "I'm burning this disk . . . in the fireplace, that is . . . and you'll be relying on testimony alone to fry Vito."

Savannah chuckled. "She's not kidding, and it's a good idea. Otherwise she'd be burglarizing the judge's house to get the DVD back and in spite of all my lessons, she's not that good at breaking and entering. She'll get caught; we'll have to bail her out and all that rigmarole."

"I'll arrest you for destroying evidence," Dirk said, waving a brownie in Tammy's direction.

"No, you won't. Because Savannah would stop feeding you, and you'd have to buy your own food or starve to death," she replied. "There, that should do it." She popped the DVD out of the computer, slipped it into a plastic case, and walked over to the sofa.

Holding the DVD out to him, she said, "The whole, sad, sordid story right there in digital format for the world to see."

"Thanks." He took it from her, getting only the merest smear of Savannah's fudge frosting on the cover. "I owe you girls. I couldn't have done it without you. None of the girls in the SCPD are cute enough to have lured any-body into that shower room."

Savannah stroked Cleopatra's glossy black coat with one hand and ate a slice of pecan pie with the other. "I wouldn't share that with the gals you work with," she told him.

"Why not? It's true."

Savannah nodded solemnly and gave Tammy a sideways glance. "And thus the mystery is solved: Why does Detective Sergeant Dirk Coulter continue to work alone since that day, all those years ago, when Detective Reid left the force?"

"To heck with that," Tammy said, nudging Dirk's shin with the toe of her sneaker. "Let's get back to that 'I owe you girls' part. What's it going to be? A day at a spa, dinner at Chez Antoine? A weekend on Catalina?"

"Get real," Dirk replied. "I'm paying you out of my own pocket."

Savannah sighed. "A hot dog at the pier. Pay yourself if you want extras, like sauerkraut or mustard."

He grinned. "That's more like it."

His cell phone buzzed, playing the theme from *The Good, the Bad, and the Ugly*—his choice of ringtone for his captain.

"Coulter," he barked into the phone.

His curt tone had a lot to do with the fact that he despised the captain, but he would have answered the same way if it had been his grandmother, the Dodgers' lead pitcher, or Santa Claus.

"Oh, yeah? Really? Hm-m-m."

Savannah and Tammy watched as his irritation faded to subdued interest and mild curiosity.

That was as close to "excited" as Dirk got.

"All right," he said. "Gimme the address." He dumped an instantly indignant Diamante on the floor, reached to the end of the sofa and got his leather bomber coat. He took a pad and pen from the inside pocket. Scribbling, he said, "Oh, yeah, I know the place. I didn't know it was *she* that lived there now. All right. I'm on my way."

He clicked the phone closed and sat there with a perverse little smirk on his face. "You're not going to believe this. You are *not* gonna freakin' believe this!"

"What?" Tammy asked.

"Who?" Savannah wanted to know.

He swelled up with the high degree of irritating self-importance enjoyed by someone who holds a juicy gossip tidbit that they haven't yet shared.

Savannah had seen toad frogs less puffy.

"Oh, spit it out," she said, "before I slap you nekkid and hide your clothes."

He crossed his arms over his chest and lifted his chin a couple of notches. "Clarissa Jardin."

Neither Savannah nor Tammy said anything for as long as they could stand it. Finally, Savannah broke the stalemate by reaching down and snatching the remainder of his brownie out of his hand.

"Hey! I wasn't done with that!"

"You are, unless you tell us what you're so danged smug about. What's with Clarissa? She's having a hissy fit about us busting a perv in her gym and giving her bad publicity?"

"Oh, no. She's happy about publicity. Any kind of publicity."

"That's true," Tammy said, "or else she wouldn't go on all the talk shows, the way she does, and talk trash about 'tub-os' as she calls them."

"Yeah, she needs a skillet beatin' for that," Savannah said. "But what's the call about?"

"Did you know she lives in the area?" Dirk said.

"Yeah, big deal," Savannah replied.

Looking quite pleased with herself, Tammy said, "I knew that, too. I read the other day she's bought that old,

old adobe mansion up in the hills between here and Twin Oaks. It used to belong to the Mexican landowner Don Ramon Rodriguez back in the mid-1800s."

"*That* place?" Savannah said. "I heard that old place is haunted."

"Well, that's where the Mistress of Pain and Gain and her hubby are living right now," Dirk told them. "Or, at least she's living there. Seems to be some question about whether he's living or not."

"What?" Savannah and Tammy asked in unison.

"Yeap," he said. "That's what the call's about. She phoned the station house tonight and reported him missing. And I just caught the case."

"How long?" Savannah wanted to know.

"Five days."

"Five days?" Savannah's right eyebrow raised a notch. "Not exactly eager to get him back, huh?"

"Maybe he leaves home frequently," Tammy said.

"You listened to her squawking all afternoon." Dirk rose and pulled on his coat. "If you managed to get away from her, wouldn't you stay gone?"

"But five days!" Savannah couldn't get over it. "Heck, I wouldn't wait a minute past four days to report *you* missing." She poked Dirk in the ribs as he passed by her. "Wait. Where do you think you're going?"

"To talk to the Mistress of 'No Pain, No Gain.' "

"Not without me you aren't. Let me get my purse . . . and my gun."

"Your gun? You probably won't need your gu—"

"Listen, if that loudmouth gives me any lip at all or even mentions the word 'tub-o' in my presence, you gotta know what's gonna happen. It'll be justifiable homicide. And if there's one overweight gal on the jury, I'm home free."

Dirk gulped and shot Tammy a helpless, worried look. At least, as helpless and worried as tough-guy Coulter ever looked.

"Yeah," he said, following her to the front door. "That's what I'm afraid of. You dispensing your own brand of Southern justice in the middle of my missing persons case. Just thinkin' about all that extra paperwork is enough to make me sick to my stomach."

He paused at the door, then darted back into the living room. In one smooth move, he scooped up another brownie and some chocolate pecan cookies.

Wrapping them in a napkin, he hurried back to Savannah. "Okay, let's boogie."

She glanced down at the wad of goodies, which he was cramming into his coat pocket. "A little something to settle your tummy?"

"Hey, whatever gets you through the night. We'll stop at the Patty Cake Donut Shop for some free coffee on the way."

Savannah could practically see the dollar bills flying out the tailpipe of Dirk's old Buick Skylark as they chugged up the steep foothills that framed the eastern side of San Carmelita. The ancient bomber was big, comfortable, practically indestructible, and got a whole whopping nine miles to the gallon.

"When are you going to trade this tanker in on something more energy efficient, something less polluting, something kinder to Mother Earth?" she asked him as she sipped her free coffee and helped herself to one of the only slightly mashed cookies from his pocket.

"I'll trade it in when you get rid of the Scarlet Pony, Miss Treehugger Environmentalist. That jalopy of yours guzzles just as much gas as this thing does."

He had her there. Her '65 Mustang with its Holley carburetor was hardly a "green machine." She kicked herself for starting an argument she couldn't win. Until . . .

"My 'jalopy' can go from zero to one-twenty lickety-split. This thing can't go over ninety downhill with a stiff wind behind it."

"It don't need to go over ninety."

She gave him a sideways glance. Even by the dim light of a half-moon and the Buick's dash lights, she could see he was stung.

She grinned. *Touché.*

Rolling down the car window, she breathed in the moist night air, scented with orange blossoms and eucalyptus and wild sage. Ah, life was, indeed, worth living.

As they traveled farther from town, higher into the foothills, the fewer houses they saw. Although there were developments here and there, some of them exclusive, gated communities, overall, the countryside had a lonely, almost haunting quality about it.

Dark, gnarled oaks and patches of desert scrub and prickly pear cacti provided the only greenery. Occasionally, through the trees, a creek could be seen, running parallel to the winding two-lane road. Its rocky bed was usually dry or held only a trickle at best. But the spring rains had been abundant so far this year, and as a result, the rivers, streams, and creeks of Southern California actually contained water.

"What do you think about this house we're going to?" she asked.

"It's not a house; it's a hacienda," he snapped.

Still pissy about the car comment, I see, she thought. Someday she'd learn not to bait him. He pouted for so long afterward that it was hardly worth it.

"I know it's a hacienda, as in, big fancy Spanish house. I meant, what do you think about the stories about it being haunted?"

"I think it's bullshit. And anybody stupid enough to believe in that kind of crap is nuts."

Boy, still really *pissy,* she thought.

She cleared her throat. "Okay. Next time I talk to

Granny Reid, I'll be sure to tell her that you think she's nuts."

"*She* believes in ghosts?"

"Big time. Calls 'em 'haunts.' Don't ever get her started about the time Great-Granny Robinson came to visit her from the other side of the grave. That story will stand your hairs on end."

He didn't reply right away, but she could tell he was dying to ask.

Finally, he gave a little. "Wasn't your great-grandma an Indian or something?"

"Full-blooded Cherokee."

Again, a long silence.

"Okay!" he snapped. "What happened?"

"Well, one night, about a month after she died, Great-Grandma came to Gran in a dream. She warned her about a giant black cat that was stalking the—"

He snorted. "Probably one of those fleabags of yours, Di or Cleo. The way you feed those things, they're the size of lions."

Savannah shot him a deadly look. "Do you want to hear this story or not? It's my family folklore. This is deep, serious, spiritual stuff that I'm sharing with you here."

"Yeah, okay. In a dream, a giant pussycat. Go—"

"Great-Grandma Robinson told Gran, 'Beware the Spirit of the Black Leopard who roams the woods here 'bouts and—' "

"Hair boats? What's that?"

Savannah bristled. "Once more, buddy, and you ain't hearing the end of this story." She drew a deep breath and dropped her voice an octave before continuing. "Grandma Robinson told Granny that under no circumstances was she to wander near the woods after sundown for the next ten days . . . until the moon had reached full and then waned. Because if she did, the demon spirit that was inhabitin' that black leopard would not only rip her throat out but also steal the soul clean outta her."

"Yeah. Right. I hate it when that happens."

"Laugh it up, fuzz ball. But even though Granny Reid warned everybody in town about her dream, old Angus Carmody went out drinking that next Friday night and got lost on his way home. And when they found him, two days later, he was in the woods, facedown, all scratched to kingdom come, deader than an aged side o' beef."

"Throat ripped out, I suppose?"

"Naw, his throat was all right. But still, all those scratches. Deep, ugly, nasty gashes and tears. Hundreds of them. All over his body. What a sight! Folks in them parts still talk about it."

They rounded several more curves before Savannah added, "'Course, the scratches might have come from that patch of blackberry briars they found him in."

Dirk gave her one quick, sideways look and a slap on the thigh.

They both laughed.

"And," he said, "I suppose ol' Angus Carmody had the soul sucked clean outta him, too."

"Well, let's just say nobody's expecting to meet up with him on heaven's golden streets after Judgment Day."

Dirk rounded a curve and slowed the car as they approached a gated driveway on the right side of the road.

"You know," he said, "one of these days you're going to pull my leg one time too many, and you're going to be a very sorry lady."

"I'm worried plum sick to death."

"Live in fear, woman. Live in fear."

"Yeah, yeah. I sleep with my eyes open all night long and a butcher knife under my pillow."

"You'd better. I could come for you any time."

"I'd turn Diamante and Cleopatra loose on you, boy. They'd scratch and bite the tar outta you."

"And suck my soul out?"

"Damn tootin'."

"Eh, those two would never attack me. I'm the guy who gives them belly rubs and tuna treats."

"True. They've got you well-trained."

As they turned onto the gravel road, she saw an ornately painted sign above the gate that identified the property as "Rancho Rodriguez."

"This is it, huh?" she said. "I've heard a lot about this place, but I've never been here."

"Me neither. I make a habit of staying away from weird, haunted places. It's a personal standard I have."

"I thought you didn't believe in ghosts."

"Doesn't mean I'd go out of my way to run into one."

Savannah recalled the television interviews with the snooty blonde who called anyone with even a few extra pounds a lazy "tub-o." She thought of the shrill, demanding and demeaning voice she had listened to far too long at the gym.

Clarissa Jardin was the personification of every kid's nightmare PE teacher from hell.

"I think," she said, "I'd rather run into a nice friendly ghost than this gal we're going to interview."

He gave her a warning look. "You be nice now. You hear me?"

"Su-u-re," she said with a nasty little grin. "Aren't I always?"

Chapter 3

Dirk drove along the gravel road and stopped just before the gate. He rolled down his window and pushed the call button on the security box.

Moments later, a female voice with a distinct Spanish accent answered. "Hardin residence. May I help you?"

"Hardin?" Dirk said.

"I think that's the español pronunciation of Jardin," Savannah whispered.

"May I help you?" the speaker box asked again.

"Yeah. Detective Sergeant Dirk Coulter with the San Carmelita Police Department here. Ms. Jardin is expecting me. Let me in."

It was a while longer—quite a while longer—before the gate finally swung open.

"That was deliberate," Dirk grumbled as he spun gravel, shooting through. "Keeping me waiting like that . . . just out of spite . . . yanking my chain . . . messin' with me."

"You were snippy with her. I keep telling you," she said, "you'll catch more flies with sugar then vinegar."

"Yeah, well, who needs more friggen flies?"

"Good point."

The Buick's tires crunched through the gravel as they drove down the long road, through dark clusters of oaks, past groves of avocado, orange, and lemon trees. On either side of the road stood ancient barns, dilapidated outbuildings, and rusting, abandoned farm equipment—all somehow picturesque in their decay, reminding visitors that this had once been a thriving, working ranch.

Ahead, they could see a long, white wall, glowing in the moonlight. And as they drove nearer, they could tell that it was a walled-in enclosure, like a small fortress. The tiled roof of the hacienda was just visible on the far side.

In the center of the wall was an arched entry with a wrought-iron gate and above the gate hung a large bell.

"Wow," Savannah said. "This is the real thing. You can just tell by looking at that wall it's been here forever. Back before California was even a state. It's probably not that different from when this was a great rancho and Don Rodriguez was the lord of it all."

"Eh, so what. The chain-link fence around my trailer park's been there since Eisenhower."

"Gee, I didn't know that," Savannah replied dryly, her bubble popped. "I'll have to look at it with renewed respect the next time you invite me over for a hot dog and a beer."

Several vehicles were parked near the gate, so Dirk pulled the Buick beside them and killed the engine.

"Are you ready to meet the Queen of Physical Fitness?" he asked as they got out of the car.

"More like the Mistress of Meanness. I'm not going to pretend that I like her, you know. Southern belle or not, I'm getting too old for that crap."

"The crap of acting civil to jerks?"

"Exactly."

"Hell, I stopped doing that years ago. In fact, I don't think I ever did it."

"Yeah, well, men are smarter than women in that way."

He stopped in mid-stride and stared at her. "I never thought I'd hear you admit that men are superior to women."

She sniffed. "Get real, buddy, and clean out your ears. That ain't even close to what I said. Men . . . they're deafer than fence posts."

Dirk tested the bell gate and found it open. He pushed it and stood aside for Savannah to enter first.

As she brushed by him, felt his body warmth, and smelled his predictable Old Spice shave lotion, she couldn't help feeling a surge of affection for him. You had to love a guy who always opened every door and let you go through first—unless there was a possible perp with a gun on the other side. And, in that case, he insisted on being first.

You just had to love him . . . faded Harley-Davidson T-shirt, battered bomber jacket, and all.

But she forgot about Dirk's attire and gallant ways the moment she stepped through the gate and into the courtyard.

She wasn't sure what she'd been expecting here on Clarissa Jardin's property. Maybe exercise equipment? Implements of torture? At least, beds of prickly cacti and roses with all thorns and no blossoms?

But the moonlight and a few carefully placed blue accent lights illuminated a virtual fairyland. It was a lush garden, planted with every romantic flower, shrub, and herb imaginable. Hollyhocks, delphinium, foxglove, and rosebushes lined the whitewashed walls of the enclosure. Carnations, asters, peonies, nasturtiums, and geraniums grew in profusion along a rock walkway that wove through the courtyard, toward the house at the far end.

The place looked more like an English garden than a California yard. Lemon blossoms and star jasmine scented the moist night air.

Savannah could easily picture Don Rodriguez with his wife, children, and servants, living a gracious life in a simpler time here in this place. And with the help of the silvery moonlight, she could easily imagine that their ghosts remained, reluctant to leave this tranquil setting.

In the center of it all stood a giant pavilion with elegant, comfortable wicker furniture that provided a seating area fit for any rancho lord and lady and their fortunate guests.

Savannah couldn't help envying anyone who could bring a morning cup of coffee or an evening glass of wine out to this paradise and spend an hour soaking in the solace of it all, relaxing with their thoughts or a good book.

"Nice," she said. "Very nice."

"Eh, your backyard is just as good," he replied.

"Yeah, sure. How can you even say that? My folding lawn chairs compared to that gorgeous wicker?"

"Your yard has your lemonade. Your yard has you in it."

She gave Dirk a sideways glance, a bit surprised. Dirk was getting mushy in his old age.

"And your beer is the coldest in town . . . and free."

Okay, some things never change, she thought.

Ahead of them, at the end of the rock walkway, on the side of the courtyard opposite the bell gate, was the house. Savannah had been expecting something larger, having heard all about the land baron who had built it.

It was a long building, two stories high, built in the Monterey style with a Spanish tiled roof, white adobe walls, and a railed balcony that stretched across the upper level, from one end to the other.

The windows glowed with golden light that spilled out in patches onto the garden flowers. And through one of the windows, they saw a couple of figures moving, walking back and forth, in what looked like a dining room.

Both the upper and lower stories of the house had several doors each, as though the rooms were situated end to end and each had its own outside door.

"Looks sorta like the Blue Moon," Dirk said, referring to San Carmelita's most notorious no-tell motel.

"I guess architecture is a little different now than it was back when guys rode horses and ladies wore corsets and petticoats."

He shot her a mischievous look. "What? You don't wear corsets?"

"Only in your dreams."

They walked up to the door in the center of the house, the one that seemed most likely to be the main door. Dirk knocked on it, using his officious SCPD knock that was just short of pounding.

In less than a minute, a short, robust, Latina lady answered. She was wearing a bright red shirt and simple navy slacks. She had an ageless quality about her—flawless, golden skin with glossy black hair—and could have been anywhere from forty to sixty years old.

She gave them a gracious, though somewhat guarded, "Hello? May I help you?"

Dirk presented his badge. "I'm Detective Sergeant Dirk Coulter with the San Carmelita Police Department." He nodded toward Savannah. "And this is Savannah Reid. We need to talk to Clarissa Jardin."

Before the woman could reply or invite them inside, a woman appeared behind her. And even though Savannah had seen Clarissa Jardin's face in the media often enough to recognize her instantly, she was shocked at the difference between the public and private Clarissa.

Gone was the hardcore, militaristic, overbearing despot of the gym scene.

Dressed in a white Victorian style nightgown and a

flowing robe of peacock-blue satin paisley, she was the quintessential demure lady. Even her signature blond mane was tied back with a blue ribbon.

"Detective," she said, as she hurried forward to greet them, "please come in. Thank you for responding so quickly. I'm so relieved you're here."

She reached around the other woman and pulled the door open wider. "Maria, please get our guests something to drink. What will you have, Detective Coulter, and . . . is it . . . *Detective* Reid?"

"No, just 'Savannah' will do," Savannah replied warily. "And I don't need any refreshments, thank you."

"Me either," Dirk added. "We should probably get down to business, you know . . . the business that you called the station house about."

Clarissa turned to Maria. "If our guests don't need anything to eat or drink, you may be excused. Good night."

"Good night, Señora."

With a slight nod of her head, the maid left. And Savannah couldn't help but feel that, in spite of Clarissa Jardin's gentle demeanor, Maria seemed all too happy to leave her mistress's presence.

Savannah and Dirk stepped through the small doorway and into the living room.

Again, Savannah was struck by the fact that this house, although it had been owned by a wealthy, powerful landowner, was quite modest, by today's standards.

The room wasn't much larger than Savannah's, but much more expensively furnished, she had to admit.

The items that Clarissa or her decorator had chosen were a strange combination. From the enormous tapestry that nearly covered the far wall, to the dark, hand-carved, Victorian furniture and the stained glass and wrought-iron sconces, to the leather mission-style sofa, it was a strange mishmash of styles and periods.

Even with her own limited knowledge of décor, Savannah was pretty sure that Don Rodriguez had never planted his tushy on anything as fancy as that dainty, diamond-tufted, velvet chair in the corner.

"This is a neat place you got here," Dirk said. "Cool what you did with it."

Savannah nearly gagged. She knew he didn't give a hoot about decorating, and that he was only kissing up to get the interview off to a good start. Either that, or he was remembering how good Clarissa looked on that gym poster . . . her and her perky hind end.

Savannah put that notion out of her mind immediately. It wasn't professional to smack your partner in front of others, and thought control was the first step to avoiding violence.

"Come, have a seat," Clarissa said, indicated the sofa with a queenly wave. "Make yourselves comfortable."

Dirk sat down first. He moved his hand over the leather, and said, "Ah-h-h, very, very nice. Soft as a baby's bottom," in a voice that Savannah could only describe as "gooshey."

She plopped down next to him and shot him a withering look. Like he would know, Mr. Never-Changed-A-Diaper-In-His-Life. She knew the ins and outs of his love life, or lack thereof, as well as her own. And she was pretty darned sure that the only butt he'd had his hand on in a long time was his own . . . which was probably part of the problem.

"Yeah, well, all that crap aside," Savannah said, turning to Clarissa, "tell me something, Ms. Jardin. Your husband has been missing for five days. Why are you just now calling the cops?"

She certainly had their attention now. Both of them stared at her with open mouths.

Clarissa's astonishment quickly turned to indignation. "I'm sure," she said, "that Detective Coulter here was just making a bit of small talk before approaching more . . . difficult . . . topics."

"That's right," Dirk added. "I was gonna lead up to it, a little more subtle-like."

Subtle? Savannah thought. *Since when?* Dirk was as skilled at "subtle" as he was at diaper changing.

"I don't mean to be blunt, Ms. Jardin," Savannah said, "but I'd think if you're so all-fired worried about your husband, we probably don't need to be wasting time, chatting about refreshments, or decorating, or which is softer . . . your couch or a baby's butt."

Dirk reached over, placed his hand on Savannah's thigh, and gave it a little squeeze. "What Savannah is trying to say is that we need to get going on this investigation as soon as possible. Five days is a long time for a person to be unaccounted for."

Savannah put her own hand around Dirk's wrist and squeezed so hard that she felt him flinch. He quickly removed it.

"That's okay," Clarissa said as she and her nightgown and her satin robe floated over to a Victorian fainting couch, where she sat down. She folded her hands in her lap. "I'm accustomed to being treated rudely," she said. "It's just part of being a celebrity."

"Really? Hm-m-m," Savannah replied. "I've never been rude to Julia Roberts or Halle Berry."

Dirk gave her another warning look.

Clarissa glanced quickly over Savannah's figure and smiled ever so slightly. Her eyes were cold when she said, "But then, Julia Roberts or Halle Berry don't take a public stand against obesity the way I do. That makes me unpopular with . . ." She gave Savannah another quick visual sweep. ". . . with some people."

A fantasy flashed across the screen of Savannah's imagination. A delicious fantasy that involved an enormous sword and Clarissa Jardin's suddenly disembodied head flying through the air, landing on a Georgia dirt road, and getting kicked into a ditch. The whole daydream took less than two seconds and ended with Savannah standing by that roadside, bloodied sword in hand, grinning down at the ditch.

It was a well-worn fantasy that had worked for her since seventh grade, when she had first thought of it—when Kathy Murdock had called her and her family "white trash" because she wore hand-me-downs.

The classics held up.

"Oh, a lot of people, celebrities and regular folks, take a public stand against obesity, for health purposes and all," Savannah replied evenly. "But they don't make a living from wounding people's spirits and encouraging them to despise themselves and their own bodies."

Dirk cleared his throat loudly, reached into his jacket pocket and produced a pad and pen. "Let me see now, Ms. Jardin—"

She batted her eyelashes at him. "Please, call me Clarissa. Everyone does."

That's not what I call you, Savannah thought, but she decided to be professional and keep it to herself. *It's a bit late now for "professional," Savannah*, the inner critic suggested. It also whispered that perhaps she hadn't accompanied Dirk on this little jaunt for the altruistic reason of helping her old friend solve his case. She might have tagged along because she was hoping for a chance to take a swipe at Clarissa Jardin—a woman who was in trouble, whose husband was missing.

She decided to shut up.

"Ah, yes, Clarissa," Dirk said. "Tell me a bit about your husband. His name, age, general description."

"Bill is forty-one, six feet tall. He used to be good-looking, but now he's gained about eleven or twelve pounds."

Savannah said nothing but mentally gripped her sword a bit tighter. Heads could be reattached and removed over and over again if necessary.

"His hair and eye color?" Dirk asked.

"Blond and brown."

"Any identifying scars, tattoos?"

"No tattoos. Bill was too conservative for anything like that."

Savannah couldn't help noting that Bill Jardin's wife had just referred to him in the past tense. That didn't bode well for Bill.

Dirk asked Bill's birthday, and Savannah knew one of the first things he would do was run a background check on Bill to see if he had a criminal record. Experience had shown them both that a sizable bank account was no guarantee that someone was a law-abiding citizen.

"What sort of vehicle does he drive?"

"A new, red Jaguar XK. A convertible."

She even supplied the license plate number, which Savannah found mildly interesting. Most people didn't know their license plate number unless it was a vanity plate.

"And what was he wearing the last time you saw him?" Dirk asked.

"Jeans and a turquoise polo."

She wondered how much Clarissa might have prepared for this moment. Her answers seemed rehearsed, her manner quite subdued for a woman with a long-absent spouse.

"What does he do?" Dirk asked.

"Do?" Clarissa thought about it a moment before answering with a totally straight face, "He drinks, gambles, and chases other women."

Dirk stopped scribbling for a moment, but continued to stare down at his pad. "Actually," he said, "What I meant was, 'How does he make a living?' "

"Bill doesn't make a living. I do."

For just a moment, Savannah saw it—the fleeting look of hurt in the other woman's eyes. Not anger. Raw pain. And she couldn't help but feel a twang of pity for her.

Pain was pain. Even for rude people.

In a gentle tone, with her heaviest Georgian accent, Savannah said, "Your Billy Boy sounds like a real peach."

Clarissa's eyes searched Savannah's, and Savannah could feel the moment when the other woman realized that she was offering genuine empathy.

Clarissa's expression softened, and it occurred to Savannah that maybe Clarissa Jardin wasn't accustomed to kindness or sympathy.

"Yes," Clarissa said, sounding suddenly tired. "Bill's a real catch. Lucky me."

"How long have you two been married?" Dirk asked.

"Eighteen years. I married him right out of high school."

"That's a long time to spend with a heavy-drinking, womanizing gambler," Savannah said softly.

"I love him." Clarissa shrugged. "There are all kinds of love in this world. Not all of them are noble."

A heavy silence hung in the air until Dirk said, "When did you last see your husband, Clarissa?"

"Five nights ago. He left the house about nine to run an errand, and he didn't come back."

"Where did he go?"

"He said he was driving to Twin Oaks, to the convenience store there, to get cigarettes."

She was lying; Savannah saw it in her eyes.

Glancing sideways at Dirk, Savannah saw him squint ever so slightly and she knew that he had registered it, too.

Being cops for years, having people lie to you at least twice every fifteen minutes—it tended to fine-tune one's internal lie detector.

"He said he was getting cigarettes," Dirk repeated, "and he didn't come back or contact you in any way since that night."

"That's right."

"So, the question that I have to ask you, Clarissa," he said, "is why didn't you call us before now?"

Again, she seemed to have her answer ready. "Because he's done this before. He always came back after a couple of days, apologizing, promising to be a good husband from then on. And he'd be my good Bill, the one I fell in love with in high school. I just thought it was one of those times. But—"

She choked, and her eyes filled with tears.

"But?" Dirk prompted.

"But he's never been away this long. Three days was always his limit before."

"So, you two had some sort of argument or disagreement before he left to go get the cigarettes," Savannah said.

"Sure. We fought almost every night about something."

"And what was the argument about that night?" Dirk asked.

"Another woman. Most of the fights were about other women."

"What is this other woman's name?"

"I don't know her name."

Another lie, Savannah noted. She was starting to have doubts about the health and well-being of Mr. Clarissa. A guy who'd been missing for five days, whose wife was lying to the cops—things were looking a bit grim for poor ol' Bill.

"What *do* you know about her?" Savannah asked.

"That she wears cheap, disgusting perfume. Too much of it. And she's forgetful."

Dirk looked up from his scribbling. "Forgetful?"

"Yeah. She forgets to put her panties back on . . . leaves them in married men's cars."

"Oh, okay." Dirk didn't bother to write that one down.

His cell phone began to ring, playing "The House of the Rising Sun." Savannah knew it was the police station house calling. He'd chosen that ring tone after one too many all-nighters at his desk, buried in paperwork.

"Excuse me," he told Clarissa and answered it. "Coulter."

Dirk had a good poker face, but after so many years looking at his mug, Savannah could tell when it was an important call or a "the captain wants to know if you're anywhere near his daughter's school; she forgot her lunch money" call.

"Yeah? Where?" He listened, gave Savannah a quick look, and then said, "Okay. I'm on my way."

He shoved the phone back into his pocket and stood. "I think I've got what I need right now, Ms. Jardin," he said. He handed her one of his business cards. "If you think of anything else or if you need to talk to me, just give me a buzz."

"Thank you."

She slid the card into her robe pocket as she searched his face, suspicious. "Is everything all right? I mean, that call you got?"

"It's just something I have to check out. But I'll start working on finding your husband right away. I'll get in touch with you as soon as we get anything new."

In less than a minute, Savannah and Dirk were out the door and walking through the courtyard garden, on their way back to the car.

Savannah knew something was up. Dirk seldom moved that quickly.

"Whatcha got?" she asked.

He glanced back toward the house, the closed door. Opening the bell gate, he said, "A new, red Jaguar abandoned up in the hills on Sulphur Creek Road."

"Uh-oh. A body?"

"Nope." He opened the car door for her, then came around and got in himself.

"Well, that's good," she said as he started the engine.

"What?"

"Just a dumped car. No dead body."

"It ain't all that good," he said. "There's blood spatter all over the interior."

"Oh."

"And brain matter on the dash."

Savannah felt her stomach do a little flip-flop. "Oh. Yeah, not all that good. Sounds like ol' Billy Bob Jardin done lost his mind."

"Yeap. At least part of it."

Chapter 4

"I can't believe we're driving down Sulphur Creek Road, and you're not accusing me of eating chili for dinner last night," Dirk said.

Savannah looked out the passenger side window at the moonlit, prickly cactus-covered hills and tried not to breathe. This area of the foothills was known for its sulphur deposits and its distinctive odor. It smelled a bit like rotten eggs, week-old cabbage soup, and Dirk after a night of chili, tacos, or anything containing beans.

For the past eighteen years, whenever they had ventured this way, she had accused him of polluting her personal airspace.

But with age she had become wiser. Less judgmental. Less accusatory. Kinder and milder.

"I know it's not you," she said, "it's the creek."

"Damn right it's not me. Glad you finally got that straight."

"Oh, yeah. Like you're above it, you gaseous, odious beast."

Okay. Just wiser.

Savannah glanced at her watch. 9:48. This was destined to be another one of those exhausting, draining, all-nighters, for which her only compensation would be the pleasure of Dirk's scintillating wit and the warmth of his companionship.

She could be home right now cuddled up in her bed with a steamy novel, Cleo draped across her feet, Diamante tucked under her left arm, a piece of Death by Chocolate cake heaped with whipped cream sitting on her nightstand.

Someday she'd learn to say "no" to these invitations of working for nothing.

But it wasn't going to be tonight. Because a moment later, they rounded a curve and she saw the blue and red flashing lights from the police cruisers parked around their crime scene. The sight of the guys in uniform milling around, checking out the area, caused a major rush of adrenaline to hit her system.

It was a hit that was stronger than any shot of espresso or slice of Death by Chocolate cake. And she knew she wouldn't want to be anywhere else in the world right now.

Dirk pulled the Buick off the road, onto the shoulder. There was barely enough room to park the car between the pavement and the steep, rocky hill that rose to their right. And to the left, on the other side of the road was a reinforced guardrail and less than two feet beyond that, a sharp drop of at least five hundred feet.

All too well, Savannah remembered when they had responded to a call out here about ten years ago because a carload of drunken teenagers had gone off this cliff.

That's when the guardrail had been reinforced. Too late, of course.

She had hated this crook in the road ever since.

The locals had given it the terribly original name of Deadman's Curve, and apparently, the notorious spot was living up to its name again. About sixty feet ahead of them, a bright red Jaguar convertible sat on the left side of the road nearest the cliff, only inches from the guardrail. It was facing the opposite direction.

They got out of the Buick and walked down the road toward the Jaguar. "Looks like somebody's awake enough to play the yellow tape," Dirk said as they stepped over the yellow plastic ribbon that was strung around the scene.

Savannah was glad that the area had been cordoned off, too, but for a different reason than Dirk. She had better, more pleasant, things to do than listen to him chew out his insubordinates—like clean her oven or visit her dentist. And since Dirk had been on the SCPD longer than almost everyone, including the captain and chief of police, the list of insubordinates he could abuse was a long one.

As they approached the Jaguar, several of the policemen nodded to Dirk and greeted Savannah. They didn't appear to be doing much except providing a "presence," meandering around the scene, chatting with each other.

Savannah knew the drill all too well. Cops were just as nosy as anybody else. Hanging out at a crime scene provided a lot better entertainment than sitting in your squad car in an all-night convenience store parking lot, sipping free coffee.

A middle-aged cop wearing a uniform that was stretched tight across his ample belly walked over to them and put out his hand to Dirk.

"Sergeant Coulter. Good to see you," he said with a modicum of enthusiasm.

Dirk gave him a grunt and a brief handshake that was dismissive at best.

The cop turned to Savannah, perhaps searching for a warmer form of communication. "Hi, Savannah. You're looking mighty fine tonight."

Savannah gave him a quick once-over, thinking that, even though he was totally bald—not a hint of a hair on his head—his appearance wouldn't have been improved one iota if he'd had a world-class toupee.

"Why, thank you, darlin'," she replied, desperately trying to remember the guy's name. "You're pretty easy on the eyes yourself."

He flushed with pleasure at the compliment. In fact, he was so pleased that she felt only half-guilty for lying to him.

If Granny Reid's predictions were right, any minute now her nose would begin to grow, and her tongue would turn black and fall out.

"Are you senior officer here, Wiggins?" Dirk asked him, waves of impatience rolling off him.

"Yeah," was the equally curt reply.

"Start a log yet?"

Rather than answer, Wiggins held up a clipboard with some forms attached.

"Okay." Dirk nodded toward the mob of blue uniforms crowding around the Jaguar. "Get all their names and tell them to stay at least twenty feet from the vehicle. Did you call CSI yet?"

"Um . . . not yet."

"What are you waiting for? Do it! They should've been halfway here by now."

Wiggins walked away and once he was out of earshot, Dirk said, "Easy on the eyes, my ass. Herb Wiggins is as ugly as a junkyard dog, but not nearly as smart."

"Herb. *That's* his first name."

"He's fat and bald."

"He's sweet."

"Hurrumph."

She could have added that Dirk wasn't as svelte around the middle as he'd once been, not to mention a little thin on top. But in all the years she'd known him, he had never once criticized her midlife spread, so . . .

Once Wiggins had delivered Dirk's message, the uniforms scattered, standing a respectable distance away, and watched, eager to see what was going to happen next.

"Tromped all over my crime scene," Dirk mumbled as he and Savannah approached the Jaguar. Then, loudly, he said, "You bunch of morons. Don't you know to respect the perimeter of a scene? All of you . . . check the treads of your shoes before you leave here. I don't want anybody walking off with evidence, like a spent shell."

Immediately, fifteen to twenty policemen began hopping on one leg, then the other, as they lifted their feet and examined their soles. It reminded Savannah of a really bad Riverdance routine, and she had to suppress a giggle.

Her moment of humor faded, though, as they neared the convertible.

The car was only dimly illuminated by the headlights and flashing lights of the squad cars. Momentarily, the moon had gone behind some clouds, and there were no streetlights of any kind up in the foothills outside of town. The red and blue lights playing over the glistening surface of the expensive automobile gave it an eerie, sinister appearance.

She felt a prickling feeling that ran along the back of her neck and down her arms, a sensation she'd had many times when approaching the scene of a violent crime.

She was prepared to admit that some of the creepy feeling she was experiencing might have been due to what she had been told about the car's interior. But many times when approaching an area—even before she knew it was the scene of a crime—she had felt the same instinctive revulsion sweep over her, warning her that all wasn't well.

And all wasn't well with the Jaguar. The top was down on the convertible and even in the poor lighting, the gory evidence was obvious.

The blood spray on the passenger's side of the windshield and the other biological matter on the fine, burled

walnut trimmed dash, told the story all too clearly; someone had been murdered in that vehicle.

"Ee-e-ew," she said, feeling her stomach turn.

"Yeah," he replied. "At moments like this I wish I'd
followed my dream and gone into another line of work."

"Dream? *You* had a *dream*?"

"Well, don't look so damned surprised."

"What was it?"

"I'm not telling you."

She gouged him in the ribs. "Tell me."

"No."

"Why not?"

"You'll laugh, and I'm busy."

He had her there. They *were* busy. With Bill Jardin's
brains on his dash, there were more important things to
attend to.

She flipped a mental switch and went into professional
mode.

A young policeman walked by, and she asked to borrow his flashlight. He handed it to her with a flirtatious
smile, and as he walked away, it occurred to her that she
did miss being a cop, being surrounded by gorgeous, vir-
ile and . . . okay . . . seriously horny . . . men all day.

She sighed and mentally flipped that switch again.

Playing the beam of the flashlight over the exterior of
the car, she said, "This vehicle hasn't been sitting here for
any five days. It's dusty and dirty up in these hills, but the
outside of this car is as clean as a whistle." She trailed the
light over the seats and doors. "And other than the blood
spatter, it's clean inside, too."

"Of course it hasn't been here," Dirk said, slightly
miffed.

She had paid attention to two other males in less than
five minutes and that was bound to put him in a huff
every time.

"You don't have to be snippy about it," she said.

"It's just obvious. This car cost more than my trailer and—"

"Well, ye-e-eah. More than your whole trailer *park*."

"Be that as it may. My point is: A car like this one doesn't sit abandoned without people noticing and reporting it, or stealing it, or stripping it, or God knows what. I don't know where it's been before, but it's been sitting here only a few hours, I can guarantee you."

She had to agree with him. While Sulphur Creek Road wasn't as heavily traveled as your average Southern California freeway, it was the main road connecting San Carmelita with Twin Oaks, a smaller inland community of about three thousand people.

"That's true," she said. "A red Jaguar convertible sitting on Deadman's Curve would have raised a ruckus, even if no one had noticed the bloodstained interior."

"Lemme borrow that flashlight," Dirk said.

She handed it to him, and he walked slowly toward the guardrail.

Knowing his fear of heights, Savannah couldn't help admiring him and snickering just a little, as she watched him tiptoe up to the edge and peek over. Her thing was snakes. His was heights. She freaked out at the sight of an over-grown worm; he couldn't go more than three rungs up a ladder.

Hey, you couldn't be a superhero twenty-four hours a day.

She joined him at the railing as he trailed the beam of the flashlight back and forth over the thick sagebrush, cacti, and large craggy rocks that covered the steep cliff.

At the very bottom, far beyond the reach of the simple flashlight, was a river. She could hear it, rushing over its rocky bed, and she had seen it before—the day the kids had gone over the cliff and landed in the water, upside down.

That was a day she would never be able to forget.

"Hell of a thing," Dirk muttered. "This happening here of all places. I thought we were done with this friggen place."

She reached for his hand and for a moment, her fingers entwined with his. She squeezed them gently. "I know, buddy," she said. "I was thinking the same thing."

She released his hand before any of the other cops could see. No point in starting rumors. And policemen gossiped worse than anybody she knew. Probably because they had more exciting tales to tell than the average accountant or store clerk.

"There's a lot of water down there," she said, stating the obvious in an attempt to change the subject. "All those rains we've had. One storm after the other last week."

"And that one last night was a doozy," he replied, playing along.

Yeah, she thought, *when all else fails, discuss the weather*.

After a few more awkward moments of reminiscing, Savannah said, "If they took his body out of that car and threw it off this cliff . . . do you think he'd hit the water down there?"

Dirk leaned forward, ever so slightly, and took a quick look. "Yeah. I do. It's pretty much straight down." He took a couple of steps back from the guardrail. "I really wish it wasn't this spot," he said. "For more reasons than one."

"I hear you."

Gently, with her best fake-nonchalant look on her face, she took the flashlight from his hand.

Stepping around him, she moved closer to the railing and shone the light down the cliff.

Unlike him, she was fine with cliffs. As long as those cliffs were certifiably snake-free.

Swinging the light back and forth, she peered into the

darkness and saw nothing at the bottom but a black void. However, as she trained the light on the cliff itself, she saw something interesting.

"I think he's down there," she said.

Phobia or no phobia, Dirk was instantly alert. He took a few steps, closing the gap between them.

"Why? What do you see?"

"Some broken cactuses, I mean, cacti or whatever. Right down there. See?"

He did see. It was obvious, several large clumps of prickly pear about ten feet down from the edge, broken— their pads torn off or crushed. And all around the smashed cacti was equally damaged sagebrush.

"Something definitely went down through there. Recently," he said. "Something big."

"Like a human being," Savannah added.

"Exactly like a human being. And even if he was alive when he went over that cliff, he sure wouldn't be by the time he hit the bottom."

Savannah winced at the very thought. The cliff with its sharp, jagged rocks and nettled vegetation, that terrible drop, and of course the river at the bottom with its rushing water and stone-covered banks and bed.

She glanced back at the luxury car, fouled by its gruesome biological evidence. "I guess the good news for Bill Jardin is . . ." she said, ". . . he wasn't alive when he went over."

Dirk shook his head. "Yeah, right. Goody for him."

Savannah looked at her watch. 10:15. "It won't be dawn for hours," she said. "And there's no way we're going to find him until we've got some daylight."

"That's for sure. We'll get the crime scene unit out here as soon as it's light to process that car, the road, and as much of this cliff as they can get to. That's gonna be great fun for them, processing a scene while hanging from ropes."

"And of course, we have to go down there to search the river—either rappel down the cliff or have a chopper drop us."

He didn't answer, and she knew he was searching his mind for any excuse to get out of doing either of those.

"Your mom could have another emergency appendectomy," she suggested.

"Naw." He sighed. "They wouldn't buy it. She's already had three in the past five years."

"That's gotta be some sort of record."

"Yeah, especially for a woman who's been dead twenty years."

She stifled a giggle. "This time you might have to fake an attack yourself."

He took another tentative look over the cliff. "Hell, if it comes down to it, I'd rather actually *have* the operation. Anything would be better than going over that cliff on a rope or hanging from a helicopter by a thread."

Turning away from the guardrail, he shuddered and added, "I hear you don't really need an appendix."

"Yeah," Savannah replied. "They're just for decoration anyway."

Savannah had considered going home and grabbing a few hours of sleep before daybreak came and the next step in the search for Bill Jardin would begin. Certainly, it would have been the sensible thing to do.

But she hadn't considered it seriously. Of all her many virtues—which, of course, included humility—"sensible" wasn't at the top of the list.

Years ago, she had discovered that she could usually circumvent the biological need to sleep, if she only had enough adrenaline, caffeine, and simple carbs in the form of baked goods or chocolate.

Now, after hours of hanging around the abandoned

Jaguar, shooting the breeze with every uniformed cop on the scene, and ignoring the increasingly testy Dirk, she was running low on adrenaline. So, she was delighted to see the hot pink Volkswagen bug pull up to the perimeter edge and a bouncy blonde pop out.

"Tammy!" Savannah shouted, as though greeting a long-lost relative at the airport. Actually, she was happier to see Tammy than she would have been to see any of her Georgia family, with the exception of her beloved Granny Reid.

And one of the reasons for her elation was the bag in her assistant's hand.

It was a white bag, with "Patty Cake Bakery" printed in red on the side. The much needed nutrition-free simple carbs and caffeine had arrived!

"Dirk! Hey, Dirk, get over here," Savannah yelled to him.

He was sitting in the front seat of his Buick, his arms crossed over the top of the steering wheel, his head resting on his forearms.

He looked the picture of dejection. But Savannah knew it was more like the epitome of barely repressed terror.

Dawn was breaking, and he still hadn't come up with a good excuse not to lead his investigation team over the side of that cliff. She was relieved that he didn't have any cyanide capsules in the Buick's glove box.

He needed food. Free food.

If that couldn't cheer him up and take his mind off his troubles, nothing could.

Oh-so-slowly, he raised his head. Just an inch at first. Then, enough to peek at her over his burly forearms.

She tried not to laugh. *Big, bad Dirk, my butt*, she thought. He'd run headlong into a room full of "considered armed and dangerous" perps, Smith & Wesson drawn, a Clint Eastwood scowl on his face. But ask him to climb up a ladder to paint some window trim? Forget about it. He wouldn't show his face at painting parties, not even for a free keg of beer and all-you-can-eat pepperoni pizza.

She knew. She had tried.

"Come here!" she told him again.

When he didn't budge, she pointed to Tammy.

He looked that way and when he saw the Patty Cake bag, he came alive, jumping out of the car and hurrying over to them.

Savannah felt a surge of affection toward him. She had often thought that the basis of their long-standing friendship was their mutual love of junk food and artificial stimulants.

But Tammy appeared less happy. By the dim light of the early dawn, Savannah could see a half-smile, half-grimace on her pretty face, and she knew exactly why. Tammy was thrilled to be here, to be part of the action. And the grimace was because . . .

"You know I *hate* having to buy this crap for you," she said as she held the sack out to Savannah with two fingers, like a dog walker holding a plastic bag with their Fido's dumpings inside. "It goes against my principles to even step into an establishment that sells poison like that to human beings and calls it 'food.' Who—"

"Smells great in there, though, doesn't it?" Dirk said, trying to pull the bag out of Savannah's hand. "I mean, you have to admit the smell of the coffee brewing, along with the fresh-baked muffins and stuff."

Tammy grinned. "Yeah, okay, it smelled great, but what's to keep them from selling at least one whole-bran muffin or something with an actual nutrient in it?"

Savannah handed Dirk his usual oversized apple fritter and a cup of black coffee. "I think Patty gets a lot more pigs like Dirk and me in her place than she does intelligent, health-conscious people like you."

Tammy opened her mouth to retort, then snapped it closed. Why continue to argue when you've already won?

She glanced around, taking in all the activity. The van with the Crime Scene Unit's logo on the side had just arrived. Technicians in their spotless white lab coats, cases in hand, were descending on the Jaguar.

But the county coroner's van was conspicuously absent.

"No body yet?" she asked.

"No," Savannah said. "Plenty of biological matter for CSU to process, but no actual DB yet."

"Are we sure he's dead?" Tammy asked.

"Oh yeah," Dirk said. "At least, if the spatter is Jardin's, it's a lock he ain't among the living no more."

Tammy brightened—far more than was decent under the circumstances. "So, we get to go mountain climbing and look for the body! Cool!"

What a ghoul, Savannah thought. Maybe she had overtrained the kid. Tammy cried at the thought of chickens losing their lives and being made into nuggets, but finding a human corpse . . . that was cool stuff?

"Yeah, yeah, mountain climbing. Yippee," Dirk grumbled. He took a long drink of his coffee and sauntered back to the Buick.

"What's the matter with him?" Tammy asked.

Savannah bit into a maple bar and closed her eyes to savor it just a moment before answering. She swallowed, opened her eyes and said, "Dirk, heights, remember?"

"Oh, right. He won't even climb onto a chair to change a lightbulb. I guess he's not big on rappelling down a cliff."

"You think?"

"*I'll* go. I'm into that stuff."

Savannah smiled, basking in the sunshine energy that her dear friend exuded. Tammy was into anything. Tammy was into life.

Nodding toward the Jaguar, Tammy said, "May I look?"

"Sure. Don't get in anybody's way and if anybody says anything to you, tell them you're Dirk's kid sister."

Tammy's face fell. "You think that would actually score me points? I mean, Dirk hasn't won any Mr. Congeniality contests in the department."

"True. Tell them you're Miss July on this year's National Law Enforcement Calendar."

"National Law Enforcement Calendar?"

"Yeah, the one they sell to benefit cops going through divorces because they availed themselves of the free services of sex workers while on the job."

"What?" Tammy's eyes widened. "They have a charity fund for *that*?"

"Of course not. Well, not that I know of. But once you say, 'Miss July,' their brains will lock up and freeze, so it doesn't matter what you say after that."

"Okay."

Savannah chuckled as Tammy strolled away, looking particularly fetching in her snug red T-shirt, denim shorts, and espadrilles, her long golden hair shining in the early morning light. No, Tammy wouldn't have any problem getting around this scene or any other scene where the population was predominately male.

As Savannah walked over to the Buick to join Dirk, she heard a familiar sound in the distance—helicopter blades, beating the air, in a distinctive staccato rhythm, rapidly approaching.

"Sounds like our 'eye in the sky' has arrived," she said as she opened the passenger's door and slid into the car beside him.

"Yes, and please, please, God, let *them* find him," Dirk said.

"Wouldn't that be good?" Savannah said. "Then you

wouldn't have to go over the edge on a rope and get all nervous and barf and embarrass yourself in front of everybody? Wouldn't that be peachy keen?"

Dirk responded with a "drop dead" look.

She took a bite of her maple bar, chewed it, savored it, swallowed, and said, "Too bad nothing good like that ever happens to you."

"Screw you."

She laughed.

He slid lower in his seat, and once again, draped his arms across the steering wheel and leaned his head on them.

"Want half of my other maple bar?" she asked, reaching out to snatch him from the gaping jaws of depression.

He was instantly alert, but indignant. "Other? Other maple bar? She got you two? How come she got you *two* maple bars? She only got me *one* lousy fritter."

" 'Cause she likes me best." She tore the pastry in two and held the half out to him. "Do you want it or not?"

Before he could reach for it, his cell phone rang. It was a ringtone she didn't recognize, a standard, generic buzz. Very unlike Dirk, who had assigned some kind of a song, usually rock-and-roll, to everyone he knew.

"Coulter," he barked. "Who's this?" He dropped his gruffness instantly and became Sunshine and Light. "Oh, right. Hi! How are you today?"

A beloved family member, maybe? Savannah mused. No, Dirk didn't have family, beloved or not.

His smile broadened. He was practically dancing in his jeans. "Wow! Fantastic!"

Perhaps someone saying he'd won some lottery money . . . or better yet, a free trip to a buffet?

"Oh, man, that's great! Thank you! Thank you! Thank you!"

Holy cow! Savannah thought. He hadn't been this happy

when she'd given him that Harley-Davidson T-shirt eighteen years ago. And she was pretty sure he'd insist on being buried in that ratty shirt.

"Okay. Again, thank you so-o-o much. I owe you one, man. I do. I won't forget this!"

He punched the "off" button, turned and gave her a big, nanny-nanny-boo-boo-smirk. "So! Good things don't happen to *me*, huh? Isn't that what you just said? I could have sworn that was just what you said. I heard you say—"

"Oh, shut up and tell me. What is it? You won a lifetime subscription to the Victoria's Secret catalog?"

"Better than that. *Way* better than that."

It must *be good,* she thought. *Dirk's nuts about Victoria's girlies.*

"Spit it out," she said. "Now."

He rolled down the Buick's window, stuck his arm out, and waved wildly to the helicopter as it flew slowly by.

She noticed that the chopper wasn't a law enforcement copter, as she had expected. It had the call letters of a Los Angeles television station emblazoned on its side. It was a news helicopter.

"It was them," he told her. "The guys in that chopper. They found him! They spotted the body about a quarter mile from here. They said it's in the middle of the river, caught on a log. We might even be able to see it from the road if we go down there!"

"Hey, that *is* good news! You don't have to send out search teams, just a couple of firemen and a CSU investigator or two with a gurney to hoist him up and out of there. Job done."

"And most important," he said with a deep sigh, "I don't have to go over the cliff myself and lead a search team, now that we know where he's at. I don't really have to even look over that damned cliff again if I don't want to. Well, at least not here at Deadman's Curve."

"It's your lucky day, buddy," she said, slapping him on the shoulder. "You dodged a high caliber bullet on that one, big-time."

"I know it." He wiped his hand across his brow. "Believe me, I know it."

"What's next?"

"Are you kidding? I'm gonna send a team over that cliff, and then I'm outta here. I'm gonna go buy a lotto ticket, while I'm on a roll!"

Chapter 5

Dirk called the County Coroner and told them to meet him on Sulphur Creek Road, about a quarter mile east of Deadman's Curve. Then, leaving half of the forensic team there with the abandoned Jaguar and the cliff covered with broken brush and cacti, he and everyone else took off for the new location.

Savannah rode with Tammy in the VW, which Savannah affectionately called the Hot Pink Barbie Bug.

"What did you think of Clarissa Jardin?" Tammy wanted to know. "Was she dressed in a black leather jumpsuit and carrying a whip?"

"No," Savannah replied. "Actually, she was wearing a Victorian nightgown and looked like Gran does when she's getting ready to climb into bed."

"No way!"

"I swear." Savannah crossed her heart. "But she was still rude and catty."

"Yeah?"

"Yeah. A major me-e-ow."

"I knew it. I knew she couldn't be a nice person."

Savannah thought it over for a moment. "Actually, I

feel a bit bad about the way I spoke to her. I was pretty much in her face."

"Good. She deserves it. She's—"

"No, it's not an issue of whether she deserves it or not. I wasn't fair to Dirk. I let my loathing of the woman override my professionalism. He really had to rein me in while we were questioning her, and that wasn't cool. I should apologize to him."

For a moment, Savannah thought that Tammy was going to lose control of the bug as she took a curve too fast and crossed well over the centerline. Thankfully, there was no oncoming traffic.

"Are you kidding?" Tammy looked positively scandalized. "Apologize to old Dirko?"

"I'm thinking about it. Why? You figure the world will come to an end if I did?"

"It might. I'm just wondering if it's a good precedent to set. He's already got such a swelled head. You saying he was right and you were wrong . . . it might just send him over the edge."

Savannah searched her soul . . . for two and a half seconds. "Okay, you've got a good point there. Forget it. I'll talk a little nicer to her next time—make up for it."

Savannah saw the Buick ahead of them begin to slow down. The television news chopper was hovering off to their left, over the riverbed.

"Dirk's pulling over," Tammy said. "I think this is it."

"Yeah. I'm sure it is. Park right behind him." Savannah took a deep breath. This wasn't part of the job she liked. It wasn't as bad as the worst part—informing the next of kin. But finding the body, even if you'd spent months looking for it, hoping and praying you'd find it, was never easy.

The women got out of the Volkswagen and hurried across the road to the edge. There was a guardrail here, but it was far less substantial than the reinforced one at

Deadman's Curve. And the drop down to the river wasn't nearly so dramatic. The water burbled wildly, foaming as it rushed over its rocky bed only about thirty feet away from them, and the slope was gradual.

Already, Dirk was at the edge of the road, looking over, and the expression on his face was that of a man who had received a stay of execution from the governor himself.

Then the smile disappeared from his face. And Savannah knew, even before she looked herself, that he had spotted the body.

"Ohmigawd," Tammy said. "There it is. I see it!"

Savannah saw it, too.

His turquoise polo shirt snagged on a jagged tree limb that was stretched across the river, Bill Jardin lay face-down in the river, the water swirling around him.

His left arm was twisted behind him in a sickening, unnatural angle. The turbulence lifted his right arm, up and down, up and down, and in a perverse way, it looked as though he were waving to someone beneath him on the bottom of the river.

Two firemen with their litter basket and three members of the CSU had already climbed over the railing and were heading down the incline toward the water with Dirk in the lead.

When Savannah joined them at the river's edge, she thought nothing of rushing right into the water, balancing on the slippery rocks where she could and wading up to her knees in other places. But when she glanced back, she saw Tammy hesitating on the bank, looking down at her new espadrilles. They were the "must have" shoes of the season—or so Tammy had informed Savannah when she'd first worn them—and Tammy had blown two week's pay on them.

Not that Savannah paid her all that much. But two

weeks' "pittance" was a major expenditure in thrifty Tammy's economy.

However, a true Nancy Drew sleuth wanna-be could never be stopped by a simple raging river or a pair of hot new shoes. In seconds, Tammy had stripped off the sandals, tied their laces together, and flung them around her neck.

Barefoot, she plunged into the river and quickly caught up with Savannah. "Br-r-r," she said. "This water is freezing, and you're going to ruin your loafers."

"Nah, I shudder to even think what these loafers have stepped in. A little water will do them good."

But she had to agree that the river was cold. Who would have thought that water, running off the Southern California desert hills, would feel like melted snow? Her toes were already numb.

Just ahead of them, Dirk, a fireman, and a CSU tech had reached the body. The technician had her camera in hand and was snapping pictures, documenting the position of the body before anything was moved or disturbed.

Dirk stood back a few feet, watching her, hands on his hips, scowling, radiating his impatience—that antsy irritability that endeared him to the hearts of all he met, especially his fellow workers.

"You got enough pictures there?" he snapped. "This ain't no *Sports Illustrated* Swimsuit Edition shoot here, ya know."

"Back off, Coulter," the feisty little redhead told him. "Go take five, smoke a cigarette, and chill out. I'll be done when I'm done."

Savannah cringed. Apparently, the tech wasn't aware that Dirk had recently joined the ranks of the nonsmokers. And that hadn't improved his irritability factor either. In fact, Dirk might be the first guy in history who had actually shortened his life by kicking the habit. As a snippy,

:ullen, nonsmoker, his odds of dying by homicide had :isen considerably.

She and Tammy made their way closer to the body, but stayed well out of the camera's frame. The other CSU tech and the two firemen also waited for the photographer to finish, busying themselves by pulling on surgical gloves, preparing the litter basket and body bag.

Savannah glanced over the remains of Bill Jardin, forming her first impressions. "He looks fresh," she told Tammy, "for a guy who's been missing five days."

"Yeah, no kidding," Dirk agreed. "No way this guy's been dead for that long. He's fresh as a daisy."

Savannah, Tammy and the photographer gave him weird looks.

He shrugged. "Well, you know what I mean. Compared to some we've found."

Savannah shuddered to think of some they'd found.

Nature wasn't particularly kind or pretty in the way she took care of business when life had ended. But she was efficient.

"You about done there?" Dirk asked the photographer. "I'd like to get this body out of here before we freeze our asses off in this cold water . . . if you don't mind."

The tech turned to Savannah. "Your ass frozen?"

"Nope," she said, "mine's toasty warm, but I can't feel anything below my knees."

Dirk pointed straight up. "And that helicopter is getting some pretty ugly shots of their own that are sure to show up on the LA evening news."

"I'm done. He's all yours." The tech stuck her camera in her smock pocket and gave Dirk a sarcastic grin. "Thank you for your patience. It's always a joy working with you."

Dirk mumbled something under his breath that only Savannah, who was standing next to him, could hear. It sounded something like, "Yeah . . . *mumble, mumble* . . . and your little dog, Toto, too."

"What did he say?" Tammy asked her.

Savannah shook her head and cleared her throat. "Nothing. He just went somewhere over a rainbow there for a moment."

Louder, to Dirk, she said, "Don't you think we'd better wait for Dr. Liu to get here? She gets mighty perturbed when you go messing with her bodies before she has a chance to even look them over."

"No. I ain't waitin' for no coroner. I'm getting this guy outta here as quick as I can," Dirk said, glancing up at the chopper overhead. It had dropped even lower, and the cameraman was practically hanging out the window by his toes to get a better shot. "If those dudes up there know who this is . . . with his wife being a celebrity and all . . . this is probably being broadcast live, coast-to-coast, right now."

One of the firemen looked up, ran his fingers through his hair, and smiled broadly for the camera.

"I see your point," Savannah said.

The male CSU tech was leaning over the body, examining Jardin's scalp.

"Here's the entrance wound," he said, brushing the hair away from an area on the back of the head. "About where you'd figure it to be, considering the spatter in the car."

"Yeah, well, get him bundled up and out of here and you can look all you want later," Dirk told them.

As they worked to free Jardin's torn polo shirt from the jagged limb it was caught on, Savannah noticed a distinctly pink area on his back.

"Look at that," Tammy said. "Isn't that lividity?"

Savannah nodded. Yes, it was, indeed, an area of congested blood that had settled beneath the skin soon after death. Within six hours or so after he had died, Jardin had been lying on his back.

But even Tammy knew the color was wrong.

"Isn't it supposed to be bluish purple, like a bruise?"

"It usually is."

"Isn't pink supposed to indicate carbon monoxide poisoning?"

Savannah couldn't help noticing the self-satisfied smirk on Tammy's face. The kid had learned a lot about death, dying, and mayhem during her association with the Moonlight Magnolia Detective Agency. But nothing took the place of experience. Years of it.

"It isn't red enough," Savannah said.

"What?" Tammy looked like somebody had popped her enormous bubble gum bubble. "What do you mean?"

"Victims of CO poisoning aren't always red. The two I saw who were . . . they were a brighter pink than that. I haven't seen anything like this before."

Dirk and the two firemen managed to work the polo shirt free, and they flipped the body over.

Savannah prepared herself for the horror of a vicious exit wound. But, surprisingly, it wasn't as bad as she'd seen. Certainly, the hole in his forehead—just to the left of center—was larger than the small, neat entrance wound to the back of his head, but minimal damage had been done to Bill Jardin's face.

Clarissa would, no doubt, be able to identify his body.

Savannah winced at the thought, feeling a surge of pity for the woman. Even nasty, condescending, rude people should be spared having to identify one of their loved ones in a city morgue. It was one of those soul-scarring agonies that was difficult even to witness, let alone experience.

Leaning over the body, Dirk studied the face, then turned to Savannah. "That wound looks really clean, for an exit," he said. "But then, I guess the river washed it clean."

"Yes, it looks very clean," she said. "I have serious doubts about how much evidence you're going to get off it."

"That's usually the point of a river dumping. Makes

me think that whoever did this knew what they were doing."

He reached into the right front pocket of the body's jeans and pulled out a thin black leather wallet. As he removed a California driver's license and looked at it, he nodded. "Yeap. It's Jardin all right."

Glancing up at the hovering chopper and over at the ever-growing crowd on the road, Dirk tucked the wallet back into Jardin's jeans pocket and motioned to the firemen. "Let's get him in that basket—quick as we can."

Savannah looked up at the helicopter that was now nearly on top of them. The downdraft from its rotating blades was kicking up foam in the water around them. The cameraman was leaning even farther out the window than before.

"You'd better hurry," she told them. "Before that guy up there, Mr. Eye in the Sky, winds up down here in the river next to Bill, and you've got two bodies to transport."

Dirk chuckled. It was the first time Savannah had seen him laugh since he had received the call about a missing person. "Yeah," he said, "live feed of a camera falling out of a helicopter with the reporter still attached. That'd be real 'film at eleven' footage, huh?"

By the time the retrieval team had recovered Bill Jardin's remains and transported the body from the river, up the embankment, and over the guardrail, they were all pretty breathless. Savannah and Dirk were particularly tired, as they had been awake over twenty-four hours.

Funny, she thought, how missing a night's sleep is no big deal for a twenty-year-old, but once you pass forty, it ruins your year.

And so could climbing over a guardrail, snagging your already-soggy pants on a rusty screw, looking up, and seeing a reporter sticking a microphone in your face.

"Is that the body of Bill Jardin, the exercise diva's husband?" asked a perfectly coiffed, overly made-up brunette with a dazzling bleached smile.

"No comment."

Savannah tried to sidestep her, but hair, makeup, and teeth brightening weren't the reporter's only areas of expertise. She was pretty light on her feet, too.

Again, Savannah had a microphone practically up her left nostril.

"We've received a report," the brunette continued, "that William Jardin has gone missing and the body you've recovered from the river just now is his. Can you please confirm this?"

Savannah glanced over at the litter basket, which was being loaded into the back of a large, white van with the county coroner's logo on the side. She also saw a beautiful, tall, Asian woman, wearing a white smock, a miniskirt, and four-inch-high stilettos, getting out of a white station wagon with the same logo on its door.

The fur was about to fly, fast and furious, and Savannah wasn't going to stand here chatting with a newscaster while it happened.

Besides, she could see at least five other reporters heading their way, like a swarm of hungry mosquitoes. The last thing she wanted was to get swamped and have to fight them off with a flyswatter.

That always looked bad on camera.

"I'm sure the police will release a statement," she told the woman, "once the next of kin is notified. Until then, 'No comment.' "

When the reporter turned from Savannah to Tammy, pushing her microphone under her nose, Savannah brushed it aside and grabbed Tammy by the arm. "She's not going to have any comment, either," Savannah said as she propelled Tammy away from the crowd and toward the white van.

"Oh, wow!" Tammy said when she saw the station wagon. "Dr. Liu is here. Dirko's gonna be in trouble."

"Yeah, and we don't want to miss a second of it."

And by the time they got to the van, the hostilities had already begun.

In her four-inch heels, Dr. Liu was eye to eye with Dirk, her finger in his face. "How many times do I have to tell you that the body is mine, mine! It's *mine*, damn it, Coulter! You are not to move it, touch it, or even breathe on it until I examine it and release it!"

Savannah cringed and felt a little sorry for Dirk. She knew he was secretly scared to death of Dr. Jennifer Liu.

Everybody was.

The county's first female chief coroner, Dr. Liu had "aggression" down pat. There was just something strangely intimidating about a woman who spent most of her waking hours dissecting dead bodies while wearing a black leather miniskirt and stilettos.

But Dirk was exhausted, and that brought out the rottweiler in him. He leaned forward and shouted back, "That's enough! Back off, woman!"

"Whoa," Tammy whispered. "He's dead now!"

Savannah held her breath.

So did Dr. Liu. She just stood there, staring at Dirk, breathing hard and seething.

"Before you go jumpin' headfirst down my throat, screaming at me like that," he continued, "you oughta find out what's going on here. The body was out there, facedown, in the middle of that river. You've got a news chopper in the sky and an army of reporters blocking the road. What were you going to do . . . wade out there in your short skirt and your fancy hooker shoes, cut him open, and shove a temperature probe into his liver with everybody looking on?"

Dr. Liu lowered her voice, but her eyes flashed fire when she said, "Watch your tone with me, Coulter."

"Then you watch yours with me," he told her. "I've been up all friggen night and all I've had is one cup of coffee and an apple fritter to keep me going. I'm tired, and I've got a full day ahead of me, which includes having to . . ." he looked around and whispered, ". . . go tell Clarissa Jardin that somebody blew her husband's brains out. So, cut me a little slack here, would ya, Doc?"

Savannah watched, amazed, as the anger faded from the coroner's face. She said nothing for what seemed like a very long time, then she gave him something like an understanding semi-smile. "Go do your notification, Detective," she said softly, "and get yourself a decent breakfast. Then drop by the morgue and maybe I'll have something for you by then."

Dirk nodded. "Thank you, Dr. Jen. I appreciate it."

They watched as she spoke briefly to the CSU techs, then walked back to the station wagon and got inside, flashing an impressive length of leg as she did so.

The reporters on the scene were quick to get it all on camera . . . every sensuous move, every inch of well-rounded calf and thigh.

Savannah grinned. Yes, Dr. Liu always provided good film footage.

Its back doors closed, its grim cargo secured, the van left at the same time as the station wagon. Several of the reporters followed close behind.

Something . . . someone . . . caught Savannah's eye.

A young red-haired woman, maybe in her mid-twenties, petite and attractive, was standing in the midst of the reporters, but she didn't have a camera or a microphone in her hand, and she appeared quite distraught. Crying, she was trying to talk to first one person, then another, reporters, police officers, firemen, and even the CSU techs. And one by one, they dismissed her.

She appeared to be growing more frantic by the moment.

Dirk sidled up to Savannah. "You wanna go with me?" he asked.

"For breakfast?" she replied, keeping her eyes on the redhead.

"Yeah, and for . . . you know . . ."

"The notification?" Savannah didn't even have to ask. Dirk hated notifying victims' families more than anything in the world—especially when the next of kin was a female. Upset women were something Dirk Coulter just couldn't handle.

Men, he didn't mind upsetting. In fact, that was his favorite pastime. Cutting another guy off in traffic worked like a tonic for all that ailed him.

But crying women—that was a different story.

"Yeah, the notification," he said.

"Gee," Tammy mumbled under her breath, "lucky Savannah."

"Oh, shut up, kid," Dirk snapped.

"Don't tell her to shut up," Savannah leaned to the left, to see around Tammy. She was watching the redhead go up to yet another fireman, tug on his coat, and try to talk to him. He, too, ignored her.

"Come on," Dirk said. "Please? I'll buy breakfast."

"Yeah, okay," Savannah replied, barely hearing him as she watched the increasingly frantic woman.

"What do you want me to do?" Tammy asked. "Am I just supposed to go home and twiddle my thumbs while you two do all the investigating?"

Savannah had just decided to go grab the redhead and find out what was going on with her, when the young woman turned around abruptly and headed through the crowd, back to where a bunch of vehicles were parked along the roadside.

"Follow her," she told Tammy. "That's what you can do. Follow that redhead and get her license plate number. And when you get back home, look her up."

Instantly, Tammy took off running—still barefoot, her espadrilles hanging around her neck, flopping all the way.

Dirk shook his head. "I wish I could get help like that. You tell her to do something, she's on it. No lip, no hemming and hawing, no lame excuses. She just friggen does it."

Savannah slapped him on the back as they strolled through the crowd, back toward the Buick. "It's called 'leadership quality,' buddy boy," she told him. "You have to learn how to inspire the masses."

"I'll inspire the masses," he said with a sniff. "A swift kick to the masses' asses, that gets 'em movin'."

"Oh, yeah. A boot to the butt. That's how to win friends and influence people."

"Works for me."

She sighed and shook her head.

Why did she even bother?

Chapter 6

"It seems like a week ago that we were here," Dirk told Savannah as they walked through the courtyard of Rancho Rodriguez.

"No kidding," she replied. "Time drags when you're working all night instead of snoozing, like nature intended. But it's nothing that a big ol' breakfast and a pot of strong coffee won't fix."

He brightened instantly. "You're gonna cook me breakfast when we leave here? Will you make grits and some of those homemade biscuits, too? Your grandma's peach preserves are great with those—"

"Eh, get over yourself," she told him. "What do you think this is, your birthday? I was up all night, too, you know. And I'm not even getting paid for it."

He grumbled, "Sorry," and she got the distinct impression that he was expressing sorrow over the loss of biscuits and grits, not apologizing.

As they approached Clarissa Jardin's door, he said, "Now remember. You promised to be good in here."

"Oh, come on." She punched the doorbell. "I told you on the way over here that I felt bad about last time. Do you really think I'm going to beat up on a woman during a notification?"

"Yeah, well . . . I think this sort of woman brings out the worst in you."

She nodded solemnly. "That's true. That's absolutely true."

The door opened and, again, they were greeted by the maid. Her manner was warm enough when she invited them inside, but she looked tired, maybe a bit worried.

It occurred to Savannah that Maria might be worth interviewing, if she could get some time alone with her, away from her mistress.

"I will tell Señora Jardin you are here," she said before disappearing through a door to the right.

Savannah looked around the room with its beautiful antiques and thought how much more cheerful the house appeared with golden morning sunbeams streaming through the windows. Though it had been lovely at night, too, the daylight seemed to dispel the ghosts of inhabitants past that she had imagined by the light of the moon.

On a table beside the sofa, Savannah noticed a grouping of photographs in gilded frames. She walked over to the table and picked up a picture of Clarissa and the man they had seen only a short time before, facedown in the river. It was their wedding picture, and even though Savannah had no affection for Clarissa, she had to admit that the woman had been a gorgeous bride. And Bill Jardin had been a handsome man, especially with the light of happiness in his eyes. They had made a stunning couple.

When Savannah recalled the unkind things Clarissa had said about her husband only hours before, she wondered, as she often did, how a once-loving relationship could disintegrate and sink so deeply into a well of bitterness.

"He sure looked better in that picture," Dirk whispered, leaning over her shoulder.

"Yeah, no kidding. It's pretty grim, what a bullet to the head and getting dumped in a river can do to—"

She swallowed her words and quickly replaced the photo as Clarissa entered the room. Turning to greet the woman, she couldn't help noticing that Clarissa looked surprisingly fresh, even chipper, in her bright yellow terry-cloth workout suit. Even her hair and makeup were freshly done.

Well, at least somebody *slept last night*, Savannah couldn't help thinking. She was sure that her own lipstick and mascara were long gone and, since her dark curls had a mind of their own even on a "good hair day," she couldn't imagine how bad it looked now.

But Clarissa let her know how bad.

With a look that all women know and despise, she quickly scanned Savannah from head to toe, smirked ever so slightly, lifted her nose a notch, and then glanced away.

At that moment, Savannah stopped fighting the thought that had been running through her head since she had left this place last night.

I hope it's her, she thought. *I hope to God it's her, and we get to bust her ass for first-degree murder or . . .*

Now, Savannah, girl, don't go wishin' evil on another. It ain't the Christian thing to do, a sweeter, kinder voice whispered in the back of her mind, a voice that sounded a lot like her grandmother's. *Not even if they got it comin' to 'em. 'Cause if you do, that curse'll come back 'round and bite you on the rear end ever' dadgum time.*

Granny Reid was both kind *and* practical. Bless her heart.

"Mrs. Jardin, we need to speak to you about your husband," Dirk said.

"Yes, I figured," Clarissa replied. "More questions, I guess. But first, come in here. I want to show you both something."

She turned around and walked out of the living room.

When they followed, they found themselves in a quaint kitchen. The lemon yellow and cobalt blue tiles glowed in the morning sunlight, and decorative bunches of red chili peppers and dried herbs hung from the beamed ceiling, scenting the air with the aromas of Southwest cooking.

A heavy, rough-hewn table was covered with stacks of T-shirts, sweatshirts, and sports bottles. All had the House of Pain and Gain logo on it, Clarissa's curvy silhouette with the slogan, "No Pain = No Gain" below.

"This is our new line," Clarissa said proudly, indicating the piles of merchandise with a game show hostess' wave. "Don't you love it?"

They were camouflage fabric with a logo that reminded Savannah of semi-truck drivers' obnoxious mudflaps. *What's to like?* she thought.

"Yeah, nice," was Dirk's subdued review.

"Here, have one—on the house." Clarissa shoved a T-shirt at him. She turned to Savannah. "And for you . . ." She held out a woman's shirt with spaghetti straps. Again, she scanned Savannah's ample figure, top to bottom. With a nasty little, fake-apologetic chuckle, she said, "Oh, sorry. That won't do for you at all."

She searched the stack on the table, found what she was looking for, and held it out to Savannah. "Here you go. A man's extra large. Do you think that would be big enough for you?"

Instantly, Dirk stepped between the two women. He moved so quickly that Savannah barely had time to form the mental image of leading Clarissa Jardin up the steps to the guillotine, fastening her head in the yoke, and releasing the blade.

"Really, Mrs. Jardin," he said, sounding exasperated. "We don't have time for this crap."

"What? What crap?" Clarissa did her best to appear confused.

"You know exactly what I mean," he snapped. "You should have other things on your mind right now than insulting my partner. You reported your husband missing. Has it even occurred to you that we might be here because there's been a new development in his case?"

"A new development?" Abruptly, she sank down onto one of the chairs at the table. "No. Maria said you were here to ask me more questions."

Before either Savannah or Dirk could answer, a door that led from the kitchen to the courtyard opened and a tall, thin, dark-haired man rushed in.

"Clarissa, are you all right? he said, hurrying to her side. He dropped onto his knees next to her chair and grabbed her hands. "I just heard, and I came right over. I'm so, so sorry!"

"What? What are you sorry about?" She snatched her hands out of his. "Theo, what did you hear?"

"Excuse me, sir," Dirk said in an uncharacteristically soft tone of voice. "I'm Detective Dirk Coulter, from the SCPD. My partner and me, we just got here a few minutes ago. We came to talk to Mrs. Jardin about . . . her husband," he added with emphasis.

Fortunately, the guy on his knees understood Dirk's implication. He leaped to his feet, his fair complexion turning a pronounced shade of red.

"Oh, uh . . . right. I'm sorry," he said. "I was watching TV and they came on with this, well . . . I . . ."

"What the hell is going on here?" Clarissa said, standing up. "Somebody had better tell me right now!"

Savannah couldn't help feeling a rush of sympathy for the woman. Clarissa's cockiness had disappeared, and she looked genuinely frightened. And although Savannah had been spared the personal experience of being notified of a loved one's homicide, she believed it had to be the worst moment in someone's lifetime.

If, indeed, Clarissa Jardin was innocent and ignorant of her husband's murder, her nightmare was just beginning.

Savannah stepped forward and placed her hand on Clarissa's shoulder. "Please, Mrs. Jardin, sit down," she told her. When Clarissa resisted, Savannah repeated, "Please," and gently nudged her toward the chair.

Once she was seated, Savannah sat on a chair next to her and turned to face her. "Clarissa," she said, "there's just no easy way to tell you this."

Clarissa began to shake her head. "No," she whispered. "Don't tell me. Don't say it. I don't want to hear that he's . . ."

"His car was found before dawn, abandoned on the side of the road," Savannah told her.

Ever so slightly, Clarissa brightened. "His car? Oh. It was just his car that you found?"

"There was evidence inside the car . . ." Savannah continued. ". . . evidence that leads us to believe that your husband was the victim of foul play."

"Foul play? Victim? What do you mean 'he *was*?' "

"The area around his car was searched. And at daybreak, we found his body—"

"His body?" Clarissa gasped, then started to cry. "His body? Are you telling me Bill is gone? He's dead?"

Savannah nodded. "We're pretty sure. He still had his identification on him. He was dressed the way you said he was, and . . . well . . . we saw your pictures there in the living room."

Dirk cleared his throat. "Yes, ma'am, it's him. I mean, you'll have to identify his bo . . . I mean . . . the remains, but we're sure."

"No, I can't!" Clarissa buried her head on her arms on the table and began to sob into her stacks of T-shirts. "I can't look at him! I don't want to remember him that way!"

"I'll do it," the dark-haired man said. "Don't worry,

Clarissa. I'll take care of that. And everything else. Don't you worry about anything."

"And just who are you?" Dirk asked him, sounding a bit irritated.

"I'm Theodore Gibby, a close friend of the family," he snapped back.

"He's my *manager*," Clarissa said, shooting Theodore a look that Savannah would not have classified as warm or even particularly friendly.

Dirk looked uneasy as he weighed his decision. "Well," he said, "the identification is usually done by a family member."

But Clarissa had begun to cry into her T-shirts again.

Dirk turned to Savannah, a perfectly miserable look on his face. She knew he would rather be wrestling a naked, dirty, sweaty perp than dealing with a weeping female.

Savannah rose to the occasion, thinking: *Some things never change*.

She said to Theodore, "How well did you know Mr. Jardin?"

"*Very* well," was his reply. "He's my best friend. We've played golf together at least once a week for years. That's how I met Clarissa."

He reached down and patted her on the back.

She shrugged his hand away. Rising from her chair, she wiped her hands across her eyes. "I'm feeling sick. I'm going to go lie down for a while," she said. "And as far as the identification . . ." She waved a hand in Theodore's direction. ". . . Theo, you take care of it. You go *manage*. God knows, that's what you do best."

Turning abruptly, she left the room, disappearing through the door that led to the living room. Apparently, the bedrooms were on the other end of the house.

Dirk turned to Theodore Gibby. "Is there someone else you can think of who would qualify as next of kin to this guy? No offense, but I'd rather have a family member."

"Not that I can think of," Theodore told him. "They don't have any relatives living around here that I know of."

"Then it looks like you're it, buddy," Dirk said. "Do you know where the county morgue is?"

Theodore nodded. "A block from the police station, by the pier. Shall I meet you there?"

"No, you go on ahead. I've got another stop to make first. I'll call and let 'em know you're on your way."

Savannah nodded toward the door. "Is she going to be okay?" she asked Theodore.

"Clarissa? Sure," he said. "You don't have to worry about her. She's a survivor, that one—lands on her feet every time."

"Somehow I knew that," Savannah replied.

"Let's go," Dirk told her. "We've gotta get across town and do that interview right away." He glanced at his watch, shook his head, and sighed. "We're way late as it is."

Theodore Gibby walked out with them, through the courtyard and to his own car, which was parked beside the Buick.

As they watched him drive away in his black Porsche, Dirk flipped open his cell phone and called the county morgue. "Yeah, Coulter here. You've got a guy named Theodore Gibby on his way there to identify Jardin." He listened for a moment, then shook his head. "No. You don't have to clean him up that much. This guy's a golfing buddy. The wife wouldn't come."

Having said good-bye, he shoved the phone into his pocket and turned to Savannah. "There," he said. "That's done."

She grinned. "So, exactly who do you reckon you'll be interviewing . . . way across town? A waffle? A stack of pancakes? Or a Manly Man's breakfast at Penny's Café?"

He flexed a biceps for her. "I'm feeling particularly masculine today. A Manly Man's Big Meat Combo Breakfast it is."

Once they were in the car and he had the engine started, she saw him pass his hand across his eyes and shake his head, trying to stay alert.

Feeling masculine, my butt, she thought. She could feel his fatigue.

"We're getting too old for these all-nighters," she said.

"Speak for yourself," he replied. "I was too old for this crap when I was twenty-five. Old's got nothin' to do with it."

An enormous breakfast of sausages, bacon, buttermilk pancakes, and sunny-side-up eggs improved Dirk's mood a smidgen, but it put a big smile on Savannah's—mostly because he had paid the tab. By the time they had walked out of Penny's Café with nearly a pot of Pen's famous, black-as-Mississippi-mud coffee surging through their bloodstreams, they were ready to take on the world, slay fire-breathing dragons, deliver marauding miscreants into the hands of Lady Justice.

Or at least walk, talk, and keep their eyes open for a few more hours.

"Amazing what six thousand calories can do to perk up a body's system," Savannah said as they walked through the city parking lot behind Penny's to the Buick.

Pausing a moment beside the car as Dirk fiddled with his CDs in the trunk, she pointed her face to the sun, closed her eyes, and breathed in the delicious, distinctive smell of San Carmelita. Moments like these were why she could never move back to Georgia. Just the smell alone was enough to bond her to this place forever—an intoxicating mixture of ocean breeze, sage from the foothills, eucalyptus and citrus from the groves, mixed with the perfume of flowers that bloomed year-round in the gentle Southern California climate.

She could hear the cawing of the gulls, the rustle of fronds in the palm trees that lined Main Street, the sound of children playing in the nearby city park. Ah, life was good. At the very least, it was well worth living.

But then her purse began to play a frenetic tune that gave her a mental image of a tiny cartoon mouse in an enormous sombrero, being chased by a hungry cat.

It also reminded her of her overly energetic friend, Tammy, which is why she had chosen that tune for Tammy's cell phone.

"Hello, Tamitha, my dear," she said as she got into the car and put on her seatbelt. "What's shakin', sugar?"

Tammy was excited, nearly bursting out of her skin. But for Tammy, that was status quo. "You're not going to believe this!" she said. "I mean, seriously, this is wild!"

Savannah looked over at Dirk, who was now sitting beside her in the driver's seat. He popped out the Elvis CD and put in his latest choice. A moment later, Charlie Daniels was "sawing on a fiddle and playing it hot," while serenading them about a boy named Johnny and his competition with the Devil.

He gave her a big smile, and she knew he was trying to score points with her. It was the "Georgia" reference in the song that was supposed to do the trick. And, since she was a fan of Charlie's, it usually did.

Today, she knew it was a matter of guilt. He felt bad for keeping her up all night with no monetary compensation.

He was also worried that, down the road, he might have to compensate her with more than a breakfast at Penny's.

Dirk was just covering his butt, which made Charlie's fiddle playing a little less sweet.

"What's wild?" she asked Tammy. "Did they get your favorite flavor of yogurt in at the health food store?"

"No, I'm still waiting for that," was the matter-of-fact reply.

"Did you get a lead on that gal at the river?"

"No, I'm still working on that. But we got a call a few minutes ago, here at the office."

Savannah smiled, loving Tammy and her ability to pretend that the cramped corner of Savannah's living room constituted a real honest-to-goodness office. "Really? And who was it?"

"Ruby Jardin!"

"Ruby Jardin?" Savannah did a quick mental computer search with no results. "Who the heck is Ruby Jardin?" she asked, giving Dirk a questioning look.

He shrugged and shook his head.

Tammy waited a moment for theatrical effect, then said, "Bill Jardin's *mother*!"

"Get outta here! Bill Jardin's mother?" Savannah repeated for Dirk's benefit. "Why would she be calling me?"

"Oh, you wouldn't believe it! You and Dirk and Clarissa and Bill have been all over the TV! They showed the footage of you guys taking his body out of the river. And then they reported that we arrested a pervert in one of her gyms, and they've been speculating that he could be connected somehow, because the guy we busted looks like maybe he's part of the mob, and—"

"Whoa! Hold on a cotton-pickin' minute. Where did they come up with that crap? He's a stupid kid with lots of muscles and an Italian last name. That doesn't make him mobbed up."

"Who's mobbed up?" Dirk wanted to know.

"Nobody. Tammy's hallucinating."

"I am not. That's what they said on TV."

"Which station?"

Tammy told her.

"Oh, please," Savannah said with a snort. "Those people can't get yesterday's weather right. Anyway, what does that have to do with Bill Jardin's mother calling me?"

"She was on TV. I saw her. She was saying that Clarissa either killed her son or had somebody do it, and that she's going to hire a private detective to prove it. And then, it wasn't ten minutes later that the office phone rang, and it was her! She wants to hire us to solve the case! She wants to give you money and everything."

"She wants to pay me for what I'm already doing for free?" Savannah chuckled. "Sounds like a plan. When am I supposed to meet with her?"

"She was in St. Louis when she called. But she was getting on the first plane to Los Angeles. She said she wants to see you as soon as possible. She'll call you the minute she gets in town."

Savannah did a bit of time travel math and for half a second she thought, *She'll probably call two seconds after I lay my head on a pillow to grab a few minutes' sleep. Who needs the aggravation?*

Then she remembered the stack of overdue bills in her desk and quickly discarded the thought. *She* needed the aggravation. A job was a job.

As Granny often said, "Make hay while the sun shines."

If the sun wanted to shine on her in the form of a woman named Ruby Jardin—especially if that woman was Clarissa's bitter mother-in-law—Savannah was going to let the sun shine in and face it with a grin.

She thanked Tammy and said good-bye.

Rolling down the car window, she breathed in some more of that unique and wonderful California seaside air. Closing her eyes she said, "So, good buddy, I've got a gig. Somebody's offered me money to prove that Clarissa Jardin is guilty of murder. Sweet, huh?"

Dirk laughed as Charlie played away and the Georgia boy, Johnny, won a golden fiddle off the Devil. "That's a real bite in the ass for you," he said.

"Oh, yeah. Awful. Plum awful. I can hardly stand it."

"Where you wanna go first? The morgue or the lab?"

Savannah mulled it over for a few moments, then said, "If we go to the morgue without Dr. Liu calling us first to tell us she's done, she'll be madder than a wet hornet. And if we go to the lab and bug them while they're processing the car, Eileen's going to get pissed and throw us out."

He nodded. "True. Very true. So . . . ?"

"I guess it boils down to a question of who you're the most afraid of—Dr. Liu or Eileen Bradley."

"Eileen's bigger," he said.

"Dr. Liu has scalpels and stiletto heels."

"And a nasty temper."

Savannah shuddered. "And she can remove your liver with one clean swipe."

He nodded somberly, pulled the car out of the lot and headed north. "O-o-kay . . . the crime lab it is."

Chapter 7

"Industrial park, my ass," Dirk said as they drove along row after row of windowless, cement-block buildings with large, sliding cargo doors. "Where's the *park* supposed to be? I don't see no swing sets, no baseball diamond, no slides for the kiddies. And not a blade of grass in sight."

Usually, Savannah felt it was her God-ordained obligation to counter the negative statements that Dirk sent out into the universe with her own Pollyanna-style propaganda. But when it came to this area of town, she totally agreed with him.

"Yeah, it sucks," she said. "I remember when this was strawberry fields and orange groves, as far as the eye could see. Now what passes for greenery is a dandelion growing out of a crack in the cement."

"And no matter how many times I come down here to the lab, I always get lost in this maze." He peered down the row to his right, then to his left, then drove to the next block and did the same.

"It's the next set of buildings on the right," she told him as she flipped down the visor mirror, ran a brush through her hair, and checked the bags under her eyes. They were now officially big enough that, if she were flying, the airlines would charge her extra to bring them aboard.

"How the hell do you know that?" he snapped. "They all look alike."

"They're numbered." She stuck the brush back into her purse and applied some lip gloss.

"Where? I don't see any friggen numbers."

"Right there, on the upper right-hand corner of each building. You mean you never noticed that?"

He squinted, looking for the numerals and letters that were, admittedly, too small. When he saw them, he snorted and shook his head. "Damn," he muttered under his breath.

She swallowed a giggle. It seemed the kind thing to do.

"The lab," she said, "is 350B. See, A's on your left, B's on the right."

"Okay, I see it. I see it already. Rub it in, will ya?"

He turned right and drove up to a building that had the Great Seal of the State of California emblazoned on its otherwise nondescript door. "That's it," she said, pointing far too emphatically. "It's right there. See it? See it?"

"See this," he said with a one-finger salute.

She grabbed his finger and bent it backward until he yelped.

"There," she said, pointing to the only vacant parking space available. "Park there. Right there, Dirk. Just pull smack dab in there."

"Woman, you're askin' for it. I'm gonna fly into a blind rage any minute now."

"Yeah, yeah . . . whatever. It wouldn't take long; you're half blind already."

"Am not."

"You need glasses."

"Do not."

"At least some prescription shades so that you can drive properly in the daytime. Just think—no more mowing down little old ladies, no more running stop signs and red lights and then claiming that you were answering a Code Three. No more—"

"Me get friggen glasses? That'll be the day . . ."

". . . when the world becomes a safer place."

They got out of the car and walked up to the door with the seal. Over the door was a security camera, pointed at them.

Dirk punched the door buzzer button, ran his fingers through his hair, breathed into the palm of his hand and sniffed it.

He had time to administer a squirt of breath freshener before a voice crackled on the speaker beside the door.

"I've got nothing for you yet, Coulter. Go away."

Savannah recognized Eileen Bradley's voice. Loud, curt, raspy, bossy—just the way Dirk liked his women.

"I've got Savannah with me," he said, pulling her closer, into the center of the camera's view range.

A few seconds later, the heavy metal door swung open and a woman in her sixties with long, wavy, silver hair stepped out to greet them. She was wearing jeans and a pristine white lab coat.

Or more specifically, to greet Savannah.

She gave Savannah a warm hug and Dirk a grunt. Then she told him, "We've only had the car less than an hour. Caitlin and Ramon are dusting it. You can go watch in the bay if you don't get underfoot."

"Me? Underfoot?" He shook his head and looked deeply wounded. "Why, Eileen, when have I ever—?"

"Oh, right." Eileen turned to Savannah. "Your pal here would never *dream* of interfering with the lab's work, hanging over our shoulders, trying to tell us what to do, getting in our way, and slowing us down by *pushing*,

pushing, *pushing* us to get every bit of evidence processed two days before we even *receive* it!"

Eileen was getting wound up, her face going from red to purple and her eyes bugging out. Savannah was starting to get scared. So, she decided to talk her down a bit.

"Who? Dirk?" she said with a nervous chuckle. "Naw, Detective Sergeant Dirk Coulter would never do a thing like that." She grabbed him by the elbow and propelled him away from the door, toward the back of the building and the oversized cargo doors of the Vehicle Examination Bay.

Over his shoulder, Dirk called out, "Uh, Eileen . . . could you phone them there in the VEB and let them know it's okay to let me in? Last time, they wouldn't and—"

"Gee, I wonder why?" Eileen said as she disappeared inside, slamming the door behind her.

"Well, that went pretty good . . . considering," Dirk said, happy, contented.

"Yeah, better than usual. No bloodshed. Eileen's a good egg."

He grinned. "She's kinda hot, actually. I mean, she's gotta be twenty years older than us, and has all that gray hair, and she doesn't wear any makeup or anything . . ."

"But she's hot?"

"Very. It's an attitude thing." He gave her a flirty, sideways glance. "I like sassy, in-your-face women. You know, a guy wonders how they'd be if you ever got 'em in—"

"Enough."

"What?"

"I said, 'Enough.' You know, Dirk . . . it's better for our working relationship if ever' blamed thought you have doesn't just come flyin', uncut and uncensored, outta your mouth."

He nodded knowingly, suddenly enlightened and filled with sage wisdom. "Gotcha."

They walked on a few more steps. "So," he said, "just to clarify—if I was fantasizing about you and me in the sack, you wouldn't want to know what we were doin' or how we were—"

"Shut up."

"Okay."

The garage door was sliding upward before they even reached it. Apparently, Eileen had phoned ahead and warned them, because, even though the opened door might have suggested they were welcome, the scowl on CSU tech Ramon Garcia's face was anything but inviting.

As they approached him, he waved a long bristled brush in Dirk's face. "We're kind of busy here," he said. "This car is covered in prints, and Caitlin and I are going to be lifting them all day."

"Lots of prints? That's great!" Dirk said as he walked by him and entered the garage. "Thank goodness it wasn't wiped down. We get a break for a change."

"*You* get a break," said a pretty young woman with long, curly red hair, who was squatting beside the car's passenger door. She, too, was holding a brush with long, soft bristles, which she was using to swirl dark, fine dust onto the door handle. "*We* don't get a break. We've got prints from one end of this car to the other."

"And I'm sure you'll do your usual, amazing job," Dirk said with just enough sarcasm to garner evil looks from both techs.

The Jaguar was parked in the center of the enormous room, which could hold as many as four vehicles at once . . . or a semi-trailer, if it entered by the enormous side door.

The bay had the appearance of a normal automobile repair garage, only spotless, and with far more clinical looking equipment. Tool chests, pneumatic machines, several compressors, a shop vacuum, squeegees, mops and brooms lined the walls, along with a sink and chemical fume hood. And along the walls, immaculate benches with microscopes, beakers, and even a Bunsen burner, reminded Savannah of her high school chemistry class.

Situated over a portable vehicle lift, Jardin's car was the only one in the bay—a fact that did not go unnoticed by Dirk.

"I don't know what you're bellyaching about," he said. "At least you've only got one to work on today. Could be worse. Remember when we had that seven-car pileup last summer with three fatalities and two DUI's?"

Neither Ramon nor Caitlin seemed inclined to stroll down memory lane with him. They just ignored him and kept on dusting.

Savannah pointed to the car and asked, "May I look inside?"

"As long as you don't touch," Ramon told her.

"I wouldn't dream of it." She decided to press her luck a little further. "And would you mind if I use that scope over there and some goggles?" she asked, pointing to a foot square, silver box on a nearby bench. It had numerous knobs and a black tube protruding from the front. On the end of the tube was a small flashlight.

Caitlin nodded, then added, "We just got that. It's top of the line and cost a fortune, so be careful with it."

"I've got my kid gloves right here," Savannah said, helping herself to some surgical gloves from a box beside the scope. "Putting them on right now."

Dirk had joined her, and without asking permission, nabbed two pairs of goggles with orange lenses, and handed one pair to Savannah.

Once they were properly spectacled and gloved, Savannah picked up the scope, and they walked over to the car.

Caitlin had moved to the driver's side, and Ramon was occupied around the rear bumper, so Savannah walked to the passenger's side. She flipped on the scope and dialed the knobs, adjusting the beam to its highest intensity. The car interior was instantly bathed in a bright, cool, white light.

Standing beside her, Dirk bent over the car door and watched carefully as she trailed the beam back and forth over the dash, seats, floorboard, and console.

"Don't you just love an interior where everything you see is either wood or leather?" she asked wistfully.

He grunted. "Naw. I have a personal rule: Never pay more for a car than your house is worth."

"Yes, this car definitely cost more than $10.99, which makes it over your budget and a major violation of your ethics."

"Hey, despite what you may have heard, I uphold certain standards."

"Not a lot of blood, considering," Savannah said as she forced herself to focus on the gory business at hand, "and almost all of it is here, on the passenger's side."

"Yeah, I was wondering about that." Dirk leaned as far into the car as he could without rubbing against the exterior. "If he was driving, you'd think it would be over there in the driver's area, or at least, more toward the center."

"And the spatter pattern is sort of low, too," she said, "not normal head level. There's a lot of it here on the front part of the door. It almost looks like he was sitting in the passenger's seat and was shot from the left."

"But his wound was back to front."

"Maybe he was sitting over here, passenger's side— had his head low, almost dash level, for some reason— and was facing away from his attacker."

"That would be pretty damned awkward."

"True. I was thinking that. He'd have to be slouched way down in his seat for his head to be that low. Maybe he was trying to hide or duck the shot."

Dirk shook his head. "No, Jardin was six feet tall and

long-legged. There wouldn't even be room for him to slouch down that far."

"That's right.

"Which brings up another question. Where's the bullet? He had an exit wound. If he had his head down low and turned, like you say, and he got it from the back, the bullet should have gone through and into the door."

"Yeah, but you know bullets," she said. "They go through a human body and all sorts of weird things happen."

"Is that true?" asked Caitlin, who had been eavesdropping on their conversation.

"Absolutely true," Savannah assured her. "You can't count on an absolutely straight line trajectory when it comes to bullet paths through a body. They ricochet off ribs, twist around inside muscle tissue, bounce off organs, all sorts of weird things."

"Are you finished dusting this door?" Dirk said, grumpier than usual. Savannah was sure his back was hurting from leaning in, as hers was. Not to mention that he was impatient to look deeper inside the car.

"I guess you can open it, since you're wearing gloves, and as long as you're careful not to mess anything up," Caitlin replied with a tone that was a bit too bossy and haughty for a tech who had only been on the job a couple of years. Dirk had been on the force almost as long as she'd been alive.

"Gee, thanks," Dirk said dryly, giving her a look that made her wince.

He opened the door and a second later, something clattered onto the cement floor.

"There you go." Savannah reached down and picked up the small nugget of metal. "Your bullet."

He took the slug from her and turned it over and over in his palm. "Looks like a 9mm."

"And it's in good shape. You'll be able to get a good

comparison from ballistics, if you get your hands on the weapon."

"Big 'if.' "

Savannah smiled. Dirk was quite the optimist. If he ever won the lottery he'd gripe all the way to the bank about the taxes he'd have to pay on it.

Caitlin and Ramon hurried over to them. Ramon had a small, brown paper sack in his hand.

"Here you go," he said as he handed Dirk the evidence bag.

"No, here *you* go," Dirk replied once he had placed the bullet inside and sealed it. "You guys can take credit for finding it."

"Wow! Thank you!" Ramon beamed with happiness and gratitude.

"Yeah, that's really nice of you," Caitlin gushed.

Savannah resisted the urge to tell him that Dirk wasn't being kind; he was avoiding paperwork. Even filling out a label on an evidence bag was enough drudgery to ruin his day.

But Dirk was already on to bigger and better things. Having taken the scope away from Savannah, he was already studying the floorboard and lower parts of the seats.

"It's pretty clean down here," he said. "Apparently this guy was a fricken fanatic about keeping his car spotless."

Savannah thought of the refuse heap in the back floorboard of the Buick and couldn't resist. "Heck yeah," she said, "he probably vacuumed it out once a year whether it needed it or not."

Dirk didn't have the time to be insulted, so he let it pass without rebuttal.

Gingerly, with one fingertip he opened the glove box and looked inside. "Whoa! Look at this!" he said, pointing the light inside the enclosure.

Savannah looked and gasped. "Holy crap!" she said. "I wasn't expecting that."

"What is it?" Caitlin wanted to know.

"We've got blood spatter *inside* the glove box."

"No way!" Ramon crowded between Dirk and Caitlin, trying to see. "How can that be?"

"It's weird," Dirk answered, "but obviously, the compartment was open when he got shot. There's blood and tissue all over inside there."

"As a matter of fact," she said, "the blood isn't exactly *all* over the inside."

"What do you mean?" Caitlin asked.

"I mean that if you look really close, there's an area on the bottom of the compartment that doesn't have any spatter at all."

One by one, the other three took turns examining the area.

"You're right," Dirk agreed. He took several pictures of the glove box's interior with his cell phone, then turned to Ramon. "I want you to luminol that area. But be ready, and once you've sprayed it on, and you hit the area with the light, take some really good pictures for me. Close-ups. If we're lucky, maybe we'll see a shape."

Savannah recalled a case she had worked with Dirk, years ago, when a woman had been found dead by the side of the road, an apparent victim of a hit and run. But when they had sprayed her kitchen floor with the chemical luminol and then shone an ultraviolet light on it, the area had glowed, showing blood smears, where the killer had failed to thoroughly clean it.

Dirk had been an enormous fan of luminol ever since, spraying everything that stood still long enough.

In fact, Savannah had warned him that if her cats ever glowed in the dark, she'd be coming after him with her Beretta.

"We'll get on that right away," Ramon was telling him. "At least, after we get done dusting the seats and dash."

Dirk gave him a doubtful look. "If you aren't sure you can do it right, get Eileen to do it. She's really good with luminol."

Savannah had taken the light away from him and was scanning the rear area of the interior. Something glinted on the rear driver's side floorboard. "We've got a casing," she told them. "Would you hand me a marker and camera?"

Caitlin gave her a yellow, tent-shaped piece of plastic with the number "5" on it and a camera. Savannah placed it beside the casing, then took a picture of it.

After handing the camera back to Caitlin, she picked up the casing and examined it. "Yeap," she said. "A nine millimeter. If the shooter was standing outside the car, beside the driver's door, and they reached in to take the shot, the casing could eject to the right and end up right about there." She pointed to the marker she had just positioned.

"But . . ." Caitlin said, "we still don't know why the spatter is so low and on that side of the car."

"He was reaching for something," Savannah said, thinking out loud.

"What?" Dirk was all ears.

"He was sitting in the driver's seat, and he was leaning down, reaching for something in the glove box."

Dirk nodded. "That's it. He was getting something out of the glove compartment. He leaned over, opened the compartment's door and . . . blam!"

"And whatever he was reaching for," Savannah said, "it was lying there inside the glove box. He hadn't picked it up yet, and that's why there was no blood in that spot. Whatever was in there, it caught the spatter."

"Maybe a gun?" Ramon added. "Maybe he knew they

were going to shoot him, and he was going for a weapon to shoot them first."

"Could be." Dirk took the casing from Savannah and put it into a second evidence sack. "You get that luminol done as soon as you can, and if you're right, the blank spot may be in the shape of a pistol."

"A pistol that's now in the killer's possession," Savannah said.

Dirk replied, "That's just what they needed, a second weapon."

Savannah felt a little chill run over her, remembering the hole in Bill Jardin's skull. "Yeah, like one firearm wasn't lethal enough."

Chapter 8

Savannah and Dirk were about ready to leave the Vehicle Examination Bay when Savannah decided to bend down and take a look at the Jaguar's tires.

Once, she and Dirk had gotten a major lead in a case because the getaway vehicle had left a distinctive tire tread in some dirt at the scene. And since then, she had been as obsessed with tires as Dirk was with luminol.

The two tires on the driver's side of the car were unremarkable. And so was the front tire on the passenger's side. But the rear passenger's tire had a material embedded in the treads that got her attention right away.

With her rural Georgian upbringing, the grayish-white substance was all too familiar. She would know it anywhere.

"There's poultry excrement back here on the tire," she told Dirk, who was giving Ramon and Caitlin last-minute luminol illumination lessons—much to their dismay and irritation.

"What?" Dirk shouted, his fatigue and resulting crankiness all too apparent.

"I said, 'There's fowl emission back here on this tire,

and I'm not talking about carbon monoxide pollution, either.'"

He hurried around the end of the car, stood, hands on his hips. "What the hell are you talking about?"

"Watch your tone with me, boy," she snapped back. "I haven't slept either and my coffee's worn off, too."

"Sorry," he said, giving in far too quickly. He really *was* tired. "What is it you're trying to tell me."

"That there's chicken shit on this tire."

He looked at her as though she'd just spoken a foreign language. "What?"

"You heard me. Gran had chickens. Lots of them. Believe me, I've stepped in enough of it to know."

He squatted down beside her. "Where?"

"Right there."

He squinted at her newfound evidence. "How do you know it's not gull poop? Looks a lot like gull shit to me."

"Oh? Have you seen a lot of red gulls? Huh? Have you?"

She reached down and pulled a bright, auburn-colored feather off the tire and held it up to him. "That, my friend, is from a chicken. I used to play tag with a rooster that color in my backyard when I was a kid. If you don't believe me, call Gran."

He held out another brown paper sack to her. "Then by all means," he said, "let's bag the bugger and get it to the lab. Or better yet, we'll just send it to Malden, Georgia, and let Granny Reid have a gander at it, get her best professional opinion. Will *that* suit you? Ow-w-w! Damn, that hurt!"

"Good. I meant for it to."

As Dirk drove down the 101 Freeway toward the morgue, Savannah beside him, they both mulled over their findings at the crime lab.

"How long do you think it'll take Eileen to run those prints, once Ramon and Caitlin get them to her?" Dirk asked.

Of course, Dirk knew the process and how long it took and what to expect as well as Savannah, but she knew why he was asking. He wasn't asking. He was lodging a complaint about the slow service he hadn't even gotten yet.

He was the same way in restaurants, and someday she was going to kill him over it.

She could see it all now. He'd say something like, "They're slow tonight! We've been here for fifteen minutes! How long can it take them to flip a friggen burger and fry up some fries? Where's that waitress with my second beer? This one's warm and flat and I hate warm, flat—"

She'd smack him upside the head with a ketchup bottle, pour the warm, flat beer on his cold, lifeless corpse for good measure, pay the tab, and walk out.

Dr. Liu would rule it: "Cause of Death—Blunt Force Trauma to the Skull. Manner of Death—Justifiable Homicide."

She sighed. "Eileen will have the prints run and results back three hours before they even give them to her."

"What?" He gave her a puzzled, then irritated look. "What kind of a stupid answer is that?"

"The only kind you'll accept without bellyaching about it. She'll be done when she's done. That's it; that's all."

"Well, that's brilliant."

"It's the best I can do on no sleep." She glanced at her watch. It was 1:25pm. "And no lunch," she added.

"Hey, that's right. No wonder I'm hungry. Why don't we go by your house and you can feed us some of that leftover fried chicken? Throw some potato salad in there and—"

"No."

"But I bought breakfast."

"If I go home, I'm going to take a hot bath and then drop into bed. Is that really what you want?"

"We could pick up a couple of dogs off that roach coach—the one that parks in the lot next to the morgue."

"Oh, yum."

By the time they arrived at the morgue, the refreshment vendor and his infamous vehicle were gone.

Savannah decided she could live with the disappointment.

The moment they entered the front door, Dirk announced that he had to visit the little boys' room and get rid of some of his coffee, which left her alone to face one of her least favorite people on God's green earth.

"Savannah! Hey, babe! You are lookin' fine, honey!"

Kenny Bates sat at a desk behind a waist-high counter, wearing a lecherous grin and a uniform that was two sizes too small—not to mention stained with some sort of suspicious greasy substance on the front of his shirt.

He was also sporting a new toupee—a very bad toupee. It sat, lopsided on his head, the flesh-colored matting exposed far too low on his brow.

Miracles did happen, after all. Kenny Bates had managed to make himself even uglier than he'd been the last time she'd seen him.

"It's been too long!" he gushed, scanning her figure up and down with the same degree of unhealthy interest that he probably showed to a double-decker pastrami and salami hero.

"Not long enough," she muttered under her breath as she approached the counter, looking for the clipboard with its sign-in sheet.

"I've missed you!" he said, standing up so quickly that

his belly banged into his desk and slopped coffee onto a stack of papers.

Lust-besotted, he didn't even notice.

Savannah signed the sheet as quickly as she could—using the name Ura Schitt—and shoved it in his direction. "There," she said. "I'm going back to see Dr. Liu."

"Wait! Wait a minute!" He yanked open one of his desk drawers and took out a magazinc. Rushing around the counter, he said, "Here. You gotta see this! I just got this yesterday, and I saw this and thought: Hey, this looks just like Savannah!"

The next thing she knew, he had opened the magazine to its centerfold and had shoved one of the ugliest pieces of porn that she'd seen in a long time directly under her nose.

She only looked at it half a second—long enough to form the vague impression of a dark-haired, curvaceous female in a most unladylike position, with her lack of modesty pretty much in your face.

Two seconds later, Savannah had grabbed the magazine away from Kenny, rolled it into a tight, hard tube, and was stabbing at him like a psycho wielding a foot-long butcher knife.

Over and over again, she used all of her considerable strength to jab him with the end of the roll. It made a surprisingly effective weapon, especially with an enraged woman on the other end of it.

"Show me that piece of disgusting filth, will ya?" she shouted at him. "Talk dirty to me? What the hell are you thinkin', boy?"

"Hey, ouch, stop it! Savannah, don't! Damn! Stop it, girl. That really hurts! I don't—ow-w-w!"

He danced around, waving his arms, tripping over himself as he tried to get away from her. But she continued to chase him, attacking him with a vengeance. He had been asking for it for years, and in her sleep-deprived condition, she was all too happy to give it to him.

Pinning him in a corner between his desk and the wall, she continued the frenzied attack with wild and joyous abandon, ignoring the voice of reason that was saying, "Don't! Savannah, stop it! What are you doing?"

"Leave me alone," she told the voice. "This trashy, lowlife peckerhead has tormented me for years and—"

She couldn't continue arguing because she had gone from stabbing to pummeling Kenny about the ears and head with the magazine, which was now coming apart in her hands, and that took every ounce of her strength. Bits of paper were sailing through the air with every whack and smack, like an X-rated snow globe.

"Savannah, you need to stop that," the voice cautioned again. The voice sounded a lot like Dirk's. "They installed a security camera in here last month. Everything you're doing is on tape."

Cold reason washed over her.

If there was anything worse than assaulting a police officer in his own station house, it was being filmed while assaulting a police officer in his own station house. Especially if the brass didn't like you anyway. And although it had been many years since Savannah and the SCPD had parted under less than amicable circumstances, all was neither forgiven nor forgotten on either side of the issue.

She turned around to see Dirk standing there, watching her, with a big grin on his face.

He pointed to the camera that was mounted on the ceiling in the far corner of the room. "Former police officer, Savannah Reid, beats desk clerk to death with a rolled-up newspaper," he said. "Film at eleven."

The moment she ceased to batter him, Kenny went from whimpering to indignant. "Yeah!" he said, straightening his shirt, trying to reaffix the toupee that was now

desperately askew. "And it's not a newspaper. It's a magazine that I paid a lot for." He held out his hand to Savannah. "Gimme that right now! It's mine!"

She held it out of his reach and stepped away from
him, toward Dirk. "Not on your cotton-pickin' life!" she
told Bates. "I'm keeping this as garbage as evidence. And
before you go daydreaming about how you're going to be
the star of the evening news, you better think how happy
the chief's gonna be when I sue you and the whole department for sexual harassment.

"Just remember . . ." She pointed to the camera. "We've
got you on tape, too, shoving that centerfold under my
nose."

"He did what?" Dirk was instantly outraged.

"Yeap. Told me she looks like me, and he's been getting off looking at it. Why? Did you think I was giving
him a beating for no good reason? To give myself a bit of
exercise?"

Dirk walked over to Kenny and grabbed a handful of
his shirtfront. "If I'd known that," he said, his nose inches
from Kenny's, "I would have just gone ahead and let her
beat the crap outta you. And if you try it again, I'll do the
job myself . . . or worse yet, sic her on you again. Got it?"

Kenny nodded, looking sick as he collapsed back onto
his desk, clutching his chest.

For a brief moment, Savannah thought he might be
having a heart attack. Then, with a great deal of satisfaction, she remembered giving him a particularly vigorous
blow to the sternum. That one was bound to leave a mark.

Good, she decided. It was a little something to remind
him of her the next time he decided to indulge in creepy
fantasies where she played the starring role. The very
thought made her want to scrub her brain with a steel
wool pad and bleach.

"Let's go," she told Dirk as she left the reception area

and headed down the hallway toward the autopsy suite in the back of the building.

He followed close behind and watched as she unrolled the magazine and shoved it into her purse. "Hey," he said. "That's the new issue. I didn't think the centerfold looked all that much like you."

Savannah shot him a dirty look. "If you look at that kind of crap, I don't want to know about it, okay? I hold you in very high regard—as in, I like to think you're above all that—and I want to keep it that way."

"The same way you like to think that your favorite Hollywood hunks never use the bathroom?"

"Exactly. Denial can be a wonderful thing."

Their footsteps echoed down the long corridor with its shiny gray linoleum and its drab gray walls. Florescent tubes flickered overhead, desperately needing to be changed.

But the county's budget didn't allow for such luxuries. If anything wasn't directly related to the tourist industry—and the county morgue's hallways weren't exactly major attractions—it didn't receive funds.

"I don't know how Dr. Liu can stand working here," Savannah said as they neared the end of the hallway and the double doors of the autopsy suite. "If they tiled these floors bright yellow and painted rainbow murals on the walls, it would still be the most depressing place on the planet."

He nodded in agreement. "At least at a hospital, happy things happen, too, like babies being born. Here . . . nothing good ever happens."

They reached the double swinging doors and found they were locked. This probably meant that an autopsy was under way. Dr. Liu didn't want anyone to inadvertently stumble through the door and see sights that would haunt them for a lifetime.

Savannah knocked on the door, and a moment later, it was opened by a scruffy fellow in his thirties, a week-old stub of a beard and uncombed hair, dressed in bloody surgical greens.

"Hey, it's Igor," she said, giving the guy a big smile.

What Igor—whose real name was Phil—may have lacked in personal grooming, he more than made up in personal warmth. And besides, he had a wealth of ghoulish jokes with which he regaled folks at the local bar and tailgate parties.

"Got a good one?" Dirk asked him.

"Mediocre," Phil admitted, "but the price is right."

Dirk said, "Let's hear it."

Phil took a deep breath and began. "A guy's mother-in-law dies and the funeral parlor wants to know if they want her cremated or buried. He says, 'Better not take any chances. Do both!' "

Savannah groaned. "Is Dr. Liu in there?" she asked, trying to see around him.

"Yeah, she's working on that Jardin dude. Wanna watch?"

"Absolutely." Dirk didn't exactly push Phil aside, but he did hurry past him and so did Savannah.

They knew not to get too close to the table without the proper hat, booties, gloves, and greens. Having been yelled at before by the tempestuous Liu, they weren't about to repeat errors of the past.

About five feet from the steel table they stopped short and waited patiently for the coroner to look up and greet them.

Normally, they wouldn't have been so respectful—especially Dirk—but the good doctor was looking particularly irritable, and they didn't want to get thrown out before they found out why.

Dr. Liu looked very different than she had in the field earlier that morning. Her high-heeled stilettos were gone, replaced by sneakers, covered with disposable booties. Like her assistant, she wore surgical greens and gloves.

The fact that she wasn't wearing a protective mask or face protector of any kind told them that she hadn't begun any sort of cutting yet.

Bill Jardin's naked body was lying on its back, staring sightlessly at the ceiling with eyes that were glazed and flat. Savannah could see a small incision on his belly, but other than that, he looked pretty much the same as he had at the river, except undressed.

Dr. Liu had placed a small white towel over his groin area, and not for the first time, Savannah was touched by the coroner's respect for the bodies—and the people who had once inhabited them—who came across her threshold.

It was common knowledge that Dr. Liu was nicer to dead folks than to living ones. She made no bones about the fact that she preferred their company.

Finally, she set aside the instrument she was using and acknowledged them. "I suppose you want answers," she said. "Where, when, what, how, all that good stuff."

Dirk brightened. "You've got all that already?"

"Not even close. You're not going to believe this. It's a weird one. I can't even get a probe into his liver to take his temperature."

Both Dirk and Savannah forgot protocol and stepped closer to the table.

"What do you mean you can't get it in?" Dirk wanted to know.

"Well . . ." Dr. Liu pointed to various reddish areas on the skin. ". . . I was wondering what that pink lividity was all about. I can't say I've seen that exact color before."

"Yes," Savannah said, "we noticed that out at the river. Tammy asked me if it's from carbon monoxide poisoning, but I told her it isn't really red enough."

"That's true. I've seen that before myself, and it looks different from this."

"What do you think it is?" Dirk asked.

"Oh, I know what it is . . . now. I couldn't get the liver probe all the way in because he's frozen."

"What?" Savannah and Dirk said in unison.

"That's right. He was frozen, and he's in the process of thawing out. That can cause whatever lividity is present to look pink, like that, instead of the usual blue, red, or purple."

Dirk shook his head, astounded. "I thought he felt pretty cold when we picked him up and put him on the gurney. But I figured it was just the river water that had chilled the body."

"No river is that cold. At least not in this area," Dr. Liu replied. "This victim was not only shot but also frozen solid."

"For how long?" Savannah asked.

The doctor shrugged. "I have no way of telling for sure. As you know, it's hard enough to establish time of death through body temp. Contrary to TV forensics, it's iffy at best. But this . . . ? I can't even go by the rate of decomposition. Decomposition would have been arrested at the time the body was frozen. The tissues would only start to break down again after they'd begun to thaw."

Phil walked to the foot of the table and looked at the body's foot. "He's starting to look bad fast, now that he's thawing out."

"Yes," said Dr. Liu, "once tissues have been frozen and then thawed, the decomp rate is faster than normal."

"Why would anybody freeze a corpse?" Phil wanted to know.

"Lots of reasons," Dirk told him. "Maybe it was as simple as wanting to keep the body from smelling until they got the chance to dump him."

"Or . . ." Savannah added, ". . . if they were really smart, they knew it would interfere with us establishing a time of death and would help them establish an alibi."

"Why even take him out of the car that they shot him

in," Dirk said, "and then leave the car where we would find it and the body nearby? It's not like we wouldn't put the car and the body together."

"I told you it's a weird one." Dr. Liu removed her gloves and tossed them into a biohazard waste can. "But for now, I need a cup of strong coffee. I want him to thaw a bit before I do my Y-incision. Phil, make sure nobody comes near him. I'll be back in a little while."

Savannah and Dirk walked with her out of the suite and back into the hallway.

"Can I buy you two a cup?" the doctor asked. "I know you've been up all night. You probably need a jolt."

"Thanks, but we've gotta get going," Dirk said, much to Savannah's surprise.

He glanced around the dingy hallway and shook his head. "Man, this place is a bummer. Me and Savannah, we were saying right before we came in here . . . we don't know how you can stand it, working in here, doing what you do."

Savannah nodded. "Like he said, nothing good ever happens in here."

"I don't agree," Dr. Liu said as she pulled the scrunchy from her hair and shook it loose, its glossy length cascading down her back and around her shoulders. "Something good happens in here almost every day."

Savannah looked around, doubtful. "What?"

"I find out the truth. And that nearly always improves a terrible, painful situation."

Remembering some of the grim truths she had seen Dr. Liu uncover over the years, Savannah said, "Even when it's a terrible, painful truth?"

"Yes, even then. *Especially* then. Most people want to know what really happened to their loved one and why. Even if it's ugly. They have a burning need to know. I find out for them, whenever I can."

Dirk nodded toward the stainless-steel double doors.

"And you're going to find out what happened to our buddy in there—the truth, the whole truth, and nothing but . . . ugly or not?"

"I'm going to try. The killer did their best to make it difficult for me." She smiled, a nasty little grin. "And, of course, that just makes me all the more determined."

Chapter 9

When Dirk pulled up in front of Savannah's house to drop her off, she gazed at the place with all the adoration of a sweetheart who had been too long parted from their beloved.

Okay, she thought, *the flower beds could use a good weeding and eventually I'm going to have to paint again, but it's still home sweet home.*

She had loved the little house the moment she'd first seen it, all those years ago—the Spanish-style architecture with its red tile roof, the white stucco walls that were common enough in that part of the world. But the charm of the home was two bougainvilleas that grew on either side of the porch steps. Their lush vines grew in profusion up the supporting pillars, to the roof and then together, joining in the middle and forming a canopy of dark green leaves and bright red blossoms.

She had affectionately named the plants Bogie and Ilsa.

When it came to stories of ill-fated romances, she was a hopeless sap. Last summer she had planted two rosebushes in her backyard and christened them Scarlett and Rhett.

Hopeless.

"I feel like I'm abandoning you," she told Dirk. "But if I can just get a shower, a sandwich, and a couple of hours' sleep, I'll be a new woman. Or at least, slightly refurbished."

"Hey, don't worry about it," he said, giving her knee an affectionate squeeze. "We're both dead on our feet, and you've done enough already. Go get your nap and your shower. You've gotta be fresh when you meet with Jardin's mom."

"Fresh? I'd be happy with 'conscious' and 'recently bathed.' "

"Yeah, that *would* be nice, wouldn't it?"

He rubbed his hand across his eyes and shook his head, as if he was fighting just to stay awake.

She couldn't help feeling sorry for him. Dirk might have his faults, but when it came to his job, he didn't have a lazy cell in his body. He would push himself far harder than anyone Savannah had ever known when he was on a case. Especially if it was a homicide. And she knew why.

Sure, it was partly the thrill of the hunt, the challenge of catching the bad guy. But she knew that, for Dirk, it was more a matter of finding justice and resolution for the family. And that was a noble cause.

With murder, there could never be true closure. But justice was a good consolation prize.

She reached over and ran her fingers through his hair, just above his ear. Then she lightly massaged the back of his neck.

"Come on inside with me," she told him. "I've got leftover fried chicken and potato salad. You can grab a shower, too, and zonk out on my couch for an hour."

"I really shouldn't," he said with a total lack of conviction.

"You really *should*."

He nodded toward Tammy's hot pink Volkswagen Beetle parked in the driveway. "The twerp's here. If I try to snooze on the sofa, she'll keep me awake trying to talk to me. You know how she is. If she can't talk, she'll pop."

"So, stretch out on the bed in my guest room. We'll draw the blinds and you'll be snoring like a bear in his cave in two minutes. I'll wake you up later."

"I've gotta call the station house and see if Jardin had a gun permit. You know, that spot in the glove compartment where there wasn't any blood . . . ? If he had a gun, then maybe—"

"You can call while I'm dishing up the chicken."

"Okay. You talked me into it."

She chuckled. "I never doubted I could."

As they got out of the car and walked up to the house, he said, "I appreciate this."

"Oh, yeah? How much?"

He looked suspicious. "Uh . . . a little . . . I guess. Why?"

"Well, if you're just plum brimming with gratitude, you could come over here on Saturday and mow my lawn."

"Did you ever get your power mower fixed?"

"Nope. You'll have to use that old reel hand mower."

"That's what I figured."

They went into the house, and Savannah tossed her purse and keys onto the piecrust table in the front hallway.

"It's us," she called out.

"Hi, us," came the cheerful reply from the living room.

They found the devoted Tammy sitting at the desk in the corner, slaving away at the computer. She was sipping from a tall glass of water with cucumber and lemon slices floating in it, along with a sprig of mint and a curl of gingerroot.

"Cleansing again, I see," Savannah commented, pointing to the glass.

"I had to, after eating that German chocolate cake of yours last night." She groaned. "I really shouldn't let you do that to me, polluting my body like that."

"I didn't exactly have to throw you to the ground, pry your jaws open, and shove it into your mouth."

Tammy laughed. "That's true."

"If you've got any of that cake left, I'll take a piece of it, too," Dirk said as he sank onto her sofa and scooped Cleopatra up into his lap. Instantly, the cat began to rub her face on the front of his T-shirt and purr.

Savannah had decided long ago that if her cats liked somebody, they had to be a good person. Dogs would slobber all over anybody; cats were more discriminating. They could tell.

"Come with me into the kitchen," she told Tammy, "and I'll fill you in while I get this guy some fuel. He's runnin' on fumes. And me, too."

"Okay, I have good news for you," Tammy said, trailing after her, "more good news, and some maybe bad news. Which do you want first?"

Savannah opened the refrigerator door and stuck her head inside. "Give me the bad first, and we'll end on a high note."

"Your grandmother called."

"That's good news. Isn't it?" She took a big yellow bowl of potato salad from the top shelf and handed it to Tammy.

Tammy took it over to the nearby dining table. "You'd think so, ordinarily. But she sounded a little concerned."

"About what?"

"About Marietta."

Savannah cringed, in spite of herself. The very mention of her sister's name was enough to set her nerves on edge, and she felt bad about that. A body ought to at least like their loved ones.

"What's up with Marietta?" she asked, knowing it would have something to do with a man or . . . God forbid . . . men. As a beautician, Marietta was a whiz at "big" hairdos, giving perms, highlights, and frostings. But she wasn't worth a lick when it came to managing the male population in her life.

"She broke up with her fiancé."

"Which one?"

So far, Marietta had been married three times, and Savannah had long since lost count of the engagements. By the third date Marietta was usually sporting a diamond ring of some sort.

She worked fast.

After a number of painful and expensive mishaps, Savannah had finally learned to wait until the day before the wedding to actually buy the bridesmaid's dresses. She had a guest closet full of fluffy, frothy, fashion nightmares that she was determined to sell on eBay someday when she was desperate for gas and grocery money.

"I don't remember this one's name," Tammy said. "Ernie or Eddie or—"

"Ellis?"

"That's it. Ellis Crocker."

"I went to high school with Ellis. A good enough guy. Not very bright, but he could run really fast."

Tammy snickered. "Apparently fast enough."

"No kidding." Savannah uncovered a plate of chicken and set it on the table, along with some bread and butter. "So, Gran was worried about Marietta's fragile mental state? Again?"

"Actually, she's more worried about your mental state."

"Uh-oh. I think I'm about to hear the bad news part."

"Gran thought you should know that Marietta decided to close the beauty shop for a week and take a vacation."

"Oh, no. Don't tell me . . ."

"Yes, she hopped on a plane this morning, and she's on

her way to Los Angeles right now. Plans on spending some days in the sun here in seaside San Carmelita."

Savannah groaned. "Just kill me now."

"Ah, just think how popular you are. You've got people flying from all over the country to see you right now."

"Popular, my butt. Marietta isn't coming here to see me. She's coming here because it's the only vacation destination on the planet where she can get free room and board. And she knows I know it. That's why she didn't call first. Thought she'd sneak up on me and take me unawares." She put her hand on her lower back, which was starting to ache. "I wonder if all doormats feel this used."

"So, tell her 'no.' "

"Yeah, right. Have you ever tried to tell a Reid woman 'no'?"

Tammy thought that one over a second or two, then nodded. "Yeah, I see your point."

"Want me to set you a plate?" Savannah knew the answer, but Southern hospitality required her to ask.

"No, thanks. I'm—"

"Purifying."

"Exactly."

"So, what's my good news? God knows, I need it after that blow."

"I got a lead on that redhead who was sobbing her face off out on Sulphur Creek Road today."

"Really? How did you manage that?"

"I phoned that gal at the police station and asked her to run the plate number for me."

"Which gal?"

"The one who hates Dirk."

"You'll have to be more specific."

"Kimeeka."

"Oh, right. She really does despise him. How did you get her to run it? She's not really supposed to do that for civilians."

"I promised to call Dirko a pee-pee head to his face."

"You do that all the time."

"Yeah, but Kimeeka doesn't know that."

"Hey, whatever works."

Dirk walked into the room, sniffing the air. "I smell chicken. And what was that you were saying about a Kimeeka? I know a Kimeeka . . . works at the records desk at the station. She's got some attitude, that one. Takes forever to run plates for me, and then when I suggest she should hurry up a little bit, she gets all snippy. Between you and me, I've never really liked her."

Tammy batted her eyelashes. "Really? Well, she likes you. She told me so today. She thinks you're hot, got a great build on you."

Dirk swelled with male self-satisfaction. "Oh, really? Hm-m-m. Now that I think about it, she's not all that bad."

"Yeah, she said you were pretty cool, you know . . . for an old guy."

Instantly, he deflated. "She said I was old?"

"So, who is our redhead at the scene?" Savannah asked, having enjoyed the previous subject matter quite enough.

"Her name," Tammy said, "is Sharona Dubarry. Twenty-six years old, single. She lives down on the beach, not that far from me on Seagull Lane. She designs lingerie."

Predictably, Dirk perked up. "Really? There's nice work if you can get it."

"Eh, probably girdles," Savannah said. She had to. She couldn't help herself.

"And . . ." Tammy said, grinning, ". . . she has a record."

"For what?" Dirk wanted to know.

"She was arrested for prostitution, two years ago. She was working for a high-priced escort service in Hollywood called Cache."

"Hey, I remember that place, a fancy joint up in the hills by the observatory," Dirk said. "It was mobbed-up. They busted a couple of wiseguys who owned it."

"So, our girl has connections to organized crime. That's interesting," Savannah said. "And Clarissa said Bill was a womanizer and a gambler. That puts him in two high-risk groups."

Dirk sat down at the table and began to heap food onto his plate. "I guess you know," he said, "I'm going to have to skip that nap. I'm not going to be able to sleep until I talk to Clarissa again . . . see if she knows anything about him owing gambling debts to the wrong people."

"Or him fooling around with some mobster's girlfriend," Tammy said. Handing him a large plastic bag, she said, "Here, have some tortilla chips, pee-pee head."

"Don't mind if I do." He took the bag, then gave her a funny look. "What did you just call me?"

"Nothing," she replied demurely. "But Kimeeka said to give you a special 'hello.' "

Savannah suppressed a giggle as she poured two tall glasses of strong, sweet tea. They would need the sugar and the caffeine. Both of them. Because, tired as she was, she wasn't about to let Dirk go interview Clarissa Jardin alone. And it had nothing to do with the way he had looked at her tight rear end either.

It was because, if he was going to get a substantial break in this case, she had to be there when it happened.

Or so she told herself.

Chapter 10

Savannah and Dirk had just been admitted at the Rancho Rodriguez gate and were driving down the gravel road toward the fortified hacienda when Dirk received a call from the police station on his cell phone.

"Oh, yeah?" Dirk said when he heard the message on the other end. "Both of them? Okay."

Savannah couldn't help cringing slightly when he hung up without a "thanks" or "good-bye." No wonder he was so dearly beloved by his fellow peacekeepers.

"Bill Jardin had a carry permit," he told her, "for a Cobra two-shot .22 derringer."

"Really? Hm-m-m . . ."

"And so does she."

Savannah mentally slapped herself for the little happy dance she was doing in her head. How sick was it to hope that a woman was a murderer, just because she was a snippy, insulting, bitch on wheels?

Bad Savannah, she told herself. *Ba-a-ad Savannah*.

"You're really hoping she did it, aren't you?" Dirk said.

"What?" She jerked herself out of her fantasy that featured Clarissa in a bright orange jumpsuit, standing in the cafeteria line with her lunch tray, waiting for her portion of prison slop. And, of course, Clarissa had gained sixty-plus pounds from the high-carb penitentiary menu.

"You're really hoping that Clarissa killed her old man so that you can nail her, get back at her for the rotten things she's said to you."

"And millions of other people."

"Yes," he said softly, "and millions of others."

Savannah thought it over as the adobe mansion came into view around the bend—an estate bought with money made by engendering self-hatred in the minds and hearts of countless people.

"I'd be a pretty rotten person if that were true," she said. "I mean . . . to wish someone was a killer just because they try to make you feel bad about yourself. How lousy and petty is that?"

Dirk chuckled and gave her a quick, sweet smile. "I'd say you're human. Hell, when she handed you that T-shirt that was too big for Kenny Bates, I thought you'd draw your Beretta and shoot her dead right then and there. As far as I'm concerned, you get major points for restraint."

She laughed. "Thanks."

He pulled up to the wall near the bell gate and parked between a pickup truck laden with gardening tools, and an ancient, maroon Volvo station wagon. As he cut the engine, he said, "Let me tell you something else, while we're at it. It's a little secret about guys."

"O-o-okay," she said, not expecting great gems of wisdom to tumble from his lips, but on the other hand, why not listen to some inside information from the opposing team?

"All that business about how a woman looks, whether she's got big boobs, or a round ass, or long legs, or a flat stomach . . . sure, guys notice that stuff. It's what gets our attention. But after the first two or three minutes, most of us get past that. And when it comes right down to it, we'd rather spend time with a nice woman who likes us, who thinks we're decent and well-meaning. A gal who doesn't act like we're stupid or up to no good."

"Even when you *are* up to no good?"

"Especially then. Being given the benefit of the doubt is a very sexy thing."

Savannah thought of Clarissa Jardin's promo poster. "Even sexier than a sleek, hard body?"

"That crap's overrated. Call me old-fashioned, but I like my women soft."

She smiled at him. "I love you."

He grinned back. "All women do. Just ask that chick at the station, Kimeeka. She's got it bad for me."

"So I hear."

As they got out of the car and passed through the bell gate, Savannah could hear Clarissa's voice just inside the wall. She seemed to be arguing with someone.

But when they entered the courtyard, they realized it wasn't an argument, because Clarissa was the only one talking. She was addressing a fellow in dirty work clothes, a straw hat on his head, and a rake in his hand.

"If you want to keep working for me," she was telling him, "you'd better not ever let anything like that happen again. When I say I want purple asters, I mean *purple*, not *blue*. Are you people color-blind, deaf, or just plain stupid?"

Dirk nudged Savannah with his elbow and whispered, "See, not sexy."

Savannah could understand his point all too clearly. Clarissa's yellow halter top and tight terry-cloth shorts might have revealed her toned, tanned body, but the harsh, critical expression on her face said so much more.

The worker with the rake stared down at the freshly planted flowers that, to Savannah, looked more purple than blue. He mumbled something that sounded like an apology under his breath, but his eyes smoldered beneath the brim of his hat.

Savannah wondered if Clarissa had any idea how many enemies she made in the course of a day. Or if she cared.

Did she know how devastating an act of retaliation could be from someone who had been so deeply insulted?

Having a husband in the morgue with a bullet hole in his head might have been a clue.

When Clarissa saw Savannah and Dirk walking toward her, the already irritated look on her face turned even angrier. "You two? Again?" she said, leaving the gardener to his asters of dubious color. "Who let you in?"

Savannah saw Dirk open his mouth, then close it, thinking fast. She knew he was trying to avoid getting the maid in trouble for buzzing them in. Why should the gentle Maria suffer the same scolding as the gardener or worse?

As usual, when Dirk was asked an incriminating question, he skirted the issue by asking one of his own. "Do you own a gun, Ms. Jardin?"

So much for dillydallying and pleasantries, Savannah thought. She had to admit, his style was improving.

"I do," Clarissa replied, putting her hands on her hips. "And I have a license for it, too."

"As a matter of fact," Dirk said, "you have a carry permit. You and your husband both."

"Well, if you knew that, why did you ask me?"

Savannah gave her a smile that wasn't particularly warm. "Oh, Sergeant Coulter often asks questions that he knows the answer to. That's what makes a conversation with him so all-fired fascinating."

Dirk motioned toward the house. "Let's go inside. I have a few other questions to ask you."

Reluctantly, Clarissa led them into the house. This time, Savannah noticed that as Dirk walked along behind

Clarissa and her yellow short shorts, he didn't even appear to be aware that her butt was society's definition of perfection. And even though she had a pretty wicked sashay to her walk, he didn't give her hindquarters a second look.

Maybe there was something to that business of guys only noticing for the first few minutes, Savannah thought. And maybe ol' Dirk was capable of spitting out the occasional gem of wisdom, after all. She'd have to pay more attention to what he said in the future.

Nah, she decided. *One diamond in twenty years . . . hardly worth the hassle.*

Once they were inside the house, Clarissa turned on them, and without the previous courtesies of offering seats and refreshments, she demanded to know: "Why are you here, really? Do you have anything new on my husband's case? Have you figured out who killed him yet?"

"It's a bit early," Dirk replied. "These things take time."

"I watch television, all those cops and forensics shows," she snapped back. "I know that you have to catch whoever does it in the first forty-eight hours or else you never will."

"That's television," Savannah told her. "Sometimes it actually takes us forty-eight hours and ten minutes to nail the bad guy."

"Don't you get smart with me!" Clarissa shouted. "You don't know who you're talking to! Nobody talks to me like that!"

"Maybe more people should," Savannah replied quietly, evenly.

Clarissa turned to Dirk. "Get her out of here. I'm a grieving widow, for God's sake. I demand to be treated with some respect and this, this . . ." Her eyes ran up and down Savannah's figure, and it was obvious she was considering whether or not to dare a weight-related insult.

Dirk stepped forward, once again interjecting himself between the two women. "Ms. Jardin," he said, sounding exhausted and exasperated, "do you want to help us catch the person, or persons, who killed your husband? Or do you want to waste our time by trying to impress us with how important you are? It's your choice. Make it. Now."

Clarissa glared at Savannah for a long time, then said, "I don't like her. I don't want her coming around here with you any more."

Savannah answered for Dirk, "If you don't want me in your home, I won't come here again," she told her. "I'll respect your wishes. I'm only here as a favor to Sergeant Coulter, to help him solve your case. But before you decide that for sure, I want you to know that I'm a pretty damned good investigator, if I do say so myself."

Clarissa said nothing.

"She is." Dirk nodded vigorously. "She really is."

Savannah continued, "And if you don't like me, believe you me, I can live with that, because I'm not particularly fond of you either. But we don't have to like each other for us to work together. And if you work with me, and with Sergeant Coulter here, we might be able to get some justice for your husband. And I figure that's what a grieving widow would want more than anything else right now . . . that and finding out what happened to her husband in his final moments on this earth."

To Savannah's surprise, Clarissa's eyes welled up with tears. She walked over to the Victorian fainting couch and sat down. Putting her hands over her face, she began to cry.

Savannah reached into her purse and pulled out a couple of tissues. She walked over to the couch and offered them to Clarissa.

Surprised, Clarissa stared up at Savannah for a long moment, then took the tissues and wiped her face.

"I really am sorry for your loss," Savannah told her. "I wish this awful thing hadn't happened to your husband

and to you. I wish we could just make it all go away, but we can't. All we can do is find out the truth about what happened and hope that'll give your heart some peace."

Clarissa whispered a halfhearted, "Thank you," and blew her nose.

"About the gun . . ." Dirk sat down on a chair near the couch, "the one you have a permit for . . ."

"It's in my purse," she said.

Dirk cleared his throat. "I'm going to have to see it."

"Ma-a-ari-i-ia!" she screamed.

Both Savannah and Dirk jumped.

In an instant the maid appeared, looking nervous as a cat in a room full of rocking chairs. "Yes, Señora?"

"Get my purse for me."

"Sí, Señora."

The maid hurried across the living room to an armoire that was a mere six feet from where Clarissa was sitting. She yanked the mirrored door open and retrieved a purse from an inside shelf.

As she handed it to her mistress, Savannah recognized the bag as a designer purse that cost more than Savannah had paid for her '65 Mustang—when it was new.

Maria left the room as quickly as she'd appeared.

Clarissa reached inside the purse and pulled out a derringer with a stainless finish and what Savannah guessed was a two-inch-long barrel.

With carelessness born of naïveté about firearms and their potential for destruction, she waved the weapon around. "Here it is," she said. "Bill gave it to me for protection. You never know, with all the crazies in the world. And some people take my message about fitness personally. Some actually hate me. I've received death threats."

Imagine that, Savannah thought as she reached out and took the weapon from Clarissa's hand.

Few things made her more nervous than a firearm in an untrained hand.

Pointing the gun away from all living beings in the room, Savannah lifted the weapon to her eye and sighted down the barrel.

At least, that's what she was pretending to do. She was actually taking the opportunity to smell the weapon and determine if it had been recently fired.

While it might be a different caliber than the shell casing in the car, it never hurt to look . . . and smell.

One quick glance at Dirk told her that he knew what she was doing. He gave her a discreet questioning look. She shook her head just enough to send him a silent "no."

Removing the two bullets from the pistol, she said, "So, you had her all loaded and ready to go."

"No point in carrying an empty gun," Clarissa answered matter-of-factly.

"That's true," Savannah replied, thinking of the Beretta in her shoulder holster with its full clip.

Handing the weapon and bullets to Dirk, Savannah sat down in a chair near Clarissa and asked her, "Do you think you could actually use that thing on another human being?"

Clarissa looked her square in the eye and said, "If I had to. To save my life or the life of an innocent person, you betcha."

Savannah returned her look and for just a moment, the two women bonded.

"Some fat-ass guy grabs me, tries to rape me, I'd blow him away," Clarissa added.

The bonding moment ended abruptly.

"Interesting how you assume the rapist would be fat," Savannah said, "I've known quite a few scrawny-assed rapists in my day."

"Ms. Jardin, I hate to have to even mention this," Dirk interjected, "but when we were here before, you mentioned that your husband was a gambler. What sort of gambling did he do?"

"Bill would bet on which drop of rain would reach the bottom of a window first," she said. "He loved it all. Private high-stakes poker games, the ponies, football, baseball, you name it. He even bet on dogfights, you know, those awful pit bull fights where they watch the dogs tear each other apart. I kicked him out of the house for a week when I found out about that."

"Yes, I can imagine," Savannah said, her skin crawling at the idea of those horrible blood sports.

"And do you have any idea how he placed those bets?" Dirk asked.

"Yeah, with a bookie named Pinky. He called here all the time, threatening Bill to pay his debts. In fact, Bill was supposed to meet with a district attorney named Walter Wilcox next week about testifying in some murder trial."

Savannah had to mentally will her jaw not to hit the floor. "Oh, really," she said. "This guy, Pinky, is going to be tried for murder?"

Clarissa nodded. "If Wilcox gets enough evidence against him. That was why he wanted to meet with Bill. Pinky claims he never met this guy named Freddie Romano, who turned up dead in Las Vegas, and Bill knew better. Bill said he's played poker with Freddie sitting on one side of him and Pinky on the other."

Savannah glanced over at Dirk and saw that he was practically dancing. "And," Dirk said, "Bill owed Pinky money?"

"Yeah, a lot of it. Bill said he was afraid that Pinky was going to kill him. Said he'd threatened to."

Savannah asked, "How much is a lot?"

Shrugging, Clarissa said, "I don't know for sure. But Bill had owed him as much as $50,000 before and didn't consider that 'a lot.' I'd guess it was probably in the six figures."

"And you know all this how?" Dirk asked.

"Bill told me. He didn't keep much from me. Our marriage was pretty much over anyway. I think he actually
wanted me to dump him. God knows, he gave me reason
enough."

"Which brings me to my next question." Dirk took a
deep breath. "What do you know about a gal named
Sharona Dubarry?"

"Nothing," Clarissa replied. "I don't know anybody
by that name."

Savannah thought she was lying, that she could see it
in her eyes. This was the second time Bill Jardin's widow
had denied knowing the identity of his mistress. Savannah decided to tuck that little mental tidbit away and mull
it over later, deciding what it might mean.

Clarissa didn't appear to be the type of woman who
would willingly remain in the dark about something as
important as her husband's fidelity.

Apparently, Dirk didn't believe her either, because he
gave her a penetrating look—the one he usually reserved
for interrogating hardcore criminals—and said to her,
"Don't waste my time or yank my chain, Ms. Jardin. I've
been up all night long and so has my partner here. I've
been very patient with you so far, but you're starting to
piss me off."

Clarissa bristled. "Well, you've got a lot of nerve—"

"Oh, you have no idea how much nerve he has," Savannah said. "You don't want to be on his bad side, believe me. He's got a nasty streak, especially when he's
tired."

"Sooner or later," Dirk told Clarissa, "we're going to
figure out what happened to your husband. And if I find
out that you've been lying to me, giving me bullshit information or not telling me all you know, I'm coming
after you."

Dirk stood and walked closer to her. She started to

stand, then seem to think better of it and remained on the fainting couch.

In fact, Savannah noticed that she looked a little pale under her tan, a little shaky, too. Maybe she would put that couch to good use.

"You haven't been straight with us," Dirk said, sticking his finger in her face. "You wait for days before you even report your husband missing, and then you just neglect to tell me that he had a bookie after him, trying to collect gambling debts—a bookie who's being looked at for murder. Why the hell didn't you mention that last night?"

Clarissa started to cry again, covering her eyes with Savannah's tissues.

"Oh, knock it off. I don't buy it." Dirk turned to Savannah. "Have you got a glove?" he asked her.

She reached into her purse, produced an examination glove, and handed it to him.

He shoved the derringer into the glove, then placed it into his jacket pocket.

"Hey," Clarissa said, "don't you need a warrant or something to take my property?"

Dirk leaned down until he was nearly nose to nose with her. "Do I need one? Are you going to give me a hard time about that, too?"

Clarissa glared up at him, but her voice was even and only mildly hostile when she said, "No, go ahead and take it."

"If any fat-assed rapist comes after you in the next few days," he said, "you've got my card. Just give me a call and I'll send Savannah to come over here to shoot him for you, okay?"

"I'm not going to be here," Clarissa replied. "I'm leaving town tomorrow. I have an interview to do in New York. They're doing a television special on me, and now that Bill's been murdered—"

"You aren't going anywhere," Dirk told her. "Until I get a substantial lead on this case . . . one that doesn't point to you . . . you're not leaving town."

Clarissa jumped to her feet and shouted in his face, "No way! You can't enforce that! I'm not under arrest!"

"You're going to be in about two seconds."

"For what?"

"Obstructing justice . . . until I can get you for first-degree, premeditated murder."

Savannah watched the two of them glare, stare, huff and puff at each other for what seemed like ten years, until finally, she couldn't stand it anymore. This time it was her turn to play the peacemaker.

"Uh, Clarissa," she said, "do you happen to have the phone number of that district attorney, the one Bill was supposed to be meeting with to discuss Pinky's trial?"

At first, Clarissa didn't appear to hear her as she continued her stare down with Dirk. Then she shook her head slightly and turned to Savannah. "What? Oh, yeah. There's a business card. I think it's on the refrigerator. Maria! Maria! Maa-a-a-ri-ia!"

Dirk held up one hand. "I'll get it myself. Just stop that damned shrieking." As he passed by Savannah, she heard him mutter under his breath, "Sheez, living with that . . . the guy probably shot himself."

Five minutes later, they had returned to Dirk's car, one derringer and one D.A.'s business card richer, when Savannah had a thought.

"Wait a minute," she said, grabbing him by the arm before he could open her door.

"What is it?" he asked.

"Chickens."

"Chickens?"

"There were feathers and crap on the Jaguar's tires."

"Yeah, maybe we should have asked her if he ever went to any farms anywhere."

"Dogfights," she said. "Clarissa said he liked to gamble on the pit bull fights."

Dirk looked confused. "But what's that got to do with chickens? I don't know what . . . oh, you mean—"

"Yeah, cockfighting."

He nodded thoughtfully. "Dogfighting, cockfighting, same sort of miserable crap. And from what we've heard about Jardin, I'd say it's more his speed than poultry farming."

"Maybe the other night he met Pinky or somebody else at one of the sites where they hold the fights."

"Maybe to pay them, or tell them that he couldn't pay them, which might have gotten him popped."

"Do you think she might know where?" Savannah nodded toward the house.

"Let's go back and ask her."

As they passed through the gate and the courtyard with its lovely garden, Savannah began to think that she could get sick of beautiful flowers in Spanish style courtyards.

At the very least, Clarissa Jardin had ruined asters for her forever.

She could feel what little energy she had left draining out of her as they approached the door. Just the thought of another encounter with the Mistress of Painful Gain was enough to make her need a nap. About a ten-hour nap.

But just as Dirk lifted his fist to knock on the door, they heard something—voices inside the house, arguing. Two women.

And Savannah was certain that neither of them was Maria.

Dirk froze in place, his hand in the air, then he lowered it.

They stood still and listened.

"I told you to stay in the bedroom when they first buzzed in at the gate," said the first voice, which had Clarissa's distinctive shrillness.

"They're gone. I could see them walking out from the bedroom window."

"I told you to stay out of sight. If somebody sees you, we'll both be in—"

"Yeah, yeah, yeah. Stay out of sight. Stay out of sight. Just disappear off the face of the earth. That's what it's always been with you. You live like a queen, while I'm supposed to be invisible."

"You've been paid well for your so-called invisibility. For years! So stop your bitching and go home. He's gone, and you're not going to find him by hanging around here."

"Fine! I'll go get my purse and coat and . . ."

The voices faded away as the women retreated to the other end of the house.

Savannah and Dirk stood there in front of the door, staring at each other, speechless as they considered what they'd just heard.

"Who the hell is that?" he whispered.

She nodded toward the rooms to the right. "One way to find out."

"You mean peek in the windows?"

"Sure. Why not?"

He shrugged. "I don't know. I guess I'm used to getting a search warrant before I do stuff like that."

"Well, I'm a private investigator, and I don't have time for foolishness like that. Let's go."

Bending over at the waist to avoid being seen from the windows, they moved along the adobe's wall, past the living room windows and the kitchen's, to the ones they assumed were the bedrooms.

When they were at the far end of the house, they could hear the murmur of the women's voices again, but they were no longer shouting at each other, so they couldn't make out their words.

Savannah was the first to take a peek into the window. It was fairly dark in the room and at first, she wasn't sure what she was seeing. Both women were standing in a bedroom. One was picking up a purse and jacket off the bed.

Clarissa seemed to be doing most of the talking, while the other one put on the coat and slung the bag over her shoulder.

It was when the second woman turned toward her that Savannah nearly gasped. She had only gotten a glimpse of her face, but that was enough. More than enough.

"Holy cow," she whispered.

"No kidding," Dirk mumbled as he took his own look, then pulled her away from the window. "Let's go. I don't want them to know we saw her."

"Gotcha."

They made it through the garden and back to the car as quickly as they could.

It wasn't until they had written down the old maroon Volvo's license plate number and were driving off, kicking up gravel on the driveway that they discussed what they'd seen.

"I've heard a lot . . . way too much, in fact . . . about Clarissa Jardin this past year," Savannah said, "what with all the talk shows and interviews and newspaper articles. I never once heard that she had a sister."

"And that gal has to be her sister."

"Sister? Hell, she has to be her twin!" Savannah said.

"Gotta be. They look exactly alike."

"You know who she *really* looks like, *exactly* like?" she said, recalling the sight of the considerably over-weight woman who had been snatching up her purse and coat from the bed. "She looks exactly, precisely, totally like the 'before' picture of Clarissa Jardin. You know, the one on all the advertisements . . . the proof that her diet and exercise program worked for her."

Savannah started to smile. A wide, toothy smile—like the smile of a barnyard tomcat who had just finished off a big, juicy rat for lunch.

"What are you thinking?" Dirk asked as he pulled onto the main road. "Whatever it is, you're up to no good."

"I'm feeling an overwhelming urge to call a tabloid. A couple of tabloids. Maybe even Eyewitness News. This is big!"

"Resist it."

"What?"

"Resist that urge. We have a murder case to close here."

Savannah chuckled to herself, just imagining the headlines on the grocery store checkout stands. "All the more reason to wrap this up," she said. "I can nail Clarissa Jardin with murder and tell my story to the *True Informer* and make a fortune."

"And ruin your reputation as a serious professional private investigator?"

"You can't buy Victoria's Secret undies or get a facial with your reputation."

Dirk sighed and shook his head. "Well, as long as you have your priorities in order."

Chapter 11

Savannah had always suffered a bit of a mid-afternoon slump—usually requiring some sort of empty calorie infusion of sugar and/or caffeine to get her over the hump. But it was amazing how such a simple thing as missing one night's sleep could intensify that sluggish feeling. A simple brownie and a strong cup of coffee weren't going to do the trick this time.

Of course, it was worth a try.

"I'm not worth draggin' behind the barn and shootin' right now," she said as she and Dirk trudged up the sidewalk to her house.

"Me either," he replied. "I'll make a deal with you . . . once you've talked to that Sharona chick, and I've had a chat with the D.A., let's both take a nap."

"It's a deal. I'll stretch out on my bed, and you can hold down my couch for an hour or two."

"And then maybe you could fix us a little dinner . . . ?"

"In your dreams. You order pizza, or I'll have Tammy make us something."

"To hell with that. I need more than lettuce and carrot

sticks to keep me going. I'm thinking one of your big, thick steaks, a baked potato, or some homemade fries."

"Think all you want. It ain't happening."

When they went inside the house, they found the faithful, if much maligned, Tammy sitting at the computer.

"Were your ears burning?" Savannah asked her. "We were just talking about you."

"With great affection and respect, I hope," she replied.

"Always." Savannah walked over to the desk, kissed the top of Tammy's glossy blond head, and said, "We just don't like your cooking, but we adore you."

"*She* adores you," Dirk said as he sank onto the sofa and slipped off his sneakers. "*I* tolerate you."

"Yeah, yeah, whatever," Tammy tossed back. "And as far as my cooking . . . I don't cook. Cooking destroys the nutrients in foods. They should be served as close as possible to their original form. Raw and whole, as nature intended."

Savannah sighed. "Our point exactly." To Dirk she said, "Want that brownie now? Some coffee?"

"Black and strong enough to bite me."

"You got it."

"Let me," Tammy said, jumping up from her chair. "You guys are tired. I can cut some brownies and brew a pot of coffee."

"Won't that compromise your standards," Dirk said, "serving all those artificial stimulants?"

"Yes, but what can you do? I live among savages."

"I'd like to aspire to 'savage.' I wish I had the energy to be 'savage,'" Dirk said. "Bring on the brownies."

Savannah reached down to scoop up the cats that were making figure eights between her ankles. With one under each arm, she headed for her favorite, comfy chair. "Do you miss mommy?" she asked them as she sat down and propped her feet on the ottoman. "It's that bad man's fault. He kept me out all night."

He took out his phone and flipped it open. "I'm going to call in that Volvo's plate," he told Savannah, "and see if we can get a line on Clarissa's twin sister. It's just got to be her car. There's no way Clarissa would drive that hunk of junk."

"It might have been the gardener's."

"He was driving the pickup with all the tools in it. Think positive for once, would you?"

Tammy stuck her head out of the kitchen. "Did I hear you say 'Clarissa's twin?' Clarissa Jardin has a twin?"

"A redheaded, not-at-all-svelte twin," Savannah told her.

"No way! And you've got her plate number?"

"We do," Dirk said. "Why? You want to run it for me, see if you can process it faster than my girlfriend Kimeeka?"

Tammy gave Savannah a look and snickered. "Oh, I'm pretty sure I'll get it for you faster than Kim-eeka . . . even though she has that enormous crush on you."

"You've got it." He tossed a piece of paper onto the coffee table. "After you've put coffee mugs into our hands, of course."

"Of course."

Once Tammy had returned to the kitchen, Savannah said softly to Dirk, "We really should give her something fun to do. She's so sweet, willing to do the boring stuff all the time."

But Dirk was already on the phone, calling the lab—or as Savannah preferred to call it, "hassling them for results and making a general nuisance of himself."

"How did that luminol go?" he was asking. "No? Why not? Are you sure? Damn." He looked over at Savannah, then toward the kitchen. "Send what you've got to me, to my cell," he said. "Yeah, now."

He was hanging up as Tammy walked into the living room, a brownie on a dessert plate in each hand.

"The French roast is brewing," she said. She served Savannah, then handed Dirk his treat.

As he took it from her, he said, "I've got something for you, kiddo."

She picked up the bit of paper from the coffee table. "I know. I'll get on it right away."

"That's not what I meant," he said, punching numbers on his phone. "I mean, run that, too, but I'm sending you something right now that's just as important. I'd appreciate it if you'd look at it for me."

"What's that?" she asked.

"The lab's shots of the Jardin's glove box. You know how we told you it had blood spatter inside?"

She brightened more than was proper, considering the conversation topic. "Yes . . . ?"

"They sprayed it with luminol and took pictures. There's a blank spot in the middle of the compartment where there was no spatter. We were hoping it might be in the shape of a gun or something. Maybe we'd be able to tell what he was reaching for when he got shot."

"Yes. Yes. And . . . ?" She was about to burst with excitement.

"Nothing."

"Oh."

Savannah giggled. Tammy could go flat faster than a popped, head-sized, Bazooka gum bubble.

"But," Dirk continued, "they're not all that good there at the lab when it comes to pictures. You're better on the computer, sharpening them, refocusing, all that crap you do. I'd appreciate it if you'd look at this one and see what you can do with it."

For a moment, Tammy looked like she might faint, as though her knees were buckling beneath her. "Me? Really? I . . ."

"There," he said, pressing the send button. "You should have it there on your computer, you know, whenever you get a chance to look at it."

The piece of paper with the Volvo's plate number fluttered to the floor like a wounded gull as Tammy sprinted to the computer.

Savannah stood, set the cats on the ottoman, and headed for the kitchen, scooping up the paper as she went.

Dirk followed her.

As she was getting the mugs from the cupboard, she breathed in the delicious, comforting scent of the coffee that was filling the room. Handing Dirk his favorite Mickey Mouse mug—he had never actually admitted it was his favorite, but she knew it was—she gave him a sweet smile.

"Thank you," she said.

He took the mug from her and for a moment, his hand closed around hers. "I did all right, then?" he asked, his heart in his eyes.

"Perfect." She smiled up at him, thinking about his admission earlier about what men like, what they need. "You're a decent, well-meaning guy," she said. "One of the truly good ones."

"Yeah, well, don't let it get around. I've got a reputation to uphold," he said, taking the mug from her and turning toward the pot that was only half brewed. "When is this damned thing gonna be finished? Is it gonna be much longer, 'cause I don't have all friggen day, you know . . ."

It took Savannah two hours, looking in five different locations, to find Sharona Dubarry.

She wasn't in her modest beach house in Tammy's neighborhood. Nor was she at the so-called lingerie factory in the industrial section of town. The place was nothing more than a small, gloomy, noisy workshop—little better than a sweatshop—where rows of tired, depressed-looking women sat at long tables, running yards of cheap lace and flimsy satins through large sewing machines.

Dirk would not have been impressed.

The manager of the shop told Savannah that Sharona had called in sick the day before. Today, she hadn't been heard from at all.

But the manager had been helpful, suggesting three different local bars where Sharona supposedly spent most of her spare time.

Savannah found her in the third one, the worst one, the one on the bad side of town, where it was wedged between a tattoo parlor and a pawnshop.

The Keg wasn't known for its décor, ambiance, or friendly staff. The dank hole was home away from home to some of the least upstanding citizens of San Carmelita. And the moment Savannah walked through the door, she wondered why a woman who was as beautiful as Sharona Dubarry would end up in a dive like this.

As Gran sometimes said, "Beauty's no substitute for good sense and good character."

Savannah tried to breathe shallowly as she stood just inside the door and waited for her eyes to adjust to the darkness. California might have outlawed smoking in public places some time back, but the miscreants who frequented The Keg weren't known for their law-abiding tendencies.

The patrons swigging beer and other potent potables at the bar looked up from their various containers and gave Savannah a thorough once-over as she entered the place. Their looks of bored, mild surprise told her that a fresh face coming through the door was a rare event.

She scanned the drinkers quickly and felt her pulse rate quicken a bit when she spotted the red-haired beauty at the end of the bar.

Savannah recognized her instantly as the woman they

had seen leaving Sulphur Creek Road earlier that morning. But apparently, Sharona didn't recognize her. She gave Savannah a quick dismissive look, then went back to drinking her beer.

She hardly even seemed to notice when Savannah sat down on the empty bar stool next to hers. Her eyes were badly swollen from crying and dark mascara smudges and mussed hair and a wrinkled halter dress completed the picture of total dejection.

"What can I get you?" the bartender asked Savannah.

He was a handsome enough kid, dark hair slicked back, a deep tan, and muscular body. But with his black polyester shirt and his thick gold chain, he had a smarmy look about him that Savannah didn't trust. Whether he was truly a wiseguy or a wanna-be, she didn't care. She didn't like him.

"I'll have an iced tea," she said, "with plenty of sugar."

"A Long Island iced tea?" he asked with a mocking grin. "Something with a little kick to it?"

"Nope. You heard me right the first time," she said. "And if you'd pass me some of those peanuts in that there bowl, too, I'd be much obliged."

He reached for the bowl of nuts on the bar, but instead of handing it to Savannah, he stuck it somewhere behind the bar. "It's not happy hour yet," he told her.

Looking around at the drab surroundings, she said, "Y'all actually get happy in a place like this? Hard to imagine."

Grumbling, he walked to the other end of the bar, where he began to stir some evil-looking brown powder into a tall glass of water.

"Oh, yum," she said to Sharona. "I can hardly wait."

"I wouldn't piss him off if I was you," Sharona replied in a lackluster voice, as she stared into her beer.

"Yeah? He doesn't look that tough . . . or big. I think I could take him."

That got her attention. Sharona looked up, locked eyes with Savannah. When she saw that Savannah was grinning, she returned the smile weakly. But only for a moment, then she added, in a very serious tone, "I mean it. Aldo's not somebody you want to mess with. Believe me. I know."

Sharona glanced down the bar at the guy who was tossing one solitary ice cube into Savannah's drink, and Savannah saw genuine fear in Sharona's eyes.

When she had first entered The Keg, Savannah had intended to interview Sharona then and there, if she found her. But something told her that Sharona wasn't going to open up to her about anything important in a place where she felt threatened. And, apparently, she had good reason to be afraid of Aldo of the Golden Chain.

"I came here to talk to you," Savannah said, keeping her voice low. "It's really important."

"Talk to me? About what?"

Savannah noticed that she was gripping her beer mug tightly and her hands were shaking.

"About Bill and what happened to him." She saw the bartender was sticking a straw and the token lemon slice into the tea. She didn't have long. "I'm going to leave now. Meet me at the service station down on the corner in ten minutes. Okay?"

The redhead shook her head. "No," she said. "I can't. You're going to get me in trouble."

"I won't, I promise. Meet me . . . ten minutes . . . the service station. Do it for Bill."

Aldo had returned and gave her a nasty look as he shoved the drink in front of her. "There you go. Iced tea. That'll be five bucks."

"Five bucks? For tea with one lousy piece of ice and no happy hour peanuts? You gotta be kidding."

Aldo gave her an ugly grin. "You're paying for the atmosphere," he said.

"Yeah, I'm going to go home, change clothes, take a shower, and wash your 'atmosphere' out of my hair." She slapped a five-dollar bill and one penny on the bar. "Don't spend that whole tip in one place. You'll upset the balance of the economy."

Ten minutes later, Savannah was standing beside the service station's air pump, leaning on the Mustang's trunk. She had checked her watch an average of every fifteen seconds since arriving, and now, forty-one checks later, she saw an older blue Honda pull into the lot. Her hopes rose as the car bypassed the pumps and headed in her direction.

"Yes! Thank you, Lord," she whispered when she saw that the woman at the wheel was Sharona.

The Honda pulled up beside her, and the car window rolled down.

"Well, I'm here. What now?" Sharona asked.

"Park right over there," Savannah told her, pointing to the back of the lot, behind the garage. "And then get yourself into my car here. We got us some talking to do, girl to girl."

A few minutes later, Savannah had taken Sharona to a park on the town's state beach. Few tourists visited this spot, preferring the more pristine beach near the city pier. With its prominent sand dunes and clumps of thick brush, there were plenty of private spots where people could park, make out, smoke illegal substances, drink beverages that were forbidden on public beaches—and, of course, interrogate subjects from time to time.

It was one of Savannah's favorite spots.

"Are you a cop?" Sharona asked as she fumbled in her purse and brought out a pack of cigarettes and a lighter.

"Nope." Savannah noticed that Sharona's hands were still shaking. For just a brief moment, Savannah thought about all the people she had seen shivering with fear over the years. Too many.

Her heart went out to people living in that much fear. It wasn't much of a life.

"You feel like a cop," Sharona said, drawing long and hard on her cigarette.

"Feel like a cop?"

"You know—you give off that kind of cop energy."

Savannah chuckled. "Yeah? Well, I was one for a long time. I guess it never completely goes away. Now I'm a private investigator."

"And you're investigating what happened to Bill, right?"

"That's right."

The redhead's eyes filled with tears. "He was murdered, wasn't he?"

Savannah studied her face closely, watching every expression. She saw only pain, sorrow, and the ever-present fear.

"Yes, he was," she told her. "I'm sorry. I gather he meant a lot to you."

"I'm in love with him. I mean, I guess I *was* in love." She started to sob, her hands over her face. "I just can't believe that he's gone."

Again, Savannah reached into her purse and produced a bunch of tissues. It occurred to her that she went through more tissues than a marriage counselor.

"I'm sure it's awful, losing someone you love like this," Savannah said, "especially in this way."

"Are you sure somebody killed him?" she asked with a pathetic, hopeful look on her face. "It couldn't have been some sort of accident?"

"No, I'm sorry." Savannah reached back behind her seat and pulled out a bottle of water. She unscrewed the top and handed it to Sharona. "And we're trying to find out who did it."

"We?"

"My cop friend and I."

Sharona took a long drink of the water and wiped her mouth with the back of her hand. "I haven't always gotten along that well with the cops."

Savannah smiled. "I've heard. I'm not interested in whatever run-ins you've had with the law in the past. I just want you to tell me about Bill, about what he was up to lately, about anybody who had it out for him."

"Bill had a lot going on," Sharona said. "He was getting ready to make some big changes in his life. People don't always like that."

"Tell me about it."

"He was getting ready to run away with me, leave that bitch Clarissa, and start a new life, just the two of us. We were supposed to leave a few days ago for Las Vegas. He was going to get a quickie divorce, and we were going to get married in one of the chapels there."

She flashed a sizable engagement ring under Savannah's nose.

"See?" she said. "He was serious, or he wouldn't have bought me a rock this size, huh?"

Savannah nodded. She had to agree a diamond the size of a doorknob could have indicated a serious commitment—or a pretty toy to keep his mistress happy and quiet.

"How sure are you that this was really going to happen?" Savannah asked her. "I mean, a lot of married guys say they're going to leave their wives, but when push comes to shove—"

"He meant it! We'd already rented a house in Vegas, a really nice house with a pool and everything! Bill was all excited about it. He said he had one more thing he had to do, and then he'd have lots of money to take care of us until the divorce became final and he got half of all of Clarissa's stuff. She's worth millions and millions with all those clubs of hers and the vitamins and the diet meals and the exercise DVDs."

"Yes, I'm sure she is. Tell me more about this thing he had to take care of."

"He didn't say what it was exactly, just that it was going to happen four or five days ago. He said he was going to score, big-time."

"Do you think it had anything to do with his gambling, like a big win, or . . . ?"

"Bill? No way. Bill was an awful gambler. He loved it, but he never won anything worth getting excited about."

"Was he into drugs?"

"Not at all. Bill was superclean when it came to that stuff. He was into health and fitness and all that. He didn't have much of a choice about it, being married to the Queen of Fitness."

Savannah wasn't particularly surprised by the amount of venom in those last three words. If Clarissa provoked hostility in most of the people she met, you couldn't really expect the "other woman" in her marriage to hold her in high regard.

It was Savannah's experience that the mistresses of married men usually looked for the worst in the wives' characters to help ease their consciences. And with Clarissa, there was just so much to work with.

"How did you and Bill meet?" she asked.

"At one of Pinky's poker games. Pinky's this guy I used to work for." She took a drink of water and turned her face away from Savannah, looking out the passenger window. "I used to be in some bad stuff, but that was before. Since I met Bill, I've only been with him." She choked up. "I was really looking forward to . . . to only being with him."

"Tell me about Pinky," Savannah asked, trying not to

sound too wildly interested, trying to look nonchalant when she was mentally shaking cheerleader pom-poms and jumping up and down.

"Pinky's a really bad guy. He's a bookie, but he does a lot of other stuff, too. He's got a lot of girls working for him. You know, like an escort service. And he's into the drug scene. He doesn't use, but he finances a lot of big deals."

She tried to set her bottle of water on the dash, but she sloshed some of it onto the console. "I'm sorry," she said.

"Don't worry about it. Really." Savannah put her hand on the redhead's forearm and gave it a comforting squeeze. "What were you saying about this Pinky guy?"

Sharona turned toward Savannah, her eyes haunted and frightened. "I think Pinky killed Bill. I know Bill owed him some money, and Bill said that once he had this other money, the big score he was working on, he would pay Pinky off. That way we could go to Vegas with a clean slate and not have to be looking over our shoulders all the time."

"When did he tell you that?"

"Six days ago. We were going to be leaving right after he took care of this business of his and once he'd paid Pinky."

"So, what happened?"

"He was supposed to call me, as soon as he'd made his big score and settled things with Pinky. But the days came and went and he never called. That wasn't like him. I was so afraid that something was wrong, really bad wrong. And then today I was watching the news on TV, and I saw that they'd found a red convertible and a body up there on Sulphur Creek Road. I just knew it was Bill. I knew it."

"I'm sorry, Sharona. It's terrible to lose anybody you love, but especially this way."

"It *is* terrible. And now I'm afraid that Pinky's going to come after me, or send somebody after me."

"Why?"

"Because they all know—everybody on his crew—that Bill and I had a thing. If he'd kill Bill over some money, he won't give it a second thought, getting rid of me because I might know something. That's why I was hanging out over at The Keg. Aldo's an old boyfriend of mine. He's a bad guy, too, but he hates Pinky. And he wouldn't let him hurt me . . . at least, not in his place."

Savannah thought of the safe house a few miles out of town that the SCPD kept just for these occasions. It wasn't much, a little cottage out in the middle of some orange groves. But it smelled a heck of a lot better than The Keg, and Sharona Dubarry looked like she could use some fresh air and a stress-free environment for awhile.

"If I could arrange for a place for you to stay, until this whole thing is settled, would you like that?" she asked her. "It would be better than running from one bad guy to another, trying to choose the lesser of evils."

"You mean like a hotel room?"

"A little better than that. It's a house, old, small, quiet. You can take walks among the orange trees and smell the blossoms. There's a porch with a swing. You can sit there and listen to the birds chirp. Not exciting, but restful."

Sharona started to cry again, but Savannah sensed they were tears of relief. And she had stopped shaking. That was a good start.

"Then we'll do it. I'll make a phone call to my partner and get him to okay it. Then I'll take you back to your car. We'll go to your house together, and I'll wait and keep watch while you pack a bag. Then I'll drive you out there."

"Thank you," Sharona said. "I really appreciate this."

Savannah gave her a reassuring smile. "I know you do, sugar. I'm glad to help."

But she wasn't all that glad. As she made the call to

Dirk, then drove Sharona back to the gas station, she had mixed emotions, mulling over all that she'd just heard.

On one hand, she was elated to have this lead that sounded like a hot one. But at the same time, she had a nagging disappointed feeling, deep in her gut.

She didn't have to do more than two seconds' worth of soul searching to know where that was coming from. She wanted hot leads, but she wanted them to lead her to Clarissa Jardin, not some wiseguy bookie.

And how sick is that? she asked herself as she followed Sharona Dubarry's blue Honda to her house near the beach. *Sometimes self-awareness just . . . well . . . sucks.*

Chapter 12

Usually, when Savannah returned home, it was a toss-up who was the most excited to see her, Tammy, Cleopatra, or Diamante. But when she walked into the house in the late afternoon, the only interested parties were the cats.

Tammy had her nose practically glued to the computer screen, and she barely gave a grunt as Savannah walked by.

A glance over her assistant's shoulder told Savannah that Tammy was slaving away on the luminol picture—the one Dirk had forwarded to her from the lab.

It didn't look like much to Savannah, just a dark, charcoal gray screen with some white dots like tiny paint spatters . . . or a starry night sky in an Arizona desert if she were to wax poetic. And she wasn't in a poetic mood. Twenty-nine hours without sleep could just sap the poet right out of a body.

"Anything new? Anybody call?" Savannah asked.

"Nope."

"Bill Jardin's mother? Marietta?"

"Nope and nope."

"Okay."

Worn out from that lengthy, scintillating, and complex discussion, Savannah went into the kitchen, poured some cat food into the ever-hungry felines' dishes, refreshed their water, and got herself a glass of iced tea. No token slice of lemon but gobs of ice.

Leaving the cats to gorge themselves on Whisker Vittles, she returned to the living room and sank into her comfy chair. Her head spun for a moment and she realized that she was getting dangerously tired. If she didn't at least grab a nap soon, she wasn't going to be able to function.

"Did you find Sharona?" Tammy asked, her eyes still trained on the screen as she manipulated the computer's mouse and worked the photo program, trying one type of enhancement after another.

"Found her, talked to her, took her to the safe house."

Tammy whirled around in her chair. "The safe house? Why?"

"She thinks that dude Pinky killed Jardin, and she's afraid he may be after her, too."

"Whoa! Get out!" Tammy looked disappointed. "And we were hoping it was Clarissa."

"*You* were? I thought it was just me who doesn't like her."

"Nope. Can't stand her. I avoid watching her on TV or reading about her in the paper because she disturbs my inner peace. I have to meditate afterward, just to cleanse my spirit of her hostility."

"Wow, I thought it was just people like me who felt that way. I didn't think that folks like you . . ."

The hurt expression on Tammy's face made Savannah swallow the rest of her words.

"Why did you think that?" Tammy asked softly. "Because I'm skinny?"

"Well, I . . . you're . . . you know . . . into fitness and all that. You aren't the kind of person that Clarissa would criticize or insult. You're more like . . ."

"Like her?"

Savannah realized she was blowing it with her friend, but she was too tired to fully understand why. She decided to shut up before she made the situation worse.

"Savannah," Tammy said, her voice tremulous, "I hope you don't think that just because I'm thin, because I like to work out and eat a certain way . . . that I approve of what Clarissa Jardin does. I think she's amassed a fortune by being cruel and sensational and controversial. She claims to be this health guru, but I think what's she's doing is wrong and unhealthy for our entire society."

Savannah was surprised at the depth of her friend's conviction and sorry that she had obviously offended her. "Tammy, I had no idea you felt that way."

"But you should have known," Tammy said softly, with no accusation, only hurt in her voice. "I try to be a good person, and good people don't condone cruelty, no matter what size they are."

Savannah got up from her chair, walked across the room, and pulled Tammy to her feet. Wrapping her arms around her, she said, "I'm sorry, sweetie. I really am. It's so easy to slide into that foolish 'us' versus 'them' mentality when it comes to this stupid weight issue. And I don't ever want to think of you that way. I always want you and me to be '*us*.' No matter what size you are."

Tammy returned the hearty hug. "And I couldn't possibly love you more, whether you ever dropped or gained a pound. Even the thought that I might seems ludicrous to me."

The office phone rang, and Tammy grabbed for it. "Moonlight Magnolia Detective Agency. Tammy Hart speaking," she said in a breathy and rather bad Marilyn Monroe impression that Savannah had always found humorous.

"Oh, it's just you," Tammy said. She mouthed, "Dirk-o,"

to Savannah. "Yes, I've got the sister's name and address and everything you asked for. That's such old news. I'm working on the blood spatter photo now." She listened for a minute, then said, "Well, don't sound so surprised. We Moonlight Magnolia ladies don't dillydally, you know."

She picked up a piece of paper from the desk and read the pertinent information to him. "Her name is Rachel Morris. Up until last month, she lived in New York—Greenwich Village, to be exact. Then she and her son—age sixteen, named Tanner—moved to Yucca Mountain . . . a little town on Interstate 15 near the Nevada border. She's never been married, doesn't have a criminal record, and she pays her bills on time." She grinned broadly. "Anything else you want to know?"

She held out the phone to Savannah. "He wants to talk to you."

Savannah took the phone and walked into the kitchen, leaving Tammy to return to her computer work. "Did you at least say 'Thank you?' "

"Of course I did," Dirk replied, sounding moderately miffed. "I know how to talk to people."

Since when? Savannah thought, but she kept it to herself. With Dirk, she really had to choose her battles. If she griped about everything he did that drove her nuts, she'd be nagging him all the time . . . and then they might as well be married and filing joint tax returns.

"Speaking of talking to people," she said, "did you get hold of that D. A., Wilcox?"

"Yeah. He's got a pretty good case against Pinky, whose name, by the way, is actually Pinky—go figure."

"No way."

"I swear, that's his legal name. Baldovino Pinky Moretti."

"What? He didn't want to go by Baldovino?"

"He's mobbed up."

"No kidding. Sharona already told me all about him, the drugs, the hookers, the gambling."

"And murder. Wilcox is sure he's gotten rid of at least three members of his crew by himself, and he's thinking Pinky did Jardin, too. What Clarissa said about Bill going in to talk to Wilcox . . . it's all true. He was supposed to give his deposition tomorrow."

"So, where's our man Pinky now?"

"Wilcox had him picked up this morning. They're holding him in county jail."

"For murder?"

"Assault. He punched a deputy sheriff when he got pulled over for a rolling stop at a red light."

Savannah grinned. "Did that deputy provoke him in any way?"

"Naw, I'm sure he didn't. But I foresee a promotion in his immediate future."

"Are you going to question him? Can I be there when you do?"

Dirk didn't answer.

"Dirk? Do you mind if I go along?"

After a few more moments of silence, she thought maybe they had lost the signal. "Hey, buddy . . . you there?"

"What? I . . . oh, damn."

"What is it?"

"I think I just dozed off there."

"I think you did, too. Are you driving?"

"Sitting at a light on Lester Street."

"Pull off somewhere and take a nap. Right now. Go to the parking lot there by the pier, lie down on the seat, and sleep for an hour or so before you kill some poor, innocent person."

"Yeah, okay . . . Mom."

"I'm getting plum swimmy-headed myself. I'm going to go upstairs and crash for a little while. I'll have Tammy call you to wake you up in an hour."

"All right."

"And darlin', before you zonk out, be sure your doors

are locked and your windows are up. There've been some muggings down in that neck o' the woods lately."

"Hu-u-rumph."

With assurances from Tammy that she would wake her if anything important developed, Savannah retired to her bedroom to get a little sleep. The sight of the room with its lacy curtains, snowy linens, and vase filled with fresh roses from her garden sitting on the dresser nearly made Savannah cry. It felt like a week since she had last been here—the place where she retreated to refresh her body and spirit.

While Savannah usually wore slacks, simple tailored blouses and jackets, and loafers, she did allow herself total female expression in two ways: sexy lingerie and a completely girlie girl bedroom.

The handmade quilt on the bed had lacy accents with its rose and lilac print fabric—a recent gift from Granny Reid. And even the smell of the room was feminine, Savannah's favorite floral perfume, mixed with the fresh flowers.

It was, indeed, a room to dream in.

Rather than tempt evil fate by actually undressing and getting into bed properly, Savannah simply kicked off her shoes, pulled the quilt back, and slipped beneath it.

Wrapping herself in the quilt, lovingly stitched by her grandmother's own hands, it was as though Granny Reid herself was rocking her to sleep.

Less than ten seconds later, she was, as Gran would say, "snorin' like a cartoon bear."

She had been asleep two minutes—or at least, it felt like two minutes—when a soft knocking at the bedroom door awakened her.

"Savannah? It's Tammy."

The door opened an inch and Tammy's pert nose appeared in the crack. "I'm sorry to wake you, but Bill Jardin's mom is on the phone. She's here in California now. In fact, she's in San Carmelita, and she wants to come over right away. Are you up for it?"

"Up? Up? Hell no, I'm not up. I just got to sleep."

"Actually, it's been over two hours. I didn't have the heart to wake you."

Savannah threw off the quilt and sat up so quickly that she nearly fell off the side of the bed.

Running her fingers through her mussed hair, she said, "Did you call Dirk and wake him up, too?"

"Over an hour ago."

"Good."

She knew she was in a pissy mood when the thought of Dirk getting more sleep than she'd gotten made her feel the need to box his ears and stand him in a corner.

Tammy walked into the room and held out the phone to her. She did her best not to sound like a groggy wolverine just coming out of hibernation when she said, "Mrs. Jardin, this is Savannah Reid. I'm glad to hear from you, and I'm so sorry for your loss."

"Thank you," said a soft voice with a gentle, Midwestern accent on the other end. "But I don't want your condolences. I want you to put my daughter-in-law in jail for murdering my son."

Savannah was a bit taken aback by the woman's candor. The voice might be soft and sweet, but there was no mistaking the bitterness and grief behind those words.

"I want to help you in every way that I can," she replied. "Let me give you my address. You come over here and we'll talk."

"Do you have any alcohol?"

"I beg your pardon?"

"Alcohol. I need a drink or two at least to get through the next few hours."

Savannah thought of the beers that she always had stashed in the back of her refrigerator, so that Dirk could have a cold brew on demand. Then there was the whiskey she kept for hot toddies and Irish coffees. Not to mention the triple sec for margaritas and the rum for daiquiris.

"Come on over," she said. "We'll see what we can do for you . . . on all accounts."

The lady who appeared on Savannah's doorstep ten minutes later reminded her of some of the women from her own hometown in rural Georgia. The pink polyester pantsuit, the floral print blouse, the oversized acrylic beads around her neck, and the silver-blue hair—they all made Savannah homesick for women with soft, Southern accents, gentle smiles, and very strong opinions about what was right and what was just pure-dee wickedness.

"Mrs. Jardin," Savannah said, gently shaking her hand. "I'm Savannah. Come right in and sit a spell. You must be plum exhausted, considering all you've been through."

Ruby Jardin turned back toward the street and waved away the cab that was sitting in front of Savannah's house. "You don't know the half of it," she said. "I'm so mad and so hurt and so tired that I can't see straight."

Savannah led her into the house and considered seating her in the living room, but then she had a second thought. "Would you like to have that drink in my backyard?" she said. "You've been cooped up on a plane for hours. It might be nice to breathe some fresh air."

"I'd like that. I was sitting next to some numbskull who reeked to high heaven. He'd taken a bath in cheap aftershave . . . like that'd take the place of good ol' soap and water." She shook her head, disgusted. "You'd think

with all this airline security hooey these days, they'd be
more discriminating who they let onboard those planes. I
don't know what this world's coming to."

Savannah looked into the woman's dark brown eyes,
which were swollen from crying, and saw the deep pain
barely below the surface. She had just lost a child to murder, and that had to be the worst misfortune that could be-
fall anyone. But, instead of screaming at the world, she
was complaining about a guy on the plane wearing cheap
cologne.

Instead of curling into a fetal position and wishing for
death herself, as most people might assume they would
do under the circumstances, she had just flown more than
halfway across a continent to find justice for her son.

So, as Savannah directed the woman through her
house—stopping in the kitchen to grab two cold beers, an
icy mug, and a glass of lemonade, and then out to the
backyard—she decided that she liked Ruby Jardin very
much. And she was determined to help her any way she
could.

Moments later, sitting on comfortable chaises beneath
Savannah's cedar arbor, draped with wisteria, Ruby let it
flow—a flood of accusations against her now-former
daughter-in-law.

"Clarissa never did love Bill. Not properly anyway,"
she said. "She only married him because he was so good-
looking and charming. He was so handsome, my Bill."

Tears filled her eyes, but she quickly blinked them
away. "He could charm any woman," she continued, "and
did. Too many, I admit it. That was his downfall. Women."

Thinking of Sharona and how heartbroken she appeared to be over his death, Savannah had to agree that
Bill had at least one woman too many in his life.

Savannah said nothing, just let Ruby talk as the grieving

mother sipped her beer and toyed with her pink and purple beads.

"I warned him when he told me he was going to run away with that one. I told him that if Clarissa found out what he was up to she might do away with him. Or hire somebody else to do it. I wouldn't put anything past that woman. But would he listen to his mother? No. He told me to mind my own business." She swallowed hard and said, "Like *he* wasn't my business. Like I didn't worship the ground that boy walked on."

"I'm sorry, Ruby," Savannah said softly. "So, he told you about her? About his plans to leave Clarissa and move to Vegas with his girlfriend?"

"Sure. He told me everything. My son and I were very close." She sniffed. "And I know what you're thinking, that I shouldn't approve of something like adultery. But you don't know what he went through, that poor thing, what that Clarissa put him through. She made his life a living h-e-double-l, yelling at him right and left, leaving him alone and lonely for weeks on end so she could run around, appearing on TV, promoting all that exercise baloney of hers. She was just asking for him to step out on her."

"So, why, exactly, do you think Clarissa killed, I mean . . . took his life?"

"Because he was going to leave her and divorce her. California's one of those states that splits everything fifty-fifty when a couple calls it quits. He would have taken half of everything she's got. And that's what she lives for, that greedy witch, her stuff. The houses, the cars, the money. That's all that matters to her. Well, that and her celebrity. Being in the spotlight and thinking the sun rises and sets for her alone."

She chugged down the last half of the beer and set her mug down on the small table between their chaises. Savannah wasted no time refilling it. She had always found that alcohol was a great lubricant when it came to keeping a fact-gathering conversation going.

Not that Ruby Jardin's wheels needed to be greased.

"Although," she was saying, "I don't know that Clarissa's replacement would have been that much better for him. She's not exactly squeaky clean herself, if you know what I mean."

"Yes, I do. I mean, we've checked her out, and I've talked to her myself."

"Already?"

"Just a few hours ago."

"Wow, you *are* good. When I saw you on TV and heard about you guys catching that pervert at Clarissa's club, I had a feeling about you. I told myself that you were the one who could help me nail Clarissa."

"Well, I'm happy to help you find out who harmed your son. We'll have to see where the evidence leads us. It may very well point to Clarissa." Savannah took a drink of her lemonade. "Mrs. Jardin, you say that your son frequently confided in you. Did he mention anything to you about him coming into a sizeable sum of money?"

Ruby looked away, suddenly deciding to study Savannah's rose garden intently. She didn't answer.

"When I spoke to his girlfriend earlier," Savannah said, "she mentioned that he had said something to her about it. I thought he might have told you, too."

"Well, of course he told me about it. And of course she knew about it, too. She was in on it. Has been all along. It was all her big idea. Bill never would have thought of doing something crooked like that, not on his own."

Savannah gazed across the lawn at her rose garden, feigning interest, too. It didn't do to appear too excited at a time like this.

"It was her idea, you say?"

"Sure. I mean, not that I mind them squeezing some money out of Clarissa. Bill deserved every penny he got from that miserable, messed-up marriage. But that other one—she'd been blackmailing Clarissa from day one, long before she and Bill ever started seeing each other."

It didn't do to appear overly confused in the course of an interview, either, but Savannah couldn't help it. "What?" she said. "I know that she's been in some trouble in the past, but blackmail? Sharona's been blackmailing Clarissa? For how long? For what?"

It was Ruby's turn to be confused. "What? Who's Sharona?"

"Sharona Dubarry, your son's girlfriend. Tall, slender, beautiful redhead . . . ?"

Ruby laughed. "Redhead, yes. And I guess she's okay looking, if that's your taste. But she's about average height and I don't think anybody would call Rachel slender."

"Rachel? Rachel Morris?"

"Yes. Clarissa's twin sister. The one who posed for Clarissa's 'before' shot, and who's been blackmailing her for it ever since she got famous."

Savannah nodded as a couple of the puzzle places clicked into place for her. "The one who's also been sleeping with Clarissa's husband. The one who thought that Bill was going to leave his wife and run away with her to Vegas . . . too."

"Too?"

Savannah looked at Ruby Jardin, a grieving mother who thought she knew everything there was to know about her precious, recently departed son. A mom who believed that her boy was, basically, a good guy, tormented by one woman and led astray by another.

The last thing Savannah wanted was to add to her pain.

"What do you mean, 'too?' " Ruby asked, unwilling to let it drop. "And who's Sharona?"

Savannah swirled the ice in her lemonade a time or two before answering. "I spoke to a young lady named

Sharona today," she said, choosing her words carefully. "And she was in love with your son and seemed to think he was in love with her, too. Of course, I only have her word on that. She may have been mistaken. Time will tell."

"Oh, she was probably telling you the truth," Ruby replied. She leaned back, resting her head on the chaise, looking very weary and sad. "I always told that boy to keep his pants closed . . . that one of these days he was gonna get it caught in his zipper. But young people, they just think they know it all. You can't teach them anything. Especially boys."

Her breath caught in her throat. She closed her eyes and began to cry. "Did I tell you that he was my only boy? In fact, he was my only child."

"No, ma'am," Savannah said softly. "I'm so sorry."

"Catch whoever did this. Will you do that for me?"

Savannah started to say, "I'll try." But she could hear Granny Reid's oft-repeated phrase echoing in her head. "Never say, 'I'll try.' 'I'll try' is a weak person's way of saying 'no.' "

"I will," she said, meaning it. "I promise, Ruby. I will."

Chapter 13

Savannah had no sooner said "good-bye" to Ruby Jardin than another taxi pulled up in front of her house. Tammy saw it through the window and shouted up the stairs, "Don't look now, but I think your sister just arrived."

Standing at the bathroom sink, her toothbrush in hand and her mouth full of so-called super-brightening paste, Savannah tried to be thrilled. It had been nearly a year since she had seen Marietta, and she wanted so much to be happy about this reunion.

The woman in the mirror looked back at her with bloodshot eyes.

"It has nothing to do with Marietta's vexing ways," she told the makeup-less hag looking back at her in the mirror. "You wouldn't be happy to see Brad Pitt right now."

"Yeah, right," the woman replied.

"I'll be right down," she shouted, spitting toothpaste all over the faucets—a particularly irritating occurrence, because spraying toothpaste everywhere was Dirk's job.

He had equally disgusting jobs, which he also did well, but she decided not to dwell on them, in the interest of plastering a fake smile on her face and greeting her sister.

"Marietta!" she exclaimed as she hurried down the staircase and found a somewhat younger and much more made-up version of herself standing in the foyer. "Why, sugar! What a surprise!"

"Surprise, my foot. Don't tell me that Gran didn't call to warn you. She always ruins everything." Marietta set her suitcases on the floor and hurried over to embrace Savannah at the bottom of the stairs.

Tammy had played hostess and let Marietta in the door, but she gave Savannah a guilty little grin as she ducked out of sight into the living room.

Savannah couldn't blame her. Marietta had that effect on a lot of people. Even in their hometown of McGill, Georgia, folks were known to dive behind produce displays in the grocery stores to avoid Marietta Reid.

She wasn't a bad person, just high-energy, and she had a lot to say even when there was nothing to talk about.

"Hey girl! Look at you," Savannah said, surveying her sister from the top of her highly frosted, highly teased, big hair, to the sequined leopard-print sweater, to the black miniskirt, fishnet hose, and purple pumps. "Ain't you just all gussied up. And for air travel, too!"

Marietta patted her oversized hairdo with one hand, and her hip with the other. "Well, I do believe in looking your best at all times. Rich men ride on those airplanes. It ain't like takin' the bus, you know. And you just might find yourself strikin' up a meaningful relationship on a long flight like that one."

"Did you meet anybody?"

"Naw. They sat me next to some old lady. And another gal was across the aisle with two noisy young'uns. If I'd wanted to spend five hours listenin' to brats bawl and carry on, I'd have stayed home and spent the day with Vidalia and her bunch."

"How is Vi these days?"

Marietta tossed her head, nearly moving her hair, and sniffed. "We're fighting again, and I haven't spoken to her in two days."

"Two whole days. Sounds serious."

"It is. She said some hard, tacky things to me, and I don't think I'm gonna be gettin' over it any time soon. Do you have something to eat? Because, you know, those tightwads don't even feed you anymore on those airplanes." She headed for the kitchen with Savannah trailing behind. "And they shove you into those tiny little seats that aren't big enough for a gopher to sit in. Nope, air travel just ain't as glamorous as it used to be when they served you those yummy smoked almonds . . ."

Dirk had always been able to tell when Savannah was putting food on the table. And no sooner had she and Marietta sat down to a bowl of beans and ham and a pan of hot cornbread than he knocked at the kitchen door.

"Oh, it's Dirk!" Marietta said, brightening at the sight of a member of the opposite gender. "I swear, he's cuter now than that last time I saw him!"

Savannah marveled at the fact that Marietta perked up even more at the sight of a man than she did at the smell of home cooking. Some women just couldn't get it straight, what mattered and what didn't in life.

As he walked over to the table and sat down, he hardly even seemed to notice Marietta, who was sitting directly across from him.

At the slight, her well-lined, ruby-red, heavily glossed lips protruded in a pout.

"Got enough food for me?" he asked.

"Always," Savannah said. "I'll get you a plate."

"Where's the kid?" Dirk asked.

"Tammy's in the living room, slaving away on that

photo you gave her. I don't think she's taken time to pee since you sent it to her." Savannah slid a butter plate in front of her sister. "Marietta, help yourself to the cornbread before it gets cold."

"Oh, hi, Marietta," Dirk said, as though noticing her for the first time. "Savannah didn't mention you were here."

Dirk had never been particularly impressed with Savannah's family members, except for Gran, whom he adored. And Savannah couldn't blame him. Dirk had better taste in people than he had in clothes.

Having performed the minimal social courtesies, he turned his attention to Savannah and business. "The M.E. called," he told her. "It's official. The C.O.D. was a G.S.W."

"What?" Marietta said. "What does that mean? I know that C.O.D. means you have to pay for a package when the mailman brings it, but what was that other one?"

Savannah set a plate and silverware in front of Dirk. Then she turned to Marietta, who could never stand not to be the center of any conversation. "We're working on a homicide case," she told her. "The medical examiner has determined that our victim's cause of death was a gunshot wound."

"Well, isn't that nice?" Marietta slathered butter on the large square of cornbread that she had cut for herself. "I got new mirrors for my beauty shop. Did I tell you that yet?"

"No," Savannah said. "I don't recall you mentioning it." She passed Dirk the butter. "Anything else?" she asked.

"And a couple of new dryers," Marietta said. "Oh . . . and I'm hiring a new nail girl. The other one wasn't good with French tips."

Marietta stuck the cornbread in her mouth, and Savannah decided to take advantage of the opportunity.

"Dirk," she said. "What else did Dr. Liu tell you?"

"I had a Dr. Lou once," Marietta said, talking around the cornbread. "His name was Dr. Vickerson, but his first name was Lou, and after we slept together, I just started calling him that. It seemed disrespectful not to address him as 'doctor,' but 'Dr. Vickerson' is a bit of a mouthful when you're in the throes of passion."

Dirk stared at her for a long moment, eyes wide, slack-jawed, then he said, "Like Dr. Liu told us before, she can't tell how long the body was frozen, so we're not going to get a time of death. But she did find a couple of other things . . ."

"I like to have froze to death one winter when I visited my third husband's mother in Peoria, Illinois," Marietta added. "Did I ever tell you about that? Boy, howdy, I learned then and there not to wear a microminiskirt and no underwear when it's ten below zero. You talk about a wicked awful draft! Why that wind came whipping off the lake and up my skirt and—"

"Mari, please," Savannah said. "Do you mind?"

Dirk seemed mesmerized as he stared at Marietta, obviously lost in thought.

Savannah could only imagine those thoughts, and imagining made her want to smack both him and her sister.

"Dirk, yoo-hoo," she said, kicking him under the table. "What else did Dr. Liu find in the autopsy?"

"Oh, right." He cleared his throat and suddenly became busy buttering his own bread. "She said that Jardin was healthy, nothing remarkable . . . other than the G.S.W. to the head. But she did find something else interesting."

"What?" Savannah wanted to know.

"Chicken shit." He glanced over at Marietta. "I beg your pardon, Mari. I mean, excrement."

"Oh, that's okay," Marietta assured him. "Gran keeps a passel of hens, you know, for the eggs, and they're always getting out of their pen, so we stepped in chicken shit every time we went in or out of the house when we was growin' up. Why I remember one time when Danny Moore came sneaking through my bedroom window at night, after Granny had forbidden me to date him anymore, and he had this big gob of—"

"Where?" Savannah asked Dirk, getting more frantic by the moment. "Where was it?"

"On the bottom of his shoes," Marietta replied. "And when he tried to climb into bed with me—"

"And a feather," Dirk said, talking over her. "A feather and some poop were on the backs of his shoes."

"The *backs*?" Marietta asked. "Are you sure she said the backs? I only ask because we had that mess o' chickens when I was growing up, and I can pretty much tell you for certain that if you step in chicken shit, it gets on the *bottoms* of your shoes, not on the *backs* of—"

"Excuse me!" Savannah said, suddenly pushing back from the table and jumping to her feet. "I . . . I just have to . . . please excuse me, because I have to go . . . I think I'm going to have to go in the other room and . . . um . . . uh . . . scream or maybe hit something really hard. I'll be right back. Help yourself to the beans."

As she ran out of the room, she heard Dirk mumble something to Marietta that sounded like, "It's been a long day. . . . hasn't slept . . . hours."

And Marietta's matter-of-fact reply, "Don't pay her no mind. Savannah always was the high-strung, nervous type. Would you pass me some of them beans?"

Having regained her composure and consumed a considerable amount of beans and cornbread, Savannah was ready to take on the world—or at least perform one more task, pertaining to the case, before falling flat on her face and possibly never getting up again.

"I'm not being overly dramatic," she told Dirk as they walked out of her house and toward their cars, which were parked in her driveway. "I feel as rotten as you look, and boy . . . that's a bad, bad thing. We both have to spend some time with our toes pointed toward the ceiling or we're gonna die. We're too old for this crap."

"I know. I don't just bounce back from this kind of abuse the way I used to when I was young."

Savannah decided not to mention that he hadn't been all that bouncy as a young guy, either. He'd pretty much always been a grouch, young or middle-aged, sleepy or wide-awake.

But in her book any guy who groaned with orgasmic delight when sinking his teeth into her cornbread was definitely worth the air he breathed.

"I've arranged to go have a talk with our man, Pinky, over in county lockup," he said when he got to his Buick.

"Wish I could go with you," she said. "He sounds like a real character."

"Yeah, but we've gotta spread out. We'll get more accomplished separate than together. You go have your little chat with Clarissa about what her mother-in-law said about her. Then we'll call it a night and start fresh tomorrow."

"We'll start, I don't know how fresh we'll be."

He gave her an affectionate smile, reached up, and brushed a lock of hair out of her eyes. "Thanks, Van. I appreciate all the help you're giving me on this."

"Hey, it's not for you anymore. Ruby Jardin gave Tammy a nice juicy check this afternoon. I'm now officially 'on the case.' Getting paid and everything. So you don't have to feel guilty anymore."

She glanced back at the house and rolled her eyes. "Besides, you know I would *pay* to get out of there. God help me, but I think if I spend too much quality time with my sister, she might wind up with hair rollers shoved up her nose and a curling wand up her . . . well . . . never mind."

"I hear ya," he said. "I'll testify for you in court. Tell them it was justifiable all the way."

She walked over to her Mustang and opened the door.

"No girl fights over there at the hacienda," he said. "No hair-pulling, eye-gouging, or crotch shots."

"You're seriously crampin' my style there, good buddy," she said. "See ya later."

When Savannah pulled up to the wall of Rancho Rodriguez, she felt as though this place had become her home away from home. And that wouldn't have been a bad thing, considering the beauty of the estate, if it hadn't been for the mistress of the manor.

She had to admit she wasn't the least bit eager to see Clarissa Jardin's face again, or, worse yet, to listen to her mouth. But work was work, and she had to keep the cats in Whisker Vittles and Tammy in celery sticks.

As she walked through the bell gate and into the courtyard, enjoying the fragrance of the garden flowers, enhanced by the evening dew, she experienced one of those brief, but beautiful, life-affirming moments.

Gran had always taught her to pause, at least a couple of times each day, and savor the pure joy of being alive. "I don't care how busy you think you are," her grandmother said. "Everybody has ten seconds to look around and notice what's beautiful around 'em. This ol' world is full of misery and suffering, but there's good in it, too, if you've a mind to look for it."

Sometimes, those moments were all too brief, though, as Savannah had noticed. And this was one of them.

Her ten-second reverie was cut to four seconds when she heard two voices, a man's and a woman's, speaking Spanish in low, whispered tones.

It was the gardener and the maid, Maria, huddled together over the bed of asters. They were working together, removing the offending plants, as they talked.

As soon as they saw Savannah, they ended their conversation, and avoided eye contact with her.

"Buenos notches," Savannah said.

They both grinned, and—as always when using her limited and rather bad Spanish—she didn't know it if was because the listeners appreciated her feeble attempt to speak their language, or if her accent was so terrible that they were trying not to laugh outright.

"Good evening, Señora," Maria said.

The gardener simply nodded.

"Is Ms. Jardin at home?" Savannah asked.

The woman's face clouded at the mention of her mistress. "No. She is not here now."

Savannah couldn't help being disappointed, but she had decided not to call ahead. She figured: Why give Clarissa a heads-up? Why give her a reason to lock the gate and post rabid rottweilers to guard it? Wasn't life complicated enough?

And when she had found the gate by the main road not only unlocked but also wide open, she was sure the gods were smiling on her.

Oh, well. So much for that theory.

"Then may I ask," Savannah said, "where she is?"

The look of fear that spread over the maid's face went straight to Savannah's heart. So did the barely suppressed fury on the man's. She could tell they were hardworking people who sacrificed their dignity to work for someone like Clarissa Jardin, and she couldn't help feeling indignant on their behalf.

It cost so little to be kind to your fellow man, especially those who served you.

"Please, Señora," Maria said, looking as though she might start crying at any moment. "Please do not ask us.

We need the jobs. We have families at home. We send the money to them, to feed our mothers, our sisters and brothers."

"I understand," Savannah said. "I won't do anything to make you lose your job."

"I'm sorry," Maria replied, "but you do not understand. If Señora Clarissa sees us talk to you, we will be told to leave. Please go away now, before she comes back."

"I will," Savannah said. "I don't want to cause any trouble for you. That's the last thing I want to—"

The man threw down a handful of the plants and said, "We have trouble already, Maria. Much trouble. Someone killed Señor Bill and this lady is trying to help."

He turned to Savannah. "The Señora is in the hills." He pointed to the foothills edging the property. "She runs. She runs and runs and runs." He smiled, but there was no humor on his lined, sun-darkened face. "She runs but she can not get away. She will never get away."

"From whom?" Savannah asked. "What is she running from?"

"From herself," he said. "She runs from herself, from the wolves inside her soul. But someday *los lobos* will catch her. They will destroy her."

Savannah felt a chill run through her as, for a moment, she sensed her own wolf pack, nipping at her heels. Everyone had wolves—one kind or another. And there were so many breeds of wolves: unfulfilled dreams, broken relationships, poor health, financial problems, addictions and obsessions . . . not to mention difficult childhoods.

"*Guardar silencio,* Hernando," Maria whispered to him.

"It's okay," Savannah assured her. "I'm going. I won't tell her that I talked to you. I promise. Thank you."

She left them to their work and returned to her car.

Ordinarily, she would have driven up to the hills to see

if she could find Clarissa, but there would be no way to do so without compromising Maria and Hernando. So, she decided to wait in her car.

The well-fortified adobe walls had been built in an age when security was a matter of life and death for the family who lived here. And, as the builders had intended it to do, the enclosure made sure that everyone entered and left the property through the bell gate.

It was just a matter of time until Clarissa Jardin came running home . . . with that pack of hungry wolves at her heels.

Savannah wondered if she had time to do a bit of snooping before she returned. And if she did, could she do so without Maria or Hernando catching her?

Something told her that, even if Hernando caught her stealing the family silver, he'd be more likely to help her cart it out of the house than prevent the burglary.

She glanced up the hill and saw no sign of any jogger on the dusty, dirt road. So, she reached into her purse, pulled out her penlight flashlight, and got ready to . . . as Tammy would say . . . "Go sleuthing."

Chapter 14

As Savannah walked around the outside of the adobe wall that protected the courtyard and hacienda, she felt as though she had stepped back in time. Antique, rusted farm equipment sat in the shade of eucalyptus trees and one area of the wall had aging leather harnesses hanging side by side next to a fenced area that appeared to be an old livestock corral.

The split-rail fence was missing a few planks here and there, but she could see places where horses had chewed on the wood. She thought of the men who rode those horses, and, of course, pictured them to look a heck of a lot like Clint Eastwood in his prime. She thought of the ladies who might have ridden sidesaddles, their skirts billowing around them.

But mostly, she thought about the fact that if Clarissa Jardin caught her snooping around her property, she'd probably stick Savannah's head in one of those sinister-looking pieces of gym equipment she was so famous for.

Near the corral, Savannah saw a large outbuilding that looked as though it might have served as a barn in its previous life. Like the house, it had been restored, and its adobe plaster and paint were in near-perfect condition.

Glancing over her shoulder, she hurried to the building, bypassed the wide doors in the front and entered by way of a small door around the corner on the other side.

As she had suspected, the former barn was being used as a garage. Wide enough to accommodate two cars, it housed only one—a beautiful black Mercedes.

Usually, Savannah didn't consider herself materialistic. But she had to admit that, as much as she loved her classic Mustang, she'd trade it for this ride in a heartbeat.

But, even though she would have loved to stand there and imagine herself stepping into that car, wearing a Christian Dior gown of billowing chiffon, bespangled with tiny crystals, driven by an expensive gigolo in an Armani tux, she had better things to do.

She glanced over the car, looking for anything that seemed out of place, suspicious, or extraordinary, and saw nothing. Some items from Clarissa's tacky new sports line were tossed onto the back seat. A stack of brochures advertising her "Houses of Pain and Gain" lay on the dash.

Savannah tried not to be disappointed that there was no gun or bloody gloves lying in plain sight on the passenger's seat. It was never that easy. At least, not if you were trying to nail a criminal with more than two brain cells to rub together. And even though she couldn't stand Clarissa Jardin, Savannah had to admit the woman was no dummy.

Savannah squatted behind the car and shone her penlight's beam on the rear tires. Then she walked around to both sides, checking the front tires.

There were bits of leaves and other assorted vegetation lodged between the treads, some sand, and a few small rocks, but no poultry droppings and nary a feather in sight.

No, it was never that easy.

"Dagnabbit," she whispered. She had risked her neck for nothing.

Noticing that it was rapidly growing darker in the building, she glanced at the window and saw that the sun was, indeed, setting. Clarissa was bound to be getting home soon. Savannah figured she should get back to her car, so that she could pretend she had just arrived when Clarissa did return.

But when she turned around to head for the door, she nearly walked headfirst into the indignant lady of the house.

Clarissa was standing there, wearing a camouflage-print, formfitting workout suit, her hair pulled back into a ponytail, perspiration pouring down her face.

"Ah! You really *do* practice what you preach," Savannah said, far too brightly. "Look at you, workin' up a sweat like that!"

"What the hell are you doing in my garage?" Clarissa asked, ice in her eyes and her voice.

"Um . . . looking for you?"

Hell, it's worth a try, Savannah thought.

"Under my car? You thought I was under my car?"

Okay, Plan B. When all else fails, disarm them with total honesty.

"I came by to talk to you, but when I realized you were gone, I figured I'd snoop around and see if I could find some sort of evidence."

"Evidence against me?"

Savannah shrugged. "Evidence is evidence. It points where it will. I follow."

"Am I going to have to get a restraining order against you?"

"Maybe you could; maybe you couldn't. But I might be just the person to find out who killed your husband. You do want to know, don't you? You were the one who was rantin' and ravin' about it being more than forty-eight hours, and how worried you were that we weren't going to solve this case, yada, yada."

Clarissa stood, staring at Savannah for the longest time, her arms crossed over her chest. Finally, she turned and headed out of the garage.

At the door, she paused and said over her shoulder, "Well, come on. Unless you want to question me in a garage. Maybe you'd like to climb under my car, check for transmission leaks, while you interrogate me?"

Savannah joined her at the door and together they headed around the wall toward the bell gate.

"Good one," Savannah said, grudgingly, but with a smile.

"Thank you," Clarissa replied.

A recently showered, remarkably relaxed Clarissa offered Savannah a glass of merlot as they settled into two of the comfortable wicker chairs under the pavilion in the middle of the courtyard.

"Not now," Savannah told her. "Maybe some other time."

Clarissa poured herself a generous glass, then leaned back and propped her feet on a cushy ottoman.

Savannah couldn't help thinking that Clarissa's yoga pants and hoodie top would be a lot more comfortable than her own blouse, slacks, and jacket. Especially with a Beretta strapped to her side. She also had to admit that Clarissa had the hard body she promised all of her gym attendees and the folks who ate her diet meals, worked out to her videos, and popped her vitamin supplements.

"Do you run every day?" Savannah asked her.

"Every single day. I have to."

Savannah thought about the wolf pack. "I'll bet you do."

"You could run yourself, you know. It would do you good."

"Punching out people I don't like would do me good, too. But I don't give in to the temptation. Discipline comes in all forms."

Clarissa took a sip of her wine. "I guess it does at that."

"And besides, I do run. I run to the grocery store. I run to the dry cleaners. I run to the mall. I run myself ragged all day long and half the night, too. Sometimes all night."

"I mean deliberate exercise."

"Occasionally, I help Dirk run down a perp, tackle him to the ground, and cuff him. When we're hittin' the pavement, that gets pretty darned deliberate."

Clarissa swirled her wine in its goblet. "So, why did you come out here to see me? Do you have any new leads . . . or whatever you call it?"

"Yes," Savannah said. "I found out about Rachel."

For a moment, Savannah thought Clarissa was going to spit wine all over the off-white cushions of her furniture.

"Rachel? Rachel, who?" Her whole casual lady-of-the-manor air evaporated.

"Oh, come on. Give me a little credit here. If I know her name is Rachel, don't you think I know everything else?"

"Who told you about her?" She leaned forward and set her glass down so hard on the coffee table that Savannah was surprised it didn't shatter. Clarissa's eyes narrowed. "Was it Ruby? That bitch! It was her, wasn't it? She always did have it in for me. I hate her."

"I'm not free to say. But, really, Clarissa . . . people do talk. Did you really think you could hide something like a twin sister forever?"

Clarissa plopped back in her chair, suddenly deflated. She sighed. "Well, I hoped so. It was easier, before my career really took off. In the beginning, when I was first starting out, it seemed like a good idea. But then, all the press, the interviews, the public exposure . . . and yes . . . the money. It, well, complicated things."

"Yeah, yeah," Savannah said. "I feel really bad for you. I saw one of those *complications* of yours parked in the garage."

"Hey, did you ever pay the insurance or a repair bill on a Benz?"

"Poor baby. I don't know how you stand it." She waved a hand, indicating the yard, which was now bathed in beautiful blue accent lighting. "All this. It must be rough."

"My husband was just murdered."

"That's true. I'm sorry."

Clarissa gave her a weird, sarcastic little smile. "Are you this insensitive to all your victims' families?"

Savannah though it over a moment before answering and decided to be honest. "No, I'm usually pretty nice. I don't know what's gotten into me lately. Really, I apologize."

"Don't worry about it. It's me. I always seem to bring out the worst in people."

Savannah was shocked at this admission from a woman whom she had assumed didn't have a humble bone in her well-toned body. She considered giving her the token argument of, "Oh, no, that isn't true." But, again, she decided to go the honesty route.

"Why do you think that is?" she asked.

"Oh, I don't know. I started it a long time ago, you know . . . getting in people's faces, giving them hell, telling them like it is. . . ."

"The way *you* think it is."

"Yeah, whatever. Back then, people told me I was strong, gutsy, determined. Now they just call me a bitch."

"But not to your face."

"Of course not. When you're at the top, nobody says things like that to your face. They just run you down behind your back, and then you hear about it later."

"Tell me about Rachel," Savannah said.

"She's my sister. My twin. But you know that already. We didn't even know each other for the first twenty-five years of our lives. Our mom gave us away."

"Why?"

"She was unmarried, poor. The usual reasons. It doesn't matter. Why would you care? I'll bet your mother didn't give you away."

"No, she didn't," Savannah said softly. "The court took us, all nine of us, away from her and gave us to our grandmother. She raised us."

Clarissa looked shocked . . . and impressed. "Wow! Did your mother fight for custody?"

"No. It was sorta a cut-and-dried case."

"Oh."

"How did you and Rachel finally get together?"

"I found her. She was working at a pizza place in Greenwich Village. I was in New York City trying to get 'discovered' as an actress. One day this guy who was in a play I was doing off-off Broadway told me, 'I know a girl who looks just like you, only she's fat.' I knew I was adopted and had a twin sister, so I went to see myself. And the rest, as they say, is history." She took a deep breath. "Actually, I was hoping it *wouldn't* become history, but now . . ."

"So, you looked her up and how did that go? Tearful reunion and all that?"

"Not really. She wasn't all that happy to see me, sort of standoffish actually."

"Why do you suppose that was?"

"She was jealous. Think about it. If you were fat and ugly, and a cute, slender, actress came into the place where you were slinging pizzas and said, 'Hi, I'm your identical twin sister,' wouldn't that piss *you* off?"

"Do you have any idea how obnoxious you sound when you say something like that?"

Clarissa looked genuinely confused as she thought it over. "I guess not. Pretty bad?"

"Odious." Savannah shook her head. "The reunion with Rachel didn't go so well. Then what?"

"I gave up the stage and came to California, Hollywood, television, movies, palm trees and all that."

"When did you come up with the idea for her to pose for your before-the-weight-loss shot?"

"Three years ago. It was my agent's idea."

"Your agent told you to lie and defraud the public?"

"Sheez, that sounds bad when you put it like that. No, of course he didn't. But when I told him I had this great diet exercise plan that I'd lost a ton of weight from, he said, 'Give me a picture of yourself before you lost the weight,' and I didn't have one, because, of course, I've always been thin."

"Of course."

"Oh . . . was that odious, too?"

"Just moderately stinky. It's more the sanctimonious tone that's the piss-off." Savannah grinned. "Please continue. You were about to tell me how Rachel blackmailed you and threatened to tell everybody about the picture when . . ."

"Oh, my God! You know about that, too?"

"You're good at what you do; so am I."

"Apparently so." Clarissa reached back, pulled the barrette out of her hair, and ran her fingers through her blond mass. "Yes, she did. But not right away. I had told her I'd take care of her, send her money every now and then. But that wasn't enough. She started demanding these big, lump payments."

"Did you pay her off?"

"Not at first. I got mad and told her to take what I gave her or go to hell. And no sooner had I said that, than I started getting these threatening anonymous letters, postmarked Manhattan. Like I'm not going to figure that out. Duh."

Savannah chuckled. "Rachel isn't as savvy as you, huh?"

"Oh, please. She's ugly *and* a moron."

"Oo-okay. And how did you handle the so-called anonymous letters?"

"I sent Bill to New York to take care of it. That was a big mistake."

Savannah thought of what Ruby had said about the affair between Bill and Rachel. Yes, she'd agree that may have been a tactical error.

In view of her recent promise to be more sensitive, she considered how to ask the next question. "How was Bill's . . . um . . . relationship with Rachel?"

Clarissa bristled. "They had no relationship! There was no relationship. He wouldn't give a tub-o like her a second look. He had *me*! What would he want with someone like *her*?"

When Savannah didn't reply, Clarissa tossed her head and gave her a dismissive wave. "And I don't care if that sounds bitchy. It's true. It's *just true*!"

"I'm not arguing with you, Clarissa. She's your sister. Bill was your husband. You'd be a better judge of all that business than I would."

"You bet I would. And it didn't happen, I tell you. Did not happen!"

"Okay. Let me ask you this. . . . How do you know for sure that the threatening letters, the anonymous ones from Manhattan, were from Rachel? You had to know other people in New York."

"The letters demanded money. We paid the money.

Bill dropped it off, over and over again. What else could we do? It would have ruined everything. We would have lost it all. We had to pay, and she knew it."

"But how do you know for sure that it was Rachel who was blackmailing you?"

"Because we saw her son one night, at the drop-off spot, taking the bag of money out of the garbage can. She sent a kid, a fourteen-year-old little boy to pick up her stinking blackmail money. How low is that?"

"Low." Savannah nodded. "I have to agree with you. That's lousy."

"Have you met Rachel yet?"

"Not yet."

"Well, you won't like her. If you think *I'm* a bitch, wait till you meet *her*. You are going to hunt her down and interrogate her, too, right?"

"Yeah," Savannah said with a sigh. "Woo-hoo. Ain't it fun, being me?"

When Savannah dragged her weary bones through her door, it was nearly eight o'clock and she was literally seeing double. On the way home from Rancho Rodriguez, she had stopped for a green light, gone the wrong direction on the 101, a freeway she had traveled several times a day, every day, for the past twenty years. And she had nearly hit her own oleander bushes, pulling into her driveway.

"I can't do it," she was telling Dirk on the cell phone. "I was thinking of driving out to Rachel's tonight and trying to talk to her. But I can't. I'm a threat to man and beast on the road right now. If I don't get some sleep, I'm gonna fall down dead in my tracks."

"Go to bed. I know I'm gonna as soon as I get home."

"Where are you?"

"The station, filling out fives."

Her heart went out to him. If there was anything worse than being on the job for all these hours, it was having to do paperwork when your eyes were crossing. "You poor baby. When do you think you'll get to bed?"

"God only knows."

Savannah put her gun and purse away in the foyer closet and walked into the living room. Tammy was still sitting at the computer, totally absorbed in her photo task.

Marietta was watching some trashy movie on the television. Looking at the screen, Savannah saw more naked flesh writhing on bedsheets than she had seen in ages. She had the sinking feeling this was a pay-per-view that would show up on her bill. You didn't get hardcore porn for free.

Marietta was never cheap to have around.

"How did your visit with Pinky go?" she asked Dirk on the phone as she walked past Tammy and patted her on the back, then continued on into the kitchen to make herself a cup of hot chocolate.

"Waste of time. He wouldn't admit anything freely, and I was too tired to beat anything out of him. I've gotta admit it, Van, I'm not as intimidating as I was in my twenties."

Savannah chuckled. "Yeah, and I don't look as good in a miniskirt and fishnet stockings as I did, either. You reckon life's still worth livin'?"

"Not at the moment."

"Tammy's still working on that picture for you," she told him. "And knowing her, she'll stay at it till the wee morning hours. So, you won't be the only one slaving away."

"Good, misery loves company and I'm really suffering here."

Savannah took a mug out of the cupboard and poured some chocolate milk into it. No fancy stuff tonight. Just a simple cup of cocoa . . . with whipped cream . . . some chocolate shavings on top . . . maybe a sprinkle of cinnamon . . .

Then she heard something on the phone. Something suspicious.

It sounded a heck of a lot like a bottle top being removed. She even heard the clatter of a bottle opener being tossed into a silverware drawer.

"What was that?" she asked, straining to hear.

"What was what?" replied Mr. I'm Working My Fingers to the Bone.

"I just heard you open a beer."

"Did not."

"I did, too. Since when do you drink at work?"

"I'm not!"

"You are! And what's that?" She could hear something else . . . an all-too-familiar theme song playing in the background. "That's *Bonanza*! I hear *Bonanza*! You're at home, kicking back in your friggen trailer, swiggin' beer and watching those DVDs I bought you for your birthday!"

"I . . . I . . . well . . ."

"You lyin' sack! You peckerhead! And to think I was mopin' around here, feeling all guilty and sorry for you! I hope you choke on that beer. I hope Pa Cartwright gets shot and actually croaks!"

Chapter 15

Savannah hung up on Dirk and tossed her cell phone onto the counter.

To appease her anger, she squirted an extra shot of whipped cream on top of the cocoa she'd been making, and walked back into the living room.

"Was that Dirk-o you were yelling at in there?" Tammy asked without looking away from the screen.

"Yeah."

"What's he done now?"

"He's being his usual, contrary, aggravating self, that's what." She rested one hand on Tammy's shoulder. "How's it going there?"

"Okay. I've sharpened the focus, increased the contrast, toyed with all sorts of special effects to try to . . ."

Savannah started to glaze over. "Why don't you call it a night and go on home, sugar? You've done way more than enough for one day."

"If you don't mind, I'd like to work a little longer before I leave. I feel like I'm close, and I hate to quit."

"You stay if you want, but I'm taking a nice, warm

bubble bath, drinking this hot chocolate, and then hitting the sheets. You can lock up when you leave, right?"

"No problem."

Savannah kissed her on the top of her head, then walked over to Marietta, who was staring goo-goo-eyed at the television screen.

"What the hell are you watching there?" Savannah asked.

"I think it's called *The Long, Hot Summer*," Marietta replied, leaning sideways to see around Savannah, who had partially blocked her view.

"Get outta here. That ain't Paul Newman there—and that sure as shootin' ain't Joanne Woodward that he's . . . ew-w-w . . ."

"It's a different version. A remake."

"It's porn. How can you watch that crap?"

"They're making love. There's nothing wrong with that."

"Yeah, well, when it comes to that sort of thing, I'd rather be a participant than a spectator."

Marietta gave her an unpleasant little snicker. "*Participated* a lot lately, have we, sis?"

She had her there. Savannah could hardly even remember the last time she had been properly . . . participated.

"Hey, you made hot chocolate!" Marietta said, when she noticed the mug brimming with whipped cream in Savannah's hand. "Where's mine?"

Reluctantly, Savannah handed it to her. "Right here. I figured you'd want some."

Watching her cocoa disappear and Marietta acquire a frothy mustache was nearly more than she could bear. "I'm going to bed," she said. "I'm sorry I had to run out like that when you first got here, Mari. Maybe tomorrow we can go to the beach or get some fish and chips on the pier, or—"

"The beach. I want to try out that new, red bikini . . . see what I can catch with it."

"A sexually transmitted disease, if you aren't careful," Savannah muttered. Then, louder, she said, "I'm going to bed now. You make yourself at home. I'll turn down the covers in the guest bedroom and you—"

The front doorbell chimed, and Savannah jumped. "Who the heck is that at this ungodly hour?"

"Savannah," Tammy said, "it's only eight o'clock. You probably just feel like it's one in the morning."

Savannah went to the door and peeked through the peephole. The sight of the man on the other side of her door was enough to set her heart racing.

The sight of Ryan Stone was enough to set her pulse and her hormones to racing any time, day or night.

She flung open the door and feasted her eyes on male splendor at its most dazzling.

Wearing a black tux, a red rose in his lapel, and a crisp white shirt that set off his handsome, chiseled, tanned face to perfection, he was simply gorgeous. And so was his partner, John Gibson, who was standing beside him.

Equally debonair, dressed in a similar tux, John was older than Ryan, with thick silver hair, pale blue eyes, and a neatly trimmed mustache. His British accent was strong and sweet as he held out a lavender rose to Savannah and said, "Good evening, milady. We've been . . ." He hesitated as his eyes swept over her, taking in the now-rumpled slacks and jacket, her mussed hair and makeup-free face. ". . . looking forward to this for weeks."

Ryan looked her over, too, and seemed a bit confused when he said, "We did mention that we were picking you up at eight o'clock?" He turned to John, looking somewhat concerned, and added, "You did tell her it's black-tie, right, John?"

"Um . . ." John shifted from one foot to the other and

cleared his throat. "I do hope I mentioned that. You know—it being the Center for Performing Arts Annual Gala—it's one of those rather stuffy affairs."

"Oh, my goodness, I totally forgot!" Savannah wished that, like some wicked witch, she could just dissolve into a big puddle of water on the floor and then disappear.

She opened the door wider and pulled them both inside. "I am so, so sorry! I can't believe I . . . oh . . . I feel lower than a skunk's belly. Or is it a toad's belly? It doesn't matter. I can't believe I let that slip my mind!"

"Quite understandable, love," John said, planting a kiss on her cheek, "and completely forgivable. We heard on the news that your past twenty-four hours have been most exciting."

Ryan put his hand under her chin and turned her face into the light. "Savannah, are you okay? You look pale and a little under the weather."

"You've just never seen me without my face paint on before. Maybelline and Max Factor are two of my closest friends."

He laughed. "I've seen you without makeup, and you're lovely either way. But you look really tired."

"As a matter of fact, I was on my way to bed, but now that I've seen you, I've perked right up."

"Me, too!" Marietta came sailing into the foyer from the living room. "And, unlike my sister here, I *do* have my face on and *am* available. You know . . . since y'all don't have nobody to escort to your shindig."

As though in slow motion, Savannah watched the looks of helplessness and horror cross her friends' faces.

They knew her sister well, having met her during one of her previous visits. She really couldn't blame them.

As though from far away, she heard Marietta say, "I don't have no evening gown with me, but I've got a really cute little tiger-striped stretchy dress that's cut way down to here and way up to there. It shows off all my feminine assets to their best possible advantage. And I can slip into it nearly as fast as I can slip out of it."

Savannah tried to think fast, fast enough to save them. But her brain was crawling when it needed to sprint.

"Well, that's a lovely, tempting offer," John said, with all the enthusiasm of a man being offered dental surgery without anesthesia. "I hardly know what to say."

"Me either," Ryan added.

"Hey!" Tammy shouted from the living room. "I've got it! Look at this, everybody!"

Savannah and her three guests all rushed en masse into the living room, where Tammy was hopping up and down in her chair.

No matter what she's got, Savannah thought, *the kid gets a raise just for rescuing Ryan and John from spending a night in Marietta Hades.*

"I was trying to sharpen the focus and all that, to define the spatter. It's so fine, and it just barely shows. It wasn't easy, you know. But I was using this new photo manipulation program you gave me for Christmas, and when I applied this one special effect to it, that sort of changes the positive image to a negative image, I—"

"Tamitha," Savannah said, leaning over her shoulder and staring at the gray-white screen with fine black dots, "I'm old and tired. Just tell us what you see there, Sweet-pea."

"It's not the outline of a gun," she said, pointing to a distinct area that was clear of any spatter. "The lines are pretty clear, and straight. When he got shot, the glove compartment was open and something was lying in it. The fine high-velocity blood spray went all over the interior of the compartment, except where the object masked it."

Savannah explained to Ryan and John, "Dirk thought it might be a gun, because it would make sense that

Jardin might have been reaching for a weapon if he felt threatened."

Ryan nodded. "Makes sense."

"But it wasn't a gun. Look at that shape," Tammy said. "It's more like something square was lying there—or rectangle, actually—something with straight edges."

"A piece of paper?" Savannah said.

"Maybe something like a brochure?" John suggested.

"Or the owner's manual?" Ryan said. "Most people keep the manual in the glove compartment."

"Or an envelope?" Tammy said.

Savannah thought that one over for a moment and a bell went off in her head. "He told his girlfriend, Sharona, that he had to pay off a debt that he owed to a bookie named Pinky before he could leave with her to go to Las Vegas. What if he had the money in the glove compartment? Maybe he met somebody to make a payment, and when he reached over to pull the envelope out of the car . . . bang."

"Girlfriend? Bookie named Pinky? Gambling debts?" John said with a raised eyebrow. "It sounds like this fellow had a complicated life, to say the least."

"Oh, you have no idea how complicated." Savannah took John by the hand and laced her arm through Ryan's. "Just park yourselves down over here and let me tell you al-l-l about it."

For the next hour, Savannah sat on the sofa between Ryan and Tammy as she filled the guys in on the pertinent facts of the case. No one seemed to mind that they were missing the society event of the season.

John relaxed in Savannah's wingback chair, while Marietta wriggled around on the floor, adjusting her back, performing semi-obscene yoga-type stretches, doing what she called "gettin' them blasted kinks out" after her long trip. With the gymnastics and the come-hither looks she kept shooting at Ryan, she was, as Gran would say, "Makin' a spectacle of herself in front o' God and ever'body."

Savannah would have blushed for her, if she'd had the energy. But she decided, instead, to just beat her once she'd rested up and had the strength to wield a baseball bat.

Ryan and John listened with rapt attention as she filled them in on the many and sordid adventures of the recently departed William "Bill" Jardin. And it was all a lot of "jolly good fun" as John would say . . . until she hit the wall.

She didn't see it coming, the wall that marked the boundary of her endurance level. She was, simply, there one minute and gone the next.

"Savannah?" Ryan said as she slid sideways and collapsed against him, her head on his shoulder.

"She's out," Tammy said with a giggle. "I knew she would be pretty soon. She was running on empty all day."

"Poor girl," John said, jumping to his feet and grabbing the well-loved, well-worn afghan that was draped over the back of her chair. He hurried to the sofa.

Ryan eased her down, and Tammy placed one of the loose cushions beneath her head. Then Ryan gently lifted her legs and straightened her out, nearly the full length of the couch.

John covered her, tucking the crocheted throw around her feet and legs. When he pulled the cover up to her chin, he knelt down and placed a kiss on her forehead.

Ryan told Tammy. "I'd bet money that she'll sleep right through the night. I don't think I've ever seen her that tired."

"Oh, tired, sh-mired," Marietta said, getting up off the floor, a sour look on her face. "Savannah always did have a lazy streak wide as the Mississippi River . . . not to mention being a big party pooper."

She sidled up to Ryan, toying with a stiffly sprayed lock

of her hair. "I, on the other hand, can go all . . . night . . . long."

Ryan shot John a somewhat frantic "save me" look.

And John came to the rescue. He looked at his watch. "Oh, dear, I had no idea it was so late. Don't we have to get back to the flat and attend to those game hens? They've been marinating much too long and will be over-seasoned for tomorrow's dinner."

"You're absolutely right," Ryan agreed, nearly running for the door. "Too much rosemary can ruin a bird."

As they disappeared out the door, the startled Marietta turned to Tammy. "Well, if that ain't a fine how-do-you-do! I never figured the two of them for farmers."

"Farmers?"

"Yeah, they're all in a tizzy, worrying about those hens. And who the hell is Rosemary? I thought they were gay."

As Ryan and John made their getaway, hurrying down the sidewalk toward their classic Bentley in the driveway, Ryan said to John, "Marinating *game hens*? You never cook game hens. Where the hell did you get that?"

John shrugged. "I don't know. Maybe it was the business Savannah told us about the chicken droppings on Jardin's tires."

"Ah. Divine inspiration."

"Precisely."

When Savannah regained consciousness the next morning, it was to the ringing of the house phone and Tammy's soft voice that was half-whispering, "Moonlight Magnolia Detective Agency. How may I help you?"

It took Savannah a few seconds to orient herself and realize she was on her couch, instead of in bed, and the sun was shining outside her windows. Faithful Diamante was at her feet, Cleopatra was curled snugly against her chest, and Granny Reid's hand-crocheted afghan was over her. The aroma of fresh-brewed coffee scented the air, along with something that smelled deliciously like home-baked cinnamon rolls.

Life didn't get much sweeter than this.

"She's sleeping, and I hate to wake her. Is it really important?" Tammy was saying from her seat at the desk in the corner.

Tammy turned and looked at Savannah. Seeing that she was awake, she put her hand over the phone and said, "I'm sorry, but it's your sister. She's all upset, almost hysterical. And she says she has to talk to her big sister."

"Hysterical sister?" Savannah groaned. "You'll have to be more specific."

"Vidalia."

"Ah, that figures. Ask her whose life and whose death."

Tammy hesitated. Being a kindhearted and truly superior human being, Tammy found it difficult to be rude. "Do you really want me to ask her that? She *is* crying."

"Vi has a kid every year and a half . . . unless she's having twins," Savannah said, forcing herself to sit up. "She's always suffering from either pregnancy hormones or postpartum depression. Hand me the phone."

Scooping up Cleopatra with one hand, Savannah relocated the enormous kitty to the other end of the sofa, next to her equally oversized sister.

"Here's Savannah," Tammy was saying into the phone as she walked across the room. "Feel better."

"What is that amazing smell?" Savannah asked as she took the phone.

"Coffee and cinnamon buns."

Savannah couldn't believe it. "Marietta brewed coffee and baked?"

Tammy blushed, as always, embarrassed to be caught doing a good deed. "Um . . . no, I did. I thought you might need some of that awful crud that you eat to get you going this morning."

"I adore you."

"Same here. I'll get some for you."

"God bless that girl," Savannah whispered as she watched Tammy scurry away to the kitchen. "Whatever did I do to deserve her?"

She took a deep breath and held the phone to her ear. "Vi," she said. "Who's about to die? You? You didn't find out that it's twins again, did you?"

Vidalia already had two sets of twins. She was pregnant again and the whole family was praying it was only one. Another set might just put her over the edge.

Vidalia pretty much pitched her tent right on the edge anyway. It wouldn't take much of a nudge to send her over.

"It ain't me who's gonna die," Vidalia said between hiccuping sobs. "It's that no-good-for-nothin' sister of yours who's gonna get a bullet through her head next time I see her."

"No-good-for-nothing sister," Savannah mused as she ran her fingers through her hair and stretched. "Could you narrow it down a bit?"

"Marietta! That's who I'm talkin' about. Mar—i—e-eta. She's pushed me too far this time; and she's gonna get what's been comin' to her for years. I'm gonna stomp a mud hole in her. You wait and see if I don't."

"Now, Vi, don't talk nasty about your sister. It ain't proper," Savannah said, conveniently forgetting that, only the night before, she had threatened to do Marietta bodily harm with a baseball bat.

"Don't you scold me!" Vidalia shot back. "You ain't Gran, so don't go gettin' bossy with me, girl."

"If you didn't want me to boss you around, why the

blazes would you call me? You know how I am." She yawned. "Why are you all riled up? What did she do to you this time?"

"She seduced Butch!"

Savannah snapped wide awake. "She what? Butch? Your Butch?"

Picturing the sweet, easygoing garage mechanic who had fathered Vidalia's brood and tolerated her moods for years now, Savannah just couldn't imagine it. Not that Butch was above it, or Marietta, either, for that matter, but Savannah was sure that he was far too afraid of Vidalia to even look twice at another woman.

A few years back she had nearly murdered him for looking once at the waitress at the Chat-n-Chew Café there in McGill.

"Vidalia, I can't believe it. Butch loves you to death."

"Yeah, well, as soon as her latest fiancé dumped her, Marietta waggled that big butt of hers in front of Butch, and dadburn him, he went for it."

"Define 'went for it.' "

"They *did it*. I know they did. I saw some of it with my own eyes. And he admitted the rest of it to me after I threatened to brain him with a skillet."

It occurred to Savannah that maybe the Reid women should stop cooking with heavy, cast-iron frying pans and take up lighter, nonstick cookware, like the rest of the world. It might be safer for all concerned . . . especially their menfolk.

"Now, Vidalia," she said, "this is not the time to tell any stories outta turn or even to embroider the truth. This is serious. Don't tell me that Butch stepped out on you with Marietta unless it's true. 'Cause if it is, I'm gonna have to go right now and whoop her tail. And you don't want all that violence and mayhem on your conscience if it's not so."

"It's true! Why do you think she lit outta here like a cat

afire? It's 'cause she knew I was gonna mop up the floor with her."

"What does Butch say about it all?"

"He ain't sayin' nothin' to me. I threw him out—lock, stock, and barrel. Put his clothes and CDs in a garbage bag and pitched 'em out the window into the yard. He's livin' over at the garage, sleepin' on a cot there in the office."

Savannah laid back on the sofa and put one hand over her eyes. Without coffee, this was just too much for a body to bear. "Vidalia, what do you want me to do about this?"

"Tell that worthless hussy sister of mine that she's living on borrowed time."

"Okay. I'll pass it along. And Vi, sweetie, try not to get any more upset than you have to. It's not good for the baby, you pitching a fit like this."

Tammy appeared with a tray laden with a coffee mug, a cinnamon bun on a dessert plate, and a daisy in a bud vase.

As she set it on the coffee table, Savannah caught a particularly fragrant whiff of the pastry and said a rather quick good-bye to Vidalia.

"You're an angel," she told Tammy. "A pure angel."

"So are you." Tammy whipped a napkin off the plate, and with all the aplomb of a waiter in a five-star restaurant, spread it across Savannah's lap.

"If I am, I'm an angel who needs wings to hold her halo up. I just rushed my sobbing sister off the phone to get to a cinnamon bun."

Tammy laughed. "If you stopped eating every time one of your sisters called, crying about something, you'd . . ."

When she didn't finish the sentence, Savannah supplied the end for her, "I'd lose a ton of weight. I'd have to run around in a rainstorm just to get wet."

She savored a bite of the bun, then a long drink of the

coffee. "By the way, where is Marietta? It's not like her to be absent when food is present, her being a Reid and all."

"She already had hers. She's out in the backyard . . . um . . . getting a tan."

Something about the way Tammy said "getting a tan" caused Savannah's antennae to rise. Sure, Tammy was big on sunscreen and limiting sun exposure, but something was amiss besides the health issues.

"Getting a tan? In her new red bikini?"

"Uh, yeah." Tammy gulped. "Half of it."

"Half of the bikini?"

Tammy nodded, her eyes wide. "It's the bottom half. And she's facedown . . . at the moment."

"At the moment? Oh, Lord. I have neighbors and low fences. What is she thinking?"

Chapter 16

Savannah got up from the couch and hurried to the back door. When she flung it open, she saw her sister, the picture of contentment, lying on her back, soaking in the rays. She could have been posing for a Southern California Tourism poster. Except that she was topless.

"Marietta! What is the matter with you, girl!"

She bounded down the porch and over to the chaise, where Marietta was stirring from her nap.

"What? What's the matter?"

"You know blamed well what's the matter." Savannah grabbed a towel off a nearby chaise and tossed it over her. "Are you trying to get yourself arrested?"

"It's not illegal. I know. I called the police station and asked them."

"You what?"

Marietta looked smug as she grinned up at her older sister. "I called them ten minutes ago and asked them if it was legal to sunbathe topless in the privacy of your own backyard."

"You didn't!"

"I sure as shootin' did. And the guy that answered, he

beat around the bush awhile and then he said it ain't exactly illegal, as long as nobody can see. And then, just to be sure, he asked me where I lived . . . well, where you live actually . . . because he said that if somebody called to complain, he'd tell them that he'd already given me the okay on it."

"And you believed that? Holy crap, Marietta. You don't have the sense God gave a rock. I'm gonna have a dozen of San Carmelita's finest over here on my property, any minute now, checking you out. You nitwitted numbskull. Put your top back on."

Pouting, Marietta reached for the string bikini top that was lying by her feet and slipped it on. "I have to tell you, Savannah, you haven't been a particularly gracious hostess since I got here. I came here to relax and get away from it all and—"

"Hooey. You came here to get away from Vidalia. She just called me, bawling like a cat stuck in a briar patch. What's this about you screwing Butch?"

"I didn't touch Butch. I ain't that hard up and never will be."

"Then how come Vi thinks you did? She says Butch confessed to it."

"Well, sure he did. She was goin' at him with kitchen utensils. You've seen the way she gets. He would've confessed to being Jack the Ripper to get her off him."

Savannah sank onto a nearby chaise. "Well, something must of set her off. What was it?"

"He patted me on my butt. That's all it was. One teeny little butt pat, which, by the way, was an accident, and Vidalia's all in an uproar about it."

"How does a guy *accidentally* pat a butt?"

"He thought it was Vidalia's butt."

"He mistook your hind end for Vidalia's?"

"That's what he claims, and I believe him. He was sitting on the floor, hooking up their new DVD player, and I walked by wearing the same kind of jeans that Vidalia wears. He reached up and gave my fanny a pat, thinking it was hers. Vi saw it, and all hell broke loose. She's been on the warpath ever since."

"So, you two were never actually . . . intimate?"

"Shoot, no. What do you think I am? Butch is an idiot. He's way too skinny and has bad skin and black grease under his fingernails. I wouldn't have him on a hot dog bun with mustard."

"Plus he's married to your sister, your *pregnant* sister. And the father of her twins. Both sets of twins."

"Yeah, yeah, yeah. That, too."

Savannah stood and said, "I'm going to go in now and take a long-overdue, much-needed bubble bath. You, Miss Exhibitionist, keep your clothes on. All of them. And stay out of trouble till I get out. I'll take you over to the beach later . . . where you also have to wear all of your clothes. This is Southern California, not Las Vegas."

She was heading up the walk to her back door when she saw a young cop looking sharp in his crisp patrolman's uniform, coming around the side of the house. He had a goofy grin on his face. She recognized him as a rookie she had met at the last SCPD barbecue that Dirk had dragged her to.

"Get the hell outta here, Gilmore!" she yelled at him. "There's nothing to see here. Nothing at all! Go!"

He disappeared so quickly that she couldn't help but snicker.

She went on into the house and nearly ran headlong into Dirk, who was standing in her kitchen.

"You're welcome to the coffee and cinnamon buns," she said, "but if you get between me and that bathtub, you're gonna get hurt."

She brushed on by him, nabbing a second roll off the plate as she went.

"You're going to eat food in the bathroom?" Dirk called after her. "Gross."

"What makes you think this roll is going to live long enough for me to get to the bathroom?"

Upstairs, she licked the frosting off her fingers before opening the bathroom door and considered Dirk's words.

Maybe food in the bathroom was disgusting, but in her opinion, you hadn't lived until you had soaked in a bubble bath by candlelight, while sipping brandy and eating Godiva dark chocolate truffles.

But she just couldn't picture Dirk doing that. If he were going to eat in the john, he'd be more of a bologna sandwich and potato chips in the shower kind of guy. And she could understand his reluctance to go there; that *would* be gross.

"Are you sure she's going to be there?" Savannah asked Dirk as they headed for the little desert town of Yucca Mountain. It was over a three-hour drive, even with Dirk's heavy foot, and Savannah wasn't sure if she was happy or not to be making such a long drive for one simple interview.

"Yeah, I called her and told her we were coming. She said she'd be home."

"And you took her word for it?"

"No, I asked the sheriff there to park down the block from her house and watch it."

"He was willing to do that?"

"Yeah. What else is there to do in Yucca Mountain? It's not like they're gonna suffer some crime wave there this afternoon to occupy his time."

"True. But somebody might run the one red light."

He reached for a plastic bag on the dash and shook out a cinnamon stick. As he stuck it into his mouth, Savannah resisted the urge to snicker. The guy was trying. He hadn't smoked in months, and she had to give him major credit for holding out this long. She was sure it was the hardest thing he'd ever done in his life, and she wasn't going to make fun of him, even if he did look a bit weird with a cinnamon stick poking out of his face.

Someday she might go on some sort of diet and she would need his support, so . . .

Yeah, like that's gonna happen, she thought. *Been there, done that. Suffered and gained it back.*

No, life was too short to deny yourself the basic pleasures of life. Like food.

Once traffic had thinned, and they were headed into the Mojave Desert, Savannah leaned back in her seat and gazed out the window at the strange, otherworldly landscape.

The cracked dirt crust was dotted with soft, colorful desert flowers, marigolds, poppies, primrose and larkspur, that grew alongside prickly pear and beavertail cacti, and the ever-present yucca.

Occasional trees, like the pinyon pine and the beautiful Joshua tree, provided a bit of shade here and there for any snakes, lizards, jackrabbits or wood rats who needed a break from the midday sun.

"Tammy was sure pleased with herself over that photo thing," Dirk said, interrupting her communion with nature.

"She was moderately proud of her accomplishment."

"Are you kidding? You'd think she'd discovered fire or invented the wheel. I think I'm going to have that photo blown up into a poster and framed. I'll give it to her for Christmas."

"The scary thing is, she'd probably like it. She'd cry and jump up and down and say, 'Thank you, oh, thank you, Dirk-o,' and hug and kiss you."

"Yeah, it's a lousy idea. Forget I mentioned it." He took a long drag on the cinnamon stick. "What did Ryan and John have to say about the case when you talked to them about it last night?"

"I don't remember a lot of it," she admitted. "John asked me about the car's GPS tracking system. I told him it had been disabled. That's what Caitlin said, right?"

"Yeah. We can probably still track the car's movements, but it's going to take a while to get the records from the company."

"They thought the poultry droppings and feather were interesting. They asked about Bill's cell phone, whether you'd found it, any calls of interest."

"No, we haven't found that. It wasn't in the car."

"At his house, maybe?"

"No, I called Clarissa, and she said she's sure it's not there, that he always had it with him. It wasn't on the body. But we already got the record from his carrier. Most of the calls are pretty run-of-the-mill. Calls to the car dealership where he bought the Jaguar, calls home, some to the country club, to some of Clarissa's business people."

"Pretty standard stuff."

"Yeah, but there was one that was interesting. It was a cell phone number, and when we traced it, we got an old lady who said her phone was missing. She was upset because her son gave it to her, and it was one of those fancy Sendai phones that does everything but feed you. It cost him a pretty penny."

"Did she have any idea where she'd lost it?"

"No. And we ran down the short list of people she'd been in contact with, and nobody jumped out as somebody who'd steal it from her."

"Give me the number, and I'll tell Tammy to see if she can hack into its records. Doesn't always work, but it's worth a try."

He rattled off the number to her, and it just happened to end with the digits "666."

"That's a creepy one," she said as she wrote it down in her notebook. "Gran would be weirded out if the phone company tried to assign her a demon number like that. She wouldn't stand for it."

"I'm sure she wouldn't. Gran takes all that stuff pretty seriously. I've been calling this number every few hours, just to see if maybe somebody will pick up. You never know."

"Can't hurt."

"So, uh, what else did Ryan and John have to say?"

Savannah grinned to herself. For someone who had taken a long time to get to know Ryan and John, Dirk had learned to respect their input about any investigation.

Time and experience had bred respect, and Savannah was happy about that. She liked it when her friends all got along. It made Halloween parties, Easter egg–dying "eggs-travaganzas," and Christmas caroling a lot easier.

She stuck her notebook and pen back into her purse. "Ryan asked about the owner's manual," she said. "He pointed out that most people keep those in the glove compartment."

"Yeah, I'd already thought about that. Ramon told me they found it under the driver's seat."

"Unbloodied?"

"Clean as a whistle. It was out of its leather folder."

"Bill, or somebody, was looking at it. Maybe finding out how to disable the GPS?"

"That's what I figured. I had Caitlin dust the whole book. The only page that had a print on it was the page about the guidance system. It mentioned how to turn it off."

"Whose was it?"

"It was too smeared to tell."

"Dangnation. But if it was clean, it couldn't have been the object that blocked the blood spatter in the glove compartment. I'd think that means it had already been removed before the shooting."

"It was probably Jardin who took it out and disabled

the GPS. I guess he didn't want anybody to know where he was going. And he had to read the manual because he wasn't used to the new car yet."

"Would you want people to know where you were every minute if you had one wife, two girlfriends, and a guy like Pinky after you?"

"Good point."

"How was Pinky, by the way? What's he like?"

"He's a hardcore dirtbag. And I found out why he was named Pinky."

"Large diamond ring on his little finger?"

"No, this was in jail, remember? He has an enormous pink birthmark across his forehead."

"No way! Good grief, can you imagine the insensitivity of parents who would saddle an innocent baby child with a name like that? Reminds me of the woman in McGill who married a guy named Harold Duck. She had this little boy, and she named him—"

"No, don't tell me. She didn't."

"She did. She said she'd always wanted a son named Donald. Can you imagine what recess was like for that poor kid? Or boot camp? He became a marine later."

"Don't tell me any more. I can't stand it."

"Then tell me about Pinky."

"He admitted that maybe Jardin owed him money. But he swore he had nothing to do with the murder."

"Does he have an alibi?"

"Says he was in bed with some gal, who vouched for him. I talked to her this morning. I think she's scared of him, so I don't know whether I believe her or not."

"So is Sharona. She was shaking like she was standing naked in a snowstorm when I was interviewing her. I felt sorry for her. I called her before we left the house. She sounded better, but we need to get this case closed so that she can go back home."

"Pinky's in jail now. What's she worried about?"

"His crew."

Dirk nodded. "Can't say that I blame her. His boys are very bad characters. If they've got some reason to hurt her, she'd better worry."

Savannah thought that over as they continued on toward Yucca Mountain, the tiny town in the middle of nowhere. She considered how it would feel to be deeply, terribly afraid, to have a gang of "very bad characters" after you who were perfectly willing to kill you because you knew too much about them and what they'd done.

She thought of Sharona and how vulnerable and injured she seemed, sitting in the Mustang, trembling and crying about her lost love and lost dreams.

"I think I'll call Sharona again," she said, "before we get to Rachel's. Just to touch base. See how she is."

"You're a good person, Van," Dirk told her, giving her a pat on the knee.

"Naw, I'm just a bossy big sister. If you don't believe me, ask Marietta or Vidalia."

He shook his head. "That'll be the day, when I ask those two bimbos for their opinion on anything, let alone on you."

They passed a sign that read YUCCA MOUNTAIN—15 MILES.

Savannah took her cell phone out of her purse and punched in some numbers. "Hello, Sugar, it's Savannah again. How's it going? Anything new? No? Yes, I know it's boring just sitting around there, twiddling your thumbs. Hey, I've got an idea. That television there has a good cable service. Order yourself a couple of movies."

She glanced over at Dirk and added, "Yeah, sure. Detective Coulter says he'll pay for them. It'll be his pleasure. . . ."

Chapter 17

The first thing Savannah noticed when they pulled into Rachel Morris's driveway was how tiny the house was. "Cracker box" was the term she had heard down South, used to describe a home that was barely large enough for one person, let alone a woman and her teenaged son.

The lots on the street were all narrow, too, with the houses jammed together. As Granny Reid would have said, "Them places was so close together, if you'd stuck your dust mop out the window to shake it, it would've been in your neighbor's front room."

A sagging chain-link fence surrounded the property and a BEWARE OF DOG sign was posted on the gate. A dilapidated doghouse of Great Dane proportions indicated that a very large canine had once called this yard home. And a strip of the lawn next to the fence was worn bare. Apparently, the dog had taken his job seriously and patrolled regularly.

"You think she's got a dog?" Dirk said, looking at the sign with a sick expression on his face.

He hadn't been the same since that Doberman had

taken a bite out of his rump a few years back. Ever since then, he had sworn off dogs and proclaimed himself a cat lover, whether it was the manly man thing or not.

"I don't think so," Savannah said. "There aren't any food or water dishes by that doghouse, and the big chain tied to the tree is rusty."

She reached over and slapped him on the back. "Don't worry, buddy. If it's a mean, ol' Dobie, I'll give him a serious talkin'-to, and you'll be okay."

"Shut up."

They got out of the car and ventured through the gate. The door opened as they walked up the cracked and buckled sidewalk, and the woman standing in the doorway was the one they had seen earlier through Clarissa's window.

Dressed in a black tunic and black slacks, her red hair cropped short, her figure full, Rachel Morris looked quite different from her sister in all ways, except one. She wore the same angry, defensive expression on her face.

She also looked deeply worried and grief-stricken . . . maybe even more than the widow herself.

"I'm Detective Sergeant Dirk Coulter," Dirk said as he walked up to her and put out his hand. "And this is Savannah Reid. She's also investigating this case."

"And you know who I am," Rachel replied with a distinctively nasal twang to her voice that identified her as being from one of the five boroughs of New York City. Rachel opened the door wider and waved them inside. "I guess you might as well come in."

"Thank you," Dirk said, not sounding particularly thankful for the less-than-warm invitation.

When Savannah entered the miniscule living room, it took a while for her eyes to adjust to the darkness. Dark sheets were hung over the windows in lieu of curtains. Cardboard boxes lined two walls, stacked five feet high.

The only furniture was a shabby sofa that looked like

an angry kitty had used it for a scratching post for a very long time.

But the other thing she noticed, far more telling than the boxes and lack of furnishings, was the pile of books. One entire wall was lined with cheap shelves made of cement blocks and crude wooden planks. And on those boards were piled books, books, and more books.

"I see you're quite a reader," Savannah said as she glanced over the titles that ranged from history texts, science fiction, murder mysteries, and more than a few that she recognized as Pulitzer Prize winners.

"Yes," Rachel replied dryly. "I'm a New Yorker. We read."

Savannah couldn't resist. "I'm a Californian. We read, too."

Rachel didn't reply. Didn't crack even a semi-smile. She just stood there, giving Savannah a deadpan, somewhat condescending look.

Okay, so much for the friendly chitchat, Savannah thought.

"Do you mind if we sit down?" Dirk asked with a nod toward the sofa.

"I mind that we're even having this conversation," Rachel replied, "but on the phone you gave me the impression I didn't have much choice."

"You really don't," Dirk replied as he walked over to the sofa and plopped himself down on it. "You can choose not talk to us. But this is a homicide investigation. A man's been murdered, so we're not just going to go away. And if you're uncooperative, then when somebody says something accusatory about you, we're a lot more likely to believe them."

She bristled. "Who's accusing me of what? Clarissa? Screw her. She's the one who'd better be worried about being accused."

Sitting down next to Dirk, Savannah said, "Why do you say that?"

"Because she's the one with a dead husband, the one with the motive to kill him."

"And what motive is that?" Dirk asked.

"She was mad at him. Outraged that he'd leave her, for anybody, let alone me—her fat, loser sister."

"And Bill was going to leave Clarissa to be with you?" Dirk said.

"Yes, he was. Is that so hard to believe?"

"Not at all," Savannah replied softly. "People choose to be with other people for all sorts of reasons. I've met Clarissa. It isn't so hard to understand why Bill might want to be with someone else."

Rachel seemed to soften a bit. She pulled an old folding metal chair closer to the sofa and sat down on it. "It was an enormous blow to Clarissa's overinflated ego, Bill choosing me over her."

"And you look all guilt-ridden about it," Dirk said with a smirk.

Rachel's temper flared again. "Not one bit. And if you knew how she's treated me over the years, you wouldn't blame me."

"Tell us about it," Savannah said. "How did the affair between you and Bill begin?"

"I prefer to call it a relationship."

"Okay, where and under what circumstances did your *relationship* with Bill start?"

A soft, dreamy look passed over Rachel's face and, for a moment, she looked much sweeter, kinder . . . even happy.

"He came to New York to see me. Actually, Clarissa sent him to straighten me out. I was trying to negotiate for a larger share of the profits from our business arrangement—"

"You and Clarissa had a business arrangement?" Dirk asked.

"Yes, we did. From the very beginning. She said that if I helped her get her fitness plan going, she would pay me a share of the profits. And she did for awhile. But then, it took off, she got to be well-known, the money started to pour in, and she really started to resent writing me out those big checks."

"So, you told her you wanted more?" Savannah said.

"I told her I was raising a kid and living in the city, which is very expensive, and if she was getting filthy rich, I didn't see why I should have to just scrape by, serving pizza in a hole in the wall in the Village."

"The village?" Dirk asked.

"*Greenwich* Village." Rachel gave him a scathing look. "Let me guess," she said. "You *don't* read much."

"Actually, I read three newspapers every morning with my coffee," Dirk said. "But none of them is the *New York Times.*"

"Imagine that." Rachel crossed her arms over her chest and leaned back in her chair.

"You were saying that Bill came to New York at Clarissa's request, and the two of you became lovers?" Savannah asked.

"Not right away. He was there for the weekend. He came to my apartment first, and we talked. Then we went out for dinner and talked. We had a lot in common."

"Like . . . ?" Savannah prompted.

"Like hating Clarissa. As it turned out, she was making both of us miserable. Her withholding money from me and her bossing him around, controlling everything he did and said. She held the purse strings for both of us, and let me tell you, she enjoyed having that power. In case you haven't figured it out, that's what Clarissa is all about, power and control over everybody around her."

"But she didn't control what happened next . . . between you and Bill, that is," Savannah said.

Rachel chuckled. "No kidding. She had no idea. She sent him across the country to scare me, to tell me to stay down in that dark hole and hide from the world, for her convenience, and we wind up lovers. It was great."

Savannah couldn't help but wonder if a large part of Rachel's attraction for Bill lay in the fact that he was her hated sister's husband. And maybe "payback" had something to do with Bill's feelings for Rachel, too.

In certain circumstances, passive aggression could be a powerful aphrodisiac.

"Let me get this straight," Dirk said. "You're claiming that your sister legitimately owed you money. Do you deny blackmailing her?"

"Blackmail? Are you kidding?" Rachel's eyes filled with fury. "Is that what she's claiming, that I blackmailed her? I only asked for what she'd agreed to give me, back when she was first starting out and needed my help."

"When you posed for the 'before' shot for her fitness campaign?" Savannah said.

"Yes. I posed for the picture. So what?"

"Well, it's a bit of a fraud, don't you think?" Dirk asked.

"I posed. What she did with the picture, that's her business." Rachel leaned so far back in her chair that Savannah wondered how much it would hurt when the chair tipped over backward and spilled her onto the floor.

"How about the threatening letters?" Savannah asked her. "Why did you send her those?"

"I didn't send her any letters, threatening or otherwise. When I wanted to talk to her, which wasn't very often, I just called her on the phone. We'd scream at each other and hang up."

It occurred to Savannah that, like her sister, Rachel

looked quite pleased with herself, as if she had her answers well-rehearsed and was happy to be delivering them.

"Let me get this straight," Dirk said. "The letters that threatened to expose this little scheme of hers, the ones postmarked from New York City, they weren't from you."

"Nope."

"You and Bill were in love," Savannah said, "and you weren't blackmailing your sister, just asking for what you had coming to you."

"Yes. And I never threatened to give her what was coming to her."

Dirk was looking more irritated by the moment, and Savannah didn't like the way this interview was going. They really hadn't learned much, except that Rachel was a liar. And they'd suspected that back in San Carmelita, before they had trucked across the desert and wasted most of a day.

"Listen," Rachel said, "you don't know what it's like, having a sister like Clarissa. Do you know how many times I was serving somebody their pizza and they'd say, 'Hey, you know who you look like? That girl on television, the pretty, skinny one with the big mouth, the pain equals gain gal.' I'd have to just smile and say, 'Yeah, I hear that a lot.' "

When neither Savannah nor Dirk answered right away, she continued, "Bill knew what that was like, living in her shadow. Everywhere he went, he was Mr. Clarissa Jardin. We had a lot in common, because of her. But he was going to leave her and be with me. He had my son and me move here from New York, just so that we could be closer to him. That way it would be easier for him to come see us. We were moving to Las Vegas. He'd already rented a house for us there. And the three of us were going to finally be a family and be rid of her."

"Right." Dirk looked around the room. "Where *is* your son, by the way?"

An instant change came over Rachel at the mention of her boy. Her eyes filled with tears, and she uncrossed her arms and clasped her hands tightly in her lap.

"He isn't here right now," she said, her voice trembling.

"Where is he?" Dirk asked.

"He's at a friend's house."

"We're going to need to talk to him, too," Dirk said. "Especially with you claiming that you weren't the one who sent those letters to Clarissa from New York City."

"Tanner didn't do anything wrong. He's just a kid!"

"Kids do wrong things all over this world every day," Dirk told her. "Where is he? Really."

"I told you. At a friend's."

"We can't leave without talking to him," Dirk said, "so we'll just wait here until he comes back. Whenever that might be."

Rachel stared back at him and clutched her hands together so tightly that Savannah could swear her fingers were turning white.

"Rachel, where is Tanner?" she asked gently.

The tears in Rachel's eyes spilled down onto her cheeks, and she took a deep breath. For a long time she didn't speak. Then she said, "I don't know. I don't. He's missing. Like Bill was." She started to sob. "I'm so scared. I'm afraid that maybe he's been . . ."

Savannah got up from the sofa, hurried over to Rachel, and dropped onto her knees beside the woman's chair. She reached for her hands and held them between her own.

"How long has he been missing?" she asked her.

"He disappeared the same night that Bill did."

"Rachel," Dirk said. "Tell us what happened that night and maybe we can help you find him."

"Okay." She fought back her tears and regained control of herself. "We had gone to San Carmelita to meet Bill. He asked me to come because he wanted to talk to me about our future, about us all moving to Las Vegas. You know, to solidify our plans."

"Did he sound positive or negative? Was he upbeat or more like . . . 'we have to talk,'?" Savannah asked.

"He sounded fine, happy. So, we drove there, Tanner and me. We checked into the Blue Moon Motel in San Carmelita and waited for him to call us, tell us where to meet him. We waited and waited, and he didn't call. Finally, I went to sleep. And when I woke up, there was a note from Tanner saying that he'd gone out for a while. Bill didn't call and Tanner didn't come back. And I haven't seen either one of them since."

"Do you have any idea where Tanner might have gone?" Savannah said.

"Yes. I do. Every time we went to San Carmelita or anywhere near there, he'd beg me to take him by Clarissa's house, that old ranch. He was obsessed with seeing it, seeing how she lived. I think he had it in his mind that, once Bill and she were divorced, we'd just slip into Clarissa's place, live her life. He really wanted to see that ranch."

"You think he went out there?" Savannah asked.

"I think so."

"How would he get out there?" Dirk said. "It's too far to walk, even for a curious teenaged boy."

"He's a New York City boy," Rachel said with more than a hint of pride in her voice. "He knows about taxis. And he took twenty dollars from my purse. He's never done that before. He's a good boy."

Savannah patted her hand. "We're going to help you find him. Do you have a picture of him that we can borrow?"

"Yes, I've got one in the bedroom." Rachel got up

from her chair and disappeared into the other room. In just a moment, she returned with a school photo of a gangly, freckle-faced boy with a mop of curly red hair.

She placed it in Savannah's hand. "I want that back," she said.

"I'll get it back to you. I promise." Savannah looked down into the child's face and then into his mother's. They looked a lot alike. They also looked like Clarissa. "Why were you at your sister's house?" she asked.

Rachel looked startled. "How do you . . . ? Did she tell you I was there?"

"It doesn't matter," Savannah told her. "We know for certain that you were there. Why were you there?"

"I had called her, several times, asking her if she'd seen Tanner. Asking her what had happened to Bill. She kept hanging up on me. So I went out there to confront her, face-to-face. You two came to the house while I was there, so she told me to hide in the bedroom. I did what she said."

Dirk stood up, came over to stand by them, and took the boy's picture from Savannah. He looked down at it for a long time, then said, "Are you telling me that you think your sister hurt your boy?"

"Hurt him? I'm telling you . . . I'm hoping that's all she's done."

Chapter 18

Once Savannah and Dirk were on their way back to San Carmelita—the desert scenery whizzing past as Dirk exceeded the speed limit by a wide margin—Savannah took the Morris boy's picture out of her purse and looked at it.

"I hate it when it's kids," she told Dirk. "I mind a little less when adults are in trouble. A lot of them deserve the trouble they're in, or at least they've done things to land them in the doghouse. But kids . . . kids break my heart."

"Mine, too." He shook another cinnamon stick out of the plastic bag. "All kids mess up. It's part of growing up and figuring out who they are. But when they do things that ruin their lives, before their lives even get started, that's sad."

She looked at the picture, the eyes wide with innocence, or maybe naïveté, the freckles and red hair, so like his mother's. She thought about Rachel, who, even though she'd never win awards for her scintillating personality, appeared to care deeply about her son.

"Why didn't she report him missing?" Savannah said.

"What?"

"If my kid went missing, I'd call the cops."

"And tell us what? That you were blackmailing your sister, screwing your brother-in-law, and were going to run away with him? That the brother-in-law's missing and . . . oh, yeah, murdered. If you're doing crap like that, you don't want to draw attention to yourself."

"She'd do it for her kid."

"If she told us what was going on, it would hit the news and then her sister's career would go up in flames. She might hate her sister, but it wouldn't be in her best interests to kill the goose who lays the golden eggs and all that."

"If she thought her kid's life was in danger, she'd report it, get us looking for him."

"So, why didn't she?"

Savannah stared out the window for a long time, looking at the scenery, but not seeing it. "I think she didn't tell the cops he was missing because she's afraid he did it. She's afraid her son murdered her lover. She's also hoping he did."

"Afraid he did it? Hoping he did it? Why the hell would she hope a thing like that?"

"Because thinking that your kid is a murderer is better than thinking he's dead."

"Lousy choices."

"Aren't they?"

Before Dirk took Savannah home, he dropped her by San Carmelita's juvenile hall facility. He waited in the car as she hurried inside, Tanner Morris's picture in her purse.

"My name is Savannah Reid," she told the young woman at the reception desk. "I'd like to see Rebecca Shipton if she has a minute for me."

"Do you have an appointment to see her?"

"No, but please tell her it'll only take a minute. I know how busy she is."

As the receptionist called Shipton's office, Savannah looked around at the stark white walls, gray linoleum tiled floor, and worn blue chairs that had seen better days—a few decades ago.

The county didn't spend a lot of money on wayward kids. At least, not decorating for them.

But then, juvie hall shouldn't be a nice place to go, Savannah thought. It was intended to be a lesson to kids who were headed down the wrong road—a lesson that even grimmer surroundings might be in their future if they didn't shape up and fly straight.

But that was the hardcore kids, Savannah reminded herself. A lot of the children who came to this place really hadn't been given a chance for a good life. And she wondered if they would find a fresh start here.

She had her doubts.

"Ms. Shipton will be with you in just a moment," the young woman told her. "You can sit down if you want."

Savannah took a seat, but had barely chosen a magazine, when a tired-looking, middle-aged woman walked into the waiting area. She was attractive, with large, expressive eyes and thick salt-and-pepper hair that lay in natural, neat waves. A tall, large-boned woman, the social worker gave off the air of someone who could be trusted, but not someone to mess with.

And seeing her, Savannah had the encouraging thought that it was the people, compassionate, tough-minded professionals like Rebecca Shipton, who made a difference in kids' lives inside this institution . . . whatever color its walls might be.

"Savannah," Rebecca said, hurrying across the room to greet her. "It's so good to see you. What a nice surprise."

She embraced Savannah warmly and gave her a peck on the cheek, which Savannah returned.

"I know you're always up to your gazoo in work," Savannah said, "so I won't keep you. But we've got an unofficial report of a missing kid, and I was wondering if you'd take a look at his picture and tell me if you've seen him."

"Unofficial report?" she asked.

Rebecca's sharp eyes and ears missed nothing. In her business, she couldn't afford to.

"Yeah, it's a long story," Savannah said as she removed the boy's photo from her purse.

She held it out to her, and Rebecca studied it carefully before answering. "No," she said. "We don't have him, and I haven't seen him."

"Would you keep an eye out for him? He was last seen here in San Carmelita, and he could be in trouble."

"In trouble or causing trouble?"

Savannah shrugged. "At the moment, we don't know for sure. Could you just pass the word for everybody to be on the lookout for him and call me if anybody sees him?"

"Absolutely."

Savannah handed Rebecca the picture, who gave it to the receptionist. "Debbie, could you scan and copy this for me and then give it back to Ms. Reid here? I'll need about eight copies."

"Sure." The receptionist took the photo and immediately stuck it inside a scanner.

"I wish we could talk longer," Rebecca said, "but I have to get back. I'm in the middle of an intake."

"I've gotta get going, too." Savannah gave her another hug. "Thanks a million."

"Let's get together at the Pastry Palace sometime soon for one of their cream puffs and a coffee."

"You got it. Thanks a bunch."

Rebecca disappeared down the hallway, and Savannah silently blessed her for the work she did. Helping kids . . . whether they wanted to be helped or not. It didn't get any more noble than that.

When Debbie gave the photo back to her, Savannah thanked her and hurried back to the car where Dirk was waiting for her, listening to Elvis's greatest hits, and sucking on his cinnamon stick.

"What's next?" she asked him as she climbed into the Buick.

"That feather and the crap on the tires—I keep thinking about that," he said. "I think I'll go see our old buddy, Julio Sanchez, the dude we busted for cockfighting a couple of years ago."

"I thought they locked him up."

"They did, but he's out on probation. Got out a few months back. I think I'll go talk to him and see if I can get him to tell me where the action is now."

"You think he's going to admit to you that he knows, him being on probation and all?"

"He's a druggie, too. Once I pat him down and find his stash, he'll probably be happy to talk to me about anything else. Do you wanna come along?"

Savannah considered it. She didn't like people who were cruel to animals of any kind, and she wouldn't mind seeing Dirk put Julio in an uncomfortable position. Like against the Buick, legs spread, hands behind his back.

But she had a mission of mercy she felt she should run.

"I'm going to go take Sharona a goody bag," she said. "Some homemade cookies and books. Things to while away the time over there. I don't want her getting bored and thinking about going home. At least, not until we know if Pinky's boys are after her or not."

She remembered her sister, sitting at home, probably

cursing her for not taking her to Disneyland or at least Sunset Boulevard. One of the perks and curses of living in Southern California was taking your visiting relatives to see the world-renowned sights. Whether it was a perk or a curse depended on which relative was visiting.

"I have to take Marietta to the beach, too. I promised her, and I've been neglecting my hostess duties. Southern hospitality standards to uphold, and all that."

"She arrived on your doorstep without warning, not a call or letter to say she was coming. I'd say that releases you from all responsibility when it comes to entertaining her."

"Yeah, well, that's because you're a barbarian, heathen Yankee, who doesn't know any better."

"And you're a pushover for pushy relatives—a friggen pansy, a doormat, a goody-two-shoes."

Savannah didn't reply.

He had her there.

Savannah loved the safe house. She loved the cottage itself with its bright white exterior and its cheerful blue roof, the flower beds planted around it that bloomed with marigolds and nasturtiums. She loved the swing on the front porch and thought of the people she had seen sitting there, relaxing and unafraid of whatever evils that might bedevil them.

She loved the whole idea of "safe."

As a girl she had been taken from an unsafe environment, along with her eight other siblings, and placed in Granny Reid's safe home. There, the young Savannah had relearned the joys of being a child again. She had gone to bed at night in peaceful surroundings and woke to the smell of coffee, sausage and biscuits, and her grandmother's kind voice.

And if placing a fearful person here in this cottage in

the middle of orange and lemon groves could give them that same sort of soul-deep contentment that she had experienced lying on her grandmother's featherbed, Savannah supported the effort any way she could.

And her support usually came in the form of her traditional "safe house basket."

She felt a little like Red Riding Hood as she took the large basket from the backseat of the Mustang and walked to the door with it over her arm. Only she had more than simple edibles in her basket. She had loaded it up with the macadamia chocolate chip cookies and fudge brownies, but she had also included an assortment of romance novels, some lighthearted movie DVDs, and a book of crossword puzzles.

She had some doubts that Sharona was the crossword puzzle type. But she was pretty sure she could get into the romance novel with the cowboy hunk on the front—the guy who was bending a cowgirl backward in his arms and gazing down at her half-exposed bosom with unabashed lust.

He looked a heck of a lot better than that creep, Aldo or Alpo, or whatever his name was.

But her do-gooder buzz was diminished a tad when she saw Sharona sitting on the front porch swing, talking on the phone.

It wasn't simply that she was having a conversation with someone on her cell phone. It was that she ended the conversation a bit too abruptly and snapped the phone closed a little too quickly to suit Savannah.

She also didn't meet Savannah's eyes for the first few seconds after she stepped up onto the porch, and that bothered her, too.

"Hi, sugar. How's it going?" Savannah asked her, trying to sound as cheerful as she'd felt a minute ago.

"Okay. Boring, but okay."

She noticed that Sharona appeared more rested. Her

hair was brushed, she had a little bit of makeup on, and most importantly, she wasn't shaking at all.

"I brought you some stuff to help with that," Savannah said, handing her the basket.

She was touched by the young woman's eagerness as she searched through her new treasures. "Wow, that's so nice of you. Thank you!" she said as she held up first the books, then the DVDs, and read the titles.

Savannah sat down on the other side of the swing. "Honey, I hate to bring this up, but the person you were talking to on the phone . . . you didn't tell them where you are, did you? Like I told you before, it's critical that you never, ever tell anybody where this house is. That's the number one condition for you being here."

"No, I didn't," Sharona assured her. "Are you worried because I was talking on the phone?"

"Well, it did cross my mind when I saw you that maybe . . ."

"I was afraid that's what you'd think. But I was talking to my sister in Indiana. She called me because she couldn't get me at my house, and she was worried about me."

"Does she know what's been going on around here?"

"Yes. She and I are close. We share everything. Well, almost everything. I told her that you'd put me in a safe house, but I explained how I couldn't tell her or anybody where it is. She understood."

"Okay."

"That's all right, isn't it? I can tell her that much, as long as I don't say where the house is, right?"

"Yes, that's okay. It's just that the fewer people, especially ones around here, who know what's going on with you, the better."

"I understand, believe me. It feels great to be here. I don't want to ruin it."

"For yourself or for anybody else in the future who might come here for protection."

Savannah's cell phone began to chime, and when she dug it out of her purse, she saw it was Ryan's number on the caller ID.

"Excuse me just a minute," she told Sharona as she walked a few feet away and answered it.

"Hi," she said, "I'm glad you called. Sorry about falling asleep on you like that. Literally, falling asleep *on* you, from what Tammy told me."

"Think nothing of it," Ryan replied. "You were exhausted. We were happy to tuck you in."

Lurid thoughts of them tucking her into bed rushed through her mind, but as always, she just let them flow in and immediately out. There was no point. Just no point at all. So why torment herself?

"I'm really sorry I forgot about the gala, too," she said. "You two looked so gorgeous in your tuxes. I can't believe I missed the opportunity to look at you all night."

He chuckled. "We'll see what we can do about making that up to you. We enjoy looking at you in an evening gown, too."

"Yeah, right."

No point, Savannah, she told herself. *No point at all. Don't even go there.*

"Actually, I called," he said, "because I might have a lead for you on that poultry . . . um . . . site."

"Really? A chicken farm?"

"Well, nothing so quaint as a farm. It was actually a poultry-processing plant."

"Yuck. A chicken slaughterhouse?"

"That's another way to put it."

"Where?" She brightened considerably.

"Would you believe, just off Sulphur Creek Road, about six miles from where you found the car and body?"

"No way!"

"Yes. I was talking to a friend of mine who grew up in this area, asking him if he knew about any sort of poultry ranch or whatever. He said his dad actually worked at this place, like thirty years ago. Said it put his father off eating chicken for the rest of his life."

"I can imagine."

"Anyway, it's abandoned now."

"All the more reason to check it out."

"True."

"Off Sulphur Creek Road, near the car dump site, huh? Which direction?"

"West. There's a sign by the road where you turn north, an old one, advertising apple cider, a dollar a gallon."

"Yeah, I've seen that."

"Turn down that dirt road, and my buddy says it's about half a mile from there."

"Dirk's gonna love you for this."

"Oh, wow . . . what I've always dreamed of . . . having Dirk's undying love and devotion."

"I'm sure. Thanks, buddy. I owe you one."

"You owe me nothing, except an evening in a slinky, low-cut ball gown."

"Yeah, sure. Toy with my heart, will ya?"

Savannah said good-bye to him and hurried back to Sharona.

"Something about the case?" Sharona asked eagerly.

"Maybe. Maybe not. Not sure yet." Savannah had learned long ago not to show all her cards to anybody. "But let me ask you something. You said you know a bit about Pinky's operations."

"Some, yes."

"Did he or any of the others ever mention anything about chickens?"

"Chickens?"

"Yes, like maybe cockfighting, betting on them, whatever . . . ?"

Sharona thought for a moment, then nodded. "Yes, I

think I did hear something like that. A couple of times I heard Pinky tell someone to meet him at what he called the 'chicken plant.' I thought that sounded sort of strange. Is that a flower or a tree or . . . . What kind of plant is a chicken plant?"

"Thank you," Savannah said. "Thank you very much. I've gotta go. Enjoy the goodies."

"Oh, I will! I will! I'm going to go do the crossword puzzles and eat the cookies right now! I do the crossword in the *Los Angeles Times* every Sunday."

Crossword puzzles, huh? Savannah thought as she rushed back to the Mustang, punching in Dirk's phone number as she went. Maybe there was more to Sharona than she'd thought.

"Hi ya," she said when he picked up the phone, "I'm at the safe house. I gave Sharona her stuff. Ryan just called me. He had something for us."

"Oh, yeah? What?" He sounded grumpy. Dirk was always grumpy, but more so when a case wasn't moving fast enough to suit him.

"An abandoned chicken-processing plant just off Sulphur Creek Road, six miles from where we fished Jardin out of the creek." She climbed into the Mustang and waited for his excited, overjoyed response.

There was dead silence on the other end. But she could hear him breathing, so she knew he was alive.

She started her engine. "And Sharona told me that she's overheard Pinky mention meeting people at the 'chicken plant.' "

Still, he didn't reply.

"Aren't you happy about that?" she said, heading down the road through the orange grove. "I was. It sounds like a good solid lead to me."

"It is," he said. "But I'm going to be bummed if it's Pinky. I was hoping it was Clarissa or Rachel. Weren't you?"

"Yes, a little, I guess. But a lead is a lead. And at least this way, it won't be the Morris kid. I'm heading out there right now."

"No, wait for me. You could run into some of his crew out there. Or some of the guys who do the cockfighting."

"If I run into some bastard who thinks it's fun to see animals kill each other, I'll beat the tar out of him."

"That's exactly why I want you to wait there at the dump site for me, and we'll go together. I don't want you hurting anybody. You don't think I was worried about *you*, do you?"

She laughed. "I want to call Ryan back and invite him and John along, too. After all, it was his lead."

"You really think this is gonna pan out?"

"Yes, I do. I have a feeling about it."

"Okay, if they want to tag along, that's fine by me."

"Later, Sweetcheeks."

"In a while, Babycakes."

In unison they blew raspberries at each other and hung up.

Ah, the sweet romance of it all.

Chapter 19

As Savannah, Ryan, and John sat in her Mustang by the side of Sulphur Creek Road, waiting for Dirk to arrive, they discussed the upcoming trek to the poultry plant.

"I'm not looking forward to this. I just want to get it over and done with," Savannah told them, resting her arms on top of the steering wheel and resisting the urge to check her watch again. "I'm an animal lover and a hypocrite. I like to pretend that the meat I eat is created back there in the rear of the grocery store. They make it out of some magical ingredients and then put it in those little Styrofoam packages with the cellophane wrap over them."

"I know what you mean," Ryan said. "I think most of us would prefer to think that what we're eating never actually mooed or clucked or swam."

"I don't mind if it swam," John added from the backseat. "But I can assure you, that if I had to butcher my own meat, I'd be eating a lot of fish."

"We're a bunch of wimps," Savannah said. "Too many Disney animal films growing up. That's what ruined us. It was Bambi and those mice friends of Cinderella's."

"True," Ryan and John agreed in unison. "So true."

Savannah's cell phone rang, and when she answered it, she had an excited Tammy on the other end.

"Got something for you," Tammy said. "I was searching on the Internet and found out who owns that property that you're going to right now."

"Oh, yeah? Who?"

"Baldovino Pinky Moretti himself."

"Really? Well, if that ain't interesting." Savannah glanced up and in her rearview mirror she saw Dirk's Buick approaching. "I'm so happy to hear that. And I'm sure the boys will be, too. Good work, I mean, good sleuthing, kiddo."

She hung up and said to Ryan and John. "Hey, fellas. The chicken plant is now owned by none other than our mob-connected friend, Pinky Moretti."

"Ah," John said, "and so the plot thickens."

"Sleuthing? The plot thickens?" Ryan shook his head. "You two need to limit how much time you spend with Tammy."

Savannah waved Dirk to drive around them, and she pulled out onto the road and followed behind him.

"There are worse influences in this world than Miss Tammy-Pollyanna Hart," she said. "But I have to tell you, she's been trying to get me to go vegetarian for years. After this little field trip, I may just have to try it."

The processing plant wasn't difficult to find, because it was the only group of buildings at the end of the long, dirt road.

One large, gray, windowless structure promised to be the actual processing center, and several equally forbidding outbuildings stood, shabby and somber, nearby. The roofs on some of them had caved in, while the walls on others bowed outward.

And yet, for all the property's rundown appearance, it didn't have the look of a totally abandoned facility. Weeds grew beside the road, but there had been enough recent traffic to keep the drive itself clear. And on either side of the road, lay a profusion of litter, mostly beer cans and assorted snack food wrappers. And those looked fairly fresh.

"There's been some recent activity around here," Ryan said, looking out the window as they bounced down the deeply pitted road. They could barely see ahead because of all the dirt Dirk was stirring up.

"I don't see any cars up there, though," Savannah remarked, squinting through the dust cloud. "Maybe we'll have the place to ourselves."

"Does Dirk have any sort of search warrant?" John asked.

"I doubt he had time to get one that quick. If we find anything good, he can get one then."

"You colonists are far more bold about these things than we are on the other side of the pond," John said.

"Oh, stop with the Limey crap," Ryan told him. "Like you and I didn't bend plenty of the rules when we were in the Bureau all those years ago."

John snickered. "I remember it well. If we'd been caught, we would have been—"

"Fired?" Ryan interjected. "You mean, like we were?"

"I thought you two were fired because you were gay," Savannah said.

"Well, let's just say that we broke more rules than just 'Don't ask; don't tell,' " Ryan replied. "They had a hard time deciding which ones to fire us for. They had quite a selection."

Dirk pulled up in front of the largest building, and Savannah parked right beside him. They all climbed out of their cars and looked around.

The dirt nearby showed the tire tracks of numerous vehicles. In fact, it was obvious that some cars or trucks had even been parked on large portions of the weeded areas as the vegetation had been flattened. Even more litter lay strewn about here than on the road.

"Looks like they've thrown some pretty big shindigs around here," Savannah said with a feeling of dread.

"Yeah," Dirk answered. "I found Julio in a pool hall on the east end of town, and he said he'd heard of some cockfighting going on in this area. Of course, to hear him tell it, he hasn't even been close to a KFC since he's been out on parole."

"And speaking of . . ." Savannah said, as she opened the door of a nearby outbuilding and looked inside. Her heart sank when she saw row upon row of tiny wooden doors. One of the inside walls was covered with what looked like stacks of tiny outhouses, three high and six across. Eighteen separate enclosures—one for each of the roosters who was awaiting his turn to fight to the death for the amusement, entertainment, and financial profit of the spectators.

The broken cement floor of the building was littered with chicken feathers, excrement, feed, and, here and there, drops of dried blood.

"It's a holding area," she told them, as they joined her to look inside. "How much do you want to bet the arena is in there?" She pointed to the largest building.

"Rather ironic really," John said. "Years ago, this place was used for killing birds. Now it is again."

"Yes, but slaughtering for food is one thing," Dirk replied. "This crap is something else."

"As bad as this is for the chickens, it breeds other crimes, too," Savannah said. "Huge amounts of money are gambled and lost. And anywhere there's a lot of money, there are guns. Homicides aren't that uncommon in these circles."

"And then you've got organized crime," Ryan said as

he walked over, opened one of the small cages, and looked inside. "Anything that rakes in a lot of dough is a magnet for those guys."

"But blood sports are prominent in many cultures around the world," John said. "In the U.K., we have our own foxhunting. Spain its bullfights."

"And cockfighting's always been part of the U.S. culture, too." Dirk turned away from the outbuilding and headed toward the main structure. The rest of them followed. "George Washington and Abe Lincoln participated," he said, ". . . or so Julio informed me when I was arresting him last time."

"Yeah, well, slavery and child labor were legal back then, too," Savannah added. "Just because it's an old cultural tradition doesn't necessarily mean it's a good one."

When they reached the door to the main building, they found it secured with a heavy padlock. Dirk fiddled with it a few minutes, then started looking around for something to pry it off with.

"Here, let me try," Savannah said.

He gave her an indignant look. "Oh, right. I can't get it off, but you . . ."

She reached into her purse, took out a lock pick, and ten seconds later, had the lock open. "And that," she said, "is how a professional does it."

"A professional what?" Ryan teased. "Burglar?"

She raised her nose in the air. "I'll have you know I have never burgled anything. Breaking and entering, yes, but Granny Reid raised me to be a lady."

As she pushed past Dirk to be the first to enter, he said, "And breaking into people's property is okay with her?"

"What Gran doesn't know . . ." she said, ". . . won't get me whooped."

There were no windows and no lights on, so at first, they had no idea of the enormity of the room. It wasn't until Dirk had felt around for a switch on the wall and thrown it that they realized the long, gigantic building was mostly one room.

And the evidence of both its past and its present was all too apparent.

Hanging from the high ceiling was a conveyor belt with many small, ominous-looking metal frames suspended from it. Savannah didn't have to use a lot of imagination to picture a chicken hanging from each of those frames as it circled the room, going through one stage after the other of the slaughtering process.

Along the conveyor line there were several huge vats. At least one of them appeared to be connected to some electrical equipment.

Savannah didn't want to think a lot about that, either.

At the far end of the room were a set of large doors, and she assumed that was where trucks could load and unload their cargo. Near that end was also another walled-off area with a particularly heavy metal door.

But it wasn't the slaughterhouse equipment that bothered her most. As Dirk had said, killing for the sake of producing meat was one thing. What she saw in the center of the room had nothing to do with providing fried chicken for the traditional American family's picnic.

"Look at that," Ryan said. "That has to be a cockfighting arena."

"Yeah," Dirk replied. "They call it a 'pit.' "

He was pointing to a large circle in the center of the room that was bordered by a short, mesh fence. Around the pit was a ring of cheap plastic chairs, and behind those chairs, on a foot-high riser, was yet another circle of chairs.

"Stadium seating," she said dryly. "How very civilized."

Together, they walked to the arena, then each went their separate way and looked around.

Dirk stepped over the wire fence and studied the pit itself. Ryan and John investigated some nearby square enclosures that were also fenced off with wire mesh.

On one side of the room, to the right and behind the pit, was a snack bar. Savannah walked over that way and scanned the list of goodies that could be purchased. She was only mildly surprised to see that, along with nacho chips, hot dogs, sodas and beer, they were selling chicken strips.

There was no real kitchen, per se, but several big ice chests for the beer and soda, and a couple of large microwaves seemed to do the trick.

Dirk called out from the pit, "There are a lot of red feathers here that look like the one on Jardin's tire."

"Over here, too," Ryan told him, as he squatted down and looked at the floor of the other pen.

"Maybe if we can get some of these to the Bureau," John said, "we can find out what breed of rooster it is. If it's strictly a gaming breed and not a run-of-the-mill domestic chicken, that would narrow down your evidence a bit."

"Yeah, that would help."

Dirk left the pit and walked toward the rear of the room, where Savannah joined him. They headed toward the large doors at the end of the room, but before they reached them, they both caught a whiff of something horrible, something putrid.

"Damn," Dirk said, putting his hand over his mouth and nose. "Where the hell is that coming from?"

Savannah's heart fell. She had smelled that terrible stench far too many times not to know what it was.

"Decomp," she said, trying not to breathe. There was something about the stink of decaying flesh that went straight to the belly and induced instant nausea. Savannah had seen things and heard things over the years that had troubled her. But it was the smell of decomposing bodies that haunted her.

They walked around for a few moments, trying to find the source.

When Savannah realized it was coming from an industrial-sized metal trash can with a lid, she froze.

"Oh, no." She thought of the missing redheaded boy in the picture. "Don't let it be him," she whispered. "Don't let it be . . ."

One look at Dirk told her that he was thinking the same thing. He reached into his pocket, took out a latex glove, and slipped it on one hand.

Normally, Savannah wanted to be in the thick of things, the first to see and do. But as Dirk stepped up to the can and gingerly lifted off the lid, she hung back, reluctant to see yet another sight that would scar her soul forever.

The kids. She just couldn't handle it when it was the kids.

He leaned over and glanced inside. Then slammed the lid back onto the can. He looked like he was about to barf.

"Roosters," he said. "Dead roosters. Apparently, they toss the losers in here and forget about them."

"Hope they were dead when they got pitched in there," she said.

"Not always, by a long shot, I've heard."

Savannah sighed. "At least it's not . . ."

"Yeah."

Ryan and John were still in the pen. "Hey," Ryan called out. "You ought to see these grisly things. Razors that they tie onto the chicken's feet. Artificial spurs."

"I nicked myself just touching one of the things," John said, wiping his hand with a handkerchief.

"Be careful," Savannah told him. "You'll get an infection from that crap. I've got a first-aid kit in my trunk."

"It's okay, love," John replied. "But I'll not be handling anything like that around here again. I'm behind on my tetanus shots."

"Anything in that can you were looking in?" Ryan asked.

"No," Savannah said. "Nothing important."

Remembering how Julio had defended his favorite sport, Savannah recalled his argument that champion cocks were often fed better than the human families who raised them. "Treated like kings!" he had argued.

Not once they lose, she thought. *Then they're garbage.*

Happy to leave the trash can and its foul contents behind, Savannah walked over to join Dirk by the large doors at the end of the room.

"This has to be the loading and unloading area," he said. "Swing those doors open and you could get a semi-trailer truck in here."

"Or a Jaguar?"

She knelt on the ground, took out her penlight and scanned it back and forth across the floor. "Take a look at this. Do you see what I see?"

Kneeling beside her, he put his head down near the floor and nodded. "Yeah, those look like tire tracks in the dust there."

"Do you figure the CSU could lift those?"

"If we can see them, chances are they can lift them. Wouldn't it be something if they match the Jaguar?"

Ryan and John had joined them in the rear of the building.

"This would be a great place to hide a car," Ryan said.

Dirk nodded. "Just what we were thinking. If you wanted to keep the body and a vehicle under wraps for a while before dumping it somewhere, this would be the perfect place."

They all turned toward the heavy metal door to the left of them.

"Processing houses have to have cooling rooms, right?" Savannah said. "You have to chill the meat before you ship it."

"Some have flash freezers," John said.

Dirk was already at the door. He jerked the thick handle and the door creaked as it opened.

"It's not cool in here," he said, stepping inside and flipping on a light. "But look at those shelves. It's got to be where they chilled the meat."

Savannah spotted a thermostat on the wall. "Yeah," she said. "It's a cooling unit, but it's turned off."

"Why waste electricity?" Ryan said. "Your man Pinky is probably a guy who watches his profit margin."

Seeing yet another smaller door on the far wall of the cooling unit, Savannah walked over to it and opened it. Instantly, she was hit by a blast of frigid air. "Bingo," she said. "Freezer, big-time. And it's on."

She found the light switch for that room, too, but she used a tissue to open it, so she wouldn't disturb any prints. Something told her they had entered an area that the crime scene techs would need to process.

By the light of one dim overhead bulb, she could see shelves with at least twenty plastic bags of ice—the same sort she bought at the liquor store when she was having a party that was sure to tax her own meager ice cube trays.

"Well, now we know where they store the ice for the sodas and ice chests at these little soirees," she said.

"Can I use your light for a minute?" Dirk asked her.

She handed it to him. Then she, John, and Ryan watched and shivered as Dirk ran the light over first one shelf and then the other.

"Hey, lady and gentlemen, look what we have here!" he said, excited.

They gathered close, and Ryan and John shone their own lights at the spot he was indicating.

"Okay," Savannah said. "It looks like blood. But in a place like this, blood's as plentiful as feathers."

Dirk grinned. "Yeah, but I've never seen a chicken with short, straight blond hair, have you?"

"It's got hair in it?"

"Right there in that one big, dark spot."

He stepped back so that they could move closer. And when she leaned into the shelf and squinted, there they were—several short blond hairs, glued to the shelf by the dried blood.

"That looks a lot like Jardin's hair," she said. "The lab will be able to tell for sure, but I'd bet money on it."

"I think they killed your lad somewhere on this property," John said, "and then stowed his car in there and his body in here."

"Until they were ready to let the world know he was dead," Ryan added.

"So why the wait?" Savannah asked. "What did those days buy them?"

"I think I'll go ask Pinky," Dirk said. "And this time I'm going to 'ask' him really, really hard."

Chapter 20

Whether it was the city jail, county lockup, or one of the state penitentiaries, every time Savannah set foot in an incarceration facility, she was struck by the sheer power of the law.

Even though she, personally, had been responsible for many arrests and subsequent convictions over the years, the fact that society could take a person's freedom from them and lock them behind bars continued to awe her.

Keeping human beings in cages was a necessary evil, but an evil, nevertheless.

Surrounded by steel bars and cement, their faces strangely blank and eyes empty, the inmates wandered about listlessly—ghosts in orange jumpsuits.

Sometimes, when they saw her, their faces would light up momentarily, the sight of a pretty woman sparking something in their souls. And usually the way they looked at her was touchingly respectful. Not so much lascivious, as one might expect, but adoring and with a longing of the spirit, rather than the flesh.

She wondered if she reminded them of the women

they loved on the outside: wives, girlfriends, sisters, and friends.

But when Baldovino Pinky Moretti walked into the small interrogation room with its four plastic chairs and its one scarred table, and its drab, unadorned walls, he scarcely gave her any look at all. He hadn't been inside long enough to need a woman, physically or spiritually.

Pinky just wanted out.

"You again," he said when he saw Dirk sitting at the table next to Savannah. "They said somebody was here to talk to me about my case. Like I told you before, it's a bunch of bullshit, me supposedly attacking that cop."

"It probably is," Dirk replied. "But that's not the case I'm here to talk about. Have a seat."

Savannah looked him over as he plopped his considerable body onto the chair across from them. He was a large man, well over six feet and must have weighed close to three hundred pounds. Most of it wasn't muscle.

The hair on his head had been shaved, but was beginning to grow out. So he had a blond stubble, reminiscent of a boot camp recruit.

But his most obvious feature, without a doubt, was the enormous pinkish-red birthmark that covered most of the right side of his face. The port wine stain stretched from his forehead, over his eye and down to his neck.

She thought of all the teasing and harassment the young Pinky would have endured with such an unusual appearance. Not to mention a name to underscore his uniqueness. It couldn't have been an easy childhood.

Of course, that was no excuse for murder, she reminded herself.

"I didn't kill that guy either," Pinky said, chewing on his thumbnail, an activity that looked particularly ridiculous since he was handcuffed and had to lift both hands to his face to accomplish it. "That DA's got nothing on me and he knows it."

"Maybe you did and maybe you didn't." Dirk leaned back in his chair and crossed his arms over his chest. "But I'm not here to talk to you about him. I still want to find out what happened to Bill Jardin."

Pinky snorted and spat out a nail fragment. "That gambling degenerate scumbag. I told you before, I don't know anything about him . . . except that he owed me money."

"Gee, for what?" Savannah asked. "Did you redecorate his house? Tailor his tuxedo?"

Pinky glared at her for a moment, then turned to Dirk. "Who's this bitch?"

Dirk chuckled. "A good friend of mine. You'd better watch what you call her, 'cause she's got a mean karate chop, and I'm pretty good with a left hook myself."

The two men had a brief stare down, and Savannah noted with satisfaction that it was Pinky who broke eye contact first.

"Let's get down to business here," Dirk said. "We just went for a little drive out in the country."

"Had a hankering for some clean *farm* living," Savannah added.

"Yeah," Dirk said to her, "my buddy Pinky here, he knows all about farming. He owns that one we just visited out there in the hills, just off Sulphur Creek Road. He's a chicken man."

"Not chickens," Pink said, his pale gray eyes narrowing. "If you've been out to my place, you know what I'm about. *Cocks*."

Savannah snickered and said to Dirk, "It's kinda pitiful, really, what a big kick he gets out of saying that. Kinda like a twelve-year-old who just learned himself a new dirty word."

Dirk laughed, then quickly sobered and leaned across the table, getting in Pinky's face. "So, why did you kill Jardin?"

"Kill him? I told you, I didn't have anything to do with that one. Nothing at all."

"Yes, you did," Dirk snapped back. "You hid his car in your building there, right next to the trash can full of rotten chickens—"

"Cocks!"

"Whatever. And you stashed his body in your freezer. The CSU techs are over there right now, lifting his tire marks off your floor and collecting samples of his blood and hair out of your freezer. Do you want to play this bullshit game with me and pretend they're not all gonna match?"

Pinky looked like somebody had slugged him in his ample belly. He began to chew his thumbnail with all the vigor of a deeply worried, multicharged felon.

But he hadn't yet uttered that one dirty word they always dreaded. The one used by more intelligent criminals. "Attorney."

No, Baldovino Pinky Moretti looked like the type who considered himself much smarter than any stupid lawyer. So, why call one?

Savannah loved guys like Pinky. And so did Dirk. His sort made life so much easier for them.

"Why did you kill him?" Dirk said.

"I told you. I didn't. I mean it! I didn't do that one!"

That one, versus the other ones? Savannah thought. No, Pinky wasn't exactly coloring with a full box of crayons.

But, sadly, she almost believed him. There was a certain indignation to his protest that struck her as sincere.

Dirk, on the other hand, didn't appear to believe him at all.

"You killed him," Dirk said. "He owed you money. He came out to your fricken chicken joint, and you blew his brains out and shoved his body in your freezer. Then, later on, you took the body and the car and dumped them up the road a few miles in Sulphur Creek. We already know that much. Now we just need to find out why. Did he do something to piss you off?"

"No! I wasn't pissed at him at all. The only beef I had with him was that he owed me money. He said he was going to pay me what he owed."

"And you believed him?" Savannah asked.

"Yeah, I did, because he knew better than to lie to me."

"When did he say he was going to pay you?" Dirk asked.

"Last Monday, the night he got killed."

Dirk grinned. "And how do you know that he got killed on Monday night?"

Even a nonintellectual like Pinky knew when he'd been caught in his own trap. He sat there and opened and closed his mouth a few times, then shut it tightly.

"He came out there to pay you off, didn't he?" Dirk said. "And something went wrong. And he wound up dead. Why don't you tell me about it?"

Pinky said nothing. Savannah was afraid he might utter that ugly word that had ended so many promising interrogations. So, she leaned across the table and gave him her most sisterly, caring, compassionate look.

"Listen, Pinky," she said with loving kindness just oozing from her voice. "You don't strike me as a cold-blooded killer. You seem like a decent guy who wouldn't hurt anybody unless they were really, really asking for it. Tell us what happened. Tell us what he did that caused you to do it."

No response from Pinky. He had even decided to give his thumbnail a rest.

"I know you want to tell us," Savannah continued, "because nobody wants to be thought of as a mean bastard who'd just kill somebody for no reason. Tell us your side of the story. Set the record straight."

"I didn't do it!" he shouted. "I did *not* shoot him! He was already dead when—"

"When you got there?" Savannah said. Again, his words had a certain, frantic ring of truth. The look of total frustration on his face appeared genuine. "You went there to meet him, to get paid, and when you arrived, he was already dead?"

"Yeah. Dead. Shot through the head right there in his car. On my property! What the hell was I supposed to do, just leave him there?"

"What *did* you do?" Savannah asked.

Pinky sighed and his shoulders sagged. "I had my boys stick him in my freezer there, just for a few days, until we could figure out what happened to him. And we put his car into the main building there."

"Did it occur to you to call us?" Dirk asked.

"Oh, yeah," Pink replied dryly. "I'm under investigation for a gambling-related murder, and I'm gonna call you and say what? 'I found this guy who owed me money shot to death at my cockfighting arena?' That would have gone over well."

"So, if we believe you," Dirk said, "you went to your property to meet with Jardin and when you got there, he was already dead in his car. The Jaguar was parked where?"

"Right there by the main building, near the front door, the one with the big, new lock on it." Pinky thought that over for a moment. "Hey, how did you guys get in there?"

"She picked it," Dirk replied.

Pinky looked at Savannah with new respect and nodded. "Okay."

"Why did you really leave him in that freezer so long?" Dirk asked him. "You don't strike me as a guy who'd take days to make up his mind what to do about something. Why were you stalling?"

As Pinky sat there, saying nothing, avoiding Dirk's eyes, as well as his question, Savannah mulled it over.

"When you found Jardin," she said, "did he have your money on him?"

Pinky shook his head. "No."

"Was it in his car?"

Again, a head shake.

"So," Savannah said, "the reason you kept him on ice was because you were trying to track down your money. You wanted first crack at finding the killer and your dough, before the cops got on it."

Dirk smiled and nodded. "I think you've got it," he told Savannah. "That's exactly why. You figured if we nabbed the murderer before you did, you'd never get your money back."

"But I still didn't kill him," Pinky said.

"And let's just pretend for a minute here that we believe you," Dirk replied. "Who do you think did it? You've been on the investigation for about five days longer than we have. You've gotta have some sort of opinions on the subject."

Pinky's face changed, from dull and witless to dark and furious. "Oh, I'm pretty sure I know. I think it's his wife, that Clarissa exercise bitch."

"Really?" Savannah asked. "Why?"

"Because she called me and changed the meet time."

"What?"

"Yeah. He'd called me that morning and asked if I could meet him there at the plant at seven o'clock. I said okay. Then, later that evening, his wife calls me. She says something's come up, and he can't make it till two hours later. Said he asked her to call me cause he was tied up doing something or the other."

"Did she say what he was doing?"

Pinky shrugged. "I don't remember. Something about the car, problems with the new car or whatever. I didn't pay a lot of attention to it. I was just pissed that he postponed on me like that. I'd already been waiting a couple of weeks to get paid."

"You don't happen to remember what number she called you from, do you?" Savannah asked. "Like if it showed her name in the caller ID or whatever?"

"No, it just said 'Wireless Caller.' And showed a number. I remember it ended with '666.' I noticed it because of all the scary movies I've seen about that number."

"Yeah, that's a distinctive one," Dirk said, giving Savannah a sideways glance.

Savannah said, "Pinky, did you ever get in touch with Clarissa Jardin?"

Pinky gave a raspy little laugh. "Yeah. We talked several times."

"On the phone, or in person?" Dirk asked.

"Both. She claimed she didn't know anything about the money, or him coming out to pay me, or any of it. She even said she didn't call me, that it must have been somebody else pretending to be her. I made her get out her cell phone and call me with me standing there. She did. But a different number showed up on my caller ID. It wasn't the '666' one."

Dirk sat still, staring at Pinky, thinking it all over. Finally, he said, "We've interviewed Mrs. Jardin a number of times. She never mentioned that she'd met you face-to-face. Why do you suppose that is?"

The already menacing look on Pinky's face turned even darker. "I asked her not to," he said with chilling coldness. "As a personal favor to me."

"I'll bet you did," Dirk replied.

Pinky lifted his thumb to his mouth and began to chew again. "She comes across all tough on TV," he said, around his mutilated cuticle. "But she ain't all that tough . . . believe me."

Savannah looked into those flat, predatory eyes. *Oh, I believe*, she thought. *I do, really do, believe.*

"But you think she killed her own husband?" Dirk asked him. "You think she was the one who made that call to you, telling you to come two hours later? You think she met him there earlier and killed him before you got there?"

"Yeah, that's what I think."

"So, why didn't you do worse than just threaten her?" Dirk said.

"Because, in spite of what people might think, or what a certain DA thinks about me, I'm not that kind of guy. I don't just go around killing people because of what I *think* they did. I have to know for sure before I take a drastic action like that."

Savannah gave him her best, Southern belle, dimpled smile. "Now that's what I like," she said, "a man of high moral standards."

When Savannah and Dirk had left the jail and were headed back to her house to grab a bite to eat, regroup, and decide on their next move, Savannah got a call on her cell phone.

It was Ruby Jardin on the other end, sounding irritated and impatient when she said, "Well? I've been waiting. What's going on?"

"I'm sorry, Ruby," Savannah told her. "I was just going to call you. I—"

"I've been watching my TV, the news channels, to see if they've arrested Clarissa yet, and not a blamed thing."

"No, there haven't been any arrests made yet. But we've come up with some interesting leads."

"Leads? I'm not paying you for *leads*. I'm paying you for *results*."

"Leads come first, Mrs. Jardin. Leads, then arrests," Savannah told her, as gently as she could. "I know you must be very anxious for justice for your son. But these things take a little time. Please be patient with me for just a wee bit longer."

A call-waiting beep came through, and Savannah looked at the caller ID. The number was Rebecca Shipton's.

Savannah's pulse rate rose. "Listen, Ruby, I've got another call and it might be important. I'll call you back this evening there at the hotel, okay? I promise."

Ruby wasn't happy to say goodbye, but Savannah had a feeling that Rebecca wouldn't be calling unless she had a lead on the Morris boy.

"Rebecca!" Savannah said. "Hey, girl! What's going on?"

"I'm here in my office, looking across the desk at your young man."

"Really! Oh, that's fantastic!" Relief flooded through her. At least the kid wasn't dead. No matter what happened to make him run or whatever he'd done, at least he was alive. "Did he actually say he's Tanner Morris?" she asked.

"No, he's being difficult and won't talk to us. But I'm looking at his picture right here in my hand. There's no doubt about it at all."

"Where did you find him? How did you pick him up?"

"We passed the picture around and one of our volunteers saw him hanging out at the bus station downtown. We called the cops, and they picked him up for loitering."

"We're on our way over right now. We'll be there in twenty minutes. Don't let go of him."

"Wouldn't dream of it. See you later."

Savannah hung up and turned to Dirk, who was eagerly eavesdropping. "Rebecca's got Tanner Morris."

"I gathered," he said. "Alive and well?"

"Well enough to be sitting in her office, refusing to tell her who he is."

"Hm-m-m. Sounds like your typical pain-in-the-ass teenager."

Savannah thought of her younger siblings, all of whom had suffered through adolescence, some with more grace than others. "Difficult teenagers," she grumbled. "Oh goody. My favorite."

"But he's alive and kicking," Dirk said.

"Yes, thank goodness for that." She remembered some times when they hadn't had such a happy ending. She still had nightmares about the endings involving kids that hadn't been happy. "He can be as difficult and surly as he wants," she said. "I learned from Gran how to handle surly."

"Does it involve a switch cut from a tree and the back of a woodshed?"

"Precisely."

"Great. That's just what the SCPD needs. A child-abuse lawsuit."

"Naw, I won't give him a switchin' . . . just a serious talkin'-to."

"Oh, no! Anything but that! We men hate the talkin'-to crap. 'Honey, we need to talk.' Those words strike terror in the hearts of American men everywhere."

"Only those who've committed dark, wicked deeds."

"Like leaving the toilet seat up, walking into the house with muddy feet, not listening to every word you women babble at us all day long?"

"Those are the main ones. The toilet seat thing, though, that's the worst."

"So I've heard. I never understood that. Women act like it's a mortal sin. We need it up; you need it down. It's not like one point of view is any more virtuous than the other."

"Listen up, buddy. Have you ever got up in the middle of the night and gone to the bathroom, thinking you're going to be able to just shuffle in there, do your business and then come right back to bed, get in, and never quite wake up? Then . . . you go in, sit down and plop! Your rear end's sticking in ice-cold water, and believe you me, you're wide awake and mad as a wet hen. And before you can go to bed, you have to take a shower, maybe even change pajamas. Takes you hours to get back to sleep. All because some lamebrain forgot to put the toilet seat down like he was supposed to, like you asked him to a thousand times before!"

He was silent for a long time. Finally, sounding a little hurt, he said, "I thought we had put that behind us . . . no pun intended."

"Some things a woman never truly forgets."

"You already yelled at me a lot. I said I was sorry, and you said you forgave me."

"Forgiving's one thing. Forgetting's another."

"Obviously."

They rode on a long, long time in silence.

"Sheez," he mumbled, reaching for a cinnamon stick. "Some women. You piss 'em off once and . . ."

"Watch it."

Chapter 21

When Savannah sat down in Rebecca Shipton's intake office and looked at the tall, skinny, red-haired kid sitting across from her, she didn't see a problem child. She saw a scared young man.

He did have the look of a man, being taller than most adults. And even though he was slender, she could see the promise of a full-fledged hunk further down the road.

But for today, Tanner Morris was a teenager in trouble, and he knew it.

"Tanner," Savannah said as she settled into one of the uncomfortable, folding metal chairs that Rebecca had provided for her and Dirk, "we know who you are. We even have some pretty good ideas about why you might have run from your mom. And we want to help you. But we need you to talk to us."

"I've got nothing to say," the teenager replied, his arms crossed tightly over his chest. "I want a lawyer."

A kid who's smarter than the hardcore criminal we just interviewed, Savannah thought. *Go figure*.

"You don't need a friggen lawyer," Dirk grumbled at him. "You're not being charged with anything."

"You have the right to have your guardian present while they question you," Rebecca said from her seat behind her desk. "If you tell us how to get in touch with your parents, I'll call them."

At the mention of parents, a look of fear swept over Tanner's face. "No, don't do that," he said. "I don't have a dad, and I don't want my mom here."

"Your mom, Rachel Morris, that is," Savannah said.

His big eyes filled with tears. Hanging his head, he started to quietly cry.

As she reached into her purse for tissues, it occurred to Savannah that, lately, everyone she came in contact with burst into tears within minutes. Maybe she should reexamine her interrogation tactics.

"We've talked to your mom, Tanner," she told the boy. "She's worried sick about you. In fact, I called her just before I got here, and I told her we have you. She's on her way to get you right now."

"No!" He jumped up from his chair. "I don't want to see her. Not now. I can't!"

Dirk stood and with a firm hand on the kid's shoulder pushed him back down onto his chair.

"Then you better tell us why you don't want to see her," Dirk said. "And you'd better start talking fast. What happened that night?"

"Which night?"

Tanner's innocent act wasn't very convincing. Savannah found it both interesting and reassuring that he wasn't a good liar. Good kids weren't good liars. Maybe he was a good kid after all.

"You know which night," Savannah said. "Last Monday night, the night that Bill Jardin was killed."

Tanner gasped and his fair, freckled skin turned an even lighter shade of pale. "Mr. Jardin was killed? He's dead?"

"You didn't know that?" Dirk asked.

"Um, no. Well, not for sure. I was hoping that maybe he wasn't."

Savannah gave him her sweetest, most understanding big sister smile and said, "Tanner, I know you're scared. I think you're in a really bad situation and you need our help. But we can't help you unless you tell us exactly what happened that night. We know part of it, but we need to know the rest."

"For one thing," Dirk said with far less sisterly understanding than Savannah, "we know that you were at the Jardins' ranch out there in the country."

Tanner gulped. "Okay. Maybe I was."

"No maybe to it. You were there," Dirk said. "And you'd better tell us all about it, because right now we're wondering what you had to do with Bill Jardin being murdered."

"Me? I didn't do anything!"

"Then you'd better start telling us all the stuff that you supposedly didn't do. Fast."

Tanner turned to Savannah with a "rescue me" look in his eyes.

"It's okay," she told him. "Just tell us what you did and what you saw when you were there."

The boy took a deep breath and plunged in. "I took a cab there. It dropped me off there on the main road, and I walked down to the house. I just wanted to see what it was like. To see where he lived, you know?"

"Bill Jardin?" she asked.

"Yeah. If he was going to be my new dad, I wanted to see what his place was like. Also, I was kind of worried, because my mom and me had been waiting for him to call and he hadn't."

"You guys were all supposed to be heading off to Las Vegas together, right?" Savannah said.

"Yeah. He'd promised that he'd leave Clarissa lots of times, but this time we thought he really meant it. My mom told him that he'd better go through with it and not back out, like he had before. She told him she'd give him twenty-four hours to tell his wife about us, and if he didn't, she would. And she really meant it, so I thought that time he'd finally do the right thing."

"It sounds to me," Dirk said, "like you were going out there for more reasons than just to check out the estate. Sounds like maybe you were curious to see why Bill hadn't called you and your mom. Maybe you wanted to make sure he was going to do the right thing by your mother this time."

When Tanner didn't reply, just stared down at his hands that were lying on his thighs, Savannah had a sinking feeling.

For all practical purposes, this kid had no father. If he had liked Bill Jardin, he'd have been looking forward to having a dad, being a traditional family of three. It also occurred to her that, if Bill changed his mind again that night, Rachel Morris wouldn't have been the only one feeling rejected.

"What happened when you got there, to Rancho Rodriguez," Savannah asked him. "Tell us everything."

"I walked up the road, and through that gate, the one with the bell over it."

"How did you get through the first gate?" Dirk asked. "The big one there by the main road?"

"I climbed over it."

"It helps to be young," Savannah muttered to Dirk when he looked skeptical. Then, to Tanner, she said, "Go on. You went through the bell gate and . . . ?"

"They've got a big yard inside the wall there," he said, "with lots of trees and plants and junk."

"Yes, I know. We've been there," Savannah said. "Go ahead."

"It was dark and the lights were on inside the house.

And . . . well . . . okay . . . I sneaked up to one of the windows and peeked in."

"All right. No big deal. We're not worried about you doing that," Savannah told him. "What did you see?"

"I saw their living room. And Clarissa and Bill were yelling at each other, and Clarissa was crying."

"Could you hear what they were saying?" Dirk asked.

"Sure. Especially her, 'cause she was the loudest. Bill must have told her about my mom and how she'd given him twenty-four hours to tell her about us, because Clarissa yelled, 'You never would have told me if she hadn't made you. You . . .' Well, she called him a really bad name and slapped him."

"She slapped him?" Dirk said.

"Really hard, a couple of times. He just stood there and took it. I guess he figured he deserved it."

"What else?" Savannah asked.

Again, Tanner's eyes welled up with tears. "I don't want to get my mom in trouble."

"She's not in trouble," Dirk told him. "What else?"

"Clarissa asked Bill if he'd known all along that the person they were paying money to was my mom. He said, 'No,' but she didn't believe him. She said he and my mom had been a team from the very beginning, ripping her off, blackmailing her. She accused him of sleeping with my mom for years."

Softly, Savannah asked him, "And how long has it been, Tanner? Did Bill know all along that your mom was threatening Clarissa and taking money from her?"

"No. Not at first. But then one night, my mom sent me up to take the bag of money out of the garbage can in a park, and Bill saw me. A few months later, Clarissa sent him to New York to tell my mom that they knew it was her writing the letters and to knock it off. That's when he and my mom started, you know. That's when they fell in love."

"So," Dirk said, "you saw Clarissa slap Bill and you heard them arguing, and what else?"

"She was all mad about some big amount of money that she'd given him. She said he gave it to my mom, that they were in on it together. She acted like my mom had demanded an extra big amount of money, even more than usual, and that Clarissa had given it to Bill to give to her. And since Clarissa found out that they were . . . you know . . . in love, she wanted her money back. She even threatened to kill him."

"She did?" Savannah felt her heart take an extra beat. "What did she say, her exact words?"

"She said, 'I should kill you for this, Bill. You screw my sister and the two of you rip me off for a small fortune. I really should kill you.' Then he . . ."

The boy's voice broke, and he started to sob hard, his shoulders heaving.

Savannah reached over and put her hand on his knee. "It's okay, Tanner. You're doing really good. You're okay. What happened then?"

"He told her that he didn't really love my mom, that she didn't mean anything to him. He said he'd just been stringing her along because he really needed the money. She said, 'For what? Your damned gambling debts?' and he said, 'Yes. They're going to kill me, Clarissa. I owe a lot of money to guys who really hurt you if you don't pay them in time.' "

He blew his nose loudly into the tissues, then continued, "Clarissa told him, 'Then you should have found some way to get it other than through my sister.' And then he apologized. He apologized and told her again that my mother had never meant anything to him."

Savannah's heart broke for the kid. She didn't need Rebecca's master's degree in psychology to know that Tanner felt that rejection as keenly, or even more so, than his mother may have.

Savannah's own father had abandoned his family over and over again. So she was no stranger to the kind of pain the teenager was feeling.

She also knew the depth of anger that pain engendered.

"What happened then?" she asked him, afraid of where this might be leading.

Tanner wiped his eyes. "Clarissa told him that he had to call my mom and tell her that he was never going to see her again. To tell her that she wanted that last payment back and there wasn't going to be any more money. He had to tell her to stay the hell away from them. She told him to do it right then."

"Did he?" Dirk asked.

"Yeah. She handed him a phone, and he did it. I heard him tell my mom it was all over, that it had all been a big mistake and that they couldn't see each other again, and that they'd have to give Clarissa back that last payment."

"And what happened after he talked to your mom?"

"I don't know. That's when I left."

"How did you leave?" Dirk asked. "You didn't have a car or a cab."

"I walked."

"You walked all the way back to town?"

Tanner nodded. "Yeah, it took me most of the night, but I did." He lifted up his foot and slipped off his sandal. On his heel was a large, ugly blister. "I've got another one like it on this one," he said, holding up the other one. "But it felt good to walk. I needed to think, you know, about stuff."

Savannah, Dirk, and Rebecca looked at each other as they digested all they'd just heard. Tanner put his sandal back on, blew his nose once more, and then tossed the tissue into a wastepaper can next to Rebecca's desk.

"You did the right thing, Tanner," Savannah said, "telling us this. We appreciate it."

"Okay. What's next?" the boy wanted to know.

"We'll take it from here." Savannah sat back in her chair and took her first deep breath in ten minutes. "Your mom is going to be here in a few hours, so you just hang here with Ms. Shipton until—"

"What? No, I don't want to see my mom. If I haven't done anything illegal, can't I just go?"

"No, you can't," Dirk told him. "You're a minor, and you've been missing for days. Your mom wants you back, and we have to return you to her."

"Why don't you want to see your mom, Tanner?" Savannah asked. "Why didn't you go back to the motel that night? Why did you run?"

A look of deep hurt, mixed with intense anger, swept over the kid's face, and Savannah didn't think it was solely because of Bill Jardin's abandonment.

"I just don't want to see her, and that's all I'm going to say about that," he told her. "I'm done talking now."

And the way he crossed his arms over his chest and the jut of his chin assured Savannah that he meant what he said. She'd seen that look of male determination on her brothers' faces, not to mention Dirk's many times before.

He *was* done talking.

And they had gotten everything out of Tanner Morris they were going to get. At least for now.

"That was certainly enlightening," Savannah said to Dirk as they walked out of juvenile hall.

"You think so? Then enlighten me," Dirk replied. "I'm more confused than ever. Who the hell shot Jardin? His wife, who said she ought to kill him?"

"And by the way, I agree with her on that one."

"Me, too. Or the girlfriend, who had high hopes of taking over her sister's husband and at least half of her lifestyle and got those hopes dashed by a phone call?"

"That phone call must have been pretty hard to hear. As a hot-blooded woman myself, I think I might've snapped if I'd gotten a call like that, under those circumstances."

"You figure both Clarissa and Rachel had good reasons to kill him?"

"There's never a truly good reason to commit murder, but that said—"

"And here, ladies and gentlemen, is her real opinion . . ."

"If a husband of mine did what that peckerhead did, I'd have shot him between the eyes, removed the parts of his anatomy that I found most offensive, buried his body and miscellaneous parts in the backyard, and planted a potato patch on top of him. And every time I had a big ol' baked potato with my bloody, rare steak, I'd think of him and grin real big."

Dirk shot her a look of alarm. "Damn girl, remind me never to piss *you* off."

"Just don't ever marry me, promise to be faithful, and then fool around with somebody else."

He gave her a playful grin and said, "I'll certainly file that away for future consideration."

As they reached the Buick, he said, "Do you think we should have another talk with Clarissa? Maybe lay some of this newfound knowledge on her and see how she reacts?"

"Okay. But I want to be back here in two hours when Rachel arrives to pick up Tanner."

"Yeah? Why?"

"Because it's bothering me a lot, the fact that he doesn't want to see his mom. I want to know why."

"That bugs me, too."

Dirk's cell phone began to jangle. Irritated, he dug it out of his jacket pocket, flipped it open, and said, "Yeah?" He listened a moment, then said, "Actually, I was on my way somewhere." He glanced over at Savannah. "Can I send Savannah instead? Okay. Bye."

"*Send* me? Can you *send* me? Like send me to get the office coffee and doughnuts? *Send* me to get your laundry or buy your mistress a black lace teddy? Who do you think you are?"

He looked totally confused. "What? I don't have a mistress."

She sighed and rolled her eyes.

"Besides," he said, "it was that Caitlin chick at the lab. She's got something she wants us to see."

"Well, hell's bells, boy. Why didn't you say so? Get me home so I can pick up my car and hightail it over there. Shake a leg. Time's a'wastin.'"

At the lab, Savannah didn't have to hunt for Caitlin or finagle a way into the Vehicle Examination Bay. Caitlin was waiting for her outside the garage door when she arrived.

Or at least, she thought Caitlin was waiting for her. But as it turned out, the lab tech had simply sneaked outside to have a smoke.

"I'm going to quit one of these days," she said, stubbing the cigarette out on the ground as Savannah walked up to her.

"At least you've got Southern California weather to smoke by," Savannah told her. "Folks in Montana and North Dakota must have it rough when they have to go outside to grab a drag on a cold winter's day."

"I can imagine. That'd be enough to make you quit."

Savannah grinned and together they said, "Naw."

"Whatcha got for me?" Savannah said, following Caitlin back into the garage.

"It may be nothing, but I had a feeling I should point it out to you, just in case."

As they walked over to the Jaguar, which by now was practically covered with dark fingerprint dust, Savannah said, "I heard you found a print inside the car's manual. On the page that tells how to disable the GPS."

"Yes, and I did my best to get a clean lift. But there was just the one, and it was really smeared. No way to get any sort of comparison from it."

She took Savannah over to a brightly lit workbench that was covered with white paper. Quite a lot of items were spread across it: an empty suitcase, numerous changes of men's clothes and toiletries, a tennis racket bag, some expensive tennis shoes, a towel and a plastic container of balls, and a Yankees baseball cap.

Caitlin handed Savannah a pair of gloves, and donned some herself. Then she picked up the cap. "The rest of this stuff is pretty mundane," she said, "but this is what I wanted to show you."

She held it out to Savannah. "I just assumed," she said, "that it was Bill Jardin's cap, since it was his car, thrown in there with his athletic gear. But then I happened to look inside it, and . . ."

Pointing inside the cap, she said, "There were three short red hairs. Two of them were on the outside of the band and one underneath the band."

Savannah felt her adrenaline rising. "Oh, really?"

"Yes. Do any of your suspects have short, red hair?"

Savannah nodded. "Yes, I'm sorry to say they do."

"They?"

"Two of them."

She thought of Rachel's short, straight crop and Tanner's curly mop and she felt sick to her stomach. For the kid's sake, she didn't want to go down that mental road with either destination.

"I've got one of them over here under the microscope. Want to see?"

"Yes, I do."

Caitlin led her to the other end of the bench, where a microscope was set up with the hair in position.

Savannah looked through the lens and saw what could have been considered neither straight nor curly. Just a short hair with maybe a slight wave to it. It had a root attached to one end and the other end was bluntly cut, not worn to a point.

There was something else about it, too.

"I'm not too up on hair analysis and all that," Savannah said, "but has this hair been dyed?"

"Yes, I'd say so," Caitlin agreed. "It appears to have a sort of coating on it and the hair cuticles are lifted, like they are when they're color processed."

Savannah felt a tiny bit of relief. She couldn't imagine Tanner Morris dying his hair. Some teenagers might have colored their hair black, green, pink, or blue. But probably not copper penny red.

Middle-aged women, on the other hand . . .

She walked back to the bench and picked up the cap again. Looking closely at the inside, she saw a faint, reddish tint on the white inner band. "I dyed my hair red once," she told Caitlin, "a long, long time ago. And for a few days afterward, the red kept wearing off on everything. I got it on my pillow, on one of my favorite white nightgowns. This sort of a reddish-orange stain. Just like this." She pointed to the band.

Caitlin looked at it and nodded. "That's what it looks like to me, too. We can have it analyzed to be sure."

"If you would, please."

"It'll be a few days though, before we get the results. They're backed up a bit there in the lab."

"That's okay," Savannah said, her face grim as she thought about racing back to the juvenile hall. She was going to be there when Rachel Morris came to pick up her son. No doubt about it now.

"You get the results as soon as you can," she said. "And maybe by then, we'll have this case closed."

Chapter 22

As Savannah was leaving the lab, she called Dirk and told him about the baseball cap, the hairs, and the dye stain. He found it as interesting as she did and said he'd meet her at the juvenile facility.

Once they had both arrived, they decided to sit in the parking lot and nab Rachel Morris before she even went in. Savannah insisted that they wait in her Mustang, claiming that she had spent as much time in his landfill of a vehicle as she could stand for one week.

"Did you get a chance to talk to Clarissa?" she asked, once they had settled in and were munching on some candy bars and sipping sodas.

"Yeah, I was there when you called and told me about the lab."

"How'd that go?"

"Once I leaned on her, she pretty much confirmed everything the Morris kid told us. Bill did confess to her that night, told her about the affair, the blackmail, and Rachel's twenty-four-hour ultimatum. She said he called Rachel in front of her and told her it was over. She also told me that she had just paid him a 'shitload' of money right before he told her about him and Rachel. But when she insisted that he give it back, he said it had already been given to the bookies he owed."

"Did she give you an actual figure?"

"No, I tried to weasel it out of her, but she just kept using the term, 'shitload.' However much that is. I think she was embarrassed that she'd actually been naïve enough not to realize that Bill was in on it with Rachel. Until that night, she thought he was just the delivery-man."

"He was delivering all right. Did she admit that she smacked him and told him she wanted to kill him?"

"I had to lean hard to get that out of her, but yeah, she spilled it all."

"I gotta tell you, Dirk, this guy with his lifestyle—he was walking a tightrope with nitroglycerin in his hand over a pit of rabid crocodiles. It was just a matter of time until somebody got their fill of him and put him out of their misery."

"But who? Usually, we can't find any suspect. Now we're swimming in them."

"And speaking of suspects, here comes one now."

She pointed to the parking lot entrance, where the old maroon Volvo station wagon was driving in, a disgruntled-looking redhead behind the wheel.

"I am not looking forward to another round with this gal," Dirk said. "And especially right on the heels of her sister."

"I hear you."

"But there's one thing about dealing with females like this," he said sweetly. "They make me appreciate you."

"Kiss my heinie all you want. You're still doing the talking with this one. I'm just along for the ride."

"Damn."

* * *

Thanks to Rebecca Shipton, Savannah and Dirk had a nice, secure interview room with no windows to jump from, or objects of art that could be used as weapons. Just a simple table with a few chairs was all they needed or wanted for their little chat with Rachel Morris.

She was already furious that they refused to let her see her son until after their conversation. And Savannah couldn't really blame her. But they had things about the case they had to ask her and, if they could, they wanted to find out why her son was refusing to see her.

"I think this is illegal," she said, pushing away the chair Dirk offered her and standing with her hands on her hips, feet spread apart in a battle stance. "You have to let me see my kid. I just drove for a long time—"

"We know how far it is," Dirk told her. "We just drove it ourselves. And if you want to see your kid sometime soon, you'll sit down and tell us what we need to hear."

"You don't have the right to hold me for anything!" she shouted at them, her New York accent even stronger than usual. Savannah noticed it seemed to intensify along with her temper.

"Oh, you'd be surprised what we've got on you," Savannah said smoothly.

" 'Got on me?' What's that supposed to mean?"

"Rachel," Dirk said, "I'm going to ask you just a couple of questions, and if you know what's good for you, you'll be perfectly honest with me. If you aren't, things are going to go very bad for you very quickly. Got it?"

She didn't reply. But she gave a curt nod.

Savannah thought she could see a bit of fear in those guarded eyes, but she couldn't be sure. The only thing she was sure of was that Rachel Morris would make a darned good poker player.

"Think carefully before you answer this, Rachel," she told her. "Have you ever been inside Bill Jardin's new Jaguar?"

"Oh, he got that? He'd talked about it. I didn't know he'd actually bought one."

"So, that's a 'no?' " Dirk said.

"That's a 'no.' I was never in Bill's new Jaguar."

"Okay." Dirk gave Savannah a satisfied smirk. Then he turned back to Rachel. "Do you dye your hair red?"

"What kind of question is that to ask a woman?" she snapped back.

Savannah glanced over the short, too-bright red hair with its even tone. She could distinctly see gray roots. "She colors her hair," she told Dirk. "You can go on to the next question."

He did. "Ms. Morris, do you sometimes wear a Yankees baseball cap?"

Suddenly, the poker face disappeared and a worried woman appeared in its place. Very worried. In fact, Savannah had seen trapped rats with happier, more contented expressions.

"Why?" was all she would say.

Dirk looked at Savannah, and she knew what he was thinking—whether to go for it or not. She gave him a slight nod.

"Because," he said, "we found a Yankees baseball cap in Bill Jardin's trunk. It had short red hair in it. I'm pretty sure that if we run DNA on those hairs, they're going to be a match to you."

Rachel's entire body sagged, and for a moment, Savannah thought she was going to faint. But she reached out and grabbed the back of a chair. Slowly, she lowered herself onto it.

"That's your cap in Bill's trunk," Dirk said. "And you just told me that you've never been in his car before. You want to tell me how it got there?"

Still, the stunned Rachel just sat there, silent, looking sick.

"And your son says that he was at Clarissa's house the

night that Bill went missing," Savannah told her. "He was looking through the window when Clarissa made Bill call you and tell you the affair was over."

"Tanner . . . he . . . he told you that?" Rachel could hardly get the words out.

"Yes," Dirk said, "so, we know that you had a good motive to kill him, scorned woman and all that."

Rachel nodded, ever so slowly, staring at the table in front of her. "Yes. Okay. I did it."

"You killed Bill Jardin," Dirk said. Savannah could see the gleam of triumph in his eyes, but he kept his voice even.

"Yes. I'll write you a confession. Whatever you need. Let's just get it over with."

Savannah stood, a bit too quickly. "I'll go get some paper and a pen," she said. She made herself walk slowly to the door. But once she was through it and had closed it behind her, she ran down the hallway to the first office she could find. "Gimme some paper and a pen," she told the startled young woman seated behind the desk. "And make it snappy! We got ourselves a hot one!"

After delivering the needed stationery supplies to Dirk, Savannah reluctantly made her way to the room where Rebecca had stashed Tanner Morris.

She wasn't looking forward to this one bit, telling a teenaged boy that his mother was a murderer. Although, something told her the news wouldn't be a total shock to him.

When she got to the sleeping room that opened onto the common area day room, she stood at the small window and watched him for a moment. He was sitting on a cot, staring at a tiny television that was mounted to the wall, high in the corner. He was hunched over, his knees drawn up under his chin, his arms around his legs.

Savannah thought he looked terribly unhappy. She felt awful that she was about to make him even more miserable. After their talk, his life would never be the same.

She opened the door and stepped inside. "Tanner," she said. "Can we talk?"

He nodded, but she couldn't help but notice the fear in his eyes. "Is my mom here yet?"

"Yes," she said, sitting on a small chair next to his cot. "But you won't be seeing her . . . for a while. She's with Detective Coulter."

"Why? Why is she talking to him?" He looked confused and nervous as he fiddled with the strap on his sandal.

"He's asking her some questions about what happened to Bill Jardin."

His eyes searched hers frantically. "And?"

"And it seems she . . . well . . . she knows what happened to him."

"She does?"

Savannah nodded. "In fact, she knows more about what happened than we do. She's filling Detective Coulter in on the details now."

"But what's she telling him?"

His big eyes were filled with dread, as though he was anticipating her answer, but that didn't make it any easier when Savannah said, "She's confessed, Tanner. She told us she did it."

He collapsed onto the bed, crying and pounding it at the same time with his fist. "It *was* her!" he shouted between sobs. "It *was* her! I knew it! I knew it was her I heard!"

Savannah let him cry for a moment, to get some of it out of his system, but then she reached over and grabbed him by the shoulders, forcing him to sit up.

"What do you mean, Tanner? What do you mean, 'It was her.' How did you know she did it?"

"Because I heard her do it. I was in the trunk!" His eyes were wild with fear and sorrow, his voice ragged as he wept.

"In Bill Jardin's trunk?"

"Yes. After he and Clarissa had their big fight, after he called my mom and told her good-bye, Clarissa came out of the house and went running up in the hills. After a while, Bill came out, too, with a suitcase in his hand. I followed him to the garage and saw him throw it into his trunk. Then he called some girl on his cell phone and was talking all mushy to her, about how much he loved her and couldn't wait to see her. Said he had to go somewhere to take care of something. And then he wanted to meet her at their special place, and they'd go to Las Vegas that night."

"That must have been very hard for you to hear," Savannah said.

"It was. I hated her, whoever she was. I wanted to see her, to find out what she looked like, why she was so much better than my mom and me." He shuddered. "Bill had walked away from the car while he was talking to her. He was looking out the garage window, probably to make sure Clarissa didn't come back and hear him. He hadn't closed the trunk all the way, so I snuck over there when he wasn't looking and got inside. Then I closed it."

"Weren't you afraid of getting locked inside?"

"No, the new cars have those special locks inside so that you can get out if you're locked in. You know, emergency releases."

"Oh, okay. I drive a '65 Mustang, but . . . never mind . . . what happened then?"

"He drove off with me in the trunk. We went for a ways. I don't know how far, because it's hard to tell when you're in a trunk. And then he stopped and turned the engine off. He sat there awhile. I could hear him fiddling with the radio, changing songs and stuff."

The boy drew his legs up to his chest again and hugged them tightly. Savannah could see he was shivering.

"And then," he said, "I heard another car drive up. And . . ."

"It's okay. Go on."

"And I heard her get out of her car and start to walk up to Bill's car. He said, 'Took you long enough. I've got things to do. Here's your—and then, blam! I heard the shot. I hoped it was a firecracker, but I knew it was too loud for that."

"You said you heard *her*. How did you know it was your mom?"

"Right after the shot, I heard her say his name, and she was crying. She said his name over and over and then she said, 'I'm sorry. But you broke my heart. You threw me away. You shouldn't have done that."

"And it was your mom's voice you heard. You're sure?"

"It was kind of muffled sounding from there in the trunk, but yeah. I was pretty sure it was her."

"And what happened, after he was shot, after you heard her say that?"

"She walked back to her car and got in. And then she drove off."

"What did you do?"

"I waited awhile. I was so scared, that I didn't know what to do. But finally, when I didn't hear anything else, I got out."

He covered his face with his hands. "And that's when I saw him, slumped over, not moving. It was really dark there, so I couldn't be sure, but I thought he was probably dead."

Gently, she reached over and took his hands away from his face. "It's all over, Tanner," she said. "You endured a terrible thing, but it's not happening now. It's done. What did you do after that?"

"I walked back to San Carmelita."

"That's a very long ways. That's how you got those blisters."

"Yeah, it took me all the rest of the night. It didn't matter. I didn't have anyplace to go. I couldn't go back to the motel, to my mom, after I knew what she'd done. I wouldn't have been able to look at her. Bill was a jerk, and he did her wrong, but you shouldn't kill a guy for being a jerk."

"No, you shouldn't, Tanner," she said. "And that's why your mom is being arrested. She'll have a trial and probably be sent to prison for a long time. I'm so sorry."

"I know. I was afraid of that," he said.

"But you'll be okay. I'm going to talk to Ms. Shipton about you, and we'll see about getting you out of here as quick as we can. You'll be placed with a good family who'll look after you for awhile, till all this mess gets sorted out."

He nodded. "Thank you."

She couldn't resist reaching over and taking him into her arms. She was afraid that a kid his size would resist being hugged by a woman he hardly knew. But he melted against her, sobbing on her shoulder for a long time.

When he finally pulled back, he seemed exhausted.

"Lay back there on the cot, sugar," she told him. "Rest a spell. You've been through a lot. Way too much for a fella your age."

He did as she told him. She reached for a blanket that lay, folded, across the foot of the bed. Spreading it over him, she said, "You get some sleep. When you wake up, you'll feel a mite better."

But as she left the room and walked through the facility, she knew that Tanner Morris wasn't going to feel better when he woke up. Or the next day, or the day after that, or the day after that.

This is a biggy, she thought. *One of life's deepest wounds that leaves a permanent scar. No, he'll never get over this one.*

Chapter 23

On her drive to the safe house to give Sharona the news about Rachel's confession, Savannah couldn't muster her usual happiness at solving the case. In fact, she couldn't recall a time she had been less pleased with her own results.

While Rachel may have deserved whatever was coming to her, having taken a human life, Savannah thought of Tanner's face and any sense of satisfaction evaporated.

Even the orange groves, the sight of the trees filled with snowy blossoms glowing against the shiny dark leaves and the heavenly perfume they created, weren't enough to lift her spirits.

Some cases just didn't have happy endings.

So much for "closure."

At least Sharona will get to go home, Savannah thought as the little cottage came into view. Dirk had gone to the county jail and personally informed Pinky Moretti about Rachel's confession. Dirk had pointed out to Pinky that Sharona didn't have his money, and Pinky and his crew were off the hook for the murder. So there was no reason why Pinky and company would be coming after Sharona.

Savannah was looking forward to this visit, a small bright spot in a dark situation. At least someone would get their life back.

When she drove up to the cottage, she saw Sharona sitting on the ground beside the house, weeding a flower bed. She looked happy and contented with dirt smeared on both knees, all over her shorts and tank top, and a big smudge of it on her nose.

She smiled and waved when she saw Savannah's car.

"Hey girl!" Savannah said as she climbed out of the Mustang and walked over to her. "Whatcha doin' there? Communing with Mother Earth?"

Sharona laughed and wiped her forehead, leaving a brown streak there, too.

"I am," she said. "I noticed that these flower beds needed weeding. It's good therapy. Sort of symbolic of what I need to do with my life in general, you know?"

"I know exactly what you mean. Sometimes you just have to get in there and figure out what you're keeping and what you aren't."

"And getting rid of the briars and brambles."

Savannah reached down and picked up a few of the discarded weeds. "Are any of these guys named Aldo?"

Sharona nodded. "He's already in the trash can over there. He was one of the first to go."

"Good girl. Sounds like all this country air has cleared your head."

"More than you know. I've already bought a ticket to go back home to Indiana. My sister says I can stay with her for a month or two until I get on my feet."

"That's great, Sharona. And I have some more news for you. We've solved the case. Rachel Morris, Clarissa's twin sister, has confessed to killing Bill. Dirk's talked to

Pinky and everything's settled there. I wouldn't hang out with those people anymore, if I were you, but I don't think you have to worry about them now. You can go home to Indiana with a clean slate."

Sharona took several moments to absorb what she had been told, then she closed her eyes and slowly shook her head. "I can't believe it," she said. "Why did she do it? Bill told me about that gal Rachel. He said she took it hard when he broke up with her a few months ago, but . . ."

"A few months ago?"

"Yeah, he dumped her for me."

"Oh, okay." Savannah decided not to tell her that Bill had been two-timing her. What was the point in adding to her burden? Wasn't it bad enough, just losing a fiancé to murder? She didn't need to know everything.

"So, when are you going home to Indiana?" Savannah asked her.

"My flight is tonight. I'm taking a redeye." She stood and brushed the dirt off her hands and knees. "I can't wait. I haven't seen my sister's new baby girl yet. It's going to feel really good to be home."

Savannah thought about her own sister, sitting at her house, pouting and waiting to be taken to the beach. She sighed. "Family. What would we do without them?"

"I guess I'd better get busy," Sharona said. "I've got things to do. Let me go grab a quick shower and rinse off this dirt, then you can take me home."

"Have you got a lot of packing to do?"

"Not that much," she said with a sad smile. "I travel light."

They walked into the house, and Savannah settled herself on the sofa with the crossword book and a pencil. "Do you mind if I finish your puzzle here?" she called out to Sharona, who was in the bathroom, getting ready to shower.

When she got no answer, she glanced over the rows

and columns, seeing if any of the answers jumped out at her. None did. Sharona had already gotten all the easy ones.

Bored and tired, she laid the book aside, got out her cell phone, and called Dirk.

"Yeah?" he answered with his usual charm.

"Whatcha doin'?"

"I just wasted an hour with that Rachel chick. I was trying to squeeze her to give up the gun, but she's got an attorney now, and she's not saying much."

"You've got her written confession. You don't need the murder weapon, do you?"

"Not really, but it's a loose end, you know. Like that '666' phone number. I don't like loose ends."

The phone on the end table began to ring.

"Somebody's calling here," she said. "I'll talk to you later."

She hung up and reached for the house phone. "Hello," she said.

A very cheery female voice on the other end said, "Hi, Sharona. It's Lucinda from Worldwide Travel. I just wanted you to know that I was able to get those first-class tickets for you and the honeymoon suite there in Casa del Sol was available, so you're all set."

"Uh, thanks."

"I so-o-o-o envy you! You and Aldo are going to just lo-o-ove Cancun! I'd ask you to take me along, but since it's a honeymoon, I guess you won't want company."

"No, I suppose not." Savannah glanced at the closed bathroom door. She could still hear the shower running. "Um, Lucinda," she said, her voice low, "I don't remember for sure . . . did I already give you my credit card number?"

"What? Boy, you *must* be excited. Don't you remember we had that whole conversation about you paying cash . . . about how we don't usually have that much lay-

ing around here at one time, but we'll take money however we can get it?"

"Oh, right. Duh. I guess I *am* a little scatterbrained
right now," she replied, trying her best to squelch her
Southern accent.

"So, we'll see you soon?"

"Yeah. Soon."

"We close at five."

"Gotcha. Thanks a lot."

Savannah hung up the phone and stood there a moment, her thoughts spinning.

She glanced around the room and spotted Sharona's
purse lying on the carpet at the end of the sofa.

Still listening for the shower, she rushed over to it, and
grabbed it up off the floor.

She didn't even have to look inside. She could feel the
heft of it. And she knew all too well what a purse that
heavy meant.

She sighed, shook her head, and said to the closed
bathroom door, "Ah, Sharona. Damn it, girl, you're good.
I'll give you that."

A few minutes later, when Sharona came out of the
bathroom, a towel wrapped around her hair and another
around her body, Savannah was sitting on the sofa, the
crossword book on her lap.

"Boy, I feel better," Sharona said. "Nothing like a cool
shower to perk you up."

"Yeah, nothing like it," Savannah replied. "Hope you
don't mind that I'm working on your puzzle here."

"No, not at all. But I was wondering, is it okay if I take
the book along with me on the plane? It's a long flight."

"It certainly is. How many hours is it . . . from here to
Indiana?"

Sharona hesitated only a second. "Oh, I'm not sure.

Three or four, I guess. And I have a few of your good cookies left over. I think I'll take them along, too. They don't feed you now on planes, I've heard."

Savannah fixed her with a level stare that Dirk called, "shooting those blue lasers." Her voice even and monotone, she said, "Oh, I wouldn't fret too much. I think they still feed the folks in first class."

Something flickered in Sharona's eyes, but it was gone in an instant. She gave a tense little laugh and said, "Yeah, but first class . . . who can afford that these days?"

"You'd better get dressed," Savannah said. "You don't want to miss that flight. I'm sure they're looking forward to seeing you back home. Your sister and her new baby girl, that is."

"Right. I'll just go get dressed."

She disappeared into the bedroom and then reappeared in record time, wearing jeans and a sexy wrap top in a colorful, tropical print. She was carrying her suitcase. "Okay," she said. "All set."

Savannah shielded the cell phone in her hand with the book as she punched the "send" button. Her phone dialed Dirk's infamous "666" number. A second later, Sharona's purse, lying on the carpet beside the sofa, began to play a merry tune.

Sharona glanced at it and seemed to freeze in place. A look that Savannah could only describe as "quite worried" crossed her face.

The song played louder and louder, and finally Savannah said, "Aren't you going to answer that?"

Sharona stared at Savannah, her eyes searching her face. But Savannah was a pretty mean poker player herself, and she had on her best deadpan expression.

"It's probably just my sister calling again," Sharona said. "She's all excited about me coming. I don't have time to chat with her now."

"You might oughta check. It could be the airline calling to tell you that your flight's been cancelled. You know the way they are these days."

"Yeah . . . okay."

Slowly, Sharona walked over and picked her purse up from the floor. Reaching inside, she pulled out her phone. With her hand wrapped around it, she glanced down at the caller ID, and her eyes widened.

She looked up at Savannah. "What . . . what are you . . . ?"

When she saw that Savannah was holding her own phone up for her to see, she shoved hers back into her purse. "What are you doing?" she asked, sounding a bit unnerved.

"I'm calling a phone number that ends with '666.' Detective Coulter's been calling it for days, trying to figure out who has the phone now. But nobody's answered."

"Okay." Sharona sat down hard on a nearby chair, her purse clutched to her chest. "And so . . . what's that supposed to mean?"

"It means that you have the phone that Bill Jardin called the night he died. The best we can figure, within an hour, or thereabouts, of the time he died."

"So?"

"But you said you never heard from him that night. You were so worried, because it wasn't like him not to call."

She shrugged. "I guess I forgot."

"I'll bet," Savannah said, "that if I were to look at that phone of yours, I'd see quite a few interesting calls, both incoming and outgoing. Unless, of course, you're smart enough to have deleted all the history."

"What are you saying? Are you accusing me of something?"

"First of all, your phone . . . it's stolen. Somebody took it from an elderly woman across town."

"I didn't steal this phone. Somebody gave it to me."

"Aldo?"

When she didn't reply, Savannah said, "Does Aldo rip off old ladies?"

"No, he certainly does not! He told me that he found it on a table in the library."

"Yeah, Aldo strikes me as a big reader, one of those intellectual types."

"He's not that bad!"

"Not exactly a weed outside in that trash can either, is he?"

"I don't know what you're talking about, and you're going to make me miss my plane if we just sit here like this."

Savannah laid her phone on the sofa cushion next to her. "Oh, I wouldn't worry about that," she said. "You've got all the time in the world. In fact, I'd say you'll get thirty, maybe even forty years. Premeditated, first-degree homicide. That's a hefty sentence."

Yes, she's getting the picture now, Savannah thought as she watched Sharona's face change from red to a ghastly gray.

Savannah continued, "We thought that Bill called Rachel that night and told her their affair was over. But it was you he called. He was the one who dialed the phone when Clarissa insisted he make the call. How was she to know who he was talking to?"

"I don't know what you're talking about. Bill never dumped me. We were in love. We were going to move away together."

"You can drop that story now, Sharona. That was never the plan for either one of you. Bill was lying to you. He was moving to Vegas, all right, but with another woman. With Rachel."

Sharona's eyes flooded with tears. "That's not true! He loved me."

"Stop with the waterworks. I'm not buying it this time. You killed him."

"I did not!"

"You're the one who called Pinky. You pretended to be Clarissa when you told him that Bill wanted to meet him later than the time they'd agreed on. Then you went to the chicken plant . . . which you know damned well wasn't a tree or a flower . . . and you blew his brains out."

The tears stopped flowing so abruptly, it was as if Sharona had turned the handle of a faucet.

"I did not," she said coolly, "and you can't prove anything anyway. You're going to charge me with murder based on what? A couple of phone calls?"

"Partly, yes. Your phone carrier's been a little slow turning the records over to Detective Coulter, but they'll get around to it pretty soon. And it'll show that it was you Bill called that night, that you were the one who got dumped."

"That's not enough to prove murder. I'm not stupid, you know."

"Well, the jury's still out on how stupid you are or aren't. But I'll bet that you took your phone with you that night when you went out to the processing plant. And if it was on, the cops can tell by the records that you were in that area."

"They can not! I mean, if a person doesn't make or receive any calls, there wouldn't be a record of where they were."

"The signal that's being sent to your phone is beamed from one tower and then another as you go from one area to the next."

"That's not true."

"It is. How do you think your phone always knows what time it is? It's receiving a signal. And there's a record of that."

"I don't believe you."

Savannah laughed. "Well, you can believe me or not,

missy. Maybe they'll explain it better at your trial. I never was all that good with techno stuff. Let's see if you're any better at explaining how you came into all that ready cash. You know, enough money to fly first class to Cancun and stay in a swanky resort . . . you and Aldo."

Sharona looked like she had just received a blow to the stomach. She clutched her purse tighter to her chest and started to shake her head. "No," she whispered, "no, no."

Savannah continued, "How much was in that envelope . . . the one you took out of Bill's glove box after you shot him? Was there a lot of blood on it, Sharona? Did you get it all off, or will the CSU find traces on some of the bills?"

Sharona didn't reply, but Savannah thought she had seen friendlier eyes on killers in a courtroom who had just been sentenced to death.

"Did it bother you at all to have to clean a man's blood and brain matter off that envelope, Sharona? Or are you just a coldhearted bitch all the way through?"

"He dumped me. We were going to get married. We were going to have a life together, but he called and said it was over, that I was never to even try to contact him again. Can you imagine how much that hurt?"

"Oh, that's going to be your defense? Crime of passion and all that crap? But that won't work either. You'd planned to murder Bill even before he called you and told you the affair was over. Pinky says you phoned him earlier that day and reset Bill's meet time to later. You did that so you could get there before Pinky, and shoot and rob Bill. You never intended to run away with the guy, just murder him and take his money. The jury's gonna take a dim view of that."

"You think I would kill somebody . . . just for money?"

"Oh, I think there was an element of payback in it, too. I'm sure that phone call from him was hard on your ego, but yeah, I'd say it was mostly for the money. You were intending to kill him that night, whether he was planning to run away with you or not."

Savannah watched her closely, weighing every expression that flitted across her face. Sharona was teetering, but not over the edge just yet. She needed another little push.

So, Savannah asked her, "Where's the gun that you shot him with? We'll find that, too, you know. And when we match the ballistics on it. They'll be able to prove that your 9mm gun shot the bullet we found at the scene. And there you go! Guilty as charged on all counts!"

That did it.

Sharona reached into her purse and pulled out a Ruger 9mm pistol. She pointed it at Savannah. "Here it is," she said, her voice as emotionless and cold as Savannah had ever heard. "Right here. This is what I shot him with."

Savannah looked down the barrel of the weapon and nodded solemnly. "Yes, that definitely looks like it would do the job."

Sharona glanced around, as though making sure no one else was present. "I can't let you live now . . . now that you know."

"I understand completely," Savannah said. "I wouldn't expect you to. If you could kill a man for money, a man you'd made love with, it shouldn't be that hard to kill me, too."

"Actually, I sort of liked you. You were nice, bringing me here, the cookie basket and all that. But you shouldn't have been so smart, figuring it all out like that."

"Yeah, well, that's what I get paid for."

Savannah reached inside her jacket, put her hand around the butt of her own gun, and started to pull it out.

"No! Don't!" Sharona shouted as she pulled the Ruger's trigger.

Savannah smiled. "And that, ladies and gentlemen of the jury," she said, "that click you just heard, was the sound of Ms. Dubarry attempting to shoot me with an empty gun."

Savannah pointed the Beretta at Sharona with her right hand and pointed to the phone with her left. "And you, my dear, have just been recorded, confessing to murder in the first degree. Oh, and by the way . . ." She nodded toward the crossword book. ". . . 21 across is 'conviction.' What do you think, is that some sort of omen? I'm sure my Granny Reid would think so."

"Savannah, you look positively stunning in that gown," John told her. "The blue satin brings out those sapphire eyes of yours and the drape of the fabric accentuates the curves of your figure so that—"

"Oh, stop. This old thing? You're just a silken-tongued lad, you are." She leaned close to him and placed a kiss on his cheek. "Now, what was that you were saying about my figure . . . ?"

They laughed, as she took his arm and he escorted her around the paradise that had, only hours ago, been her backyard.

The festivities had begun before noon, in the form of a party rental company, bearing an Arabian-style tent with sumptuous carpets, satin cushions, and faux-fur throws.

Then a florist appeared and filled the erected tent, as well as the rest of the yard, with sprays of pink and lavender roses as well as at least a hundred white candles.

Next, the caterer arrived and by dinnertime, silver trays, laden with cheese, fruit, olives, shrimp kabobs, mushroom strudel, and crostini, covered the tabletops. The exotic aroma of Bisteeya Moroccan Chicken Pie filled the air. And in the place of honor in the center of the tent, a fountain was flowing with warm, Belgian chocolate, surrounded with fresh fruits and other sweets for dipping.

A violinist, a flutist, and a cellist performed classical music as Savannah, Tammy, and Marietta descended the back stairs in their evening attire.

Savannah wore a deep blue silk wrap gown, Tammy a bright green, full-length kimono, and Marietta her tiger-striped, stretchy dress that, as advertised, was cut down to here and up to there.

All three of them had "big hair." As "big" as Marietta, a teasing comb, and a can of hair spray could get it.

They looked magnificent.

And so did their escorts. Ryan and John were at the foot of the stairs waiting for them, looking simply delicious in their tuxedos, with roses in their hands for each woman.

There was time for a few dances before the other guests began to arrive.

"Is Dirko going to wear a tux?" Tammy asked Savannah.

"Absolutely."

"I don't believe it. I've never seen him in anything but a T-shirt . . . oh . . . and the maids-a-milkin' costume you made him wear that Christmas."

"He asked me what he owed us for helping him with the case. That was my price."

And when Dirk did appear, wearing not only a tux, but an *opera* tux, complete with white cummerbund and white wing-collar shirt, Savannah thought her heart would stop.

"Lord have mercy," she said as she hurried across the lawn to greet him, her hand on her chest, "you clean up go-o-ood, boy! You look plumb fit to eat!"

"Well, enjoy it while you can," he grumbled, " 'cause this damned thing is friggen uncomfortable. You'll never get me in one again."

She glanced around quickly, to see if anyone was watching. They weren't, so she wrapped her arms around his neck, stood on tiptoe, and gave him a warm, long, sweet kiss on the lips. When she finally pulled back, she flashed him a dimpled smile, tapped him on the chest with her forefinger, and said, "Yeah? Well . . . we'll see about that."

She left him, stunned, his mouth hanging open and walked back to join Tammy and John who were nibbling on crème fraiche and caviar on cucumber slices.

"Have the guests of honor arrived yet?" Tammy asked.

"Not yet," Savannah replied. "But they sounded so pleased to be invited, I'm sure they'll be here soon."

"That must have been most fulfilling, restoring a mother's and son's relationship," John said. "Was it difficult, convincing young Tanner that his mom was innocent, in spite of her confession?"

"Not at all. I explained to him that, in her mind, she thought she was protecting her son. A mother will even confess to murder to save her child. She really believed he'd done it. Once she found out about Sharona, she denied it all."

Dirk had joined them, a glass of white wine in his hand—also a first.

"Well, aren't you suave and debonair tonight?" Tammy said, admiring his physique-flattering tuxedo.

"Quite sharp, old boy," John agreed. "Is that a Hugo Boss?"

"No, it's my brother-in-law's. He just got married, and he hadn't returned it to the rental place yet, so I borrowed it from him."

"Ah, I see." John developed a sudden coughing fit and had to excuse himself for a moment.

"I never really believed that confession anyway," Dirk said, anxious to stir the conversation to his own area of expertise. "Rachel never could tell me where the murder weapon was. She wouldn't even tell me what part of his body got shot."

"There are a few things I don't understand." Tammy licked some caviar off the end of her finger. "How could Sharona walk up to Bill like that and him not know it was her?"

"It was a moonless night," Savannah told her, "and that area is really dark. No streetlights or artificial lighting of any kind. She could see him when he opened the glove compartment because of the little light inside it. But she was standing in the dark. Besides, he thought he was meeting Pinky or one of his flunkies. He never would have expected it to be her."

"And the phone calls," Tammy continued. "We know it was Sharona he was phoning when he made that call in front of Clarissa. But how about the other call, the mushy one that Tanner overheard him make in the garage, when he told someone he wanted to meet them when he was done with Pinky? Who was that?"

"That call was to Rachel," Savannah said. "That's what makes all this ugly business even sadder. Apparently, he really was in love with Rachel and leaving Clarissa to make a home with her and Tanner. If Sharona hadn't killed him, the three of them would probably be in Las Vegas together right now."

Dirk sniffed. "Well, before you make this guy 'Man of the Year,' remember that he was juggling women right and left, and had a major gambling addiction. He wasn't exactly family material."

"That's true," Savannah said. "They're probably better off without him in the long run."

"How is Ruby Jardin?" John asked, rejoining them with his wineglass refilled. "Was she terribly disappointed that Clarissa didn't turn out to be the killer?"

"Terribly," Savannah said. "In fact, she was so disappointed that I sent Tammy to the bank right away to cash

her check. I think she'll get over it, though, once she real-
izes that she really did want to hear the truth about her
son. She really did want justice for him."

"But for right now, she's pissed?" Dirk asked.

"Oh, big-time."

Over her shoulder, she heard Marietta saying, "Why
now, don't you look just cute as a dumplin' with all that
curly red hair, and in that grownup man's tuxedo . . ."

"Oh, no. They're here and Marietta's at 'em!" Savannah turned and rushed out of the tent.

She found Marietta gushing over a very embarrassed,
formally dressed Tanner Morris. He was the picture of
adolescent awkwardness in his tuxedo. His only youthful
expression consisted of a pair of suspenders with skulls
and crossbones on them.

Rachel was dressed in a simple black dress with a
waist-long strand of simple white pearls . . . New York el-
egance all the way. She looked more relaxed and happier
than Savannah had ever seen her.

She even gave Savannah a hug and air kiss for a greeting.

Looking around the lavishly decorated yard, she said,
"Wow, do you guys always celebrate like this when you
close a case?"

"No. This is all a lovely gift from two of my dearest
friends." She laced her arm through Tanner's. "Come
along, and I'll introduce you to them. And after that, you
can raid the chocolate fountain."

Tanner lit up. "A chocolate *fountain*?"

"Young man. You haven't lived yet. But you're about
to experience life to its fullest."

An hour later, Savannah was dancing with Dirk, her
head resting comfortably on his shoulder, his arm warm
around her waist, holding her close.

"This is almost worth getting dressed up for," he said, pulling her even a bit closer.

"Wear a pair of three-inch heels for a few hours, buddy," she told him, "then tell me about 'uncomfortable.'"

"Those two are having fun," he said, nodding toward Tanner, who was enthralled with Tammy and had been discussing computers with her for the past half hour. Rachel was between Ryan and John, and the three of them were embroiled in a hot, literary discussion.

"Yes, they are. I'm glad," Savannah said. "They have some healing to do, too."

"Did you invite Clarissa to this?"

"I did. I wasn't at all surprised when she turned me down. I don't know if I could forgive my sister for something like that, either. It's a bit much to ask."

"At least Clarissa isn't going to press charges against her for the blackmail."

"Yes, but that's as much to Clarissa's advantage as it is Rachel's. Clarissa is going to have enough bad press, just explaining how her husband got shot by a girlfriend while paying off his cockfighting debts to a bookie. I shudder to think what the *True Informer* is going to do to her."

He laughed, "Yeah, I'm sure you're sick about it."

"Clarissa's not as bad as I thought. She's a bitch, but that's not an altogether bad thing to be."

"If you say so." He nodded toward Marietta, who was sitting, dejected beside the fountain, drowning her sorrows in Belgian chocolate. "And speaking of sisters, how is yours?"

"Cranky. She had it out today with Vidalia on the phone, but in the end, they made up. She promised not to ever wear jeans like Vi's in front of Butch again. Vi apologized for calling her a 'godforsaken, brazen hussy slut.'"

"Whoa, tough words."

"We Reid women aren't known for holding back. I'm

taking her to Santa Barbara tomorrow. We'll go to the pier, hang out on the beach, and she can try out her new red bikini as a pickup tool. I'll make it all up to her, see that she has a nice vacation after all."

She looked up at him and saw that he was smiling down at her, his eyes soft and kind. She had the distinct impression he hadn't been listening to her, which was nothing unusual.

But for tonight, that was okay. She was in a forgiving mood.

He really did look gorgeous in that tux.

"What were you thinking about just then?" she asked him.

"Actually, my mind had drifted," he admitted. "I was thinking how nice you smell."

"That's Marietta's hair spray. She darned near drowned me in it this afternoon."

"No, it's not hair spray. You always smell like this."

"Oh, thank you."

"And I was thinking how nice it is to dance with you. We don't dance together enough."

"I think this is the first time we've ever danced."

"That's what I mean. We should do it more." He gave her a quick spin that nearly lifted her off her feet, but he caught her, steadied her, and pulled her against him again. "You asked me about my dream before," he said, suddenly looking quite vulnerable.

"What?"

"Before, you seemed surprised when I said I'd had a dream, too. You know, something I'd wanted to do, besides be a cop."

"Oh, right. What was it?"

"Don't laugh."

"I won't. I promise."

"I wanted to be a dancer. And if you ever tell anybody, I'll deny it and get you back, big-time."

"I won't tell a soul. I swear. A dancer? Really?"

"Well, not like John Travolta. More like Fred Astaire, when he was waltzing with Ginger Rogers. I always thought that would be cool, to be able to glide around a floor like that with a pretty lady in your arms."

She put her face against his and gave him a kiss on the ear. "I think that's a wonderful dream to have. And I'm glad you shared it with me."

"It's not the sort of thing I'd want the guys at the station to hear."

"Of course not."

"Or Ryan."

"God forbid."

"Or John."

"It'll just be our little secret."

"'Cause if any of them found out, I'd have to move to Mexico and take up deep-sea fishing or bullfighting or some other overtly masculine occupation."

She sighed. "Fred, just shut the hell up, and dance with me."

"Okay, since you asked so nicely, and since you smell so good . . . Ginger."

"Ah-h-h . . . nice," she said, snuggling into his warmth. "Nice, Fred. Very, very nice."

Savannah Reid may have a few extra curves on her full-figured body, but that hasn't stopped her from becoming one of California's most successful private investigators. Her latest case puts her hot on the trail of a shady weight loss therapist who's made a killing treating—and cheating—his overweight patients. The question is, did he kill his wife, too?

Dr. Robert Wellman claims his breakthrough hypnosis techniques can help anyone shed unwanted fat in record time. But while countless weight-challenged folks have flocked to his popular clinic, most have only lighter wallets to show for it. Still, Dr. Wellman seems to have it all, until his wife Maria is found dead at the bottom of a cliff outside the Wellmans' seaside estate—and it's clear she didn't go down without a fight.

Savannah is more than happy to help her good friend, Detective Sergeant Dirk Coulter, investigate Maria's untimely death. The clues all seem to point to murder, from the broken statuary to the trampled flowerbeds surrounding the deadly precipice. And since Dr. Wellman appears to be the only viable suspect, Savannah is sure it's an open and shut case. But she's about to learn that appearances can be oh-so deceiving. Pound for pound, this is shaping up to be one of Savannah's toughest cases ever. But she'd better find the killer soon . . . or else the bodies will just keep piling up . . .

Please turn the page for an exciting sneak peek of G.A. McKevett's newest Savannah Reid mystery WICKED CRAVING coming next month!

Chapter 1

Savannah Reid rolled down the window of the rented pickup, breathed in the fresh sea-scented air, and decided it was a perfect day in sunny California. But then, barring earthquakes, mudslides, and brush fires, most Southern California days were pert nigh perfect.

She vacillated between being deeply grateful she had moved from rural Georgia to the picturesque seaside town of San Carmelita, and being bored to death with "perfect." She missed the drama of an old-fashioned, southern thunderstorm, complete with all-hell's-done-broke-loose lightning crashing around you and the scream of tornado sirens going off, warning you to shake some tail feathers and get your tail—feathers and all—into the nearest storm cellar.

Ah, yes, she thought, watching the palm trees glisten in the tropical noonday sun. *There is nothing quite like huddling with your granny and eight siblings in a spider-infested tornado shelter at two in the morning, storm raging above you, to bring a family together.*

"And we are close," she whispered, thinking of her

loved ones in Georgia, so far away. "So close it's a wonder we haven't murdered one another yet."

"Murdered who?" Dirk asked as he guided the pickup truck away from the downtown area and headed toward the poor side of town. The part of San Carmelita that didn't have perfectly matched palm trees lining the streets. The part where windows had bars, not flower boxes, and the only fresh paint on the building walls was gang graffiti. The part where you were more likely to see a pit bull chained to somebody's front porch than a Chihuahua poking its head out of somebody's purse.

"What?" she said to the guy sitting in the driver's seat next to her. Detective Sergeant Dirk Coulter was still with the San Carmelita Police Department.

She wasn't. And on most days, she was grateful for that. Occasionally, she waxed a bit bitter about the fact that she had been dismissed. But those days only came along about once a month . . . like most of her truly dark moods. And a bar of chocolate or a dish of ice cream usually put her world right again.

"You were talking to yourself," he told her.

"Was not."

"Were, too."

"Well, do you have to bring it up and make me feel like a nitwit who's losing my marbles?"

"Don't snap at me. You told me to tell you . . . said you wanted to break the habit."

"Oh, right. Sorry." She sighed and wondered if she could blame her forgetfulness on perimenopause. After all, now that she was solidly in her mid-forties—and if she didn't admit that she'd been forgetful her whole life—it could float, excuse-wise. And it would carry her through to menopause and past to senility.

"I'm forgetting stuff lately," she said, "because I'm approaching the 'change o' life.' You wouldn't know anything about it. It's a woman thing."

"I know it's not why you're talking to yourself. You've been doing that for twenty years." He slowed the truck down to drive over a particularly deep drainage dip in the road and checked his cargo in the mirror. "But that might be why you've been extra irritable lately."

She shot him a look. "Ever consider it might be because you've been exceptionally irritating?"

"No."

"No, you haven't been irritating?"

"No, I haven't considered it might be me. I'd rather blame it on you and your hormones."

"A dangerous thing to do, blaming anything on a woman's hormones."

"You brought it up."

"True."

She didn't like this—him winning two arguments in a row. She decided to just keep quiet and say nothing for a while.

That never lasted long.

"It's just that I've been bored lately," she said, fifteen seconds later, as they headed deeper into a valley that stretched from the sea into the dry, brown, scrub brush–covered hills.

The tattoo parlors, pawn shops, porn stores, and junk-yards had given way to tiny, dilapidated stucco houses and yards covered with dead, brown grass, surrounded by sagging fences.

Many of the inhabitants sat on sagging sofas on sagging porches, wearing saggy clothes and saggy facial expressions—much like many of the inhabitants of the poor, rural town where she had been raised.

Savannah understood despair. She knew, all too well, the toll it exacted on the human spirit.

"Do you miss being on the job?" he asked. "Is that why you're bored?"

She considered his question honestly before answering. Did she miss being a police officer? The constant adrenaline rushes? The camaraderie with the other cops? The fascinating view of ever-changing human drama? Having drunks throw up on her shoes?

"I do sometimes," she admitted. "Mostly when I don't have any clients. Private investigation can get pretty mundane when you don't have a single case to investigate. It's been a bit lonely at the Moonlight Magnolia Detective Agency lately."

"And that's why you hang with me," he said, giving her a grin and a poke with his elbow.

"That and all this philosophical, mind-expanding conversation." She looked him over, taking in the Harley-Davidson T-shirt that had, in a former life, been black, but had gone through a navy blue stage and was now a muddy chocolate brown. "And your sense of style."

She glanced at herself in the truck's side mirror and saw a woman who wasn't exactly a fashion plate herself. Her thick, dark hair had a mind of its own, so she pretty much let it do its wayward-curls thing. Clean skin with a bit of lip gloss and mascara, hastily applied, were the extent of her daily beauty rituals. And her wardrobe was only a notch above Dirk's on any given day—a lightweight blazer over a simple cotton shirt with jeans or linen slacks. The blazer hid the Beretta strapped to her side. And the cotton and linen kept her cool under the California sun.

Years ago, when they had first met, both Savannah and Dirk had turned heads, especially when they were in uniform, before their detective days. And even though Dirk's T-shirt might be faded, and they both had gained some extra poundage here and there, in Savannah's mind, Dirk was still a stud, she was a babe, and as a pair, they were both pretty darned hot stuff.

On the seat between them lay the empty sack that had

recently held two apple fritters and two cups of coffee, all compliments of the Patty Cake Bakery.

Patty, the blonde bimbo baker, liked the way Dirk filled out his worn jeans and, apparently, didn't mind the old T-shirt, because she was always generous, doling out the sugar and caffeine. She was also a major cop groupie, which irked Savannah and pleased Dirk to no end.

Since Dirk was also in his mid-forties—a tad past his "glory days"—he was constantly starving for attention from the opposite sex, wherever he could get it. He wallowed in every bit that came his way, even from a moderately desperate, blatantly oversexed donut clerk.

Long ago, Savannah had gotten sick of the goo-goo eyes and the silly tittering and the deliberately deep bending over the counter while Patty was waiting on them. But Savannah kept her mouth shut. Patty was as well known for her generously frosted maple bars as she was for her appetite for the boys in blue, and Savannah was a woman with her priorities in order . . . having a healthy appetite of her own.

She glanced down at her ample figure and wondered briefly how many of Patty's maple bars and apple fritters she was toting around with her on any given day. Several pounds worth, to be sure. But Savannah liked to think that most of her "extra poundage" was well placed. And the admiring glances she got from quite a few guys told her that Patty's pastries were being put to good use.

The guy sitting beside her was one of those. Frequently, she caught him giving her a sideways look that wasn't very different from the ones Patty gave him when she was sacking up the goods. And, considering how long Savannah and Dirk had worked together—first as partners on the San Camelita Police Department and then as investigators of numerous homicide cases—she found it most complimentary that he still noticed and enjoyed her curves.

But then he sped up a bit too much and hit a pothole, jarring every bone in her body.

"Dangnation, Dirk," she snapped. "If I had dentures, they'd be in my lap. Would you take it easy?"

He loved it when she criticized his driving. "Hey, I didn't do nothin' wrong! You know they never fix the road out here. Besides, I can't drive like an old lady if you wanna nail this guy."

He had her there.

Savannah was just as eager as he was to slap a fresh pair of handcuffs on Norbert "Stumpy" Weyerhauser. And just because Stumpy's mom, Myrtle, had told them he was home an hour ago, didn't mean he would hang around. If he smelled a rat—or a cop sting operation— he'd be making tracks out of town.

"Do you think she bought it?" Dirk asked for the fourth time.

"Who? Myrtle?"

He nodded.

"Oh, yeah." Savannah chuckled at the memory of the telephone call her assistant had made on Dirk's behalf earlier. "You should have heard Tammy laying it on thick." Savannah dropped her southern accent and donned Tammy's valley-girl tone. " 'Yes, Mrs. Weyerhauser, it's true! Your son, Norbert, has won a forty-one inch, high-definition, flat-screen television! If you can assure me that he'll be home to sign for it personally this afternoon, your entire family will be able to watch the Super Bowl in style this weekend!' "

Dirk frowned. "She said forty-one inch?"

"Yeah, I think so. Why?"

"I don't think they make a forty-one-inch. I told her to say it was forty-two."

Savannah shrugged. "Oh well. So, Stumpy gets shorted an inch. He's probably used to it."

"What?"

Grinning, she said, "Didn't you ever notice that Stumpy and his limbs are normal height and length?"

"uh . . . yeah . . . I guess."

"So, where did he get that nickname? I'm thinking from a former wife or girlfriend, someone who knew him intimately."

Dirk smiled. "You're a nasty, evil woman, Van. I like the way you think."

"Well, you know me." She shrugged. "I have a soft spot in my heart for nimrods who break into elderly ladies' houses, steal from them, and smack them around. I think about Granny Reid, and then I have this overwhelming need to beat them to death with a brick of week-old cornbread."

"Yeah, me, too. I can't tell you how happy I was to hear that this dude had violated his parole. I begged the captain to let me be the one to bring him in."

As they neared the street where Stumpy, robber and senior-citizen abuser, lived, they both dropped the casual banter and assumed an all-business demeanor. Stump wasn't known for carrying deadly weapons or assaulting anybody who was actually big enough or strong enough to fight back, but he was still a convicted felon. And they were pretty sure he'd have pretty strong objections to going back to prison. So, they couldn't exactly sleepwalk through the act of nabbing him.

"When we get there, you go to the front door," Savannah said. "I get to cover the back."

"No way!"

"that's the price I charge for going along."

"But he always runs out the back door!"

"I know. I read his sheet. Why do you think I want to cover the rear?"

"Hey, I'm the cop and—"

"Don't you even go there, buddy. If I wanted to *watch* cops doing their thing, I'd be home with my feet up, eating Godiva chocolate, and staring at the TV."

"Damn," Dirk grumbled. "I should have had Jack Mc-Murty or Mike Farnon come along instead of you. They take orders a lot better."

"Yeah, but they wouldn't have come. They don't like you."

Actually, nobody in the SCPD liked Dirk. Most respected him, even envied him; he was a gifted detective. But he never received invitations to hang out at the local bar after hours or drop by for a tri-tip sandwich when somebody in the department threw a barbecue.

Normally, Savannah wouldn't have mentioned that to a person. She wasn't cruel, as a rule. But she knew Dirk didn't care. He didn't have a people-pleasing bone in his body. And long ago she had decided to be Dirk when she grew up. He saved so much energy . . . not giving a flying fig what anybody thought of him.

"But *you* like me," he said with more than a touch of little-boy vulnerability in his voice.

Okay, he cared a little what a few people thought—the people he loved. And he could count those on one hand.

She gave him a dimpled grin. "Oh, I'm plumb crazy about you, but I still get the rear of the house. End of discussion."

Dirk pulled the truck over to the curb. "Then get out here. The house is up there on the right. The yellow one."

As she started to climb out of the truck, he added, "Watch yourself. He's got a pit bull in the backyard."

She froze, one foot on the ground, staring at him, mouth half-open. "Are you yanking my chain?"

He grinned broadly. "Yeah."

"You lyin' sack!" She got out, slammed the door, and said through the open window, "I'll get you back. See if I don't"

She strolled along the street, picking her path among chunks of broken concrete that had once been a sidewalk, tree roots, weeds, and the leavings of dogs whose owners didn't carry pooper-scoopers.

Glancing up and down the block on both sides of the street, she didn't see anyone looking out the window, sitting on the porch, chatting with the neighbors, or trimming any hedges. Not a lot of hedges got trimmed regularly in this neighborhood.

As she got closer to the yellow house, she eyed the blue one next to it. There were no cars in the driveway. Instead of curtains, faded, flowered sheets covered the windows. The back yard was accessible and, from what she could see, there were no signs of a watchdog.

Looking back, she saw that Dirk was still waiting, watching her through the pickup's dirty windshield, grinning at her. He shot her a peace sign. She shook her head and chuckled. *Some old hippies never grow up,* she thought. But she wouldn't have him any other way.

After one more glance around to make sure she wasn't being watched, she darted down the side of the blue house. It was a small, shotgun affair, long and narrow, with rooms arranged end to end—not unlike the one she had been raised in.

Less than five seconds later, she was in the backyard. From there, she could see the rear of their suspect's house.

She reached into her pocket and retrieved her cell phone. She punched a couple of buttons, and Dirk answered.

"I'm here," she said as she walked through the tangle of weeds, past a collapsed, rusty swing set, and through a broken chain-link fence.

"I'm driving up to the front," he said.

She could hear the truck approaching as she scrambled up to the yellow house and positioned herself at the corner. From here, she couldn't be seen from any of the windows, and she had a clear view of the side of the house and the rear. "I can't see the right side of the house," she whispered into the phone.

"My right or your right?" he asked.

"Your right."

Knowing Dirk, she had already done the "math." Why confuse the poor guy? He confused so easily.

"The right if you're in the house looking out, or . . .

"Dirk! Are you still in the truck, on the street, looking at the house?"

"Yeah."

"Then I'm at the left back corner of the house. I can't see the right of the house, so you'll have to keep an eye on it. *Your* right. You know, like your right hand. That's the hand you scratch your ass with."

"Jeez . . . you really *are* irritable today."

She heard him cut off the engine and open the truck door.

"I'll keep my phone on," he said, "and put it in my pocket, so you can hear what's going on."

"Thanks," she said. "Good luck."

"You, too."

Her ear to the phone, her eyes on the back door and the side windows, she listened as Dirk walked up to the front door and knocked. It took longer than usual—or at least, it seemed like a long time as her adrenaline levels soared and her heart raced—before the door finally opened.

She heard Dirk say, "Hi, are you Myrtle Weyerhauser?"

"Yeah," was the reply.

"I've got a delivery, a wide-screen television, on the truck there. It's for a Mr. Norbert Weyerhauser. Is he your husband, ma'am?"

"No, Stu—I mean . . . Norbert is my son."

"Well, if he can sign this form, I'd be happy to—"

"He ain't here."

"But you told our office on the phone that he is. I'm afraid I can't deliver it unless Mr. Weyerhauser signs for it."

"Gimme that paper. I'll sign for it."

"No, ma'am. Can't do that. And besides, I'll need Mr. Weyerhauser to help me unload it. See, my partner was sick today—out with the flu—and I can't carry it in by myself."

"Are you a cop?"

"A cop? Me? Why would you say that? Do I look like a cop?"

"Yeah, actually, you kinda do. What's in that box in the truck? Is it really a TV?"

Savannah went from "vigilant" to "high alert" in an instant.

The voices on the phone faded as she lowered the phone and listened intently to a new sound . . . a scraping noise . . . coming from the other side of the house.

Ducking, so that her head would be below the windows, she hurried across the back of the house. She paused at the opposite corner, then took a quick peek around.

At first, she wasn't sure what she was seeing—a flash of silver in the sunlight. Some sort of metal was sticking out of the upstairs window.

Then more of it protruded . . . and more . . . tilting down toward the ground.

A ladder.

She grinned, closed her cell phone, and stuck it in her pocket. She unsnapped her side holster, freeing her Beretta . . . and waited.

She didn't have to wait long. No sooner had the end of the ladder reached the ground than a hairy leg popped out of the window, and then another followed.

Dressed in baggy shorts that hung low on his hips,

flip-flops, and a T-shirt large enough to use as a tent for a backyard campout, Stumpy Weyerhauser was making his getaway.

Or at least, Stumpy thought so.

She waited until he was halfway down the ladder before she sauntered around the corner of the house and over to the foot of it.

He was huffing, puffing, and unsteady as he descended. The flip-flops didn't help as he tried to get solid footing and kept sliding off the backs of the sandals.

So intent was he, hanging on tightly to the sides of the ladder and casting furtive glances toward the front of the house, that he didn't even notice Savannah as she walked up behind him.

He didn't realize she was there until she reached up, grabbed the hems of his shorts, and jerked them down around his ankles.

Instantly, she regretted the action, because his underwear came down, too, and she found herself "face-to-face" with one of the least attractive features of an unattractive man.

"Hey! What the hell!" he yelled as he whipped his head around and nearly fell.

He tried to grab at his shorts with first one hand, then the other, while clinging to the ladder, and again, it was nearly his undoing. The side rails bent and the entire contraption wobbled as he tried to maintain his balance and re-dress his backside.

Her hand on her still-holstered pistol, Savannah laughed at him and said, "Careful there, Stump. You don't wanna take a tumble with those britches down; you could skin something important."

"You stupid bitch!" he shouted. "What's the matter with you?"

"Whoa, Norbert! Watch who you're calling names

there, good buddy. You're in no position to make enemies."

She reached over and nudged the side of the ladder. Not enough to knock it down, but definitely enough to get a rise out of the already stressed Stumpy.

"Hey! Knock it off! You're gonna make me fall and—"

Again, he reached for his shorts, while trying to step down one more rung. Apparently, multitasking wasn't Norbert Weyerhauser's strong suit.

He tumbled off the ladder and landed on his face in a particularly muddy area of a flower bed. Adding injury to insult, the ladder slid sideways with him and landed on him, smacking him soundly on the head.

A small, inch-long gash opened in his scalp, and bright red blood began to ooze out.

"Hey, Stump . . . you've sprung a leak, boy," Savannah said as she stepped across him, straddling his body, then sat down on his back.

The wind went out of him in a whoosh.

He struggled only a moment as she pulled his arms behind him. Taking some handcuffs from her slacks' waistband, she called out, "Hey, Dirk! Back here!"

"What . . . are you?" Stumpy asked struggling to breathe with her weight pinning him. "A . . . cop?"

"Close enough," she replied as she saw Dirk come running around the corner.

He looked infinitely alert, ready for action, body taut with tension . . . until he saw her sitting on the face-down Stumpy. Stumpy with mud on his face, his shorts still pulled down to his ankles, his butt bare as the day he was born—only hairy and not half as cute.

Dirk froze, staring at them, his mouth open, taking in the scene.

Then his eyes locked with Savannah's.

"What the hell are you doing?" he asked her.

"Apprehending your suspect for you. And you're welcome," she replied with a grin.

"She . . . she . . . sexually assaulted me!" Stumpy whined, thrashing around. "And she's . . . squashing . . . me."

Dirk considered the words for a moment, shook his head as though he simply couldn't process the information, and walked over to them.

Savannah stood and pointed to the cuffs. "After you're done with him, I want those back," she said.

Instantly, Dirk was indignant. "Hey, I gave you a pair to replace the ones I—"

"Don't get all huffy with me! You gave me one pair for my birthday after ripping off three pair from me over the years. So, by my calculations, I'm short two sets and a birthday present."

Dirk reached down, grabbed Stumpy, and hauled him to his feet. In another quick move, he hoisted his prisoner's shorts back up to their original position. "There you go, Norbert," he said. "I just improved your appearance tenfold."

"I'm telling you," Stumpy whimpered, "that crazy woman sexually assaulted me!"

"No, she didn't." Dirk took him by the arm, leading him toward the front of the house. "I've known her for twenty years," he said, "and in all that time, I couldn't convince her to sexually assault me."

Dirk glanced back over his shoulder at Savannah, who was following close behind. "And . . ." he added, ". . . as we've all seen, I have way more to offer her in that respect than you do."

A woman with pink, foam hair curlers, a lavender chenille robe, and a cigarette hanging from the corner of her mouth, came running up to them. "Norbert!" she yelled around the cigarette, "I told you it was a scam. There's ain't nothing in that box they brung. I checked it! It's empty as your head. You ain't never been lucky enough to win nothin'!"

"Ah, shut up, Ma," Norbert replied, shuffling along as Dirk led him toward the pickup.

Savannah wondered where the woman had found antique, pink, foam hair curlers. She wondered how old that chenille robe was. She wondered if every time Norbert had abused one of his elderly female victims he had been thinking of his mommy.

But there was something else that piqued her curiosity even more.

She had to ask.

Turning to Mother Weyerhauser, she said, "I have to know . . . who was the first person to call him 'Stumpy'? Was it you?"

"Hell no." The cigarette, stuck to her lower lip, bobbed up and down a couple of time. "It was that idiot bimbo that he dropped out of high school to marry. She started calling him that right before she divorced him. I've always called him 'Norbert.' "

Savannah gave Dirk a big smirk as she opened the truck door and helped him tuck the bloody, grumpy, Stumpy inside. "Told ya so."